In the Company of Shadows

The Night's Road: Book One

Red Company

Andy Monk

All rights reserved. No part of this publication may be reproduced, distributed, or transmitted in any form or by any means, including photocopying, recording, or other electronic or mechanical methods, without the prior written permission of the publisher.

Copyright © 2019 Andy Monk
All rights reserved.
ISBN: 9781697628340

Part One

Fire

Chapter One

The Wolf's Tower, Tassau, Upper Saxon Circle, The Holy Roman Empire - 1630

Solace stood atop the castle and watched the village beyond the winter-sheared trees burn. Dreams of fire had haunted her sleep for weeks and now it had come to pass, as her dreams so often did. Fear, sharp and painful, speared her.

Blood had drenched those dreams too...

Across the frozen woods the church bell tolled, the only sound to break the heavy silence of a deep winter night. The villagers were calling for help. She pulled her fur-lined cloak tight against the cutting cold. At her side Torben stared towards the western sky; a furious orange glow silhouetted the barren trees of the woodland separating The Wolf's Tower from the village.

Torben's usually restless gaze didn't move from the distant fire. He ignored the licks of long unkempt hair the swirling breeze teased back and forth across his large, unblinking eyes. Despite the bitterness of the night, he wore no hat or hood, the cold never troubled him. Unlike so many other things.

"I dreamed of fire again last night..." her sigh turned into a shiver.

Fires were common. An untended cooking pot, a spark from a hearth, a dropped rushlight. The village was just wood and straw. It didn't take much to set a building ablaze, especially during summer when the sun dried everything to kindling. But this wasn't summer. It was midwinter. Ice gripped the land, snow dampened thatch and timber. But clearly, things still burnt.

Below, mounted men clattered across the bridge. Soldiers from The Wolf's Tower's garrison sent by her father to aid the village. It probably *was* just an accidental fire caused by a dozing peasant, but this was a time of war, so the men always carried arms outside the castle walls.

Her father's soldiers, particularly the old, grizzled ones who displayed their scars like pennants, insisted war did not come at this time of year. They'd been saying it since the leaves fell. She suspected they wanted to reassure themselves as much as her; the tales of what was happening in the north were brutal.

Armies and warbands did not move well in snow, they explained. There was little food to scavenge from the land, daylight was in short supply, the cold would kill more men than any enemy. So, the fire beyond the woods would be due to an accident rather than the war finally reaching their tiny, insignificant barony.

The riders galloped down the icy track towards trees backlit by the fire's glow. The dread within her had swelled even further by the time they entered the woods and its deep shadow enveloped them.

The old soldiers said war would not come to The Wolf's Tower, not in winter. Solace believed the old soldiers, because old soldiers knew more about the business of war than a seventeen-year-old girl ever would.

And yet, as she stared at the dancing horizon, the weight in her stomach grew. Something was wrong. Very wrong. Whatever the old soldiers said, the dread stone sitting in her guts whispered something else...

She glanced at Torben. He was rummaging through the leather satchel he always wore, long tousled hair hanging about his frost-pale face, the frown furrowing his brow not melting until he found what he was looking for.

Shoving his hand under her nose he opened his palm to reveal The Hen. Carved from oak like all his little figures, years of constant handling had polished and blurred its lines.

"Yes..." she nodded, looking up to meet his eye, "...I'm scared too..."

*

The column of mounted men slowed as they entered the wood, the road was a sorry thing and even worse where it cut through the trees. Nobody wanted to break their horse's leg for the sake of a peasant's hovel already beyond saving.

After a few minutes, the size of the fire became apparent. Orange tongues licked the sky, casting distorted shadows through the tapestry of twisted trees woven around them. Smoke hazed the moon, its stink heavy in the freezing air.

"Whole damn village's ablaze!" Holger, who was riding next to Ulrich, shouted.

Holger was an idiot with a taste for exaggeration. Given the choice Ulrich avoided talking to idiots, so he didn't bother replying. The fact he thought idiots filled the world to its brim had helped earn him a reputation as a taciturn and uncommunicative young man.

Buildings should burn slow when the winter's damp hand lay so heavy upon the world. Slow enough for a panic-stricken peasant or two to run to The Wolf's Tower for help, but no one had. A guard atop the battlements raised the alarm when the church bell started ringing.

But if men had taken torches to the village...

It would be a desperate band who raided at this time of year, renegades and runaways most likely. Desperate *and* stupid. If you went a pillaging, better to pick somewhere not sitting next to a castle with sixty armed men inside it.

The world, however, *was* full of stupid people.

Captain Kadelberg slowed the column further. Probably all they'd find would be the local simpletons milling around, watching their village burn until someone with enough wits to organise them to fetch water from the frozen pond arrived. But Kadelberg was a cautious man and wouldn't want to charge merrily into trouble.

If there had been a raid, the attackers would likely have disappeared with whatever they could carry away by now. Unless they were *really* stupid, of course.

To Ulrich's way of thinking, the only things of worth in the village were a couple of plump whores and some thin beer. Still, in such dark times there were plenty of men prepared to kill for a lot less than a plump whore and a thin beer.

Ulrich eyed the trees on either side of the narrow track. It wasn't a dense or fearsome wood; charcoal camps regularly thinned the trees in the summer. But now, frosted white by old snow frozen to the bare branches, between the orange glow of the fire and silver moonlight, it was distinctly sinister.

Several times, out of the corner of his eye, he thought he saw shadows move in ways shadows shouldn't. Although whenever his head snapped around there was nothing to see amongst the skeletal birch trees bar snow and ice.

The column was silent save for the occasional nicker or snort from the horses. Frosted breath and steam rose from the beasts, who didn't relish the cold any more than the men.

Beyond a stream edging the woods, peasants had long since cleared the trees for farmland, but they still grew dense enough here to conceal an ambush.

Admittedly, it was unlikely. A raid on the village wouldn't be by soldiers. Armies didn't campaign at this time of year. However, the war had stripped the land of order. After one side or the other had plundered and burned their homes, many desperate souls turned to brigandry in preference to starving. Perhaps things had become so bad in Mecklenburg men were roving further south for food. Such desperate rogues might raid a village in winter, steal whatever was at hand and then run away. They wouldn't linger to face men capable of fighting back.

And yet...

He felt uneasy. The kind of unease that ran deeper than a sour mood from Sergeant Lutz hooking him out of bed on a freezing winter's night. Even idiots like Holger could sense *something* was amiss.

"Gonna grab me an ale in *The Bear Pit* when we're done..." Holger slapped his hands on his arms to ward off the cold.

Ulrich rolled his eyes towards the heavens.

"It might be a pile of ashes by now..."

"Fuck..." Holger spat, "...only decent thing about the shit hole."

That was one thing they could agree on. The village tavern was well frequented by soldiers from The Wolf's Tower, if it burnt to the ground life was going to be even more miserable for the garrison.

He'd become a soldier to fight. To find wealth and glory on the battlefield. To prove his mettle and honour, which his father had taught him were the only things of worth a man ever truly possessed. Instead, he found himself guarding a small castle of no significance, serving a lord intent on keeping his tiny barony out of the wars at all possible costs. It was not what Ulrich's dreams had amounted to.

As the trees started to thin, he made sure his sabre was clear to draw.

Always be prepared.

His father, who had once owned the sword, had forever growled those words in his ear on the practice yard.

Holger picked his nose and examined the findings with interest.

How the man, who was twenty years his senior, still had all his major body parts roughly where they should be, was a mystery to Ulrich.

The column moved forward at walking pace. Smoke hung about the trees, distorting the shadows further. The only sound was the soft pad of hooves on snow and the incessant call of the church bell.

The glow of the fire grew brighter as the trees thinned. The village was a simple affair, consisting of two rows of cottages looking across a muddy excuse of a road. At either end stood the only substantial buildings, serving the village's most pressing needs - *The Bear Pit* tavern and *St John's* church. A rudimentary wall of wooden stakes, built more to keep wild animals out than men, enclosed the buildings.

A murmur rippled along the column as they crossed the stream separating the village from the woods. The blaze centred on the church and the surrounding cottages. Giddy swirls of fire engulfed *St John's*. Smoke billowed from the spire towards the cold stars above.

And yet its bell still tolled.

"Who the fuck is ringing the bell?" Ulrich muttered. As Holger was the only man in earshot, the question had been very much rhetorical.

"At least the tavern's safe..." Holger grinned.

Ulrich ignored him. Another question clambered for attention as insistently as the church bell. Where was everybody?

The village was deserted. There wasn't a soul about. No rushlights burned in the cottages, even *The Bear Pit* was dark. He'd expected confusion and disorganisation, idiot villagers milling around without making even a half-arsed attempt to fight the fire. But not this.

"Where is everyone?" he called, but no one answered. He'd a reputation for eagerness and seeing enemies in every shadow. Being one of the youngest and newest men in the troop didn't lend his words much weight either.

Kadelberg drew to a halt at the edge of the village, the simple wicker gate in the stake wall hung open, creaking in the breeze. The only other sound was the frantic ringing of the bell. All else was still.

The Captain ordered half his men forward to investigate the burning church. Ulrich was in the group sent on. As he came alongside, he reined in his horse next to Kadelberg's.

"Captain, should we not hold back and send scouts ahead?"

Kadelberg studied him with tired, grey, seen-it-all eyes, and cocked a greying eyebrow beneath the rim of his helm.

"Pray why, young man?"

"Whoever did this might still be here... waiting for us!"

"Did what?"

"Attack the village!"

Kadelberg cast his eyes around, before swivelling them back upon Ulrich.

"There has been no attack."

"The church-"

"Is on fire. We must deal with it."

"But where are the villagers?"

"Staying out of the cold, I would imagine."

"But-"

"If there'd been an attack, there'd be bodies, there'd be blood on the snow. There'd be signs of a fight. Are there any?"

The snow, which had last fallen days ago, was a grey broken churn. But no blood or bodies soiled it.

"No..."

"There is nothing here to make us run back to The Wolf's Tower. If there are brigands, we will put them to the sword. I have my orders. You have yours."

Ulrich looked at the men plodding towards the church, and then the others arrayed behind their Captain. Could no one see this was wrong apart from him? No matter how cold it was, the peasants would never cower in their hovels while their church burned.

"But who stays in a burning church to ring the bell?"

"Perhaps the Devil is about his business..."

"The Devil?" Ulrich shifted in his saddle. Kadelberg was a religious man who never invoked Satan's name in jest.

"I fear him more than any ragged band of brigands. Whatever is afoot here..." both the Captain's words and eyes filled with scorn behind his frosted breath, "...I'd like to find out before we all freeze to death."

The Captain returned his attention to the church, hands folded over the pommel of his saddle. Ulrich was dismissed.

"Yes, sir..." he prodded his horse on.

Ulrich headed after the other soldiers. He'd been eager

for action since joining von Tassau's men, assuming the *Freiherr* would hire out his soldiers to one Prince or another to fight in the war. Instead, his life here consisted of nothing but practice and polish, idle time in *The Bear Pit* and pursuing Erna, a pretty scullery maid in the castle, without success. Now he eyed the shadows haunting the silent, empty village uneasily.

The armies rampaging to the north had stripped the land bare in recent years, had things become so bad they would scavenge this far in search of food in the midst of winter?

The orange glow of the fire and cold silver moonlight painted the village. It was not where the light fell that held his eye, however, but the places it didn't. The gaps between the shuttered windows and ill-fitting doors, the gloomy reaches separating each little wooden dwelling from the next.

He felt eyes upon him. The villagers cowering in their hovels? Perhaps. But why would they hide from the *Freiherr's* men? They knew the soldiers well, the men's coin bought ale and provisions, the village's crops and animals fed the garrison. They had called for their aid by ringing the bell. So why hide?

Perhaps the Devil is about his business...

It was too cold for armies and warbands. But Satan? It might be hot in Hell, but Old Nick didn't mind the winter. The dark cold months brought him a surfeit of souls to roast and the long nights provided cover for his mischief.

Keeping the reins tight in his left hand, he pulled a pistol free with the other.

He urged his horse on. The gelding wasn't happy, tossing its head and snorting.

The rest of the men had reached the church and he suddenly felt very alone away from his comrades. None had made any move to dismount as they clustered before the burning church, grey wraiths of smoke floating around them. Their long shadows danced across the dirty snow to greet him.

"God in heaven! God in heaven!" Holger cried when Ulrich drew his horse to a halt aside him.

No one else spoke.

The bell tolled and the fire crackled. Beneath those sounds came another. And it chilled his soul. The villagers were not hiding in their homes. They were in the church. And their screams floated out of the flames.

Planks of wood barred the doors of *St John's*, sealing the burning building.

And a spread-eagled man was nailed to them.

"Pastor Jonathan..." Holger gibbered.

For once, Holger was right, the blood-soaked corpse was the village pastor. A man who'd never been slow to tell the soldiers Satan was waiting for them with his roasting fork to reward their drunken, fornicating ways.

Only the smoke pouring from the church clothed the pastor, shrouding him in billowing sheets of grey. Blood smeared his nailed wrists and ankles, his throat too, which appeared to have been torn open.

"We must get them out!" Ulrich jumped from his saddle. Slipping in the slush, he grabbed hold of the pommel to stop himself falling. No one followed suit.

"Devil's work..." someone cursed.

"They're dying in there!" Ulrich yelled. The fire's cackle was growing louder while the screams began to fade. Even the bell seemed to be tolling less frantically, a wounded beast nearing the end.

"'tis men who nailed the Pastor to the door, not the Devil, and 'tis men who are dying in there!" Ulrich screamed at the dumbstruck idiots glued to their saddles.

That was when the Devil made him look a fool, by stepping out of the flames and striding towards them...

Chapter Two

"The Devil is about his business!"

Her father looked faintly amused. When it came to amusement it was the only look he ever managed. It wasn't the response Solace had been hoping for.

"My dear, the Devil is *always* about his business."

She glanced at Torben in the hope of support. Despite knowing him all her life, she still sometimes forgot. The flames dancing in the hearth engrossed her brother, his mind had retreated into the other world it spent most of its time in.

She didn't know where the phrase had come from or what she really meant by it. She just felt the *rightness* of the words. The Devil was about his business, and her father had sent their men out to meet him.

"We should be prepared for the worst."

The look of amusement on her father's face faded.

"I am always prepared. I know how bad the world is, I have seen much more of it than you, after all."

"The rest of the men should be on the battlements,

they-"

"The Wolf's Tower is well defended. It always is. Whatever is happening in the village will not threaten us. There is no need to fret, my dear."

She raised her chin, "You do not seem overly concerned."

Another, colder, expression surfaced on her father's narrow face, washing away the last vestige of amusement.

"Of course I am concerned! The village provides our food, our labour and our servants. The peasants pay our tithes and dues. This fire, I have no doubt, will prove a great inconvenience."

"But what if-"

"No one is attacking the village! And no one will attack the castle either. 'tis winter and a bad one. Such things do not happen. I have lived through far more than you have. The war is not close. Neither our fellow Protestant Princes, the Imperial army, the Swedes or anyone else are responsible. 'tis just an accident."

"How can you know that for certain?"

"I don't. Hence, I sent Kadelberg to establish the truth of matters. He will deal with whatever has happened, be it an untended stove or the Devil himself."

Solace shifted on her feet and resisted the urge to slap her hands against her thighs in exasperation. She was no longer a child - her father's ongoing search for a suitable husband for her was evidence enough of that.

"Father, I have a bad feeling..."

"We all have bad feelings from time to time. Mine are often the result of Herman's undercooked meat."

"No. You are not listening! I have a bad *feeling...*" her eyes flicked to her brother who had edged closer to the fire "...and so does Torben."

Her father threw back his head and stared at the shadowy ceiling of his study. A long slow breath escaped before his gaze returned to her. His eyes narrowed as he pressed his lips into thin pale lines.

He looked like he regretted not yet finding anyone suitable for her to marry even more than normal.

"I have warned you many times. Do not say such things."

"You know my feelings come true. Torben's even more so."

"I have told you!" He jumped to his feet fast enough for her to want to step back. She didn't. She *wasn't* a child anymore.

"No one is going to burn us."

"If such talk reached the wrong ears, I pray you are not foolish enough to believe being my daughter would save you. The children of far richer men than me have gone to the flames," his expression softened as he turned his gaze to Torben, "and ones not touched in the head either."

"I was right about the harvest, I was right about Rahel's baby, I was right about ghastly *Graf* Bulcher's true interest, I-"

"Enough!"

She pressed her own lips into thin lines, aping her father.

"And I am right about tonight."

Her father shook his head, placing a hand on each of

her shoulders, "You are as stubborn as your mother..." he sighed, "...but you must not talk like this, please."

"I watch my words, I am not stupid," she kept her chin raised and eyes fixed on his, "and I am not a witch either."

"No, you are not. Neither was your mother, but I worried myself sick about her... *feelings* too."

"And she was always right too. Wasn't she?"

Her father didn't answer. He didn't have to.

"Something terrible is happening... please get the rest of the men ready to defend the castle."

"Solace... we are safe. The only way anyone can take this castle is with cannon and a lot of men, and if an army hauling cannon through the snow had been heading in our direction, I would know about it. Such a force would be slow and large. My every waking moment involves keeping you, Torben and our home safe from this wretched war. No one is getting into The Wolf's Tower."

They both turned to the familiar sound of wood clicking against wood. Torben was sorting through his bag. Twisting his head around, he stared at them with his unmoving, unblinking eyes that always seemed so sad. He held out two wooden animals, one in the palm of each hand. The Fox and The Goat.

The Fox meant *clever* or *sly*.
The Goat usually represented *bad* or *wrongdoing*.
Or it meant *The Devil*.

*

The figure emerged from the smoke, unconcerned by the flames spurting and turning around it.

The man was by far the tallest Ulrich had ever seen. A long, sinewy stretch whose head would bump the ceiling of all but the grandest rooms. Despite the freezing night he was bare-chested, numerous tattoos twisted around his arms and torso, stark against his pale skin. White-blonde hair hung in long plaits around sharp, feral features cut by more tattoos.

Amusement played across his face as he stood before Pastor Jonathan's smoking corpse. Planting the haft of a huge halberd into the slush, he rested easily upon it. At first Ulrich thought mud smeared his skin. When he realised it was blood, he drew his sword.

"I hope you've enjoyed your lives, gentlemen..." the giant grinned. The words were softly spoken, but Ulrich heard them well enough above the crackling flames and faltering screams. They chilled him more than the frigid air.

"Who the hell are you?" Sergeant Hammerl, a bald, surly Hessian, demanded, inching his horse forward.

The giant smiled.

"Death."

Almost too fast to see, the giant hefted the halberd in both hands and swung it from left to right. Hammerl's horse didn't have time to flinch before its head hit the ground. A prodigious gout of blood shot over the snow as the horse's body, and the Sergeant, folded into the half-melted snow.

One of the other soldiers, Reichart, charged, but the giant ducked out of his way and the massive halberd almost cut Reichart in two as he went by.

The giant was laughing. A tremendous booming noise,

ill-fitting his willowy frame. And he'd changed, Ulrich realised with a start. His face had grown both unnaturally long and thin, what little pigment dusted the devil's flesh was gone, leaving his already pallid skin as white as the snow under the moonlight.

Muzzle-flashes sparked from the darkened cottages as musket shot punched men from their saddles. Horses reared in panic. Shapes erupted from the shadows to fall upon the Tassau soldiers, plucking men from their horses and tossing them to the ground.

Hammerl was pinned beneath his headless horse, "Kill him! Kill him!" the Sergeant screamed as the giant demon, if he wasn't Satan himself, bore down on the prostrate soldier, its mouth gaping open to reveal elongated fangs within.

Nobody was paying attention to the Sergeant's orders; everyone was too busy screaming and dying themselves.

Something dragged Holger from his saddle, so fast there was no time for the fool to raise his sword.

Horses and men screamed all around Ulrich, there was the occasional clash of steel on steel as some of his comrades managed to find a foe to fight, but, for most, their assailants were too quick. Just blurs in the darkness, dragging men down to bloody damnation in the snow.

Like many young and foolish men before him, Ulrich had yearned for battle since the day his father had first let him hold his sabre. The stories behind each nick and scratch on the dull steel of the blade and the scrolling metalwork of the handguard, enthralling a young boy who still worshipped his father. Now, at last confronted by battle, all he wanted to do was flee.

When he tried to remount his horse, he found the animal had bolted in panic. He turned one way and a headless corpse collapsed into the blood-soaked snow at his boots, he turned another and a riderless horse blocked his path. He made a grab for the reins, but with a pistol in one hand and his father's old sabre in the other it was impossible. The horse was gone before he could toss a weapon away.

Two figures staggered out of the smoke, one was Wiebald, a foul-mouthed oaf from Brandenburg who still owed Ulrich money from a dice game, the other a demon, shorter than the thing with the halberd, but with the same long, bloodless face. Fangs tore into the Wiebald's neck. That was three talers he was never going to see.

Ulrich raised his pistol, but someone clattered into him before he could fire. Whirling around he found it was Holger, hands pawing his throat, blood spurting between his fingers.

Ulrich stepped away from the dying man. Holger was far beyond help. Another demon appeared, a long fur-lined coat flowing behind him. Ulrich managed to half raise his pistol, but the creature knocked it from his hand.

"Pretty thing come to me..." the creature hissed, its voice soft and almost feminine. It closed on Ulrich with incredible speed, its gaping mouth baring fangs. Ulrich's foot gave way on a patch of ice and he fell to one knee. The demon stumbled over him. He slashed furiously at the thing with his sabre, but found only air as the demon swivelled around, dark locks flying about its hideous, too long, face. It was laughing. Laughing the way a man might when playing with a child.

It came again, but a panic-stricken horse charged between them, knocking the thing aside.

Ulrich turned and ran.

Kadelberg and the rest of the men danced a dark dance through banners of smoke, silver in the moonlight, at the other end of the village. Things swarmed over them too. No help was coming from that quarter. A gun fizzed and barked nearby. Ignoring it, he kept running.

Behind him the church bell still rung weakly above the screams of the dying.

He aimed for a gap between two shacks, behind them and the simple staked fence built to keep out wolves and boar, was the little stream and the trees. If he reached the woods, there was a chance he could get back to the safety of The Wolf's Tower.

A man appeared out of the shadows, reloading a musket. Putting his head down, Ulrich sprinted. There was still a loaded pistol in his belt, but he left it there. He bellowed as he ran, he didn't know what, it was just terror given voice.

The musketeer's head jerked up. He didn't look like a demon. And he didn't look comfortable either. A screaming man charging you with a sabre could do that. The musketeer fumbled his powder. He should have cast away the musket and drawn his sword, but some men preferred distance between them and their killing.

Realisation dawned that he wasn't going to get the musket loaded in time. With every stride Ulrich expected other musketeers to appear and gun him down. None did.

The man took a two-handed grip on his musket and managed to block Ulrich's sword with it, but the force of the strike, which carried all Ulrich's terror and fury, slid the blade down the musket and cut away at least three of the man's fingers.

The musketeer screamed as he staggered backwards. If this was a demon too, it was a feeble one. Ulrich slashed through the man's heavy jerkin, and he went down. He left him bleeding on the snow, hopefully he was dying, but he dared not risk the time to finish him.

He hurtled between the shacks. Skidding on a patch of ice and slamming into a wall hard enough to shake snow from the roof. Just about keeping his footing, he dodged a snow-capped barrel and made it past the little buildings.

Silver birch, as stark as bleached old bones in the fey light of the full moon, beckoned beyond the crude stakes of the village wall. No sound of pursuit came from behind him. The speed the demons moved, if one were chasing him, they would have their hellish teeth in his neck by now.

Each home had a small plot behind it where the peasants grew vegetables or kept chickens, but now snow blanketed everything. Shouts and screams still came from the village, but they were diminishing. It was never going to be a long fight.

Running in mad flight from his first real battle. Not the glory of his boyhood dreams, but he would take seeing the dawn as a victory. His father, who had spent every sober moment, and a lot of the drunken ones too, giving him advice, had never faced a foe like this.

He was sprinting towards the stakes of the village wall, which would provide only a modest barrier to one terrified man, and the stream and treeline beyond when two riders emerged from the wood.

At first, he thought they were from The Wolf's Tower, but they both wore lobster tail helmets with long nose guards rather than the open burgonets favoured by most of the *Freiherr's* men.

Both riders were pistoleers and had a gun in hand. A well-equipped pistoleer might have another four or five loaded guns on him. Seeing Ulrich, they cried and spurred their horses on to a gallop and jumped the simple fence.

Changing direction, he sprinted parallel to the cottage plots, looking for cover before they rode him down.

The carcass of an old wagon sat behind one of the cottage gardens, sagging on broken wheels even before being laden with snow for the winter. Behind him the horses thundered. Despite the noise growing louder as they closed, he forced himself to keep jigging from left to right rather than running in a straight line. The first crack of a pistol was followed immediately by a second.

As the frozen earth shook with the fury of iron hooves, he flung himself towards the wagon. The swoosh of a blade cut the air above his head. He kept on going down till he got himself a mouthful of snow.

He could wriggle beneath the wagon, but it wouldn't take the riders long to winkle him out from under there. His only hope was that the two riders, like the musketeer, were not demons. The way those things moved he was dead, but against men... Well, all men died.

Scrambling up, he pushed himself hard against the side of the wagon, crouching behind one of its broken wheels. The moon was over the woods and he was deep in shadow. He kept the sabre in view and slipped his remaining pistol free, keeping it out of sight beneath his cloak. Best the pistoleers thought he only had a sword.

He was a lot better with a blade than a pistol, but they had their uses. Even a good pistol wasn't effective beyond thirty to forty paces (and he didn't have a good pistol) but he was going to struggle to beat two mounted pistoleers with only a sabre.

He needed to reduce the odds and fast. More of the bastards would be here soon.

The gap between the crude drystone wall marking the end of the cottage plots and the side of the wagon where he crouched was only a metre, far too small a space for both horsemen to charge together.

The riders conversed for a moment, perhaps discussing whether to dismount or not, before one of the men made a circling motion with his hand and the other nodded, before spurring his horse back along the other side of the wagon. They planned to come at him from both sides at once in the hope of flushing him out into the open. Or hacking him to pieces where he was.

His father had made him practice with blades for hour after hour, but the old man had never trusted pistols. "All flash and piss," the familiar sneer would come whenever one was produced, "Fuck em and stick to your blade, boy. A blade will never misfire when you need it most. It won't ever explode in your face either. And a blade will go exactly where you want it to, not like those fucking devilish contraptions..."

Old Man Ulrich's growl was loud in his ear.

Ulrich wished he'd the time to dredge up a more reassuring memory.

He didn't. The second rider wheeled his horse around and was now behind him. Ulrich glanced over his shoulder once and then ignored him. They would both be arriving at the same time, give or take, and he still only had the one shot, so he concentrated on the first rider. He'd ordered the second to come around, so he had rank.

Always kill an officer first...

More sage advice from Old Man Ulrich.

Neither rider was coming hell for leather, they wouldn't want to ride into each other. Still, the sound of hooves slapping through the snow grew rapidly louder. They were coming hard enough for him all the same. He wanted to pull the trigger as much as he'd ever wanted to do something in his life. He forced himself to wait.

The first pistoleer had opted for his sabre, Ulrich wanted them to think he was cowering like a mouse in the shadows and about as defenceless. Perhaps they worried about shooting each other as they came at him from opposite sides.

A pistol ball splintered wood behind him.

Perhaps not so worried about shooting each other then...

He risked another glance over his shoulder. The second pistoleer was hard against the stone wall, smoothly changing his spent pistol for a loaded one. They were trying to flush him out.

"He's not going to hit me..." Ulrich muttered, it was dark and he was a small target at that range. And the first pistoleer was almost on him. The horse was huge, an enormous black shadow blotting out the sky.

It was difficult to hit a moving target. Pistols weren't precision weapons, pistoleers used them to break up enemy infantry formations, firing and turning, firing and turning at massed ranks. A hundred men behind pikes was a big target, one horseman, especially one wearing a heavy breastplate, was much harder to kill.

So, Ulrich shot the horse instead.

Raising his pistol at the last possible moment, he waited half a heartbeat before firing into the horse's chest. Despite his father's misgivings, the wheel turned and clicked, the powder ignited, the muzzle flashed and coughed smoke.

The horse screamed, half turned, then collapsed thrashing onto the snow.

Another pistol ball slammed into the wagon by his head, but Ulrich was already up and running. The first pistoleer was trying to pull himself to his feet, but he snagged his ankle in a stirrup and stumbled to his knees. Ulrich hollered as he swung his sabre, aiming for the man's neck, but hitting the side of his helmet. The helm stopped the blow, but it was hard enough to knock the man flat to the ground, exposing his unarmoured back and Ulrich hacked at him. The pistoleer screamed, jerked, twitched and fell still.

Spinning around, he found the second pistoleer

charging him down, sabre raised and primed to take off his head. Instead of trying to parry the blow, he threw himself under the swing. The air sung with steel.

While the rider wheeled his mount around Ulrich, scrambled over to the fallen pistoleer's twitching horse. Two pistols hung from the saddle. Plunging his sabre into the snow he scooped them up and prayed they were loaded.

He wheeled and fired both guns together as the remaining pistoleer yelled a curse about the mother Ulrich had never known, one shot cracked into the man's breastplate, the second hit him in the face. Jewels of blood sprayed the snow as he tumbled from the saddle.

Dropping the spent pistols and grabbing his sabre, Ulrich sprinted for the now riderless horse which had stopped a dozen paces away, looking back as if wondering where its master had gone.

"Just stay there..." Ulrich panted from behind plumes of frosted breath as he laboured through the snow. His light breastplate seemed to have tripled in weight and his heart was echoing inside the thing.

He was sure the horse would trot off, but the animal stood its ground and eyed him curiously as he sheathed his sabre and found a stirrup with his boot.

Grabbing the pommel, he was about to boost himself into the saddle when something seized him from behind, lifted him into the air and tossed him to the ground.

The breath whooshed out of him as he slammed into the snow. A figure loomed over him before he could scramble back to his feet.

"You go nowhere, pretty thing..." a voice hissed.

Then something hit him in the face and the white world went black.

Chapter Three

Sergeant Lutz was even older than her father.

Craggy, saggy, baggy. His face had always fascinated her. How did someone end up looking like that? He couldn't have been born so... worn and weathered. Could he? Were his looks the result of the life he'd lived or just bad fortune? Either way, he suffered the appearance of a man God had not taken kindly to.

As he burst into her father's study, it was apparent something in addition to the normal crags, sags and bags weighed down Sergeant Lutz's face.

Concern.

"Freiherr!"

Lutz bellowed as the doors crashed behind him.

The Sergeant had never been a quiet man...

"Lutz?" Her father raised an enquiring eyebrow. Lutz had served the family a long time and, if she didn't know better, Solace would have said her father was fond of the old soldier. Fonder than of her and Torben anyway.

"Dolman reports hearing gunfire coming from the

village. Dolman is a half-witted puppy not to be trusted with anything more than cleaning out the latrines and stables, but the arse-" he spotted the *Freiherr's* children and baulked in mid-profanity, "My lady, excuse me..." he offered her a nod of the head. Torben he didn't bother with. To most of the inhabitants of The Wolf's Tower her brother was invisible. It was quite a trick. She often wished she knew how to do it.

"Gunfire, you say?" Her father pushed himself up from behind his desk.

"According to Dolman, who isn't the most... erm... ..." Lutz glanced at her, a smile bloomed somewhere deep in the valleys of his face "...reliable of men."

Solace hoped her father noted she was staring at him in a significant fashion.

"How much gunfire?"

"More than a few isolated shots, the boy said, but it didn't go on for long. By the time he sent word there was nothing. I've put more men up top."

"And no message from Kadelberg?"

Lutz shook his head. His jowls, chins and cheeks followed suit.

Her father sighed, balled his fists and leaned on the desk. For a moment he stared at the scrolls and parchments he'd been working on, then raised his eyes back to Lutz.

"Break out muskets and pistols, get the remainder of the garrison into firing positions around the Barbican, rouse the servants and place men on each wall of the battlements. A musket and shot for every man who knows how to use one, and a blade for everyone who doesn't. Bring oil and quicklime to the Barbican too."

"Has been a long time since anyone used oil in this place."

"Let's hope it isn't needed."

"Soldiers, my Lord?"

"Not likely. Just brigands making merry in the snow. No doubt the gunfire was Kadelberg running the vermin off, but..." his eyes flicked towards Solace "...'tis best to be careful in such dark times."

Lutz nodded but didn't look reassured. It appeared Torben and her were not the only ones enduring bad feelings, "I'll see to it at once, my Lord."

"And fetch Udo, I'll need my pistols and sword too."

The Sergeant managed a small bow and waddled out of the room as fast as his short, bowed legs could carry him.

"I'm sure 'tis nothing, but best you stay in your rooms till we know what is afoot," her father sank back down behind his desk and picked up a quill. He had always been a great believer in scribbling, whatever the situation.

When he noticed his children still loitering, his eyes rose, "Yes?"

Torben was holding The Lion. When their father continued to stare blankly, he pointed to himself and then The Lion.

Her father's grey eyes moved to Solace for a translation.

"He's saying he's brave. He wants to fight."

"There isn't going to be a fight. Kadelberg will return

soon and we'll all be able to go to bed."

"Then he wants to freeze pointlessly on the battlements until Kadelberg's return..." she matched her father's stare, "...just like the other men."

Her father carefully put down his quill.

"Torben can't fight," he directed his words to her rather than his son. Like almost everybody else, her father usually chose to treat Torben as if he wasn't in the room.

Torben put The Lion back into his bag before punching his open palm to show he could.

"He is my son and heir. He cannot be risked in a situation to which he is not accustomed."

Her father thought Torben too simple and clumsy to fight and hunt like other men, but he still clung to the hope his son might be able to get a suitably high-born young woman pregnant and secure his lineage. No one knew if Torben was capable of fathering a child. Practising with the scullery maids was another manly pastime he wasn't allowed to try.

"He is a man," she insisted, "and he wants to take his place with the others to defend The Wolf's Tower. To defend his home."

"That," her father said sternly, "isn't possible..."

The words hung. He didn't need to finish them. Despite turning twenty-one, Torben was no man in their father's eyes, he was a child and always would be. He had the body of a man - albeit a gangly awkward one - but the mind of a child. He was too stupid to trust with anything more demanding than a bag of wooden toys.

Solace, however, knew her brother better than anyone

and she didn't think him stupid at all. His mind just worked differently to other people's. She didn't know if his mind worked differently because he couldn't talk, or he couldn't talk because his mind worked differently. Either way, he wasn't stupid.

And he wanted to prove to their father he was a man.

"We may need every man we have."

"Perhaps, but probably not. And if you are correct, then Torben will have the most important job of all. Protecting you. Can you do that for me Torben? Protect your little sister?"

It was the kind of thing you said to a small boy, which was how their father still saw his son, despite the fact Torben was taller than him and had grown a beard. The beard was a patchy sorry looking thing that didn't suit him, but their father had a beard, neat, clipped and shot with threads of storm-grey, so Torben had wanted one from the moment the first downy bristles sprouted on his chin too.

Fire sparked in her brother's usually placid eyes as he pulled The Lion and The Ox from his bag. *Brave* and *strong*.

Freiherr von Tassau smiled.

She knew he loved Torben, but she also knew his love, just like the smile fading from his face, was always going to be one tinged with sadness and disappointment.

*

Dragged through the snow, the toes of Ulrich's boots carved furrows behind him. He was dimly aware of being slumped between two men. Their rasping breaths echoed either side of him. He drifted in and out of consciousness.

Which was probably best. He heard voices but couldn't focus on them.

He should be thinking about how to get away, but the hard reality was his chance had vanished. Whatever their reasons for not killing him yet, he suspected he wasn't going to end up being grateful.

His face hurt. The warmth of his blood set his cold skin a tingling. His nose felt broken.

He couldn't decide whether to concentrate on the pain in order to bring him around and pray a cunning scheme to escape his captors would soon follow, or just to let his mind drift away and hope he never woke up again.

In the end the choice wasn't his.

He hit the ground like a sack of turnips. Peeling open an eye, he found the floor was wood and sawdust rather than snow and ice.

"The last one?" A voice demanded.

"Aye, Master," came the reply.

Both voices spoke in accented German.

"Get him up," the first voice commanded.

It sounds like he's in charge. I should try to kill him first.

His new friends hauled him to his feet again. It seemed a bit of a waste of time to have thrown him to the floor in the first place. But nobody was asking his opinion. His knees buckled as soon as he was back on his feet. Rough hands grabbed either arm to keep him upright. The stink of the men assaulted him. Old sweat, the acrid tang of gunpowder and rotten teeth being the most immediately identifiable odours. Others didn't come so readily to mind, but they were pungent enough to clear his throbbing head a little.

Opening his eyes, he tried to take in his surroundings. Knowing where he was and who he faced would no doubt help his cunning scheme along no end.

Know thy enemy... Another favourite from Old Man Ulrich's lexicon of military wisdom.

After looking around the room, he decided he didn't want to know anything about this enemy.

A man with strikingly blue eyes watched him. Tall, well-built and handsome. Broad shoulders tapered to a slender waist; his thick dark hair caught in a black ribbon at the base of his neck. He wore a long velvet coat over a silk shirt, black britches and very fine boots. A leather baldric crossed his chest and an expensive looking sword hung from it. He had the cut of a gentleman and the air of someone familiar with commanding any room he walked into.

It was the eyes that captured the attention, however.

They sparkled. So blue and bright they appeared to cast their own light rather than just reflecting the candles scattered around the room. There was humour and mirth in those eyes. Laughing eyes, they seemed, but Ulrich knew better.

These, he'd wager, were liar's eyes.

"Give our guest a seat," the blue-eyed man nodded. The men dragged Ulrich a little further before dumping him onto a stool.

He was in *The Bear Pit*. Kadelberg sat next to him. The Captain favoured him with a baleful glance. His helm was missing and blood caked his mouth. Ulrich resisted the urge to tell him he'd been right about sending scouts into the village.

Three red-cloaked soldiers stood behind them, though none saw the need to draw a weapon. Ulrich wondered if he could grab a gun. Then the blue-eyed man moved to one side to talk to another grim-faced pistoleer. Revealing the rest of the tavern.

Ulrich decided if he got hold of a pistol the best course of action would be to use it to blow his brains out.

The Bear Pit was well known to all the men of The Wolf's Tower, such a small village would not have sported so large a tavern without the coinage of the *Freiherr's* troops. The tavern's two whores had often drawn Ulrich's eye. Neither Edna nor Gerty were particularly fetching but both were very obliging. He'd lost his virginity to one of those girls, but he'd been too drunk to remember which.

Once more the two girls captured his attention.

Strung up by their ankles they hung naked from the rafters, their fingers scraping the top of a table as they swung back and forth on one of the tavern's many draughts. Rivulets of blood, running from scores of tiny wounds, smeared their pale fleshy bodies.

As he watched, the bare-chested giant appeared. Biting deep into Edna's thigh he slurped loudly for a second or two. The girl moaned and her fingers twitched, but she made no further struggle.

The giant pulled away and his demonic face became human again. His rattish features wrinkled in distaste before hawking up a gob of crimson spit.

"She tastes of grease and spunk..."

Laughter filled the room.

Around the shadowy periphery of the tavern, armed figures loitered. Most surrounded a group of young women and children from the village huddled in one corner. They were only men. Others lounged at tables with more casual demeanours, they had less armour and carried fewer arms. Some had helped themselves to Gustav's thin beer. Most had blood smeared around their lips. The demons, Ulrich decided.

The blue-eyed man finished talking to the soldier, who, like the other armed men wore a red cloak over his cuirass or jerkin. They were well-equipped, their armour gleamed in the weak candlelight, they carried modern, well cared for weapons. None appeared hungry or sickening. This was no half-starved band of brigands.

The red-cloaked soldier picked up a stool and placed it before Kadelberg and Ulrich. The blue-eyed man eased himself on to it. The soldier remained at his shoulder.

As the giant sauntered over and sat on a table, the blue-eyed devil regarded them in silence. He was the only one of the demons not to have blood either around his mouth or on his hands.

Two of the other men Ulrich thought to be demons came over. The one responsible for breaking his nose, who he only recognised from his unruly curls, now wore a human face that was round and handsome in a boyish way. A slight figure with high cheekbones and a brooding, melancholy face sat down with him.

Once the demons had settled themselves, the blue-eyed devil spoke.

"What are your names, gentleman?" he asked, pleasantly enough.

Over the blue-eyed devil's shoulder, the two plump whores continued to swing...

"Tell him nothing, he is Lucifer himself!" Kadelberg cried, before Ulrich could answer.

The blue-eyed devil gave a gentle snort of amusement.

"I am not Lucifer."

"Then you are his minion. An accursed demon from the bowels of Hell!"

"I am not a demon," his smile faded, "and I am no one's minion."

"Then who are you?" Ulrich asked. Kadelberg shot him a venomous glance. He ignored it. The days he had to worry about his commanding officer's opinion of him were over.

"I believe I asked first?" Amusement sparkled in his eyes, but it didn't fool Ulrich. One of the other demons started sucking blood from Edna's breast in the background. Hungry wet slurps filled the shadowy tavern. He swallowed. No, he wasn't going to be fooled.

The blue-eyed devil pursed his lips when neither of them replied. A wise man didn't give his name to the Devil, which, until he found out more, was who he thought he was dealing with.

"If you don't talk, I have no use for you..." he glanced over his shoulder at the whores hanging upside down. The demon who'd been drinking Edna's blood, gave her tit a playful squeeze before pushing her away. Wiping the back of his hand over his bloody mouth, the demon wandered off to wash down the whore's blood with a flagon of ale. The blue-eyed devil looked back, "...well, almost no use."

"You'll get nothing out of me devil."

"I'll slit your throat and drink you dry," the blue-eyed devil said, still amiably.

"You'll send me to heaven to be redeemed by the love of Our Lord Jesus Christ. I welcome death..."

The blue-eyed devil sighed, "And what if I kill him instead?" He nodded in Ulrich's direction.

"He is a good Christian man. He would welcome death too."

Ulrich wasn't sure he agreed with Kadelberg on that point...

The blue-eyed devil gave a thoughtful nod, "Very well... what if... I brought over those children in the corner and started chopping off their limbs until your tongues loosened? Would they go so happily to Your Lord, Jesus Christ? Piece by squirming, screaming piece...?"

Kadelberg swallowed but didn't reply. Those blue eyes weren't laughing now.

"Bekker, bring me a child..." he said to the red-cloaked soldier, "...we'll start with a small one, if you please..."

No expression crossed Bekker's face. He turned toward the villagers in the corner without hesitation. The other demons fell silent as women pulled children closer to them. Ulrich's stomach turned. This was no idle threat.

"My name is Ulrich!"

The blue-eyed devil held up his right hand, index finger pointing to the rafters. Bekker stopped, his boots squeaking on the worn old boards of the tavern floor. It was the only sound bar the two plump whores swinging in the draught.

Kadelberg didn't raise his eyes from his boots.

"Kadelberg. Captain Niklas Kadelberg..."

"Kadelberg. Captain Niklas Kadelberg..." the brooding demon repeated.

Bekker returned to the blue-eyed devil's shoulder.

"Now we can be friends," he smiled, as friendly and affable as any fellow could be, and clapped his hands.

A Red Cloak brought over two ale pots and pushed them into their hands.

"'tis just beer," he said, when Ulrich stared into the froth.

"More like piss!" One of the demons shouted.

Ulrich shrugged, if the demons had murder in mind there were many more straightforward ways than poisoning them. He downed the ale. His parched throat was the least of his current discomforts, but it was the only curable one.

"I like things with a thirst..." the curly-haired demon purred, pecking at his thumbnail.

"Thank you," Ulrich said.

"Don't sup with the devil!" Kadelberg dropped his own untouched pot to shatter on the floor.

The blue-eyed man rolled his liar's eyes, "As I've explained, I'm not the devil. My name is Saul. Saul the Bloodless to some," he smiled radiantly, "but you may call me Master..."

Chapter Four

One of The Wolf's Tower's many rules stated no man could enter Solace's bedchamber. She didn't know what her father would do if anyone ever broke that rule, but she suspected the consequences would be severe. However, as no one considered Torben to be a man, her brother came and went as he pleased. Just like he did in the rest of the castle.

"'tis just brigands, as father says..."

Stretched out on her bed, fingers entwined across her stomach, she stared at the ceiling. The hour was late, any other night sleep would long since have taken her. But not tonight.

"...no doubt Kadelberg has strung them up by now. The poor souls. They're probably just hungry."

She glanced at her brother, sitting on the floor in his favourite corner. He liked corners. His chin rested on knees he'd drawn up and hugged. A candle sat in front of him, its pirouetting flame entrancing him. He often carried no expression on his soft face, but an air of particular melancholy had hung about him these past few weeks, punctured only by fleeting anger when his father had refused to let him defend the castle with the other men. On anybody else she would have said something had been troubling him, but you couldn't judge Torben by the usual rules of facial expressions and demeanour.

"Do you not think?"

Torben heard her well enough but didn't respond. Her words had reached his ears, but his mind was elsewhere. Some place where candle flames whispered more eloquently than she ever could.

Next to the candle sat The Goat.

The Devil is about his business tonight...

"Do you think the Devil is coming?" The question was just a whisper. It was best not to say that name too loudly in case he heard and came a calling.

Torben picked up The Goat and placed it next to the flame. Its horned shadow danced upon the wall.

"What do we do when he comes?"

Torben put down The Goat and rummaged in his bag. He stood The Knight next to The Goat.

"How do we fight the Devil?"

The Fox reappeared.

"By being clever. But the Devil is clever too, isn't he? Clever and sly."

Torben rose to his feet and moved to the door. Shuffling across the room, his boots scuffed the floorboards. He hunched forward, hands held out slightly before him, right laid on the left. With his sad knowing eyes and shuffling gait, her brother often looked like an old man trapped inside a young one's body.

He stood before the door, staring at it intently before reaching out and turning the black iron key. The lock clunked shut.

"I think it might take more than locking a door to keep the Devil out."

Torben remained motionless, his big clumsy hand resting on the key. He would often do that. Just stop. Sometimes she thought nothing was going on inside him. Other times she suspected there might be too much. Eventually he twisted the key and the heavy metal mechanism opened again.

When Torben turned back, his eyes glistened. His fleshy lips trembled on the verge of tears.

Solace jumped from the bed and went to him. She wanted to hold him, but he hated being touched. However, this time her big brother lowered his head, bending his gangling frame until his forehead rested upon her shoulder.

"What do you see, brother?" she asked, patting down his unkempt fair hair.

And he did see things. She never spoke of it, not even to their father, for he was right. If people suspected he had the *sight,* Torben would burn. She shared a little of it, just occasional hunches and feelings she struggled to express in words. Sometimes she just *knew* things. Mostly she kept them to herself. Sometimes, if important enough, she would tell Father, whose face would harden. Not with displeasure, but fear.

Their mother had died giving birth to Solace. The wag-tongues whispered, not to her face of course, but the rumours found her ear often enough regardless, that she'd predicted her own death. She'd had the *sight* too. Her father refused to believe in such things, he was a practical man after all, but belief had come after his wife died in childbirth exactly as she had told him she would. Or at least enough belief to fear for his children.

Whatever Solace had inherited from her mother's blood, Torben had inherited more. He knew things yet to pass. His curse was he could not talk or grasp the ability to write, but she recognised what flashed behind the motes of his eye well enough.

He saw what was coming. She had a sense of it, but he saw it. Clear enough to terrify him.

"What do you see?"

Torben shuffled back a pace and pulled another little carving from his satchel.

The Raven.

The Devil was coming to The Wolf's Tower. And death rode at his shoulder.

*

"My only masters are the Lord Jesus Christ and *Freiherr* von Tassau," Kadelberg said.

"My only masters are the Lord Jesus Christ and *Freiherr* von Tassau..." the brooding demon repeated.

Saul the Bloodless tilted forward on his stool, "The Lord Jesus Christ offers you eternal life. *Freiherr* von Tassau gives you silver for your sword. I can do both."

"I have no interest in your deceits," Kadelberg sat ruler-straight, his eye holding the demon's. He was a brave man. Or a fool.

"Tell me..." Saul let the Captain's defiance pass without comment "...how many men guard The Wolf's Tower now?"

"And don't lie to us," the giant added, "we can sniff out lies as well as we can sniff out virgin cunny."

"I will tell you no lies..." Kadelberg's gaze turned to the tall man with the sharp, rat-like features, "...because I will tell you nothing at all."

"...tell you nothing at all..." the brooding demon echoed. Ulrich's attention flicked to him. Hadn't his hair been longer and darker before?

"You are a brave man, Captain. I can admire that, but, trust me, everybody tells me what I want to know..." Saul's smile, as amiable as ever, widened, "...in the end..."

"Then kill me now and save yourself the disappointment."

"Disappointment..."

The Captain's defiance hastened their deaths and Ulrich knew he should be paying some attention to them. Better still, he should be trying to conjure that cunning scheme he was relying on to save his skin. Failing inspiration, he would be well served praying to the Lord for salvation from the monsters they'd been cast down among. Maybe he should just be screaming from the madness and horror of this night. Instead, he found himself transfixed by the brooding demon repeating Kadelberg's words.

His hair *was* shorter, while strands of dusty grey now threaded the black. And his face had grown a gauntness not there before and...

"And what of you, young Ulrich, are you as keen for death as your stubborn Captain?"

Saul's voice snapped him back.

"You are going to kill us, whatever we say," he felt an absurd flush of pride no quiver or quake tarnished his answer. Of all the demons, even the savage-looking giant, the blue-eyed devil scared him the most.

"Perhaps," Saul admitted, his grin both charming and chilling, "perhaps not."

"Better to die like men than treacherous cowards!"

"Treacherous cowards..."

The Captain's eyes darted towards the brooding demon for the first time, uncertainty playing across his face.

Not only was the demon's appearance changing, but his voice also. It was deepening and the accent, one Ulrich had been unable to place, was gone. He sounded like a native Bavarian now.

"Don't worry about Wendel. He's quite mad," Saul gave the barest of shrugs.

One of the other demons, with skin like frost and spiky flame-red hair, had started pushing the two whores back and forth, like a bored child playing with a swing. One of the girls, Edna he thought, gave out a low pitiful moan. The demon giggled.

"Now," Saul slapped hands on his muscular thighs, "are you going to start talking or should I get Jarl here to chop up some children with that big old axe of his?" The giant grinned, his teeth as sharp and feral as the rest of him, "What do you say, Captain?"

"I say better them than the people in The Wolf's Tower.

Not that it makes any difference, without cannon you'd never get through the gate. And you don't have cannon, do you, Devil?"

Saul laughed, "Oh, I don't need cannon, good Captain Kadelberg. I have you!"

"I do not fear you. The Lord will protect me."

"He has wittered enough."

Wendel had spoken, but the voice had been Kadelberg's.

"Jesus..." Ulrich breathed. The brooding demon didn't look *exactly* like Kadelberg, not close enough to fool a mother or lover, but his hair had reduced to grey bristle, his face drawn and eyes sunken behind heavy livid bags. Just like the Captain's. Even the demon's frame had broadened to match Kadelberg's.

The Captain frowned and cocked his head. Kadelberg didn't strike him as the type of man to over frequent a looking glass, but the change was unmistakable. An entirely different man now sat before them.

"Excellent. He was starting to bore me anyway," Saul clicked his fingers and Wendel's face changed again, this time instantly to one of the hideous demons that had ambushed them. Long, bloodless and terrible.

Wendel moved with astonishing speed. One moment perched comfortably on a bench, the next he was at Kadelberg's throat. The Captain screamed and toppled off his chair backwards, blood spraying from his neck. The men behind him shuffled aside as Wendel pinned Kadelberg to the floor, mouth clamped to the Captain's bloody neck.

Kadelberg cried out, tried to punch Wendel's back and

roll him off him, but nothing he did had the slightest effect. His cries grew weaker as Wendel's slurping grew louder.

Ulrich found himself on the floor. He couldn't recall how he'd got there any more than he remembered Kadelberg's blood splashing his face.

"Well then," Saul beamed, turning back to Ulrich, "you were about to tell me how many soldiers remain in The Wolf's Tower, I believe..."

Chapter Five

Torben clamped a hand against his neck.

He stopped in his tracks. His eyes both glazed and bulging. A low keening moan escaped his lips for a few seconds before he returned to his usual silent state.

"Torben?"

There was no response, he remained rooted to the spot, staring glass-eyed at thin air, hand still pressed against the side of his neck.

"What is it?"

He had moments like this. Now and then he would become a statue, frozen in time. People said his broken mind simply stopped working, but Solace didn't think so. Her brother's mind still worked when his body froze. It just went somewhere else.

They were on the third floor of The Wolf's Tower's North Wing. Candles flickered in niches hacked from the cold stone. Other than their footsteps, no sounds disturbed the darkness. If she didn't know otherwise, she'd have thought they'd the castle to themselves. As Father had ordered them to their rooms it was better no one saw them, but, still, the thought they were alone unnerved her in a way it rarely had before.

Solace had been born within the castle's stark sanctuary. Her mother had died here, giving her child life with her dying breath. It was cold, dark, dank and countless draughts stole through the ancient stonework. It stank of tallow, wood smoke, damp stone, dry ashes and musty spent years.

She loved it almost as much as she loved Torben.

She loved its age, she loved its height and heft, she loved its solidity, and she loved its hollowness. She loved its little corners and shadowy places. She loved the view from the battlements, she loved the arrow slits filled with leaded glass when a forbearer, in more peaceful days, had decided it needed to be a home more than a fortification. She loved the cobbled courtyard, around which the four sides of the castle rose, that was always choked with horse dung, clatter and chatter. She loved the dusty crypt where her ancestors rested and waited for her. She loved the moat around the tower, deep and dark and full of mysteries, so she'd thought when she was younger and hadn't realised it was where most of the castle's shit went.

She loved looking at The Wolf's Tower from afar, a great grey, square slab, solid and defiant against the sky. Built by her family centuries ago, before cannon and gunpowder made high walls far less secure than they'd once been. She loved it from its stone-slabbed floors, to its chilly rafters and lofty battlements. She always had and always would. It was home.

But tonight, the deep shadows and deeper silence unnerved her in a way she hadn't experienced before. The thick walls usually made her feel safe from the violent world swirling around them, now they just made her think of a tomb.

They'd snuck away earlier, unable to find rest or ease. Going first to the West Wing to peer through the thick leaded glass of a narrow window. The sky above the village had still glowed orange. Afterwards, Torben trailed in her wake to the South Wing housing their chambers, climbing the spiralling stairs and visiting the small family chapel to pray.

She thought prayer might provide comfort and guidance, but it had done neither. Torben had fidgeted on his knees and made little sucking noises. He liked the Chapel, the services entranced him, but kneeling together before the darkened altar had unsettled him. His head swivelling back and forth between the altar and the door instead of praying.

She'd prayed for the safe return of the gruff, dour Captain Kadelberg and his men. She kept telling herself the Captain would have little trouble dispatching a few brigands. Her father might even bestow a rare smile to reassure her there was nothing to worry about and she could go to bed chiding herself for being a silly child.

But the sense of unease that had been growing for weeks would not dissipate any more than the dreams of fire and blood had gone away. And seeing Torben acting so strangely only made the feeling grow stronger.

Something *was* wrong. She felt it. She just didn't know

what it was.

Her feelings had proved right enough times for her to trust them, even if she didn't understand them. And she had a terrible feeling she would never see Captain Kadelberg or his men again. They hadn't ridden off towards a burning village, they'd ridden off towards the fires of Hell.

They had ridden to their damnation.

*

The possibility he was a coward was one Ulrich had never previously entertained.

He'd yet to face a real battle, just a few skirmishes with half-starved brigands, but he'd never doubted, when the time came, he would show the world his quality. He would charge the enemy line without flinching, he would resolutely defend a breach against whatever odds, he would best his enemies, demonstrate his mettle and above all fight with honour. His father would be proud.

In his boyhood fancies he'd imagined testing himself against the French, the Ottomans or the Catholic League, not the forces of Satan himself. However, when his moment had arrived, he'd run rather than standing and falling with his comrades and now, he knew, he would betray *Freiherr* von Tassau and The Wolf's Tower. He would tell Saul whatever he wanted to know.

He would tell him because he was scared beyond reason.

Wendel pulled himself to his feet, yanked a silk handkerchief from his pocket and wiped Captain Kadelberg's blood from his lips. His demonic face hidden again. In its place was Kadelberg's.

"Witchcraft..." Ulrich said. His words sounded a lot like a sob to his own ears.

"Call it what you will, but 'tis quite the trick, isn't it?" Saul beamed, "Few can perform it so well as dear Wendel here..."

Wendel circled a hand airily before him and bowed. When he straightened, he smiled in a way Kadelberg never had. Fulsome and smug.

Ulrich glanced at the real Kadelberg, who was staring sightlessly at the ceiling, blood pooling around his head.

Saul held out a hand, palm up. The frost-pale skin of the demon's palm started blistering as if something red-hot pushed against it. The blackening skin took the shape of a cross. Saul the Bloodless laughed.

"Not in the same league as Wendel, of course, but amusing nonetheless, don't you agree?" Saul's smile faded, "A woman I once loved taught me that little trick..." he closed his hand to a fist and let it drop to his side.

Ulrich couldn't imagine what the Devil knew of love.

"It was a long time ago..." Saul admitted, seemingly catching the thought.

No one stopped Ulrich as he pulled himself back onto his stool.

"Twenty soldiers remain in The Wolf's Tower..." Ulrich betrayed his oath quietly, not wanting Kadelberg's shade to overhear his treachery on whatever wind carried him from this world to the next.

Saul nodded, as if there had never been any question Ulrich would betray his friends. Betrayal was no doubt a familiar currency to him. He was the Devil after all.

"Plus the *Freiherr*."

"Of course, an accomplished swordsman, I understand?"

Ulrich nodded.

"And he has a son... is he at home?"

"Torben? You needn't worry about him. The boy is a half-wit, a mute simpleton. Give him a sword and the fool would most likely just stab himself."

"And a daughter?" The casualness of Saul's question was entirely false. Wendel, Jarl and the curly-haired demon had grown still too.

"Yes. Solace. As far as I know she isn't much use with a sword either."

Saul laughed like Ulrich had conjured a clever witticism.

"This girl, Solace, she is beautiful, no?" Jarl asked, the fingers of his right hand tracing back and forth along one of the tattoos spiralling down his left arm.

A flicker of something that might have been irritation momentarily replaced the mirth in Saul's eyes.

"Yes. A great beauty. The fairest maid in a hundred leagues of here. Some say."

"You disagree?"

"I haven't seen all the maids in a hundred leagues of here."

The demons laughed. Ulrich's stomach rolled and he fixed on Saul's face. Kadelberg's boots were visible out of the corner of his eye. The toes pointed towards the rafters...

"A virgin?" Wendel asked from behind Kadelberg's face.

The leering hunger alien to the Captain's lips.

"I'd imagine the *Freiherr* would have something to say about it if she wasn't."

"The condition of her cunny is not our business..." for once a hint of ice frosted Saul's voice and Wendel sat down with a shrug, "Who else is in The Wolf's Tower?"

"Just servants; maids, cooks, footmen, stable boys. None trained in arms, but anyone can drop a rock off a wall. Twenty men with muskets and a dozen servants could hold the castle from you with ease."

"I know..."

The tavern door crashed open and red-cloaked men laden with helms, armour and tunics bearing the *Freiherr's* coat of arms staggered in. They kicked snow from their boots and cursed the cold as they started piling the booty on the floor. The blood of Ulrich's dead comrades stained all of it.

Saul's grin stretched wider...

Chapter Six

The Barbican was the only interruption to the imposing grim-grey walls of The Wolf's Tower. It still housed an ancient drawbridge, wide enough for a single wagon or cart to cross. When lowered, the drawbridge connected with a stone bridge crossing two-thirds of the castle's moat.

The family had talked about replacing it and completing the stone bridge, which was old and in constant need of repair, but they never had, whether through cost or nostalgia she didn't know.

The Barbican presented a considerable obstacle to anyone attacking the castle. The thick oak of the raised drawbridge, reinforced by a heavy iron portcullis behind it, was protected by numerous firing slits in addition to the crenelated battlements atop the three-storey structure. If attackers breached the Outer Gate, a second, even thicker door, confronted them at the other end of an enclosed passageway, where they could be fired upon from all sides, as well as having rocks, oil and other unpleasant objects dropped on them through murder holes in the vaulted ceiling.

It was the only entrance to the castle and, therefore, most of her father's remaining men gathered there.

Solace and Torben stood in the North Wing on the fifth floor of the tower, watching the approaches to the castle safe from the eyes of disapproving fathers.

Armed men criss-crossed the roof of the Barbican. Piles of rocks had long since gathered moss in readiness for any attack. While they watched, men rolled out barrels of oil, quicklime and gunpowder. At least her father was taking things seriously.

Without cannon to blow a hole in the gates, a few dozen soldiers could repel all but the largest assault. So Sergeant Lutz had assured her every time she asked if the war would come to The Wolf's Tower. When she'd asked what would happen if an enemy with cannon arrived at their door, the old soldier had shrugged his heavy shoulders. No one with cannon would come. Their small castle had "no strategic value."

That was fancy talk for not being important. She hoped they were right. The Wolf's Tower was very important to her.

She'd been pressing her nose against the leaded glass of what was once - and with the aid of a musket butt could be again - a firing slit. There was nothing else to see. The muddy track cutting through the snow was as deserted as it had been since Captain Kadelberg and his men had ridden down it. Beyond, the birch trees of the wood rose like deformed bony hands clawing at the sky.

Wrinkling her nose, she twisted around to check on

her brother. He still clutched the small wooden carving of The Goat in his right fist, but at least he'd stopped holding his neck and whimpering.

"The soldiers look cold."

If the worst the defenders of the castle suffered were red noses and numb fingers come morning, she'd forgive all their complaints and bad language. Soldiers, she'd long since discovered, loved complaining and bad language.

Torben didn't respond. On a good day he might nod or smile, on others it was like he wasn't aware of the world around him at all. Today wasn't a good day.

Forcing a thin smile, she turned her attention back to the window.

Still nothing.

No shouts, no screams, no crackle of musket fire. The Wolf's Tower was its usual silent, brooding self. Which was good. Shouldn't Kadelberg be back by now though? Or at least have sent word as to what had happened in the village? But no word had come. And that wasn't good at all.

Without warning Torben pushed her away from the window. He was the gentlest of souls and never meant harm, but sometimes he forgot he now had a man's strength and she yelped in surprise.

His nose replaced hers against the glass.

He went rigid, eyes widening. His mouth flapped open and then closed again, silent but for a faint wet plopping noise.

"What do you see?"

Torben, of course, didn't reply.

"Let me look!"

When he didn't move it was her turn to shove.

Torben shuffled aside at her second, harder push.

Riders were coming out of the wood. Just shadows emerging from the snow-laden trees. Scudding cloud had reduced the full moon to a fuzzy suggestion, the horsemen, dark against the snow, rode two abreast in no apparent hurry towards the castle.

They looked like Kadelberg and his men. They certainly weren't hauling any cannon with them. She counted the horsemen. Fourteen pairs. Twenty-eight riders. Forty had ridden out. Twelve men had not returned. Dead or left behind to help the villagers. It must be Kadelberg, yet...

Something sick and intangible twisted inside her.

A tapping noise pulled her eyes away as the men on the Barbican's roof ran to the battlements to watch the approaching riders. Torben had crossed the corridor to stand before one of the doors, the rooms on this floor were mostly empty, nominally guest rooms, though The Wolf's Tower received few guests in these days when travelling anywhere was perilous if you couldn't afford to pay a lot of armed men to travel with you.

He was tapping The Goat against the door.

"'tis Captain Kadelberg returning," she said, too brightly. She wasn't sure if it had been a question or a statement. Torben stared over his shoulder. His big soft unmoving eyes held no comfort. He started tapping the little carving more insistently against the door.

The feeling of wrongness intensified. She spun back to stare at the approaching riders.

Tap-tap-tap-tap...

The Devil was knocking on the door.

*

Tap-tap-tap-tap...

Ulrich's gloved finger tapped the pommel of his saddle. Of course, it wasn't his saddle. Or his horse. But as the owner now resided amid a pile of naked corpses stacked before the burning remnants of *St John's*, he was unlikely to complain too much.

He forced himself to curl his fingers into a fist. The demons watched him, he knew. The curly-haired devil, called Alms, rode behind him. He wore a dead man's clothes and rode a dead man's horse. Like the rest of their troop the bloodstains didn't appear to bother him any. Alms' eyes bore into the back of his neck. That demon watched him more closely than any of the others. He didn't know why and had no desire to find out.

He rode at the head of the column, next to the demon wearing Kadelberg's gaunt face. Wendel. The demon whistled tunelessly. Kadelberg never whistled. Tunelessly or otherwise. He didn't know if he should tell him. It wouldn't make him any more or less of a traitor, but he kept his mouth shut. If the whistling somehow alerted the guards bloodthirsty demons approached, then hurrah for them. The demons couldn't blame him for that...

The great block of The Wolf's Tower rose steadily against a cloud-smeared, star-sprinkled sky. The moon was currently obscured, perhaps too ashamed to cast its soft light upon such cowardice.

"Will you take me back to Hell with you when you are done?" Ulrich spurted, eyes flickering sideways.

Wendel stopped whistling, "I don't come from Hell... I come from somewhere much worse..."

"There's a place worse than Hell?"

"Certainly."

"Where?"

"Meath."

"Is that another of Satan's domains?"

"The protestants would probably say so..." Wendel grinned, "...'tis a miserable collection of bogs, inbred peasants and endless fucking rain in Ireland."

"But if-"

"The only thing you need to know," Wendel snapped, his good humour scurrying into the night like a cat avoiding a bucket of piss, "is that if you're an asset to us you'll live, if you're not... you're food."

Ulrich thought of the two plump whores swinging from the rafters. He swallowed and returned his eyes to The Wolf's Tower.

"I want to live..."

"Of course you do... now tell me, would you normally be chatting to your Captain as you rode back with him to yonder pile of shite and stone?"

"No."

Wendel squeezed Kadelberg's mouth into a sneer, "Then shut the fuck up."

The way Wendel's teeth snapped together to conclude the sentence made Ulrich think of a dog clamping on a bone. He shut up. And fought the urge to rake his spurs on his mount's flank.

He would never make it into The Wolf's Tower. It would be impossible to open and close the gates again before the demons and their company caught him. Even if he could persuade the guards it wasn't Captain Kadelberg and the rest of the garrison returning, but bloodthirsty demons and their minions.

But he *could* warn them.

It would be the honourable thing to do. The thing his oath, sworn to the *Freiherr* himself, insisted he should do. But would they pay any heed if he did? Wendel, through some vile witchery, wore Kadelberg's face and spoke with his voice. No. They wouldn't listen. They'd open the gates and he'd have thrown his life away for nothing. Perhaps by staying alive he would have an opportunity to thwart them later.

He spat at the snow.

Of course, by then, everyone in The Wolf's Tower would be dead.

Still, as long as he was alive...

Charging the enemy line, defending the breach against all odds...

It had taken only a matter of minutes for the demons to strip away every illusion Ulrich had managed to conjure about himself. He was no hero, he'd no honour, he'd no quality.

He was a coward. Plain and simple.

Shutting his eyes against the world, he felt the night's cold breath scour his face, the throb of his broken nose and the warmth of the horse between his legs. If he didn't open his eyes again, he could pretend none of this had happened. It was all just the worst of nightmares. Of course, if he kept his eyes closed long enough one of the demons would probably just rip his throat out. If he wasn't an asset, he was food.

He opened his eyes.

Something was wrong.

"The drawbridge has been raised..." he said out of the side of his mouth, barely loud enough to hear himself over the shuffling, snorting horses.

"So?" Wendel demanded. There was nothing wrong with the demon's hearing.

"I've been here for nearly a year. I've never seen the drawbridge up; they rely on the portcullis to seal the castle at night..."

Did they think they were under attack? Had word somehow got back to them? The demons seemed confident all the men at arms dispatched from The Wolf's Tower were accounted for, but, perhaps, a villager had escaped the initial attack and made it to the castle?

Would he feel better dying from a friend's musket shot than from a demon's fangs?

No. But if the castle did open fire, he might be able to escape in the confusion. A slim hope given he was riding at the head of the column, but a slim hope was better than a choice between death and damnation.

Planning to run away again?

He ignored the voice, which sounded like Old Man Ulrich piping up from the depths of his conscience.

"Heard the damn muskets. Said we shouldn't have

used the fucking things... keep riding, keep looking normal..." Wendel said.

Shaking in his saddle hard enough to rattle his bones would appear normal given the temperature, so Ulrich rode on in silence. With each step his horse took he expected either the drawbridge to clank down or for muzzle flashes to light the black firing slits of the Barbican. Neither happened.

"Why aren't the shite-begotten bastards opening the fucking gates?" Wendel demanded.

"I don't know..."

"If you don't get those gates open..." Saul, who was riding behind him, alongside Alms, said pleasantly "...I'm going to rip you to shreds and feed you to the pigs."

"That would be a terrible shame..." Alms sighed, "...it's such a pretty thing..."

"Halt the column when we reach the moat, raise your right fist and shout "Kadelberg and company returning," as loud as you can..." his betrayal was but a whisper, but the demons seemed to hear everything well enough. God probably did too.

Wendel did as instructed, pulling his horse to a halt as soon as its hooves clattered on the icy stonework of the bridge jutting out over the moat. Raising his right fist, he bellowed. Just as Kadelberg would have done.

Ulrich kept his eyes front. The moon was brightening, but even if it burst from the clouds there wouldn't be enough light to reveal none of the men behind the first two looked the same as the men who had ridden out from the castle, some wore armour that didn't fit properly and most were smeared with blood.

Braziers and tar torches glowed atop the Barbican, but, otherwise, The Wolf's Tower remained dark and silent. No answer came and the drawbridge didn't budge. If they didn't open the gates, what would happen to him?

Two plump whores, drained of blood, swinging naked from the rafters...

What should he do?

Charge the enemy line, defend the breach against all odds...

Why weren't they opening the fucking gates?

Chapter Seven

The cold slapped her face as they burst out onto the roof. Slipping on a patch of ice, she barely managed to regain her footing without falling.

Men gathered behind the crenelated battlements, resting easy on their muskets or cradling crossbows as they warmed themselves around braziers. They didn't appear to be preparing to fight.

Her father and Sergeant Lutz stood directly over the Outer Gate, watching the riders approaching The Wolf's Tower. Given the time it had taken Torben and her to get down the stairs the column must almost have reached the moat by now.

Solace hefted her skirts and run to her father. Torben padded along at her side, The Goat still clutched to his chest.

Their father spun around, scowling at the unexpected sight of his children racing across the Barbican's roof.

"What on-"

"Do not let them in!" she panted, louder than intended.

Eyes flicked in her direction. Men's eyes lingered on her more these days, although never when her father was present.

"What are you doing out here?" Father looked annoyed and cold. But mostly annoyed.

She probably looked annoyed too. As usual he wasn't listening to what she said. She took a deep breath of frigid air. Getting angry would not get what she wanted. Sometimes it did, but this wasn't going to be one of them.

"Do not let them in, 'tis a trick!"

Her father's attention bounced between Solace, Sergeant Lutz and the approaching riders. Sergeant Lutz appeared bemused. The riders were closer. Much closer. They would soon be at the moat.

"Have you taken leave of your senses?" her father's annoyance melted into concern. He had one soft-headed child, he appeared worried she was turning out to be another.

"No."

"Then why would you say such a thing?"

"I just know..." glancing at her brother, who stared out into the winter darkness, mouth hanging slackly open, she dropped her voice "...and Torben knows too. We *know*..."

Their father glanced at Lutz, but the big soldier had found something important amongst a brazier's glowing coals.

"This is no time for games."

"This is no game!"

"We have talked about this before..." he hissed out a plume of frosted breath.

Like Lutz, the rest of the men had found things requiring their urgent attention, but they both knew the soldiers and servants pressed into service on the battlements were all listening.

"I know. And if this were not so important, I would not be telling you so boldly. Father, please, believe us, you must not let those men through the gates."

"'tis just Kadelberg and his company. Do you want me to leave them to freeze out there?"

"It isn't Kadelberg!" She didn't know any such thing, but the weight of the words on her lips held a truth she couldn't deny. Blood had soaked dreams lit by fire every night for weeks. This had to be why. Didn't it?

"Then who, pray tell, is it?"

Torben swivelled his head, slow as an old man rising from his slumber. He raised his hand, The Goat still clenched in his fist. His eyes, big and soft, shone with a rare clarity.

"'tis the Devil, father, the Devil himself!" Solace insisted.

Several of the soldiers stopped whatever they were pretending to be doing and looked sharply up. Whenever someone mentioned the Devil, people paid attention. Everyone knew Satan walked the Earth sowing misery and discord. What other explanation was there for the brutal wars, famine, pestilence and death that had befallen the realms of the Empire?

Lutz cleared his throat, "Given there *was* gunfire, my lord, perhaps it would be prudent not to make assumptions..."

"Do you think Lucifer is coming to supper too, Sergeant?" Father asked, raising an eyebrow.

"The Devil takes many guises, my lord."

Solace nodded, grateful the old soldier at least gave some credence to her warning.

Her father rolled his eyes and sucked in cheeks reddened by the cold.

"My lord!" a soldier called. They all turned, save Torben who was looking up at the fuzzy patch of silver-fringed cloud hiding the moon, to see the column of riders had reached the moat.

Solace followed her father and Lutz to the battlement. Resting a hand on the freezing stonework she raised herself on to tiptoes to peer between the merlon and her father. The riders below looked like The Wolf's Tower's men, as much as she could see in the half-light of the shrouded moon anyway.

The column stood for a moment, before the lead rider - who did look a lot like Captain Kadelberg - raised his right fist and shouted, "Kadelberg and company returning!"

The tension eased out of her father, for all his harsh words he knew well enough the uncanny way his children, like their mother, sensed things they had no right to know.

"See! 'tis just Kadelberg! Lower the bridge and open the gates."

"No!"

Her shrill command teetered on the edge of panic. It was enough to still her father, his brow crumpled as his voice softened, "Solace..."

"Ask them... please, ask them what happened in the

village? Ask before you let them in."

"Why?"

"You know why," she leaned into him to avoid the listening men, "I have had dreams. Dreams of blood and fire. So has Torben."

Her father's face hardened. Then wavered. He didn't like to speak of such things. He had lost his wife to childbirth. He didn't want to lose his children to the witchfinders. She could understand that. But this was too important. She didn't know why; she couldn't articulate the feelings and dreams she had any more than Torben could ask about the weather or for more salt in his soup. But she knew well enough to trust them.

Something inside her screamed and screeched not to let Kadelberg in. Something that had never been wrong. And she could see from the restless distress in Torben's distant eyes, that he felt the same. And probably more besides.

Her father pursed his lips. He had always denied his children's uncanny knack of knowing when things were going to happen, refused to countenance it or speak of it. Nevertheless, he knew it was real. Just as he knew his wife had endured dreams and portents that had come to be. Including foretelling her own death. And he was trapped between those two contradictions.

What he wanted to be true and what he knew to be true.

"Father, please believe us..."

"My lord," Lutz interrupted, "Shall I open the castle?"

Her father's eyes darted back and forth between them.

Then settled on his son.

Torben still stared at the moon.

*

"What happens if they don't let us in?"

"No need for you to worry about that," Saul piped up behind him, "we'll kill you first and then decide."

Some of the company, he didn't know whether men, demons or both, seemed to find this funny.

If he wasn't an asset, he was food. He could pretend there was another, secret, way into the castle but dismissed the idea. He doubted such a ruse would keep him alive for long.

Looking up at The Wolf's Tower, he groped for inspiration, but nothing came. Figures shuffled atop the Barbican, dark against a handful of burning torches. Most of the remaining garrison appeared to have gathered there.

What was the best he could hope for, sat here in the cold trying to betray his Lord and his comrades to the Devil? The gates staying shut and him escaping the demons. Certainly. But how could he achieve that?

He didn't have a clue.

"Does it always take this long to open the gates?" Wendel asked in Kadelberg's voice.

"No..." he admitted. There was no point lying. Maybe an opportunity would arise later and his honesty now might buy his lie more credibility when he needed it.

"Then what is the problem?" Saul hissed, so close Ulrich was sure he could feel the his baleful breath in his ear, but when he jerked around he found the demon still sat astride his horse. Smiling coldly.

"I... don't know... perhaps they got word from the village."

"They didn't," Wendel said out of the corner of his mouth as he continued to stare expectantly up at the castle, "you can be sure of that, so you can."

"How would the lately deceased Captain react to this?" Saul asked.

"He would await orders."

"An obedient dog. I like that. By the way, the next time you fail to refer to me as *master,* I will rip your throat out. Understand me, boy?"

"Yes... Master..." the word clung to his tongue like rancid grease, but he didn't doubt Saul's promise. He'd sold his soul in return for a few more heartbeats. He belonged to the demon now.

Staring up at The Wolf's Tower he blinked back a tear, hating himself even more for snivelling.

"Captain!" A voice boomed from the battlements, "What happened in the village?"

"Brigands!" Wendel shouted back in Kadelberg's voice, the mimicry so perfect it made Ulrich shiver as much as the freezing night, "We have put them to the sword!"

"Who is that?" Again, Saul's voice sounded like a whisper in his ear, again Ulrich jumped, but this time he didn't turn around.

"Lutz, Master... Sergeant Lutz..."

How easy it is to betray your honour, your oath, your friends...

"Is there a problem, Sergeant?" Wendel shouted again

when no immediate response came back.

Figures moved atop the Barbican. Ulrich got the impression a conversation was taking place up there, but they might have been playing dice for all he knew. He eyed the distant trees and sought the courage to ride for them.

"The village still burns?" Lutz's voice came again.

"They burned the church, 'tis lost!"

Another pause.

"Do you have prisoners?"

"No. The brigands are either dead or fled."

Again, a hesitation. Lutz wasn't thinking up these questions. Someone else was telling the old bastard what to ask. The *Freiherr* presumably. Why?

"And the villagers? Are they safe?"

"Yes, I left some men there and have brought the women and children for safety. They are following!" Wendel waved Kadelberg's hand behind him.

Ulrich looked over his shoulder. The following group emerged from the woods with two ox-drawn wagons. Saul had spared the women and children. Perhaps he had some mercy in him.

Two plump whores, hung upside down, swinging back and forth...

But probably not.

The cloud was thinning, more of the fat moon's light brightened the night, the snow-crusted land glowing under its kiss. There was still a fuzzy halo about the moon and clouds raced around it, dimming it almost as soon as it brightened. If it emerged fully, would there be enough moonlight for the men atop the Barbican to realise the soldiers behind him were not the same ones who'd ridden out to the village? And if not the men, then some of the horses (the demons had replaced the horses killed in the ambush with their own)?

Ulrich doubted Lutz or *Freiherr* von Tassau would be able to tell the difference in the men, but if Stablemaster Rohr, who loved the horses far more than he did his sons, was up there...

"Why are they dithering like old women?" Wendel spat.

Saul answered before Ulrich could, "Keep calm and await your orders, like the good Captain would have done..."

Wendel hissed air between his clenched teeth.

No response came from the Barbican. Ulrich felt the cold seeping into his bones, his horse tossed her head and snorted a plume of breath. He pulled his cloak around him.

He shouldn't complain, it would be warm enough when he got to Hell...

Chapter Eight

Solace stood in silence at her father's shoulder, his angry, glaring eyes told her eloquently what he thought. She'd spoken more than enough tonight. No doubt he wished, not for the first time, the Lord had blessed him with one of those daughters who understood she was supposed to be seen but seldom heard.

Torben still clutched The Goat against his chest, his head raised to stare at the teasing moon, too shy to reveal herself from behind the banners of cloud smearing the night sky.

As a way of communicating the danger they both sensed, it wasn't the most supportive of poses.

Still, at least Father had listened, however reluctantly.

Lutz bellowed down at the men shivering under the coy moonlight. And Kadelberg answered. The Captain had commanded the Tassau household troop for twenty odd years. He was a gruff, glum man of few words. A man who had little time for children, but he was part of the fabric of The Wolf's Tower, the backdrop to her entire life. Maybe only a grey ghost on the periphery of her childhood, but she knew him well enough to recognise his voice. Her father gave a snort of satisfaction as Kadelberg answered the questions Lutz recited.

And yet...

The sense of dread persisted. It burned deeper than the cold, frost-bitten air in her lungs. Something was wrong. Something was not as it should be. Her eyes and ears told her Kadelberg and his men waited at the gate. The rational part of her mind insisted she was being foolish. But her other sense, the one she shared with her brother, the one that could not be spoken of for fear it would set them on the path to the pyre, whispered something else entirely.

Keep them outside until the sun rises...

She saw the second group on the road, two wagons of huddled forms flanked by riders. Villagers saved from the flames. Her father would give them shelter, of course he would. He was a good and kind man, as much as he tried to hide it. He was fair to the peasants under his care, even in these hard times when everything was in short supply. He would never turn them away from his hearth.

But would Kadelberg bring them without asking? Kadelberg was a loyal man, but was he a decisive one? In the midst of battle yes, but otherwise he deferred every decision to his lord and master.

"See?" her father turned and smiled, "There is nothing to be afeared!"

"Is it not strange Kadelberg did not send word? Did not ask if the villagers should be brought to the castle?"

Her father sighed and rubbed a hand over the bristles of his neat beard, "He is showing charity, as any Christian man should."

"'tis your charity to give, Father, not his," she felt the dread bubbling into panic, "would the Captain not have asked first?"

"The village is under my protection. Kadelberg is doing his duty."

"Father, please listen-"

"Enough of this! Would you see my men and those poor souls spend the night in the snow? See them freeze because... because of your wretched... *imaginings!*"

His eyes blazed and the fury in his voice made her take a step back, but he reached out and gripped her shoulders, his fingers digging into her arms through her heavy winter cloak.

"No more! You will not speak this kind of nonsense again. Do you understand me?"

She bit her tongue and kept his eye, thinking he was going to shake her, but instead he shook only his head and released her.

"Lutz, get the gates open!"

"Father!" she cried, as he showed her his back.

Lutz ordered men down the stone steps to the Wheelhouse, which housed the mechanisms for the drawbridge and portcullis and more still off to the courtyard to open the Inner Gate.

She looked to Torben for help, but he was staring down at the riders. She went to him and whispered, "What do we do?"

Torben's only response was to show her The Raven. Death. Death waited patiently outside their gates.

Gripping the lichen-mottled stone of the ramparts she stared at the men waiting below. Clouds of steam rose from the horses and soldiers as they waited. Beneath her feet, the ancient mechanisms of the Wheelhouse groaned like an old beast rousing itself from slumber.

"What do we do?"

When Torben didn't respond, she glanced to her side and found he'd slipped away. Her eyes returned immediately to the column of riders.

The moon finally cast aside the veiling clouds, bathing the frozen land in silvery light. Her eye run up and down the waiting soldiers, trying to identify the men, but even in full moonlight they were unrecognisable beneath the dull, beaten metal of their helmets. They could be anyone.

Inching forward, she leaned out into the darkness to get a better view.

Kadelberg sat straight-backed, hands upon the pommel of his horse, the soldier next to him appeared particularly cold and miserable, head lowered and shoulders sagging, but she could make out nothing else. Likewise, the next two men were indistinguishable, faces hidden betwixt helmet and shadow.

And yet they made her flesh crawl.

Keep them outside until the sun rises...

The dread stone was whispering the words over and over, an urgent, desperate demand. They would see them better in the sunlight of course, but it wasn't just that...

As the drawbridge cranked and creaked down to meet

the stone bridge jutting into the moat, Kadelberg turned his head and said something. The miserable-looking man next to him replied, his frosted breath billowing out with his words.

A coldness seeped deep into her soul.

When Kadelberg spoke again, no steaming breath accompanied his words. Nor when the rider behind him replied, a powerful-looking man, tall in the saddle. Only the rider next to Kadelberg had breath. The others...

"Dead men..." she mouthed "...they're dead men."

Of course! The dead couldn't walk in the sunlight.

Solace spun around. Her father was speaking to Lutz; men drifted away, eager for their beds. They thought matters resolved.

"Shut the gates!" she screamed, "There are dead men outside! Dead men in the moonlight!"

Her father whirled around, his face crumpling in anger.

"Solace! I told-"

"Look father, please look, they're dead men!" She stabbed a finger at the riders. The clanking groan of the drawbridge ceased. Now came the sound of hooves from below.

"Stop this at once!"

"Father-"

"Lutz, take my daughter to her room. Keep her there. If needs be you have my permission to sit on her."

"Yes, my lord," Lutz laid his hand on her elbow, but she shook him away.

"Do as I tell you, young lady. We will talk in the

morning," her father ordered.

"No, we won't," she backed away from Lutz and her father till she was hard against the cold stonework of the ramparts, "we'll all be dead by the morning!"

"Quiet this nonsense!"

The remaining soldiers openly gawped at the scene now and they stared even harder when she slapped Lutz's hand away, "The Devil is coming, can't you see? They have no breath; the Devil has brought the dead to kill us all!"

"Lutz, get her to her room!"

She tried to dodge the burly old soldier, but he caught her arm. When she kicked him, her father ordered two of his men to help the Sergeant restrain her. All the time the sound of hooves and snorting horses came from below.

A young soldier, Lothar, made a grab for her other arm, but she pulled free and twisted back towards the rampart. She must get them to look, to see what she'd seen in the moonlight.

The men were wide-eyed and fearful, but it was Solace von Tassau, not the Devil and the dead men below, who scared them. She was raving like a mad witch.

"Father, just look, *please* just look..." she sobbed. Both anger and sorrow mixed on her father's face, but no understanding.

She went limp and stopped struggling, the riders had passed the Outer Gate and into the tunnel running beneath the Barbican and the North Wing of The Wolf's Tower. The Inner Gate still had to be opened from the Courtyard, but, once it was, the castle would be lost.

There was nothing she could do to stop them.

Then she saw her brother.

In the commotion that had drawn all the remaining men atop the roof to her, Torben had rolled one of the barrels of oil next to a wooden hatch set into the flagstones. A murder hole. His hair flopped across his face as he hauled it open. For once his hands were free of his little carvings, free of his words. But his actions spoke loudly enough.

He knew death rode into the castle below them.

And this would be their only chance to send the Devil back to Hell.

Solace started screaming.

*

The drawbridge began to fall, clanking and groaning, towards the frozen moat.

Behind him, Saul laughed, a good-natured, back-slapping bellow of contentment. Ulrich couldn't remember hearing a more terrifying sound in all his life.

"We shall have some games tonight right enough, eh?" Wendel turned in his saddle.

"What are you going to do?" he asked.

"That's no concern of yours, boy," Wendel snapped.

"No... Master..." Ulrich cowered.

"Serve us well and you will live," Saul said, "I suggest that is what should be of concern to you."

"How can I serve you best, Master?" The words burned his lips. He tried to tell himself he just played along to stay alive and when an opportunity arose, he would escape, but when you chose to sit down and play with the Devil, there was only likely to be one winner.

"Stay close to me and do as I command."

"Can't it stay close to me and do as I command?" Alms purred.

Saul chuckled, another blood-curdling sound.

The drawbridge banged into place on the stone buttress. The portcullis was up, the Outer Gate open and the black maw of The Wolf's Tower beckoned.

"Ride on! Nice and easy does it!" Wendel commanded, still in Kadelberg's voice. The column moved slowly onto the bridge crossing the ice-covered moat.

The Inner Gate remained closed, and no torches burned inside the Darkway. There was enough room for two horses side by side, but with little to spare.

The Inner Gate remained shut and the darkness rushed in around them as they entered the Barbican. The passage was known as the Darkway with good reason. Seeing nothing, he let his horse follow the familiar cobbles.

"Why isn't the inner gate open?" Saul hissed in his ear again. It was even more unsettling in the darkness.

"All the men will be up on the battlements, Master, they have to send some down to the courtyard to unbar the gate."

His horse came to a halt. He'd only a sense of the Inner Gate in front of him. He looked about, panic rising. It was too much like a tomb. A dank stink lingered here, where the stonework never felt the sun's caress.

Once the Inner Gate opened the killing would begin. He dreaded it, part of him still demanding he do something to warn the castle, but right now he wanted those gates to open more than anything. It felt too much like being buried alive down here.

"Don't be scared, Pretty Thing, I will comfort you later..." how Alms could see anything, Ulrich couldn't imagine, but the demon's soft words churned his stomach.

Alms laughed like a flirtatious girl.

Then, distantly, a woman began screaming...

Chapter Nine

"The Devil is here! The Devil is here!"

She started bucking and thrashing, throwing her head from side to side so violently her long blonde ponytail whipped the faces of the men holding her. She screamed so hard it felt like her throat might split.

"My lord, she is possessed!" someone cried.

They could think what they liked, so long as they all kept their eyes on her rather than Torben.

"Solace! Stop this!" No anger hardened her father's voice now. Just fear. But that fear was for her rather than the fact men with no breath had entered the castle.

Aside from her father and Lutz, six men at arms remained atop the Barbican, two of them tried to help Lutz control her, the other four simply stared, mouths agape.

She was a slight girl, slim of frame and shorter than any of the men. She should have presented few problems to three soldiers, but she was the *Freiherr's* daughter, so they were reluctant to treat her roughly. She managed to pull her right hand free and raked the face of a grizzled toothless soldier called Clement, though her nails only scraped the cold metal of his helm.

Behind the men clustered around her, Torben pulled aside the cover to the murder hole that allowed the defenders to rain missiles down on any invaders who breeched the Outer Gate.

She ranted, not knowing what poured from her lips, nonsense and gibberish, anything to keep the men away from her brother as he rolled the barrel over the open murder hole.

As she screamed and wailed, her father shouted back at her, but she heard his words no more than she heard her own. The dread that had been swelling within her for weeks gushed from her body in torrents. She swore and cursed, she kicked and spat. She was indeed possessed, but not by any demon. It was fear controlling her. Fear and the absolute certainty the men below would slaughter them all if they got through the Darkway and into The Wolf's Tower.

Torben was trying to pull off the barrel's lid. A

hatchet or lever would have helped, but neither was to hand, instead he was tugging at the lid so hard the barrel rocked back and forth.

Her father joined Lutz and the soldiers. Between them they pushed her back against the scarred stonework. Her father forced a hand over her mouth to stop her ranting.

"Solace! Solace!" he repeated her name, all but sobbing. A wave of shame washed over her, but she couldn't allow it to stop her. So, she sank her teeth into her father's hand.

As he yelped, Torben managed to yank the lid free of the barrel. Staggering backwards, he almost slipped on the ice. Regaining his balance like a newborn foal, he tipped the barrel over as carefully as he could. Oil rushed eagerly over the lip and disappeared into the murder hole.

Just a little longer. Torben needed just a little longer.

"Jesus save us! Jesus save us from the Devil at our door!" she wailed. Her father shook his head but seemed reluctant to risk his hand near her mouth again.

"Gag her!" he ordered "Tie her up and get her to her room."

"My lord!" Lothar shouted, pointing.

Her heart sank.

Torben grabbed a torch from a metal ring set into the battlement, but he still needed to get back to the murder hole to ignite the oil.

"Stop him!" her father bellowed, running towards his son himself. All the soldiers, even fat old Lutz, followed him. Solace, suddenly forgotten, slumped back against the stonework.

Her father grabbed Torben before he reached the murder hole, grappling with him to wrest the flaming torch from his hand. Torben was slim like her, but he had a wiry strength and kept moving forward even when two more soldiers piled on top of him.

"Torben..." she whispered, as her brother went down under a pile of bodies, a terrible keening wail escaping his lips as he disappeared. He hated being touched above all things, it was such a torment no one was allowed to put a hand upon him. He would run to his room if anyone so much as brushed against him. Only she could touch him. Once in a while, he would let her hold his hand if he was frightened or distressed by the nameless things haunting his soul. But never anyone else.

It would drive him half mad.

They pulled the torch from his hand and tossed it away. He continued to struggle like a wild boar and it took all the men to keep him down.

She forced her eyes away. On the merlon next to

her another torch burned.

Grabbing it without thinking, she sprinted across to the murder hole, and pushed aside the now empty barrel.

"No!!!" Someone screamed. It was too late. Dropping the burning torch, she watched it spark and fizz as it tumbled into the gloom of the Darkway.

"Go back to Hell..."

*

"Oh, it sounds as mad as a bag of weasels," Alms giggled.

"You should know," Wendel sighed.

Ulrich heard the distant screams but made out little of the words. He thought he heard her say "Devil" a couple of times and the hairs on the back of his arms stood up.

"Any idea who that jolly lass is?" Saul asked, again it felt like the demon whispered in his ear. Ulrich jerked his head away as if bothered by a fly.

"No... Master..." he lied.

"I might cut off all her fingers and then shove them up her arse one at a time..." Saul mused "...then we'll see how she sounds when she really has something to scream about..."

At least Saul hadn't picked up on the lie. That was something, wasn't it? He was sure the screaming girl was the *Freiherr's* daughter, the Lady Solace. People whispered, very, very quietly and never anywhere the *Freiherr* might hear, that his daughter had the *sight*.

Something seemed to have unsettled the *Freiherr* enough to keep the gates closed, if his daughter had somehow foreseen the coming of Saul and his demons, perhaps that was the reason.

And now they were in the Darkway, although the Inner Gate remained barred in front of them.

Ulrich glanced upwards; it was too dark to see the vaulted arches above their heads. Too dark to see the arrow loops and murder holes too...

He edged his horse forward till she would go no further, nose against the gate that was barely a suggestion in the darkness. The faintest of glows from the torches burning in the Courtyard snuck around the edges of the thick oak.

"You seem eager," Wendel growled. The hissing sigh of metal on leather accompanied the words as the demon drew his sword.

Ulrich wondered who would be opening the Inner Gates. Someone he would have smiled or nodded to that morning, and even if it was someone he'd ignored, it wouldn't have occurred to him he would see them die a few hours later. Even less that it would, in part, be due to him. He could still shout a warning, but he wouldn't. Fear held him too tightly to do anything other than obey his new masters.

"I just want this to be over."

Such dark good humour bubbled in Wendel's reply it made Ulrich close his eyes against the shadows, "Oh, me boy, this is going to be a long, long night, so it is..."

The sound of boots on cobbles broke the following silence, men coming to open the Inner Gate. Men coming to die.

Then someone cursed behind him, a horse nickered in alarm.

Wendel shifted in the saddle, leather and metal creaking as he twisted to look back.

"What's wrong?"

"Oil!" Came the cry from further back along the column.

More curses rolled out of the darkness, horses snorted and men shouted, but there was no room to turn and go back. Only forward. The sounds coming from the other side of the gate grew louder.

"Hurry!" Wendel called out in Kadelberg's voice, "Get the gate open!"

"Yes, Captain!" Came a voice too muffled by oak a man's hand thick for Ulrich to recognise.

"I can smell oil," Alms giggled, "do they mean to cook a midnight roast down here?"

Twisting around he saw little, though a faint shaft of grey light fell from the vaulted ceiling where none had been when they'd rode into the Darkway. Someone had opened the hatch of a murder hole. And poured oil down it.

"Do not fear..." Saul's smooth voice floated out of the darkness, "...we burn slow..."

Then someone shouted a warning as a torch fell from the ceiling. Turning end over end, it plummeted towards the oil-soaked riders below. A moment later the tunnel was no longer dark.

And screams rolled along the Darkway on a dragon's breath.

Chapter Ten

The torch fell into the darkness. For an instant, its light revealed the helmeted faces of men looking upwards, their mouths stretched into black circles.

Then the murder hole blinked white and a whoosh of scorching air shot into the frigid night. She stepped back, unsure whether to smile or cry.

"What have you done?" Father seized her shoulders and shook her fiercely, "In the name of our Lord, what have you done?"

"I have brought hellfire down upon Satan, Father," she was surprised how calm she sounded. And how mad.

"You have killed my men!" The heat of his breath on her face was almost as hot as the wave of air gushing out of the murder hole.

She blinked but said nothing. He would find out soon enough the men below were soldiers of Satan, not The Wolf's Tower.

Screams echoed up from the Darkway. Lutz and the

other soldiers either stared dumbly at her or dumbly at the murder hole, out of which wisps of black greasy smoke started to curl.

"Go and help get them out of there!" When everyone continued to stare dumbly, her father jabbed a gloved finger at the murder hole, "Now!!"

Lutz, jerked out of shocked torpor, started pushing men towards the stairs. When the Sergeant moved to follow them, the *Freiherr* shook his head, "Get these two to their chambers."

"Yes, my lord," Lutz, who'd known her all her life, eyed her like she might slit his throat given half a chance.

"I'll speak to you later," her father dropped his hands from her arms and turned to go.

"If you open the Inner Gate, you will never see me again..."

Where those words came from, she didn't know, but she felt the weight of their truth.

Torben hadn't risen since the soldiers grappled him to the ground, he sat hugging his knees. Shaking as whimpers escaped his trembling lips. His tears glistened in the moonlight. They all thought he was crying from being manhandled. But he wasn't. He knew her words would come to pass too.

It wasn't enough. One barrel of oil wouldn't kill enough riders, even in the tight confines of the Darkway. If they were only regular soldiers, then maybe they could fight them off, but they weren't regular soldiers. They were the Devil's own rogues.

"You do not see the future, Solace, if you did, you

would not have set light to my men. Do you have any idea how much danger you're in?"

"I do, Father, the Devil is at the door and you are too blind to see. And we are all going to-"

Her father hit her. His open palm across her face, hard enough to finally stop her talking. She rocked backwards but managed to keep her footing.

In all her life Father had never struck her. He was not a violent man and she'd never been a mischievous child. A disapproving look or a stern word were always enough to check any errant behaviour. Her father's disapproval was a scalding, withering thing. She loved him and always wanted to please him. Now the days of pleasing him were over. She was too busy trying to save his life.

"Why don't you believe me? You know we can see things, Torben and I? You *know* we can. Just like mother could."

The mention of his wife drained the anger from his face. Sadness rushed in to fill the void it left behind.

"You don't possess foresight, Solace, just ignorance. Your mother was a sick and troubled woman..." he spun on his heels, "...and clearly so are you..."

*

The Darkway had become the gateway to Hell.

Fire and demons surrounded him. Where else could he be? Horses and men screamed, the stink of burning oil and roasting flesh filled his nostrils while grotesque shadows danced across the ancient stonework.

He fought to control his terrified mare. It bucked and

kicked as the horses behind tried to force their way forward, away from the flames at the back of the column.

He was far enough from the oil to be safe from burning. The frenzied animals trampling him to death, however, was a very real possibility if he fell from the saddle. If he wanted to live - and the betrayal of his master, his father's memory and his comrades all suggested he did - he had to keep atop his frightened horse.

Somewhere behind him, betwixt the manic shadows and the rapacious flames, came the sound of snapping bones. Someone hadn't managed to stay on their horse. That particular scream was cut short.

Any moment he expected the wet, sticky kiss of oil gushing from a murder hole, the cackle of muskets from the old arrow loops, or perhaps rubble dropped onto his head. The Barbican had more than one murder hole and the castle certainly more than one barrel of oil. If it was a trap, why weren't they being slaughtered? And why did it still sound like the Inner Gate was opening?

Saul shouted something. Ulrich ignored him. One job at a time. Staying alive was all that mattered. Oh yes, all that mattered indeed.

"Open the fucking gate!" He couldn't tell if he'd muttered the words or screamed them. Part of him begged to shout the exact opposite, to warn his comrades, but the desire to live was too strong. The greasy stink of roasting fatty meat filled the Darkway now. He focused on the gate, his own shadow flickering across the ancient oak.

The Inner Gate was two fists thick and the bar the size of a tree trunk. It took half a dozen men to lift it, which was why they rarely closed it.

His mare bucked again, then kicked her hind legs at the horse behind. Another horse slammed into her and Ulrich almost slipped from the saddle. The panicked horses couldn't turn in the tight confines of the Darkway and they trampled over each other to get away from the fire at their backs.

"Well, this wasn't supposed to happen..." Saul whispered in his ear again, suddenly enough for Ulrich to cry out. He twisted around to make sure Saul hadn't somehow vaulted onto the back of his horse. However, Saul was no longer behind him, there was just a maelstrom of men, horses and flames bleeding into one another to create some monstrous apparition, fit for only the worst nightmares and the deepest pits of Hell.

"I do hope you had nothing to do with this?" Saul asked, affably enough, given the circumstances.

Ulrich gripped the mare's flanks harder with his thighs and looked wildly about. There was no sign of Saul. Until he glanced upwards. The demon clung to the stonework above his head, arching his back and looking over his shoulder. Burning mad eyes, incongruous above a boyish look-at-me grin, fixed on Ulrich.

"No... Master!" Ulrich managed to cry, looking away. The stone blocks of the Darkway were old, pitted and broken from centuries of dripping moisture, freezing winters and the tireless work of insects, but there was nothing a man, let alone a man weighed down by arms and armour, should have been able to cling to.

Twisting back the other way he saw Wendel and Alms

had found similar sanctuaries above the sea of maddened horseflesh.

They look like bats...

Another useless thought. They were demons, not men. He doubted he'd seen a fraction of what they were capable of.

His mare screamed and nearly threw him. Tossed forward he flung both arms around the animal's neck. He got a face full of hair and horse sweat for his trouble. His right foot slipped from the stirrup, and he was desperately kicking backwards to find it when the Inner Gate finally swung open. The mare lurched into the gap.

The sudden movement hurled him forward again and he clung to the horse's neck as they exploded into the courtyard. Pale faces flashed by as his terrified horse charged across the cobbles, only stopping when it reached the far side where the steps led up towards the Great Hall.

The maddened animal skidded to a halt, then reared up, wild white eyes not recognising the familiar surroundings of The Wolf's Tower and the stables that made up the ground floor of the castle's West Wing.

Ulrich somehow found himself on the smooth cold cobbles of the Courtyard. He didn't know if the horse had thrown him or he'd jumped. He wasn't sure if he should get to his feet and run or just curl up in a ball and wait for the madness to end.

The Courtyard was full of horses, a few still had riders, most didn't.

He was sitting up, hands on the cobbles, he'd lost his helmet somewhere. His ears felt cold, he realised, suppressing a giggle.

"Ulrich!" A voice cried. It was Vinzenz. When really bored, he played dice with the young Bohemian soldier.

"What madness!" Vinzenz gasped, crouching down next to him, one hand resting on Ulrich's shoulder.

He stared past Vinzenz to the open Inner Gate as a figure walked out of the Darkway, burning from head to toe.

Albwin, one of the stable lads, grabbed a horse blanket and ran to the flaming figure. Ulrich wanted to yell at the boy to keep away; the burning man wasn't screaming in agony. He was laughing. But more figures emerged from the Darkway, Saul and the other demons. Shouting warnings would not please his new master.

He looked at Vinzenz, who stared in bog-eyed horror as the burning man's arms enveloped Albwin and pulled the boy into his embrace. His clothes began to smoke and blacken as the burning man lowered his mouth to Aldwin's neck. The stable boy's scream was never going to be mistaken for laughter.

Ulrich reached for his dagger. If he plunged it into Vinzenz's throat his new master would be pleased, wouldn't he? And it would be a quick death. Taken completely by surprise. A mercy.

The remaining mounted horsemen had drawn their swords and fallen on the unsuspecting men in the Courtyard. It was no battle.

Hand still lingering on the hilt of his dagger, Ulrich hissed, "Run, for God's sake, save yourself..."

Vinzenz didn't hear him, instead he yelled, "Come,

Ulrich! At them!"

The young Bohemian sprung to his feet and drew his sword. It was an ancient falchion, almost as long as he was. Ulrich had never gotten around to asking why the boy carried such an unwieldy weapon. As Vinzenz charged the demons, Ulrich knew it was a question he'd never get to ask now.

Vinzenz bellowed as he ran at Saul, swinging his sword two-handed.

He charged the enemy, he defended the breach...

The demon just grinned, his own weapon still in its sheath. Ducking under the swing at the last possible moment with incredible speed, he grabbed Vinzenz's wrist and twisted the young soldier's arm. The splintering crack of bone echoed around the courtyard, along with the clatter of steel on stone as the sword tumbled from the boy's grasp. For a moment Vinzenz screamed, but then Saul had the young soldier's head between his hands. Another simple twist, another crack of bone.

Vinzenz's body crumpled to the cobbles.

Six corpses littered the ground. There would be more soon.

"Where are the rest of them?" Saul demanded, striding towards Ulrich.

In the background, the burning man discarded Aldwin's corpse and started rolling in a heap of dirty snow shovelled off the courtyard after the last significant fall.

Spying his helmet Ulrich scrambled over the cobbles to retrieve it before clambering to his feet. Nothing seemed broken, everything seemed to hurt. Including his soul.

"Most of the men will be in the Barbican, the rest on the battlements or in the North Wing," he indicated the unassuming door to the side of the Inner Gate that led through the North Wing to the Barbican.

"Bekker!" Saul shouted; the Captain of the Red Cloaks was one of the few who had managed to stay in the saddle. Dismounting in one smooth movement, he hurried over.

"Master!"

"We need to take the Barbican; I don't want them dropping the portcullis before Jarl arrives with our bounty. Leave two men here, gather the rest and go with Wendel and Alms."

Bekker mustered his men, and they headed off with the two demons towards the Barbican. Several other figures slipped silently away into different doors. Demons all.

"Young women and children alive if you please!" Saul shouted after them, "Hunt everyone else down and kill them, we'll find the girl when the castle is secure."

Once they clattered through the door leading to the Barbican, Ulrich found himself alone in the courtyard with Saul, the burning demon and the two soldiers Bekker had left behind. Plus the corpses of his comrades.

The burning man sauntered over, rubbing handfuls of grey snow into his blackened flesh, which was still smoking.

"Frankly, 'tis an improvement," Saul grinned.

"Don't make me smile," the burning man growled back, "this stings a tad."

Ulrich stared. How could he still be alive? He must have been directly beneath the murder hole when the oil rained down. His face was charred like an overcooked roast and nothing remained of his hair bar some blackened clumps of bristle. His jerkin was just scraps of burnt leather and his cuirass looked like an old cooking pot.

Seeing Ulrich's attention, he shrugged, "Looks worse than it is."

"Don't worry about Callinicus, he is exceedingly ugly at the best of times," Saul gave the demon a playful slap on the shoulder.

Callinicus snarled. His lips cracked as he curled them back.

Saul positioned the two soldiers in the mouth of the Inner Gate, "Anyone sticks their head into the courtyard, kill them," he ordered. The men both nodded.

Saul and Callinicus stepped into the Darkway. The stink of burnt meat was overpowering. A few flames still licked around heaped forms further along, but the darkness had flooded back into most of the tunnel.

"You," Saul said, turning to Ulrich, "Go to the Outer Gate and give Jarl the signal to come through, then check for anyone still alive in there and drag them out."

Several thoughts competed for Ulrich's attention. What was the signal? What if someone decided to drop something else through a murder hole? Why bother dragging anyone out of the Darkway? A pistol ball in the head would be kinder? None of them reached his lips.

"Yes, Master," he said instead and moved down the Darkway as obediently as the dog he was. Vinzenz had charged the enemy. He'd defended the breach against overwhelming odds. He'd been a man. The kind of man

Ulrich had foolishly thought he'd been until a few hours ago.

And now he was dead.

Ulrich swallowed, glanced at the vaulted ceiling and the black silent shafts of the murder holes, and shuffled into the darkness once more.

Chapter Eleven

Her face stung.

She resisted the urge to place a hand against her cheek and feel the smarting heat. A *Freiherr's* daughter was probably supposed to be stoic about such things. She didn't know. No one had ever given her advice about what to do after your father slapped your face. No one had ever needed to.

Instead, she walked. Torben on her right, Lutz behind, where he could keep an eye on them in case they tried to kill anybody else.

"You need not worry, Sergeant..." she spoke quietly, calmly, eyes fixed forward, "...I have no intention of setting you alight."

The only response was the clip of nailed boots echoing along the corridor.

Lutz was upset.

She tried not to concern herself. The Sergeant was going to be a lot more upset when he found out she and Torben were right. Still, it rankled.

"Do you think me a lunatic, Sergeant?"

"I'm a soldier, my lady, I am paid to follow orders. Not think."

"Perhaps we would not be trapped in this awful war if people did more thinking..." she looked over her shoulder without breaking stride "...and less following orders."

Lutz's features crumpled beyond their usual level of dishevelment.

They continued in silence. Her words had sounded calm and sane, but nobody listened to her. Ever. She was just the pretty daughter, waiting patiently to be married off to whoever her father considered most advantageous. That was what her world had comprised of since it had become evident she would be pretty. Given Tassau's insignificance, an ugly daughter would be far harder to marry off to someone of benefit.

It didn't matter. Now she was the pretty daughter waiting patiently to die. Though perhaps a quick death would be too much to hope for...

She swallowed and closed her eyes for a moment. When she opened them again, she found Torben had stopped.

"What's wrong?" she asked, hurrying back to her brother's side. His eyes stared sightlessly ahead of him; his head cocked to one side as if listening for something. He was still trembling.

"Come along now..." Lutz said. He knew as well as anyone how difficult it was to get Torben to come along anywhere if he didn't want to.

A faint mewling noise escaped Torben's lips, his head

moving back and forth as if looking for something hidden in the shadows of the corridor.

"Can you hear something?"

The walls and doors of The Wolf's Tower were thick; sound didn't always carry true amongst its vaulted ceilings, stone corridors and narrow, twisting staircases. Sometimes you couldn't hear people talking outside your door, other times you could follow a conversation from floors away. When little she'd blamed the strange noises The Wolf's Tower made on restless spirits, but now she knew it was just the wind finding its way through holes in the masonry, the subtle shifting movements of stone and timber, the weight of accumulated centuries pressing down on the castle. Usually.

But Torben's ears were exceptional. They heard a lot more than hers did.

Torben didn't respond. He still clutched The Goat but didn't make any move to express himself. Not that he really needed to. Whatever it was he'd heard, it only meant one thing. The Devil and his rogues were in The Wolf's Tower.

A profound sense of despair descended. She was without hope. Either the Inner Gate had opened, allowing the Devil and the Dead inside the castle, or she'd set innocent men afire.

"Come along, no dawdling," Lutz was trying to sound stern.

"They're here, aren't they?"

"Who?" Lutz thought she was talking to him, not Torben.

Her eyes swivelled to the Sergeant when it became

clear her brother was not going to respond.

"The Devil."

"My lady, the Devil is not-"

The crackle of gunfire echoed up from the bowels of the castle. Faint, but unmistakable.

"Perhaps you will believe me now?"

"Horses," Lutz said, none too assuredly, "putting down horses. From the fire."

"Perhaps..." she conceded.

Lutz held her eye until a scream rolled out of the shadows. It wasn't the scream of a horse. The silence that replaced it when it abruptly cut off was heavy.

"Perhaps not..."

Lutz looked back down the corridor. The only movement came from the flickering candles, their light struggling against the greater weight of the darkness filling The Wolf's Tower.

"Should we go and wait in our chambers?" she asked, "I fear my father will not be joining us."

Lutz swallowed, concern ploughing deeper furrows across his forehead.

"This way," he barked, turning for the nearest door and pushing it open. Solace pinched Torben's sleeve, when he didn't tug it free, she pulled him gently after the Sergeant.

They were in the family rooms, not far from her own and Torben's chambers. Once the family had been much larger, now the only other occupied rooms were her father's. The room Lutz had entered had been empty for many years. It smelt of dust and disuse.

Like most of the rooms of the castle its windows faced the Courtyard.

It was unlit, but Lutz moved through the shadows, navigating the shrouded furniture to the room's only window, a narrow slit, deeply recessed in the thick wall. He placed a hand on the stonework on each side and leaned forward till his broad, flat nose pushed against the glass.

"What do you see, Sergeant?" Solace asked as Lutz stood motionless.

"Horses..." he replied in a whisper "...untended. And bodies."

"Of the men I burned?"

"No, my lady..." he eased himself away and leaned against the wall, shadow veiled his expression, but the despair in his gravel-scoured voice was unmistakable, "...the men we sent to open the Inner Gate."

"And the Devil's rogues?"

Lutz shook his head, "I can't see anyone else."

"Then they must be in the castle already."

"I must find the *Freiherr*!" Lutz exclaimed, brushing past them and back into the corridor.

"There were twenty-eight men in the column, Sergeant. How many did I kill?" Solace hurried after him. Torben trailed behind without prompting.

"Some... The Darkway is narrow," Lutz stopped outside the room, one hand resting on the hilt of his sword, his big head sweeping back and forth along the corridor. It was empty save for shadows.

"So there may not be many of them. But there was a second group."

"The ones with the villagers?"

"Who knows who sat in those wagons. But they may not be here yet."

"They soon will be."

"Not if we drop the portcullis."

"The *Freiherr* will-

"We don't have the time to find my father."

"But-"

"If more of them get inside, we are lost. 'tis probably too late, but if we can get to the Wheelhouse before they do..."

Lutz nodded, "I will go, you must retire to your chambers, my lady. Lock the door."

"A locked door will not save us. Dropping the portcullis might."

"My lady!"

"Sergeant, this is our home, my family have defended it for centuries..."

Indecision played across Lutz's craggy face. His first and last duty had always been to protect the *Freiherr's* family, but he knew she was right. His eyes moved to Torben. Her brother's face was blank, but he reached out and put a hand upon the hilt of Lutz's sword. Solace smiled a grim, bitter smile for him.

"We can fight for our home too..."

*

The Darkway reeked of death.

It led out to the snow-choked approach to The Wolf's Tower, but it might have been the very gateway to Hell itself.

Why did he send me?

Ulrich took a few hesitant steps towards the smouldering forms littering the cobbles before the Inner Gate. Was it a test? To see if he could follow an order? To see if they could trust him? To see if he would try and run?

Perhaps.

Should he take the opportunity to prove himself to the Devil or the chance to save himself before he did more harm? More harm to others like Vinzenz, more harm to whatever fragment of his immortal soul remained his own?

"Ulrich!"

Saul's voice sliced through his thoughts. He jumped and twisted around in one movement, his boot sliding on a smooth, blood-slickened cobble. The demon stood beneath the arch of the Inner Gate, a flaming torch in one hand.

"Take this!" Saul's eyes were hooded, as if the torch blazed as bright as the summer sun. He threw it with a casual flick. Ulrich managed to catch it without burning himself. One test passed.

Saul slunk back into the shadows, but Ulrich felt those blue liar's eyes lingering on him all the same.

Holding the torch aloft, Ulrich crept forward, its uncertain light flickered over the carnage. A horse lay across the Darkway. As he tried to pick a way around, it jerked its head and flailed out a leg. An iron hoof sparked against the stone wall.

Drawing his sword - which the demons had returned to him after leaving the tavern - he hacked the stricken beast's neck. Blood spurted up his arm. The horse twitched once before stilling. Other mangled horses blocked the Darkway, the next had a man pinned beneath it. Neither required putting out of their misery.

The smell of burnt meat grew stronger as he approached the point where the oil had ignited under the murder hole.

He searched for the vengeful faces of his old comrades peering down, ready to douse and burn him too. Perhaps they might favour quicklime this time? Or some other horror from the castle's armoury he was unfamiliar with? However, there was nothing but shadow and the thinnest slither of sky.

He paused over another broken and trampled corpse; the head pulped like rotten fruit at the end of market day.

There was no question the man was dead, but Ulrich crouched as if to confirm it. Quickly scooping up a pistol from the cobbles, he slipped it into his belt and swept his cloak over it as he straightened up. He didn't know if it was an act of defiance, a forlorn hope or to use on himself. It was merely instinct and that was all he had left.

He moved on.

More corpses, some still licked by faltering flames, all beyond help.

Why hadn't they poured more oil? Why had they opened the Inner Gate?

No demons had died, but Saul's company had paid a heavy price to gain entry and the old castle's defences could have made them pay more.

Someone had tried to stop them. Devil's trickery hadn't fooled everyone in the castle. But it appeared they had been acting alone.

He wondered what Saul would do to them if his piercing eyes fell upon their soul?

Ulrich hoped, whoever it was, they'd saved a pistol for themselves too.

Chapter Twelve

The Wolf's Tower wasn't actually a tower. It was four, six-storey wings built around a central courtyard, but from the outside it looked like a solid construction, grey and foreboding.

There were no turrets, no outer walls or a keep as you might find in other, grander fortifications. It had been enough to protect the von Tassau family, but it's location - of little strategic value remember - had never warranted the expansion.

The family apartments resided in the South Wing along with the Chapel, rooms for personal servants and the Great Hall which occupied the ground floor, it's high ceiling, vaulted with Bavarian oak, meant the South Wing had one less level than the other three sides of the castle.

It was also about the furthest you could get from the Barbican and the Wheelhouse within The Wolf's Tower.

They had made the journey once; they were returning more urgently.

Lutz huffed and puffed, leather creaking against a

cuirass made for him when he'd been a younger, slimmer man. Solace held her skirts up to scurry alongside him in a manner most unbefitting a lady. Torben, silent and effortless, at her side. He could have sprinted ahead of them without breaking sweat, he'd always been fast and strong despite his slender, fragile appearance.

Solace cursed herself that she'd been unable to persuade Lutz earlier that dropping the portcullis might keep the bulk of the Devil's men out of the castle.

She tried not to linger on the thought they would also be locking themselves inside with the ones already here.

One problem at a time...

In the corners of the castle, narrow spiral stone staircases linked each floor. The entrance to the roof of the Barbican was on the third floor of the North Wing.

They chose to stay on the fifth floor till they reached the north-east corner stairs, before dropping down. The enemy should all still be below them, so it seemed the safer choice. She hoped her father and the remnants of the garrison still fought on the lower floors, allowing the three of them to reach the Wheelhouse. She hoped, but she didn't know.

Her *sight* was telling her nothing about what was happening elsewhere.

She'd hoped they would run into others of the household to bolster their motley little army, preferably ones with weapons, but so far there'd found no one. Most of the remaining men had been in the Barbican and the lower windows. If they still were, then they would be heading towards the fighting, but, equally, there might be no fighting. Everyone else might be dead by now.

She thought Father then. Felt the heat in her cheek from his hand, heard his angry words. He might be dead too and the last memory she would have of him would be his anger and pain.

She could not think that. She must not think that.

Despite the dread clawing her, despite the dreams of fire and blood she'd endured with increasing intensity, despite the dead men she'd seen riding into the castle, she could not give up hope. She would carry hope to the end, for hope was always the last thing to wither before the body's final breath and the heart's last beat.

They hurried along the corridor, their footsteps echoing around them. Each pool of darkness beyond the candlelight seemingly masking a figure ready to pounce upon them, but each one they passed proved to be nothing more than empty shadows. Old friends who'd lined the corners of the castle all her life. They watched, silent and unmoving. Providing no threat but offering no help either.

If she were really a witch, she would cast a spell to bring them to life, to command them to fall in step and be ready to throw themselves at the invaders. An army of shades and ghosts risen to repel the evil defiling The Wolf's Tower.

But she was not a witch and all she had to fight the Devil with was one fat old man and her mute brother. Plus whatever she offered herself. Which, she feared, amounted to nothing.

They reached the north-east corner and paused in front of the heavy oak door concealing the stairs. Lutz nodded to them and then opened the door.

A figure hurtled out of the shadowy stairwell and barrelled into the portly soldier, who fell backwards and crashed to the floor in a whirlwind of thrashing limbs.

It was Karina, one of the maids.

"Ye gods!" Lutz pulled himself to his feet, "Are you a banshee, woman?"

Karina looked wildly about. Cobweb-coloured hair had come loose under her cap to hang limply about her face, which was as grey as morning ashes and skimmed with sweat. The maid was a mouse of a woman who mostly worked in the kitchens. Solace had long made it her business to know the names of everyone in the castle, but she doubted she'd ever exchanged more than a couple of words with the woman.

Some of the wildness faded from Karina's eyes and she heaved in deep shuddering breaths. Running up the narrow twisting stairs was not something you did unless you had to.

"My... lady...?" she finally panted.

"What has happened, Karina?" Solace put a hand on the woman's trembling arm. The maid appeared surprised both by the informality and the fact the *Freiherr's* daughter knew her name.

"Demons, my lady! Monsters from the pit!" The terror flooded back over her pudgy features, "They're killing everyone!"

Karina's words dispelled any lingering doubts in Lutz's mind. He drew his sword and leaned through the doorway to peer down the shadowy steps.

"Where are they now?" Solace asked.

"Everywhere, my lady!" Karina sobbed, looking about like a trapped animal again, "We're all going to be taken to Hell and tormented for eternity for our sins!"

Apparently, no one had told Karina about hope.

"No, we're not," Solace scolded, "we're going to fight them and, with God's good grace, beat them. We're going to the Wheelhouse to close the gates. There are more of them outside."

"More!" Karina gasped, eyes widening even further, "But there are hundreds of them! They are everywhere!"

Given the surrounding silence, Solace doubted that. The woman had been scared beyond her wits and thought every shadow a monster.

"No, they are not. I burned a lot of them in the Darkway, there are only a few who made it inside and we can overcome them. But you must come with us to the Wheelhouse.

Karina shook her head violently and stepped away from Solace as if she were mad. It wasn't an unreasonable deduction.

"Come!"

Karina moved further away.

"My lady..." Lutz shook his head.

The Sergeant was right. They were wasting time. They had precious little to spare and it was far more valuable than any assistance one terrified scullery maid could provide. But that didn't mean she couldn't help.

"Very well. Go up to the roof. There should be men still up there. Tell them what is happening. Tell them... tell anyone you see to head for the family chapel, we will gather there to make our stand. Understand me, Karina?"

"Yes, my lady, the family chapel..." the maid nodded, the idea of finding soldiers apparently less terrifying than heading down towards the demons slaughtering everyone on the floors below. She probably had a point.

Solace gripped her shoulders, "I'm relying on you."

"Yes, my lady!" Karina nodded again, more firmly, took a deep breath and allowed herself to be turned around.

Before the maid disappeared into the shadows, Solace asked, "My father, have you seen him?"

"No, my lady," Karina called back, then there was only the sound of her footsteps slapping on stone.

"Perhaps we should go that way, if there are men on the roof..." Lutz muttered, still peering down the stairs.

"We do not have the time. Besides, they may have already gone down if they saw what happened in the Courtyard. We must get to the Wheelhouse. And we must do it now."

Lutz nodded, pulled out a pistol and headed down the stairs.

Solace and Torben followed him.

*

One man was still alive.

Legs crushed in the panic, he whimpered and begged for help. Ulrich resisted the urge to spit. Blood soaked the man's clothing, but it was impossible to tell whether it was his or from the corpse of their previous owner.

Who had it been?

He counted few among the castle garrison as friends. He'd never been a man who made friends easily, some he liked well enough, but he kept his distance from them all. He had always felt more comfortable with his own company, which was a trick in the confines of a small castle.

Now the distance he had from his fellows had become a chasm. A chasm filled with corpses and demons.

"I'll be back..." he told the injured soldier. He might as well wish him the slow and painful death he deserved; the man was too delirious with pain to comprehend. He'd no compulsion to lessen the man's suffering though, the horse he'd killed had been innocent, this bastard wasn't.

Something dripped on his face. He jerked back, fearing oil, but it was only water. The fire had melted the ice and frost coating the innards of the Darkway. The sound of water softly slapping on stone had started to replace the final crackles of the dying puddles of flame.

Reaching the Outer Gate, he stepped onto the drawbridge. Beyond the castle the air was crisp and didn't stink so strongly of death. In the distance Jarl's men and the wagons waited for the signal to approach. More of Saul's company lurked in the trees, out of sight of the castle.

He could run. Head around the moat and across the southern pastures to where the trees rose again. They might decide he wasn't worth the trouble of chasing...

And he might reach a town before freezing to death or the brigands hiding in the forest killed him. Still, better than selling your soul to a demon. Surely?

Waving the blazing torch over his head, he willed his legs to run. He was fast. He was young. He might make the trees before they rode him down.

He could... he could... he could...

"We need to clear the bodies from the road..." a voice said in his ear. Ulrich cried out and dropped the torch. Spinning around he found the blackened face of Callinicus on his shoulder.

"Did I scare you?"

"I didn't hear you," Ulrich spluttered, dropping to retrieve the torch.

"You should pay more attention, almost everyone inside this castle can conjure a fine reason to slit your scrawny gizzard," the demon said. His voice was a dry rasp, whether he always spoke like that, or it was because of the fire, Ulrich didn't know.

"Including you, I presume?" Ulrich grabbed the torch and straightened up, Callinicus didn't step back from the flaming brand.

"I need more blood to heal, yours would do as well as any."

The demon was tall, not as freakishly tall as Jarl, but still half a head above Ulrich and broad with it. Even without the burnt face and being a demon, he would have stood out as a man best not to annoy.

"I doubt I could stop you."

White teeth flashed through Callinicus' blistered lips.

"Saul wants you alive for now. I think he likes you."

"I'm honoured..." Ulrich looked over his shoulder, the horses and wagons had started to move, crawling through the snow at the pace of the labouring oxen. More riders emerged from the trees behind them.

It had been a test. If he'd tried to escape, Callinicus would have run him down. His scorched skin didn't appear to be troubling the demon much.

"Come..." Callinicus ordered "...we need to clear the road."

Ulrich didn't know how the two of them could possibly drag the bodies of armoured men and horses clear between them, but he kept his mouth shut and followed Callinicus back into the scorched charnel house of the Darkway.

"There's a man still alive," Ulrich pointed.

Callinicus headed for the wounded soldier, who managed to raise a hand towards the demon, "Master..."

Callinicus crouched down, resting effortlessly on his haunches.

"There's nothing we can do for him," Ulrich said.

The demon didn't reply, but when he drew a dagger Ulrich expected him to slit the wounded soldier's throat. Instead, Callinicus drew the blade across his own palm, formed a fist and squeezed it over the man's mouth till blood dripped out. The soldier opened his mouth and drunk as greedily as any rum-starved sailor arriving in port after months at sea.

"What... are you doing?

"Saving his worthless life. And if you ask me any more stupid questions, I'll end yours."

"Yes... Master..." Ulrich swallowed. The threat had not sounded idle.

With a grunt of satisfaction, Callinicus scooped the

man up into his arms like he weighed no more than a small child and carried him to the Inner Gate. Unsure what he was supposed to do, Ulrich lingered amongst the broken bodies littering the Darkway, spluttering torch held before him.

Muffled cries came from above. He glanced up at the murder holes and arrow loops, but there was nothing to see. His new brothers were still clearing The Wolf's Tower of his old ones, it seemed.

"Good luck..." he muttered under his breath before hurrying after Callinicus.

Chapter Thirteen

They found the first body near the stairs on the third floor.

It was Rafael. The old man had been with the family for decades. Her father had lacked the heart to discharge him from service after he became too frail for menial work. As he knew some letters, he'd charged Rafael with looking after the library instead.

The harmless old man's throat was a ruin. Blood darkened the long white hair sprayed across the flagstones where he'd fallen. His eyes were wide and, even in death, he looked terrified.

Rafael was forever sucking on a lump of rock salt with his fleshy gums. He said salt kept the Devil away, though Solace had always suspected he just liked the taste.

She wanted to find his lump of salt and put it in his mouth in case the Devil was looking for his soul. Instead, she turned her eyes away and continued to follow Lutz. It was too late for that. Rafael had already met the Devil tonight.

Lutz insisted they both walk slowly and quietly in his wake. They'd edged forward only a few paces, Torben still looking over his shoulder at Rafael, when a scream rolled out of the darkness.

Solace pushed herself against the wall, as if the stonework could somehow protect her now as it had her family for centuries.

The scream might have been close, or it could have been from the other side of The Wolf's Tower. It was hard to be sure. The shadows told no tales. When no figures emerged, they continued in silence.

The entrance to the Barbican was an unmarked stone arch. As ever, a solid oak door, reinforced with strips of black iron, barred the way. If locked, there would be no way through, but when Lutz pushed against it the door swung open with only the faintest of sighs. The cold of the night rushed in to greet them.

The roof of the Barbican was as they had left it, save for a single corpse sprawled on the ice-flecked stones. It was one of their men, the blood from a gaping wound across his chest steamed in the frigid air.

His name came after a moment. Bastian.

Lutz hissed through his teeth but moved past the dead soldier without comment. Solace struggled to pull her eyes away. Something had shattered Bastian's cuirass, splitting the metal diagonally from his left shoulder. What force did it take to smash a breastplate asunder? What man had such strength? She suspected they would find out soon enough.

Torben hesitantly bent over the fallen man and

plucked the sword from his dead hand. It hadn't saved poor Bastian and he'd known how to use it. Torben straightened up and stared at her. He looked like a little boy holding a wooden sword in the expectation it would make him a man. Nodding, she hurried after Lutz. What did she know? Perhaps it would.

They reached the steps leading from the roof of the Barbican down to the Wheelhouse without incident. While Lutz and Torben crouched next to the stairs, she padded over to the battlements and peered around a merlon. The rest of the Devil's men waited at the edge of the woods. They still had time.

Before she could turn back, however, they started to move forward. The riders keeping pace with the two oxen-drawn wagons. As she watched, more shadowy horsemen emerged from the dark woods. She didn't linger to count them. They needed to seal the castle and they needed to do it now.

Solace returned to Lutz and her brother. The Sergeant raised a finger to his lips and then pointed down the stairs. At the bottom of the steps another wooden door sealed the entrance to the Wheelhouse. From behind it came muffled voices. And then what sounded like laughter.

She didn't know how many men were down there. Just that they had to kill them. And fast.

Lutz pursed his lips and spat. When he made to move down the steps, weapons drawn, she shook her head vehemently.

Lutz raised an eyebrow.

Several barrels of oil remained on the roof, but they

would do them no good this time. They could set the Wheelhouse alight, but it would stop them from getting in to seal the castle even if it did kill the men inside. Her eye moved to the piles of rocks stacked around the rooftop. A simple deterrent if you dropped one on a man's head.

She pointed at the rocks and then the door.

If Lutz's eyebrow raised any further, it would catch up with his receding hairline.

She pointed at the door, made a walking motion with her fingers and then mimicked dropping a rock. She rapped a knuckle on her head to make sure they got the concept. Lutz grinned.

Ushering Torben to help, the pair of them brought a rock each and carefully placed it on the ground above the door to the Wheelhouse and then fetched another one each. When Torben went to get more, she shook her head. She doubted they would have the opportunity to use a second rock each. They wouldn't get a third.

"I'll flush them out..." Lutz whispered.

"I'm faster."

"My lady!" Lutz protested, but she was already heading down the stone steps.

Solace didn't look back and hoped Torben was following what she planned. Sometimes he grasped the most complex of ideas in an instant, at other times it took four goes to get him to pass the salt.

Ten stone steps led down to the door. When she reached it, she glanced up at Lutz and Torben, who stood above the door on either side of the stairs looking down at her. Each held a rock the size of a man's head in their hands. Lutz nodded, Torben looked like he might burst into tears.

Flashing a grin of encouragement, she mouthed, "I love you," to her brother. Then she took a deep breath and pushed the door.

It was locked.

She glanced at the two men and pulled a face.

Hurry! Lutz mouthed back silently.

Solace hammered on the door and cried, "Help me! Please! There are demons everywhere!"

She sounded convincingly terrified to her own ears, due primarily to the fact she *was* terrified. She didn't know how many of them were inside or even what they were. Or if dropping a rock on their heads was going to do them much harm.

Solace slapped her palm against the cold oak, before scuttling backwards at the rattle of bolts being drawn.

The door swung inwards revealing a tall young man with close-set eyes and a thin slash of a mouth. He wore no helmet, which was something. He bore the colours of her father's men, but the tunic and cuirass fitted poorly enough for them to unmistakably belong to someone else.

Someone whose blood now smeared the dented breastplate.

"Demons you say, Fraulein?"

A second man appeared at the shoulder of the first, shorter and older, he still had his helmet on, "Maybe guarding the gates won't be as dull a job as we thought..." hungry feral eyes ran over her.

She backed up another step. The younger man came

forward, his companion hung back.

"Come, pretty Fraulein, we'll protect you," the soldier held out his hand.

"I'm scared... people are being killed..." her heel found the worn stone of the next step and she went up it.

"No one's going to kill you. We'll take good care of you."

"Really good..." the older man added, tongue making a serpentine flick at his cracked lips.

"Can you get me out of the castle?" She tried to look as wide-eyed and guileless as possible. Her hands shook so much she had to clasp them together before her to still them.

She may have lived a privileged and protected life, but not one so sheltered she didn't know what men like these would do to her given the opportunity.

Forcing herself to keep her eyes fixed on the two soldiers wearing dead men's clothes, she ignored Lutz and her brother waiting, rocks in hand, above the doorway. If they smelt the trap they would bolt back inside, and then they'd never winkle them out in time.

"Yes! Of course we can!" the younger man, who seemed to be the talker of the two, said, adding a fulsome smile as an afterthought. If the smile was meant to be reassuring, he needed to practice it more. It gave him the air of a slobbering dog.

The older man, who was more of a looker than a talker, finally edged out of the door.

The steps were too narrow for two men to walk abreast, Solace didn't have to stretch to touch the cold lichen-flecked stone on either side of her.

She backed up another step. The younger man came forward, but the older soldier suddenly grasped his shoulder.

"She's no maid, see her finery...?" he hissed.

The younger man paused; one boot poised on the next step. Another step and the pair would both be completely clear of the doorway's arch.

"What's your name?" the younger man demanded, eyes narrowing.

"Please help me!" she sobbed, still playing the terrified girl.

"'tis her, I'm sure of it!" the older one insisted, "the one the Masters want."

"The Lady Solace..." the younger one sighed, "...that's a pity, right enough..."

Then he made a grab for her.

As she turned to scramble up the stairs, her foot slipped on icy stone and she went down, only just managing to keep her face from hitting a step. As she pushed herself up, a hand grabbed her ankle.

"Gotcha!" the younger soldier brayed.

Solace twisted around to see his leering face looming over her. Then a wet, crunching thud sprayed blood over her face. He toppled forward with a confused expression and sightless eyes.

The second soldier staggered, crying out as a rock hit him on the back of his neck. He managed to put out a hand against the stone wall on his right to stop himself falling and another rock clipped his helmet. It was only a glancing blow, however, and he stumbled back towards the door, yanking a pistol free from his belt.

The next thing to hit him was a fat old soldier.

The man's legs buckled, the pistol spinning from his grasp as Lutz landed on him. His cry turned to a scream and then a wet gurgle as the Sergeant slammed a long dagger into the man's neck all the way to its quillons. More blood warmed the cold stones.

Still twisting the knife into soft flesh, Lutz looked up, "My lady?"

She had to pull her legs out from under the body of the younger soldier, whose head had split open like a bloody melon. She tried to stand but found she was sitting on the steps with no recollection of turning around.

"I am well..." she said, unable to drag her eyes from the dead men. She wiped her face and found her fingers came away smeared in blood. She wiped her hand on the stonework. The blood wasn't hers.

Lutz disentangled himself and clambered over the body to confirm the younger one was dead. She supposed you had to be sure about such things.

Torben squatted down behind her, his hand tapping her shoulder like a curious cat pawing a ball of string. She wanted to reach back and hold his hand in return, feel the warmth and comfort of it, but Torben could not abide another's touch. She was surprised he wasn't still shaking from being manhandled earlier. The fleeting brushes of his hand, barely noticeable beneath her thick, fur-lined cloak, was as unusual as it was welcome.

Instead of reaching for her brother's hand, she stared at the corpses sprawled across the steps below where she sat, "They were looking for me... why?"

It was, of course, Lutz who answered, grimacing as he wiped his dagger clean on the cloak of one of the dead men, "We have no time for questions..."

He was right. They had no time for anything, certainly not sitting around. She climbed to her feet and Torben did the same. Behind him, the upper floors of The Wolf's Tower rose, stark against the clouds and stars. The roof of the Barbican was still empty, the flickering dances of the remaining torches in their iron sconces was the only movement, the occasional hiss or crackle from the braziers the only sound.

Until another scream echoed in the distance.

"We have work to do," she announced, trying not to wrinkle her nose as she picked a way past the dead men without slipping on the blood-slickened steps.

"Aye, my lady," Lutz nodded, hurrying through into the Wheelhouse before her, pistol drawn.

No one had seen them, but the scream reminded her as unambiguously as the dread stone in her stomach that other enemies remained inside the castle. The Masters. Who they were and why they wanted her, were questions that would have to wait.

For now, they had to close the gate and ensure the rest of the dead men's comrades couldn't join them within the grey walls of The Wolf's Tower.

*

Callinicus set the injured man down under the arch of the Inner Gate.

He didn't quite drop him onto the frost-grouted cobbles, but Ulrich had seen men take more care unloading sacks of grain from a wagon. The man mumbled something, but didn't scream, which probably had a lot more to do with being delirious than stoicism.

"Where's Saul?" Callinicus demanded, wiping burnt hands on burnt britches. His eyes swept the Courtyard. Only a few bemused horses moved amongst the corpses.

"In the Great Hall, Master," one of the two soldiers left guarding the Inner Gate replied.

"Eager to get the banquet started," the big demon spat a gob of black phlegm.

Neither of the soldiers replied.

"Any trouble?"

"Nothing," the same man said through a thicket of greying beard.

"Shame. I need more blood. Call me if any meat appears."

"Yes, Master."

Deciding the company of corpses might be safer, Ulrich started to edge back into the Darkway.

"You!" Callinicus barked, "Drag the dead off the road. I'll deal with the horses. We don't want the women and little ones freezing to death, do we?"

The two Red Cloaks snorted dark laughter.

Ulrich was going to ask how he intended to pull the horses on his own but remembered Callinicus' earlier advice about asking questions.

"Yes, Master..."

The demon leaned in close enough for Ulrich to smell

his charred flesh, "You're a fast learner, aren't you?"

In the torchlight of the Courtyard, Callinicus' burns seemed to have begun hardening to crusty scabs, as if his injuries were a week old. It might have been a trick of the flickering light, but, then again, Callinicus was not a man.

Something he demonstrated by striding into the Darkway, grabbing a hind leg of the horse Ulrich had put out of its misery in each big hand and dragging it behind him like it was a lightly loaded handcart.

How strong were these monsters?

The urge to run for the distant trees was both growing and diminishing with every heartbeat he spent in their bloody company. He wanted to be away from these abominations, but each moment with them convinced him further it was impossible to outrun or outfight them.

He reached the first dead man, who hadn't coped with having his face melted by burning oil half so well as Callinicus. Ulrich managed to drag the corpse about ten paces, the metal of the corpse's cuirass screeching and clattering against the cobblestones, before the big demon sauntered back for his next horse.

"Just roll him up against the wall, idiot," Callinicus growled, "they'll be enough room for the wagons to get by."

Callinicus shot him a baleful look from behind his blistered face. Ulrich hurried himself rolling the body against the pitted stonework of the Darkway.

Why had they kept the women and children alive? Was it mercy? From the way the two Red Cloaks had laughed, that didn't seem likely.

He focused his energy on moving corpses and getting

out of the way when the demon sauntered past with another carcass in tow. The two of them worked in silence, the cries and screams from the castle kept jerking his head up, but he tried not to think too deeply about what was happening and who was dying.

It seemed he didn't care much for questions either these days.

"Go see how long before the wagons get here," Callinicus snapped, returning for another horse. Only two awaited hauling away. The horses had fared better than the men in the panic. The demon wasn't even breathing heavily, while sweat had soon dampened Ulrich's hair beneath his helm, despite the cold.

"Yes, Master," he panted, after pushing another vacant-eyed corpse against the stonework.

He padded down the Darkway to the Outer Gate. The column was not as close as he'd expected. The oxen labouring hard to get through the slush, mud and ice the track from the village had been reduced to. Fifty or so riders accompanied the wagons, but they remained with the women and children rather than riding ahead.

They didn't know the first group had lost so many men. They would assume the demons could deal with the garrison unaided. Aside from Jarl, whose unnatural height might have drawn a questioning eye, all the monsters had travelled in the first party. And none of them had died in the Darkway. Even Callinicus, who had been roasted alive.

Ulrich touched the hilt of his sabre and wondered what you had to do to kill one of them.

The fact they'd been happy to give him his sword back,

suggested the feat was beyond the likes of him.

Everything dies...

Old Man Ulrich growled from the shadows of his memory. Another of his father's favourite sayings, oft recited from behind a frothy mug of ale as he recited tales of battle and adventure.

But Old Man Ulrich had never met Saul the Bloodless and his merry band of butchering demons.

The men serving the masters died like any other men. The blood now staining his gloves demonstrated that. Still, if he drew his father's sabre against the demons...

He imagined swinging the sabre at Callinicus while the demon bent over a horse's carcass. Maybe if he took his head clean off... or would his sword just bounce from the monster's neck as if it were iron rather than flesh, sinew and bone? And if he did kill him, somehow, then there were all the others...

The wagons inched closer, their cargo of terrified women and children huddled within.

Whatever fate awaited them at the hands of Saul the Bloodless. There was absolutely nothing he, or anyone else, could do about it.

A grinding noise reverberated out of the arched roof of the Outer Gate, followed instantly by a rattling, tortured roar that shook the castle around him. He remained rooted to the spot, eyes widening. As he stared upwards, the great metal lattice of the portcullis started falling out of the darkness towards him...

Chapter Fourteen

She expected more bodies in the Wheelhouse, but the room was empty bar the wheels, tackle, blocks and chains of the mechanisms that raised and lowered the gates.

The men who'd opened the castle at her father's order must have left before the Devil's rogues arrived. Would they have sent just two? She didn't think so. She wasn't much of a soldier, but she'd listened to enough of her father's soldiering tales to know the gate of a stronghold was of tremendous importance. Whoever held the gates, held the castle.

So why had these Masters, only left two men?

Because they were thin on the ground, and they wanted to hunt down the rest of the soldiers in The Wolf Tower. Hunt them down and kill them before they knew what was happening and could offer organised resistance. And perhaps they had other goals too.

...the one the Masters want...

Solace shivered. Fire and blood. She had dreamed of them for weeks. Felt the dread stone growing in her guts.

She had feared for The Wolf's Tower, for her home and her family. But had she misread the portents? Was the one she should have been most afraid for herself?

Had they come here for *her?*

It was preposterous. Who was she? A minor *Freiherr's* daughter? You got a dozen of them to the silver taler. It didn't seem likely, but all the-

"My lady?" Lutz's gravelled words yanked her attention back to where it belonged.

"Let us seal the castle, Sergeant," she ordered, raising her chin to suggest she had been pondering significant matters of strategy.

"That is easy, my lady," Lutz replied, "but what is to stop them opening it again? We can't hold the Wheelhouse for long. Not with just the three of us."

Clearly, she hadn't been thinking about strategy at all. The door to the Wheelhouse was as thick as any in the castle, but without further distraction the attackers would get it open sooner rather than later, mainly as kegs of gunpowder for the muskets of the castle's defenders still sat conveniently atop the Barbican's roof...

Her eyes widened.

"You couldn't raise the portcullis without the mechanism, could you?"

"It would be difficult, my lady," Lutz agreed, "that great lump of iron weighs even more than I do after a feast day!"

"Torben!" She spun around. Her brother had found the helmet the younger of the Masters' men had ill-advisedly removed. It was too big for him; the burgonet half covered his eyes and he had to tilt his head back to see. With

Bastian's sword still clutched in his right hand he looked even more like a little boy playing at soldiers. He beamed at her. She smiled back, despite everything. Even if he looked like a boy, he felt like a man at last.

"We need the kegs of gunpowder from outside, the oil too. As much as you can carry."

"My lady, perhaps I should-"

"No," she snapped at Lutz, "he can do it, can't you Torben?"

When her brother continued to stand, chest puffed out and smiling from ear to ear, her heart sank. However, her brother's smile soon faded and his eyes found focus. Nodding, he clipped his heels together in the way soldiers did and hurried out of the door. She listened to his footsteps slapping on the stone steps before turning back to Lutz.

"My lady, 'tis dangerous..."

"Nowhere is safe anymore and you can't be everywhere."

"No, but until we have the oil and powder, we can't lower the portcullis."

She hurried to one of the arrow loops overlooking the moat and road. Unlike the arrow loops in the main castle, no glass filled the slits to keep out the biting wind. The column was still only halfway down the road, the oxen toiling to haul the wagons through the snow. Thankfully, none of the rogues had ridden ahead to reach the castle. They didn't expect the gates to be closing any time soon.

Turning back to Lutz, she nodded, "Help me pull the bodies inside to clear the stairs, then go and help Torben."

"My lady, I-"

"Are you going to question every order I give you?" Solace asked. As far as she was aware being the *Freiherr's* daughter gave her no military authority whatsoever, but she wasn't going to let that get in the way of doing everything possible to defend her home.

Lutz contained a smile beneath his whiskers, "No, my lady."

If he had any reservations about the lady of The Wolf's Tower soiling her hands on a dead man's boot, he kept that to himself too.

Both taking a leg, they dragged the first man inside the Wheelhouse. Before they returned for the second, Torben came padding down the steps, a keg of gunpowder under each arm.

"Is there more?"

Torben shook his head.

"The rest is in the armoury," Lutz carefully took the kegs and placed them under one of the two great wooden wheels filling most of the room. One was for the drawbridge, the other the portcullis. She didn't know which did which. They both looked the same to her.

"Oil, Torben, fetch oil!"

Her brother scampered out of the room before she could ask if anyone was up top. She assumed he would have let her know if there was, but her brother's mind didn't work like most people's.

Resisting the urge to see how much closer the enemy - the Masters' men she supposed - had advanced, she helped Lutz drag the younger man's body into the Wheelhouse.

The dead soldier's head left a trail of bloody goo on each step as it cracked against the stonework.

"Go!" she commanded, when Lutz continued to hover by the doorway, "They're dead and we will be too if we don't get this done!"

Lutz scowled but did as she said. Once his scuffing footsteps had faded into the night, she found it awfully quiet in the Wheelhouse with nothing but corpses for company.

The older of the dead men stared up at her with flat, sightless eyes, blood still dripping from the savage wound in his neck. She wondered, as a good Christian, whether she should feel remorse. She didn't know these men or why they had come here, but they were killing her people. No matter how helpless and pathetic they appeared in death, they were killers. She spat on the corpses.

It didn't make her feel any better.

Both men had two loaded pistols, which she requisitioned and laid out on a small table by the door. She snatched one up and went back to the arrow loop.

The riders were edging closer, and she gave thanks to God the snow had choked the road and slowed the wagons to a crawl. They would already be through the Darkway otherwise. A brief break in the cloud freed the moon, dousing the land in silvery light. Within the wagons, figures huddled together, not more soldiers, but women and children. From the village? Or the enemy's own?

The thought the two dead men on the floor might have wives and children flittered through her conscience, but she stamped down on that. Most men had wives and children. All men had mothers. It didn't stop them being evil killers who would do the most despicable things if you didn't...

...set them on fire, crush their heads with rocks, slit their throats...

...stop them first. Any way you could. Mercy and conscience were concepts without currency when men came to destroy your home. To rob and kill and rape.

Or whatever actually had brought the Masters and their rogues to The Wolf's Tower.

The Wheelhouse was silent. A couple of tallow candles and a single lantern burned, but they only pushed the shadows back to the corners and the spaces behind the winches and gears clogging the room.

Her eyes returned to the two dead men. She didn't believe the dead could do you any harm, or at least hadn't. She was sure some of the men who had ridden into the castle hadn't been breathing, no plumes of breath had left their mouths despite the coldness of the air.

It had been enough for her to set them alight.

But these two had breathed well enough. Now they were dead, would they stay dead?

It was a ridiculous thought, but the dread stone in her stomach, that feeling of wrongness that had grown day by day and nightmare filled night by nightmare filled night, thickened and swelled in her gut.

She knew what she'd seen. And she knew what she felt. And these two, they were only the foot soldiers. They weren't the Masters. Whoever they were, the dread stone whispered, she would find out soon.

Solace drew her cloak about her. The ancient stones of the castle sucked in the winter's breath and blew it into her bones. Would she ever be warm again?

Would she ever see her father again?

Solace felt a tear welling and wiped her eye roughly with the back of her hand. That would not do. She was her father's daughter. She was a von Tassau. She would not cry. No matter what. She would not.

Instead, she focused on the corpses and thought of their comrades inching through the snow towards them, guarding their cargo of women and children. A cargo too precious for them to gallop away from.

The sound of footsteps on stone snapped her attention back. She raised the pistol. The weapon was heavy and clumsy, but she knew how to use it, after a fashion. A von Tassau must know how to fight. Father had always told her that.

She'd never been much interested in fighting and weapons, but she'd always been a studious and serious girl, so she'd paid attention.

The gun shook in her hand at the thought of more rough, leering men coming to drag her off to their Masters.

Ducking behind one of the winch wheels, she braced her trembling hand against it. The mechanism shifted ever so slightly at her touch. Despite the immense weight of the portcullis and drawbridge they were cunningly counterbalanced, allowing them to be raised or lowered with relative ease.

A figure loomed out of the darkness, panting like a monstrous beast. For a moment it made no sense to Solace, it appeared inhuman and distorted, something twisted from nightmares that had dragged itself up from the Pit to shamble across God's Earth.

Before she pulled the trigger, the creature staggered into the flickering light, revealing itself to be Lutz backing into the Wheelhouse hunched over one end of a large barrel while Torben carried the other.

"The Lord be praised!" Lutz gasped as they deposited the barrel onto the flagstones.

Solace dropped the gun to her side before Lutz could turn and realise she'd nearly shot him.

"This is the largest one up there," Lutz wheezed, hands on his knees. Torben stood on the other side of the barrel in his familiar old man's stance, right hand resting on the left, hunched slightly forward, breathing no harder than normal.

"We need more."

Lutz opened his mouth to protest, but she turned her attention to her brother before he could say anything.

"We need a really *big* fire this time, do you understand?"

Torben's too large helm jiggled about his head as he nodded and then he was bounding up the stairs, his old man's posture evaporating in an instant.

"They must be close," Lutz straightened up, "and the longer we tarry here, the greater the risk."

"I did not realise you were such an old woman, Sergeant?" she said, stepping out from behind the big wooden wheel of the winch. Lutz blinked and Solace fought down a grin, despite everything.

"My lady..."

Lutz's eyes flicked to the pistol at her side.

"Do not fret, Father showed me how to use a pistol. I shall make every attempt to shoot neither you nor myself. Now, how soon can we lower the portcullis?"

Lutz scooped up the other pistols she'd recovered from the dead men and started shoving them into his weapon belt, "It can be lowered slowly by turning the left wheel or quickly by knocking the latch away," he indicated a wooden block wedged beneath the winch mechanism.

"And the drawbridge?"

"The right wheel, my lady, but it will take a minute or two for us to wind it up. Perhaps it would be better-"

"No. We drop the portcullis, then the drawbridge. With the drawbridge down they can work on the portcullis from the outside, with it up they must cross the moat to get at it. The ice is not thick on the moat this winter, is it?"

"I would not care to try crossing it, my lady, but then I am heavier than most men these days."

She looked over as Torben shuffled down the stairs, carrying a keg of oil only a quarter of the size of the one he'd brought in with Lutz earlier. Placing it next to the first, he turned his head to fix his eyes upon his sister.

"More."

He scurried away without question.

"My lady, if we cut things too fine, we'll have neither the time to light the oil or retreat before more of these..." he poked a toe in the direction of the corpses growing cold on the flagstones "...rogues arrive. They will start heading here the moment the portcullis drops."

"I know..." she smiled darkly, "...I am hoping they all come..."

*

For an instant, just an instant, Ulrich thought he wasn't going to move.

As the black iron points of the portcullis came rattling out of the darkness, the idea flashed through his mind that such a death would be quick, merciful and more than he deserved.

Instead, he threw himself across the cobbles of the Darkway. Landing hard enough to knock the wind from him as the crash of metal on stone reverberated through the passageway. His bones vibrated along with the surrounding castle as the echo rolled out of the Darkway.

Heart still hammering, he looked back over his shoulder. His right foot lay between two of the metal spikes of the portcullis. If he'd been standing a little to either side his foot would now be a bloody pulp and he'd be screaming in agony.

As he gingerly pulled himself to his feet, another creaking, clanking noise filled the passage. In small increments, the moonlight-washed landscape of glowing snow and distant trees - as well as Jarl's men and the wagons - disappeared behind the jerkily rising drawbridge.

Someone was still fighting back.

Ulrich glanced up, above the vaulted ceiling of the Darkway the Wheelhouse held the mechanisms which sealed the castle. There, at least, resistance persisted. He didn't know whether to admire or pity them.

How did you fight demons? How did you fight the Devil?

The only answer he could conjure was by being less of a coward than he was.

"What have you done!?" A voice boomed above the echo of nailed boots pounding the cobbles. Callinicus didn't sound happy.

"I haven't done anything, Master!" Ulrich protested, taking a step back.

"You lowered the fucking portcullis!" Callinicus loomed over him, his face a welter of sores and blisters, but, between them, small patches of unburned skin were now visible. Ulrich would have pondered this miracle at more length, if not for the fact the demon seemed tempted to yank his head off and throw it into the moat before the drawbridge slammed shut.

"You can't lower the portcullis from here!" He jabbed a finger upwards, "The winch is up there... in the Wheelhouse!"

The demon's wide eyes, starkly white against his still damaged face, flicked around the passageway. There was nothing in sight that might control either the portcullis or the drawbridge.

Callinicus' nose, which looked like something that had half melted before refreezing in the shape of a squashed toad, flared a couple of times and Ulrich got the distinct impression the demon was considering not letting the facts get in the way of an excuse to kill him.

After a couple of rattling, phlegmy breaths the demon's eyes rose to the ceiling and then to the Outer Gate. Ulrich glanced over his shoulder, only a reducing square of cloud-smeared sky remained visible.

Callinicus seized his arm and shoved him down the Darkway towards the Inner Gate where the two Red Cloaks stood watching, silhouetted against the glowing torches of the courtyard.

"Take me there, maggot. Now!"

No matter how fast he ran, Callinicus stayed at his shoulder, shoving him forward. At one point his foot caught on something - something dead undoubtedly - and he went sprawling. Only Callinicus grabbing him by the collar saved him from hitting the cobbles.

"I have little patience," the demon spat in his ear, before pushing him on again.

"You two, with me!" Callinicus roared when they reached the Inner Gate.

"Shall we fetch Saul?" the bearded Red Cloak asked.

"I can deal with this," Callinicus spat back.

"We have orders-"

"And now you've got a new fucking order! Do you want a new hole in your head to go with it?"

The bearded Red Cloak blanched and decided, probably wisely, to keep his mouth shut.

The injured soldier Callinicus had carried from the Darkway sat propped up on the cobbles, his back against the arch of the Inner Gate. His eyes were closed, but he appeared to be breathing without difficulty.

"What about him?" Ulrich asked, before he could stop himself.

Both the Red Cloaks shot him looks of withering

contempt, Callinicus didn't even bother with such a courtesy.

Instead, he grabbed Ulrich by the shoulder, "Take us to the gatehouse."

It was actually called the Wheelhouse (to the inhabitants of The Wolf's Tower at least) thanks to the two great winches that operated the Outer Gate. However, as Callinicus didn't strike him as one who bore correction well, Ulrich hurried across the courtyard without further comment. The demon and the two Red Cloaks on his heels.

The door next to the Inner Gate opened directly onto a narrow spiral staircase leading up to the Barbican roof, it was the only staircase in The Wolf's Tower not situated in one of the castle's corners.

However, Ulrich suspected it wasn't the only one to have become a slaughterhouse that night.

He'd directed the demons and their surviving Red Cloaks this way earlier, and they must have run into some of the castle's men at arms coming the other way. Ulrich counted six bodies, though such was the contorted mass of corpses splattered over the narrow stone steps it was difficult to be precise in the meagre candlelight.

"As usual, I miss all the merriment," Callinicus growled behind him.

The stairs spiralled to the right as you climbed them, giving an advantage to a defender coming down the stairs as their right arm had the space to swing, while an attacker (assuming he wasn't left-handed) had his sword arm fast against the stonework.

It hadn't helped his former comrades much. All the

bodies were garrison men. They'd died like something had ploughed straight through them. Blood dripped from the walls, along with, here and there, what looked a lot like brains in the half-light. Blood trickled down the steps. Sightless, accusing eyes stared back at him, the corpses that still had things as recognisable as faces anyway.

"What are you fucking waiting for?" Callinicus shouted. Unlike Saul, the big demon really was in his ear. His breath reeked of charred meat.

When he tried to find a fraction of step not covered by a corpse, Callinicus shoved hard enough for Ulrich to topple forwards. His outstretched hands found blood splattered armour, while the face of a Moravian called Bertram filled his vision. Death had not much improved Bertram's ugliness, but it had washed away all traces of the man's innate cheerfulness

"Just walk over them, they're past caring!"

Ulrich scrambled upwards. Sometimes he felt armour beneath his boots, sometimes something softer. The clank of metal mixed with squelching noises as they clambered over the bodies. Then something snapped under his boot.

Several times he slipped and, eventually, he was clambering over the dead on all fours, hands slickened by cooling blood. By the time he finally reached cold, unbloodied stone again he sobbed with relief.

He didn't stop climbing the steps, nor did he look behind him. He heard Callinicus and the Red Cloaks well enough.

The steps finished on the third floor and Ulrich tumbled out of the stairwell. Along the corridor a bundled form lay motionless. Another corpse. It was too far away to recognise in the dim light, but it didn't look like one of the garrison. A servant probably.

He remained crouched, panting and staring at his gore-soaked gloves splayed across the time-worn flagstones. Footsteps echoed up the stairs, someone had started whistling.

As he climbed to his feet, a woman's scream rolled through the castle like satanic thunder. Ulrich winced.

When the portcullis had fallen, why had he jumped back into the Darkway? He might have been able to escape. He would still have had to get away from Jarl and the main body of the Company, but all the other demons would be trapped inside the Wolf's Tower for hours.

But he'd jumped *into* the castle. Into the slaughterhouse. To where his new masters waited. Why?

Too much of a coward to even run away...

Callinicus emerged. Fresher pink skin had appeared on his face as the blisters and seared flesh retreated. He was healing before Ulrich's eyes.

"I shall soon be my old, beautiful self," Callinicus favoured him with a rare grin, noting Ulrich's wide-eyed stare, "it will be good to get the stink of burnt meat out of my nostrils. I couldn't even smell the blood down there."

The stink of blood, offal, piss and shit still caked his own nostrils. He wondered if he'd ever be rid of it. He'd grown up believing there was glory in battle, heroic deeds and noble deaths. He'd seen neither this night, just the terror of men having their lives ripped from their broken bodies. The men on the stairs had left no glory behind them. Just their blood dripping down the old stone steps, mixed with the piss that had escaped their bladders as they'd died.

The two Red Cloaks appeared in the doorway. Unlike Callinicus they breathed heavily. Their blood-splattered boots squeaked as they walked. So did his, he noticed, without looking.

"Where next?" Callinicus demanded.

They could have left the stairwell on the second floor and accessed the narrow galleries running around the Barbican, where defenders could rain torment upon any invaders trapped in the Darkway below. In his terror and disgust, he hadn't considered that option, he'd just kept moving. The doorway opening to the Barbican roof however was now in front of them across the corridor. It gave direct access to the Wheelhouse and Callinicus wouldn't know the difference.

He pointed to it and the demon strode over without hesitation.

"If there are defenders in the Wheelhouse..."

They were likely to be waiting on the roof to shoot anyone who came through the door.

"Good point..." Callinicus nodded and stood aside, "...you go first."

"I-"

The demon smiled. Menacingly.

The bearded Red Cloak nudged the small of his back, none too gently, with the muzzle of his pistol.

Ulrich swallowed and moved to the door. If he'd lowered the portcullis, he would be expecting the enemy to converge here to take back the Wheelhouse. This would be where he would make a stand. This would be where he would defend the breach.

The hollow laughter of Old Man Ulrich floated up from some distant backwater of his mind.

The door could be barred from either side, but it was unlocked on the corridor side. When he pushed it, he found no one had barred the door from the other side either.

No musket balls or crossbow bolts smacked into the wood of the door. Only the cold frigid air of a winter's night rushed in. He made to peer around the edge of the door, but a hand shoved him through. Off balance, he staggered out on to the flagstones, slipped on the icy stone and tripped over a corpse sprawled on the ground.

Once more he hit the cold stone floor.

No muskets crackled from the shadows; no former comrades fell screaming upon him with swords. There were no shouts, no battle cries.

The roof was deserted save for the corpse he'd stumbled over. Bastian. A man he knew a little and had never wished to know better. He'd been a frequent visitor to the two plump whores in the village. Now they could spend eternity together cavorting in Hell.

Callinicus and the Red Cloaks followed him onto the roof. The two soldiers crouched behind swords and pistols, the demon straight-backed and as casual as a lord taking a morning stroll around his rose garden.

Pushing himself to his feet Ulrich, took his place at the demon's heel.

"Where do we go?"

Ulrich pointed to the steps on the other side of the roof, descending into shadow, "The door at the bottom of the steps is the Wheelhouse."

The four of them walked slowly across the roof. There were no obvious places for anyone to hide. A couple of piles of rocks, some barrels and kegs, but none large enough to conceal a man. Torches fixed into sconces on the battlements flickered in the weak breeze. A couple of braziers still warmed the air, though the men who'd lit them were probably all cold now.

The only sound was boots crunching on ice.

They reached the top of the steps. The moon had slipped behind cloud again and the door at the bottom of the stairs was just a suggestion in the thick shadow, save for the pale slivers of light that snuck around its edges.

"If my nostrils weren't so charred, I'd smell how many rats hid in there..." Callinicus spat.

"Perhaps they fled after closing the gate?" the Red Cloak without a beard offered, his own nose, long and crooked, twitching as if trying to sniff out enemies in the shadows too.

"Maybe... I can't hear anyone in there."

"You could *hear* people in there?" Ulrich asked, his inquisitiveness getting the better of him.

"A vampire's senses are very keen. I could hear a heartbeat through that door," he turned dark eyes on Ulrich, "I can hear yours well enough. It beats very fast, little man."

Vampires? Is that what these demons call themselves?

Ulrich said nothing and waited for the demon to send

him down the steps first. Instead, Callinicus drew his sword and walked down himself. The two Red Cloaks followed, crouching behind their pistols and swords.

The demon paused near the bottom of the steps, staring at something. He crouched, brushed his fingers over the stone and raised them to his lips as he straightened. Blood, Ulrich thought, though Callinicus said nothing.

The demon reached the door, head tilted to one side. Listening for heartbeats? With no instruction to follow, Ulrich stayed where he was.

A sword hung at his side and the pistol retrieved from the dead man in the Darkway was still in his belt, he could draw weapons and fall upon them.

Come Ulrich! At them!

That had worked out well for young, brave Vinzenz, hadn't it? A glorious death. Like the one he'd always dreamed of before he'd seen death was not at all glorious. It just stunk of shit and piss.

His hand stayed at his side. He looked about him, but the roof remained empty, the castle silent.

Was everybody dead?

No. He was still alive. And that was the most important thing. Wasn't it?

Callinicus tried the door, it rattled on its iron hinges but didn't budge.

The defenders had either locked it and fled or waited inside to repel anyone who came through. That might take a while. The door, like all in the castle, was thick oak, reinforced with strips of iron. Designed to slow any attackers who breached the castle. It would take a long time to batter down. There were other ways into the Wheelhouse, doors on either side led to the two galleries overlooking the Darkway, but it was likely whoever had sealed the castle had locked them too. They could get gunpowder from the armoury...

Callinicus moved back a step and kicked the door, the sound of splintering wood split the night. Ulrich's eyes widened; the oak was as thick as a man's index finger was long! A second kick and the door sagged inwards, a third and something cracked inside. The wooden bar sealing the door? Not possible, surely?

Ulrich leaned over for a closer look, not believing what he was seeing. How could they be so strong?

One more kick and the door crashed open, Callinicus, unbalanced. staggered through after it.

Ulrich heard the demon mutter, "Oh, fuck..."

Then light and sound devoured the night.

Chapter Fifteen

It took Lutz two blows with the hammer to knock the latch clear of the winch and send the portcullis crashing down into the Darkway, sealing the Outer Gate.

After that, matters moved swiftly.

Lutz scurried over to the second wheel, where Torben waited, and the two of them began turning the winch together, one on either side of the big wooden wheel. The chains groaned as the drawbridge started to rise.

"Bastard is heavier than it used to be," Lutz hissed through clenched teeth as he lent into the wheel, before remembering who he was with, "sorry... my lady..."

"Curse all you want, just get the drawbridge raised before we have guests."

She peered through the doorway but couldn't see the entrance onto the Barbican roof without venturing up a couple of steps. Tightening the grip on the pistol held awkwardly in both hands, she told herself she'd hear them approaching well enough without sticking her head up the stairs.

She thought of Bastian, cold on the flagstones just out of sight, his cuirass shattered like an eggshell. What kind of a man could do that to tempered steel? She didn't know. But it was the kind they'd just given their presence away to by dropping the portcullis.

Behind her the groan of the winch and the clank of chains intermingled with Lutz's grunts and Torben's panted breath as they put their backs into turning the wheel. She bit down on the urge to tell them to hurry up.

Everything was ready, once the drawbridge was up, they'd pour the oil and be gone. Then matters would come down to luck and the grace of God. She couldn't believe the Lord would not be on their side, but this was the Devil's business and God, she suspected, didn't always win that game.

The cranking continued behind her interminably. A wailing cry announcing their presence to the Masters and their rogues. Despite telling herself there was no need, she darted up a couple of steps to check the Barbican roof. Bastian still lay dead by the door into the castle. The freezing wind making the torch flames writhe bit her face; nothing else moved.

It would take time for men to get here. Only the ones in the Courtyard would immediately realise what had happened. They only needed a few minutes. They would have that much, surely?

The steps were wet with blood. With luck and God's grace, there would soon be more.

The clanking mercifully finished with a resounding clunk. Ducking back inside she found Lutz hammering the latch into place. Hopefully it would never be used again.

She locked and barred the door.

"You are sure, my lady?" Lutz asked as she placed the stool behind the door. Torben was already opening the big barrel of oil, the liquid inside sloshing over the rim.

"I am sure."

"It will take time for them to batter down the door. Time for them to smell the oil or for the candles to go out."

"Time for more of them to get here," she'd explained this before. She placed a candle carefully on the stool.

There were two other doors into the Wheelhouse, one to the right, one to the left, both led to the galleries overlooking the Darkway. A candle burned on a stool by the left one which she'd locked earlier with a heavy iron key. She moved to the right door; another stool stood in front of it.

The open kegs of gunpowder sat under the winches. Lutz helped Torben pour the rest of the oil over the floor. Solace stood by the one remaining unlocked door, her thumb tracing the scroll work along the side of the pistol she held. Waiting for the sound of boots on the bloody steps and fists pounding on the door.

Torben and Lutz shuffled backwards towards her, flooding the room with oil. She feared it would be too pungent and their enemies would sense the trap, but the Wheelhouse smelt of grease and machinery anyway. It was worth the risk. They could set it afire now and keep the rest of the Masters' men from the castle for a few hours, or they could gamble on killing more of those already inside as well.

She'd thought of Bastian's raptured cuirass and decided to roll the dice.

"We are done, my lady," Lutz straightened up with a grimace. Her brother nodded his agreement. His oversized helmet nodded its agreement too.

Lutz had squeezed three of the captured pistols into his weapon belt, he'd let her keep the other, Torben he didn't trust with a loaded pistol. Standing aside, the two men passed through the door, she gave the Wheelhouse one last look and pushed aside the thought she was destroying the machinery that had helped protect her family for centuries.

Half closing the door she dragged the chair across to sit behind it. Lutz passed a lit candle which she, very carefully, placed on the stool. Then she pulled the door shut and locked it.

Whichever door the enemy battered down to get into the Wheelhouse they would knock a candle onto a floor flooded with oil. It should ignite. And when the flames reached the kegs of gunpowder...

She thought of old Rafael gumming his lump of rock salt, a mischievous glimmer of approval in his eye.

It would be a small vengeance for what had happened to her people. But small vengeances were all they had left. Slipping the key into a pocket in her cloak, she turned and hurried after Lutz and her brother into the shadow-haunted gallery.

The darkness consumed them.

*

The light consumed them.

Pouring out of the Wheelhouse, accompanied by a whooshing noise and a hard fist of heat that knocked Ulrich backwards and tipped him on to his arse. Someone was screaming; he was too dazed to know if it was him. Then came a roar that shook the world, or at least the part of it he sprawled on.

The screaming stopped.

He stared at the sky. A star, bright and cold, peeped out from behind a cloud. Ulrich focused on it until the fringe of the next cloud consumed it. Flames crackled nearby and an acrid tang coated the freezing night air. He blinked, the star hadn't disappeared behind a cloud, smoke billowing from the Wheelhouse had obscured it.

His ears rung and his face tingled. If he were on fire, he'd probably know about it by now. He touched his cheek all the same. Nothing seemed burnt. Scorched a little perhaps, but not burnt.

Putting his palms on the cold stone, he pushed himself into a sitting position. Smoke, thick and black, poured out of the Wheelhouse, the doorway was all but lost behind it, tongues of orange flame licking its edges.

Two dark bundles laid on the stairs. Neither moved. Bodies. The Red Cloaks. Was it possible the demon - the vampire - survived? He scanned the roof. He was alone.

If Callinicus was alive it didn't seem likely he'd still be in the Wheelhouse, an inferno raged inside now. Even if he could survive the heat, the winches must have been destroyed. The portcullis wouldn't be coming up again anytime soon.

Clambering to his feet he brushed himself down. A few charred cinders floated to the ground. If he'd been on the steps instead of lingering on the roof...

"Anybody there?" he called from the top of the now blackened steps. The flames crackled an answer. The fire was taking hold.

He recognised the stink from the Darkway. Oil. It had been a trap. And it had worked. Another two of the invaders - at least - were dead. And Saul's reinforcements could no longer enter the castle.

Whoever had lured them to the Wheelhouse was making a fair fist of defending the castle. But Saul and the other demons remained very much alive. He couldn't see them getting lucky again.

Someone is prepared to defend the breach till the end though, eh, Ulrich, me boy?

He called again. No reply came from the Wheelhouse.

He was alone.

Gingerly he moved to the battlement over the Outer Gate and peered down. Smoke pouring out of the arrow loops in the Wheelhouse partially obscured the view, but he could make out Jarl and the rest of Saul's company clustered around the moat, no doubt scratching their heads and wondering what was happening. He could see the two wagons as well. Full of women and children from the village. His eyes didn't linger on them. He had enough problems of his own.

It was possible to scale the twenty metres of icy wall with ropes to reach the Barbican's roof. Assuming they got across the moat without drowning. Likewise, he could climb down. But that served no purpose with Jarl waiting at the bottom.

His gaze moved up to the main battlements of The Wolf's Tower, if he climbed down the far side of the castle, however, he'd escape out of sight of Jarl's men...

Or perhaps if he hid?

If they thought him dead with the others in the Wheelhouse, nobody would be looking for him. Whatever Saul the Bloodless wanted here, he doubted the demon intended taking up permanent residence. When the demons left, he would be free...

Or he could stay and serve his new masters.

His gaze returned to the women and children below.

"What should I do?"

In the twisted wreckage of the Wheelhouse, wood crackled and spat, but neither God nor the Devil saw fit to furnish him with an answer.

Spinning on his heels he strode across the roof. He had no plan or purpose, but walking kept him warm at least. He passed Bastian, who stared sightlessly at the smoke curling heavenward, without a second glance.

The explosion, which must have been gunpowder, would be bringing all the remaining demons here. And they would have questions as to why he still breathed, while Callinicus and two more Red Cloaks were dead. And hadn't he been in the Darkway when the portcullis had fallen? Perhaps in such circumstances Saul the Bloodless would no longer think him an asset.

And if he wasn't an asset...

Run. Hide. Wait for his new masters.

Three choices. All likely to end with his death.

Back inside The Wolf's Tower he stared at his gloves. Blood and gore stained the rough leather. Not his most immediate problem, but he ripped them off and shoved them in his belt all the same.

How soon till someone got here? Not long.

A body lay in the corridor in one direction, so he went the other. If the demons came, he would say he was looking for them to report the trap and hope for the best. If not... he would keep walking.

Where?

The demons and Red Cloaks left inside would go toward either the Wheelhouse or the Outer Gate. Presumably their priority would be to open the gate and allow Jarl and his men inside. Then crush whatever resistance remained. In all likelihood they didn't need the extra men, but whoever was fighting back had proved a resourceful and dangerous foe they would do well not to underestimate again.

He wondered who it was...

Chapter Sixteen

She'd never suspected two kegs of gunpowder would make quite so much of a bang.

They stopped in unison. The explosion reverberated through the old stones of the castle, as if something had startled The Wolf's Tower itself, jolting it to life, blinking and confused as to what had just happened to it.

Sorry...

She stroked the cold stone wall as if reassuring a faithful old hound.

Lutz chuckled and spat. Her brother followed suit, though his chuckle was silent.

"It worked, by the Lord's mercy, it worked!" Lutz slapped Torben on the back. Her brother couldn't have looked more discomforted if the old soldier smothered him in bristly kisses.

"It only worked if it killed all of them," she said, her voice flat in the narrow stone gallery, "I do not think it worked..."

The smile faded from Lutz's battered face; he nodded

in understanding. Her father would no doubt say something about every victory, however small, being worth celebrating. Good for morale. But she wasn't her father.

"We should keep moving. More of them will be here soon and as yet I have not devised a plan for killing them."

"Somewhat remiss, my lady."

"Indeed..."

"Where should we go?"

"The Chapel."

"You think Karina found anyone? And if she did, she remembered your instruction? I fear she is not the brightest woman in the world."

"Have faith Sergeant. Have faith."

They hurried on in silence. The gallery ran along the east side of the Barbican. They passed alcoves on their right with arrow loops angled down on the Darkway. She could see nothing below, though the stink of acrid smoke and burnt meat from the murder she and Torben had wrought earlier hung in the damp air.

No candles or lanterns burned, a little grey light snuck in through the arrow loops on the outer wall of the gallery, brightening and darkening in rhythm to the moon's dance with the clouds.

If anyone waited for them ahead...

She concentrated on the black shadow of Lutz's back, the faint creak of leather and metal as he moved, his breath the only noise. Her brother made almost no sound at all. His silence went beyond his inability to speak. Occasionally, she made out the soft hiss of his boots as they dragged over the flagstones. Otherwise, nothing.

She glanced behind her as they passed one of the external arrow loops. Her brother was a silver ghost in the transient moonlight. He didn't look ridiculous in his ill-fitting helmet, with his shuffling hunched-back gait, right hand atop his left. He didn't look like a child pretending to be a man anymore either.

He looked like a wraith or some other strange creature of the shadows.

In the grey-silver light no expression hung upon his face, his eyes just dark pits beneath the rim of his helm.

What manner of a man would he be now if he hadn't been born so afflicted?

Solace returned her gaze to Lutz's dark bulk. She couldn't love him more than she already did. So, what did it matter? Nothing mattered. The dread stone in her stomach suggested they were both going to be dead by morning. Torben was what he was. Who he was. And he would die a man whilst all the small-minded fools who'd sniggered behind his back had died like pigs in an abattoir.

Only Torben had fought back. Even she had only followed his lead. She wouldn't have thought to have poured the oil. But Torben had. And maybe that gave them the slimmest of chances. Whatever the dread stone said.

As they reached the end of the gallery it turned right to run parallel to the outer wall of the castle proper. Ahead, a lantern hung by the door to The Wolf's Tower, a beacon in the night, heralding them home.

She'd feared they might run into the enemy in the gallery, but the group who had broken into the Wheelhouse, knocking the candle from the chair and igniting the oil-soaked floor and the kegs of gunpowder, must have taken the direct route across the Barbican roof from the third floor. They'd broken down the door much quicker than she'd hoped or expected. She'd wanted as many of them as possible drawn there to get the Outer Gate open, and as many of them blown to smithereens as possible. But they'd only been a few minutes clear of the Wheelhouse when it exploded.

Which meant more of the Masters' men would still be heading towards them. So far, they had heard no one, but as they reached the door the sound of running feet came from the other side.

Lutz stopped, pressing himself against the stonework and easing a second pistol from his belt. Hurrying to the opposite wall she raised her own pistol with both hands. They waited to see if the door would fly open.

The corridor was just wide enough for two men to stand abreast. The lantern, hanging from a crude metal hook by the door, burnt as low as it could without being extinguished. Past the door, the corridor returned to darkness. Beyond the reach of the feeble lantern, it turned right again, following the western wall of the Barbican and then back to the Wheelhouse.

Whoever they were, and it sounded like more than one, they were running. The hard clip of heavy boots pounded the stone floor. Predator or prey? It could as easily be her own people running from the invaders as the Masters' rogues. If the door burst open, she would have but an instant to decide whether to use her one shot or not. An instant in poor light. An instant with shaking hands.

The running feet grew louder... and then faded. She glanced at Lutz, who stood with both pistols before him, staring at the door, his face set hard beneath its bristles. Torben remained behind them, his sword drawn and gripped in both hands.

She started to speak but Lutz shook his head. She strained her ears, hearing nothing beyond her own heartbeat. Lutz's old ears were unlikely to be better than hers, so she looked at Torben. He stared back blankly, then lowered his sword till its tip brushed the floor. That was good enough for her.

"Let's go."

Lutz nodded at the door, not wanting to put one of the pistols back in his belt. She opened it for him.

The Sergeant rushed through, both guns raised. Solace followed, stepping out of the gloom of the Barbican into the only marginally better-lit corridor of the castle. The second floor of the North Wing was empty. She let out a breath she hadn't realised she'd been holding.

The running feet had - as far as she could tell given The Wolf's Tower's unreliable acoustics - been heading east. Opposite them stood the stairwell leading down to the Courtyard and up to the Barbican roof. She turned right to head in the direction the running feet had come from when Torben tugged at her sleeve and waved his sword at the floor.

Two sets of bloody footprints, faint but distinct, ran along the corridor and into the stairwell.

Torben poked his head inside. He stood there for a moment, then slowly backed out again. His face was ashen.

She moved to see for herself, but he shook his head hard enough to rattle the burgonet about his ears.

From where she stood, she could see more blood covered the stone steps. A lot more blood. A stink drifted out of the stairwell. She'd never walked on a battlefield after the fighting was done and she'd never visited a slaughterhouse, but she suspected the smell wafting out of the shadows wouldn't be too different. It was the rich and ripe stink of death.

Lutz closed the door and slammed the bar down to lock it.

Lutz was a man who had walked a battlefield after the fighting was done and had probably visited a slaughterhouse or two in his time as well. From the look on his face, he recognised the smell too.

They hurried down the corridor, retracing the steps of the bloody footprints.

The castle garrisoned its soldiers on this floor, sleeping four to a room. Most of the doors along the corridor were closed. They followed the footsteps back to one that wasn't. A corpse, as broken and discarded as a child's old doll, was crumpled inside, a woman, blood flowing out to form a lake in the corridor. Bloody footsteps led in the opposite direction. The boots they'd heard.

It seemed the men had run through the blood rather than being responsible for killing the woman - her face was so pulped Solace couldn't even tell who she was. One of her own maids she suspected. They moved on without pause. Whoever she was, she was far beyond their help.

A heavy door sat at each end of every corridor. All

could be bolted and barred from either side to seal off a section of the castle, slowing down any invaders. Someone had closed and barred the door at the end of this corridor.

And someone else had smashed it off its hinges.

The thick wooden planks of the door now splintered the corridor, shattered by ferocious blows, reduced to kindling as if they'd been rotten sun-bleached driftwood rather than seasoned oak.

She exchanged a glance with Lutz.

It explained how they had gotten into the Wheelhouse so quickly. The old soldier rolled his shoulders before picking his way through the wreckage. Torben stared at the shards of wood scattered over the ground as if they meant something. Or he just found the pattern they made interesting. Trying to work out what thoughts danced inside her brother's mind was a game she'd never quite mastered.

"Torben... come..." she waved him forward.

Her brother continued to stare for a second or two before the light returned to his eyes and he followed them.

At least this stairwell didn't stink of death.

It was too narrow to walk abreast, so they hurried upwards in single file. They'd twisted around two spirals and the door to the third floor had emerged out of the shadows when Torben tugged her sleeve. He cupped his ear as she turned around. She managed to grab the tail of Lutz's cloak. The Sergeant stopped and looked quizzically over his shoulder.

That's when she heard the other footsteps too.

Boots clipping on stone. Slow and unhurried. Coming down the spiral steps towards them.

Lutz raised his guns. By the time the owner of those footsteps came into view around the tight turn of the stairwell he would be on top of them. It would be hard for Lutz to miss... but something stalked the halls of The Wolf's Tower that could smash down a solid oak door...

And if two pistol balls couldn't stop it in its tracks...

Even if it did, the sound of gunfire might bring more of their enemies down on their heads.

Solace squeezed past Lutz and onto the third-floor landing. It was a little wider and held two doors. Candles flickered in niches cut into the stone by each door. Both were shut. If locked, they'd have no choice but to revert to Lutz's plan. The three of them could batter one of those doors for hours and make no impression on it.

The boots still clicked on stone, their refrain growing louder as the stairwell brought their owner twisting down towards them. Lutz moved onto the landing, pistols levelled at the next curve of steps rising into the gloom. Torben hung on her shoulder.

The east door would open onto the corridor containing the entrance to the Barbican's roof. That was where the enemy was probably heading. Pushing the south door, she mouthed a wordless prayer it was neither locked nor had anyone coming the other way.

The door opened onto an empty corridor, its heavy iron hinges creaking as it swung.

The footsteps stopped.

"Oh, please don't run away, warm things..."

The words made her shiver, as if they floated out of the darkness on a bitter winter's breeze.

Torben slipped past her and through the door, Lutz stood at her side, eyes flicking between her and the steps winding up from the landing.

"My lady..." he breathed, wanting her to follow her brother. But that voice held her. Speared to the spot by a dread fascination, the sudden, all-consuming desire to see the man standing on those shadowy steps just out of sight.

"My lady..." the voice repeated, dripping both amusement and contempt.

Lutz had whispered in her ear, but the man on the stairs had heard him well enough.

If man was the right word.

"Who are you?" she called, ignoring Lutz's wide-eyed glare and Torben's tug on her sleeve, "What are you doing here?"

"We are death, Lady Solace..." the cold voice came again, "...but not for you, sweet little thing..."

"How do you know me?"

"So many questions, just come to me and I will answer them all."

"Are you... the Devil?"

Laughter rolled out of the shadows.

Lutz pushed her through the door, hard enough for her to stagger and fall to her knees. As soon as Lutz followed her, Torben slammed the door shut, but not before she got a glimpse of a figure rushing out of the darkness. Tall and thin, with a pale bloodless face too long and too sharp to belong to any man. Its mouth gaped open, revealing gleaming white fangs. Its head tilted to one side and long flowing curls, absurdly feminine against the monstrous face, flew out behind the creature.

"Sweet Little Thing..." it hissed as the door slammed in its face.

Torben thumped the bar down in place and Lutz pushed home the bolts.

She pulled herself to her feet, unsure if her knees would still support her.

"You can't run forever, Sweet Little Thing..." the words floated softly from behind the door, "...this place of stones and shadows is not big enough."

They stood, staring at the door. No one spoke, as if afraid their words might make the nightmarish apparition real and not just a trick of light and shade.

Then the door began to shake as if all the lunatic creatures of Hell were flinging themselves against it...

*

His ears were making a peculiar sound.

A deep resonant ringing coupled with a buzzing noise that made him think an insect might have got itself trapped inside his skull. There was also a pounding he didn't much like the sound of. It was the explosion, of course.

Perhaps it had knocked something other than his hearing out of kilter, as it wasn't until he opened the door to the stairwell that he realised what the pounding noise actually was.

There was a demon smashing down the door to the East Wing corridor.

The thing swivelled around in a heartbeat, hissing through a mouthful of fangs, body tensing to pounce.

Well, at least the pounding wasn't my ears, after all.

He'd often wondered what his last thought might be. That was one he'd never considered.

However, the demon didn't pounce. Instead, after a moment, it straightened and twisted its grotesque mouth into something that might have been a smile.

"Ah... the Pretty Thing..."

The demon's face changed into the features of Alms, who would have looked almost cherubic, if not for the blood dribbling down his chin.

"Ulrich... Master..."

"I know your name. Your name is Pretty Thing. All mortals are just things, you see? What is the point of you having real names? It gets confusing..."

Alms sauntered across the landing. Realising he still gripped the door handle, he peeled his fingers away from the cold metal and let the hand fall to his side.

"Yes, Master..." When in doubt it seemed best to agree.

Alms' eyes, a startlingly vivid green, slid past him to the empty corridor behind.

"You are alone?"

Ulrich nodded.

"You were left with Callinicus. Why aren't you with him?"

"He's dead... I think."

Alms burst into laughter, hard enough to shower Ulrich with a fine mist of cold spittle and still warm blood.

"Callinicus is not dead."

"Is it impossible for you to die, Master?"

The smile faded from Alms' face, "No... 'tis just very

difficult... if we do not die in an instant, we will heal... what happened?"

As Ulrich told him, he found he was unable to pull his gaze from the demon's eyes. One moment the green of emeralds in the flickering candlelight, the next like new spring growth in the woodlands, the next bottle glass held up to the sun. They shifted with every twirl of the candle flame. They were, he noticed with giddy realisation, completely entrancing.

"I did wonder what that noise was..." Alms sighed.

Ulrich hadn't been aware he'd finished recounting events.

"Callinicus did not come out of the Wheelhouse. The fire is like an inferno. I... left to look for help."

"I'm sure you did," Alms looked amused. The demon's fingers were brushing his cheek, Ulrich realised. He hadn't noticed him raising his hand. The creature's skin was ridiculously soft against his.

"Who do you serve, Pretty Thing? Your old masters or your new ones?"

"I serve myself," Ulrich heard himself say in the distance, "I serve whoever will keep me alive."

"We will keep you alive, for a long time if you serve us well. Gold, women, power, long life. Whatever you desire. All can be yours. Would you like that?"

"Yes..."

Alms had a scent, not unpleasant, but not entirely wholesome either. Something meaty, rich and exotic Ulrich couldn't name. It dawned upon him the scent was so strong because Alms had moved close enough for their noses to be brushing against each other.

"Then you must give yourself to us and our beautiful cruelty..."

Ulrich had the absurd notion Alms intended to kiss him then, but instead the demon slowly turned his head to the door he'd been in the process of reducing to kindling with his fists.

"I must go and see if that buffoon Callinicus has finally managed to kill himself or not - he's been trying for centuries, but that's another story - however, the Lady Solace is on the other side of that door."

"Lady Solace?"

"The Sweet Little Thing... bring it to us. We have a use for it."

"Why do-"

Alms' hand fixed around his throat, fingers as cold and hard as iron, "You must decide who you serve. Us or them. Bring the Sweet Little Thing to us and you will have proved yourself, and that will be good. Try to help it escape and we will find you and eat you. That will be good too," Alms' eyes widened and his smile cut like the north wind, "that's the thing you need to understand. Whatever the outcome, we *always* win..."

Alms' tongue slithered out from between his full sensual lips and licked Ulrich's face, for a second the demon tightened his grip on his throat, squeezing so hard Ulrich feared his eyes might pop out of his head.

Then he stepped back.

"I will enjoy you serving me, Pretty Thing," the demon said, in his high, sibilant voice, before turning away. As he ducked out of the door to the North Wing he called back, "If the Sweet Little Thing needs any encouragement, tell her Saul the Bloodless has her father in the Great Hall. If she hurries, she might see him again while he still has a few bits and bobs we haven't tossed on the fire or strung up for decorations."

Alms grinned, before leaving Ulrich alone to stare at the half-shattered door beyond which the young woman he'd sworn an oath to protect was running for her life.

Chapter Seventeen

The sound of cracking wood echoed down the corridor as they ran.

We are Death, Lady Solace...

That cold hissing voice, those teeth, that face, the blood-smeared lips.

It knew my name.

Solace refused to look back until the dreadful pounding abruptly ceased. Then she turned on her heels and raised the pistol she'd been cradling with both hands, expecting to see that monstrous figure bounding down the corridor towards them, teeth snapping in expectation of their flesh.

The corridor was empty, and the door remained in place. That awful thing had failed to break through. It had given up. For now.

"What... what was *that?*" Lutz gasped, the visible skin between beard and helmet flushed alarmingly dark. She didn't think it was solely from the running.

"Not a man," was her only reply.

Torben produced The Goat from his satchel and held it out with a shaking hand.

"Perhaps the Devil," she breathed, "certainly the Master of the rogues we killed. One of them, anyway..."

"One of them?" Lutz scanned the corridor.

"So I fear..."

Torben put The Goat away, then he reached over, careful not to touch her skin, and tugged her sleeve. His head however, remained turned towards the door, his eyes wide and glistening. A rare flush had risen in his cheeks.

"Yes..." she glanced back at the door, even from halfway down the corridor the splits in the thick old oak were all too visible. "...we must keep moving."

Turning her back on the door, she wondered whether the thing had its eye to the cracked wood, tongue slowly licking its bloody lips as it spied on them.

"To the Chapel, still, my lady?"

"Yes."

"Do you think the Lord will protect us there?"

"We will protect ourselves, Sergeant, any assistance the Lord can provide will be, of course, very welcome."

The words sounded like hollow bravery to her own ears. A stupid child refusing to accept the realities of a cruel world. She'd been an infant when the war started and, despite the reassurances of her father, she'd always known the horrors unleashed upon the world by the endless conflict might one day arrive at the gates of The Wolf's Tower.

But this wasn't the horrors of pious men trying to impose their beliefs and ideals. Or Kings, Emperors and

Princes squabbling for power and wealth. This was something else. Something even worse.

We are Death, Lady Solace...

Lutz stared at her as if waiting for more. That, somehow, a seventeen-year-old girl might know how to deliver them from evil. She didn't. But if they reached the Chapel, she might be able to keep them and whoever else had survived the attack alive. And it didn't depend on God's assistance.

It would be thanks to her long-dead ancestors.

*

The door bulged outwards. The iron bands reinforcing it bent from the assault it had endured. Cracks split the thick oak planks as if a giant had been turning it into kindling with an axe.

Alms hadn't been using an axe, though. He'd been using his fists.

Ulrich pressed a hand against the wood; splinters scratched his palm. Bending down he put an eye against one of the larger cracks and peered through.

Almost lost in the shadows, three figures headed into the next stairwell at the end of the corridor. A big man who rolled as he half ran, that was Sergeant Lutz, who'd shouted baleful curses about Ulrich's mother every time he'd done something wrong, which in the old soldier's eyes had been every time Ulrich drew breath. A slender young man, with a slight stoop and a strange shuffling gait. Lord Torben, the half-witted simpleton and heir to the von Tassau estate. And the Lady Solace.

Why did the Masters want her?

Did they intend to string the girl up by her ankle and drink her blood like the two plump whores in *The Bear Pit*? She was beautiful, with hair like silver thread, a soft, pouting mouth that captivated the eye and a budding young body that captivated everything else. But they hadn't gone to all this trouble for one high-born wench, however comely. Had they?

They disappeared into the dark before he straightened up.

It didn't matter. It wasn't an important question.

What mattered was whether he was going to do what Alms asked of him.

The door rattled and groaned when he pushed it, but it would still take significant effort to get through it, even with his sword.

He didn't need to.

The Lady Solace and her companions had been heading away from the Barbican when they ran into Alms, barring the door behind them and fleeing down the corridor. They were going to the family apartments. The rich always fled towards their gold in times of danger.

The rich care more for their baubles than they ever will for the likes of you and I...

His father had told him that more than once, the words reeking of ale and bitterness as he slumped over a flagon in a dark corner of one flea-bitten tavern or another. Old Man Ulrich had no love of the rich, even if he'd secured his son a post in the service of the *Freiherr* just before he'd finally succeeded in drinking himself to death.

Spinning away from the door Ulrich ran up the spiralling steps. He could betray them or help them. Or do neither and try to save his own skin. He didn't believe Alms' promises of riches and rewards. Why should he? Saul the Bloodless wasn't the only demon who possessed liar's eyes.

All he really wanted to do was find a dark corner and hide. Maybe he should head in the other direction, the cellars and old dungeons boasted lots of nooks and crannies for a new-born coward to cower in.

A man has nothing but his honour...

Old Man Ulrich had slurred that one a lot too. Like most boys Ulrich had believed his father without question, following him from one company to the next and not seeing the bloodshot eyes the old man peered at the world through, the way his sword hand shook, the way his tongue stumbled over words, the way he stank of bile and stale vomit.

The men he worked for never possessed enough honour, enough glory, enough valour for Old Man Ulrich, so they never stayed anywhere long. It was only as he grew older that he realised they never stayed anywhere because it didn't take long for his father to miss a watch, or fall asleep on one, or not return from a tavern or bad mouth someone or start a brawl. Then they would pack their horse and mule before their frayed boots and worn hooves took to the road again, looking for someone willing to hire an old soldier and his boy who insisted they sought honour and glory, when it was just beer coin he wanted.

In the end, even in these desperate times when every nobleman wanted men to protect their lands and every mercenary captain wanted men to help plunder them, no one wanted Old Man Ulrich Renard anymore.

Ulrich spat as he ran up the steps.

Why was he thinking of his father so much?

Why should he worry about disappointing the shade of a man who'd fouled every opportunity life had offered? Maybe he really had been a great soldier once. But it must have been a long time before Ulrich had been born because he'd never met that man.

He reached the fifth floor. The door hung open and he hurried through into the East Wing. There were no demons and no corpses. If any of Saul's company had come this far, they would surely have turned back after the portcullis sealed the castle

These were the family rooms. The candles brighter and more numerous, beeswax rather than tallow, supplemented by oil lanterns. Tapestries and drapes softened the cold stone walls. The floors were polished oak as opposed to stone that might chill a noble foot. No one slept four to a room up here.

The private chambers of the *Freiherr* and his children were in the South Wing, a part of the castle the likes of him were usually strictly forbidden from entering.

Usually, of course, was something that had stopped applying a few hours ago.

Passing the rows of closed doors, he didn't think about what treasures might sit behind them. Gold was no use to the dead.

The door at the end of the corridor, which opened onto the south-east corner stairwell landing hung open, beyond that would be the entrance to the South Wing, the inner sanctum of the von Tassau family. A place not meant for a common man at arms like him.

He slowed his pace and then pulled up short as a shot rang out from the narrow confines of the stairwell. Then a woman screamed...

Chapter Eighteen

They locked and bolted the door to the south-east corridor behind them, sealing off that floor of the East Wing. It wouldn't slow one of the demons down for long, but the margins the hunted survive on are slim. Of course, it would also cut off their own people's escape, her father included, but the doors were supposed to be locked if enemies ever breeched the castle. Everybody knew that. Her father made sure he told everyone from the scullery maids and stable boys upwards.

They did the same to the door to the third floor of the South Wing. She thought she caught an echo of laughter, high-pitched and maniacal, before Lutz slammed the heavy door shut, but she couldn't be sure. The Wolf's Tower tricked the ear when it was in a playful mood, even those of someone who'd spent her entire life within its draughty embrace.

They climbed the stairs in silence. As she strained her ears, the darkness seemed to swallow even Lutz's laboured breathing and the hiss of Torben's dragging feet.

Then came a voice. They all froze. It had been too muffled and quiet to understand. But it'd come from below them. Hadn't it?

Lutz was looking down at her, half turned from the waist, craggy face a mask of concern. Solace placed a hand on his back and pushed gently to indicate he should go on. The furrows deepened. He seemed less sure the voice was below them. The castle playing more tricks with sound.

Wherever the voice had come from, it had now fallen silent. They couldn't just stand on the spiral steps. Eventually, someone *would* come.

Twisting around she stared at her brother's blank face, half-cloaked in shadow below her. There was no help there.

Doing something was always preferable to doing nothing. Better to make a bad choice than stand cowering in the dark making no choice at all. That would mean death for all of them. She pushed Lutz again, more insistently. *Go on.*

Lutz didn't look happy, but he headed upwards, albeit slowly. Hauling himself up the stairs one laboured step at a time, left shoulder pressed hard enough against the stairwell's inner curve for the metal of his cuirass to scrape the stonework.

Then the voice came again. Or rather voices. Still faint, but this time it sounded like they were above them, not below.

Lutz froze. Right foot on the narrowest slither of the next step, head jutting forward as if to see further around the tight bend of the spiral stairwell.

She twisted around again. Her brother, half-obscured

by the old, pitted stonework of the stairwell, stared back. Were there men in front *and* behind them. That wouldn't be good.

Mimicking walking with her fingers she jabbed her head forwards. No expression crossed Torben's face, but he turned his head to look behind him. And to listen. When he twisted back his face was still slackly expressionless. He shook his head, only a slight movement but enough to rattle the helmet about his ears.

Lutz nodded down the stairs. *Turnaround. Find another way.*

She shook her head forcefully. They could go back down to the fourth floor and then along the corridor and up the south-west stairs to the Chapel. But that would squander priceless time and they might well run into even more of the demons before they got anywhere near the Chapel.

Of course, she didn't know who the men above were. They might be her own soldiers or servants. The dread stone in her stomach, however, insisted otherwise. Her people wouldn't be calmly chatting given what had befallen The Wolf's Tower. And if they were the enemy, were they men like the two in the Wheelhouse or would they be monsters like the thing in the north-east stairs?

It was a terrible gamble. Men they could kill, with a fair wind. The creature that had all but smashed through a thick oak door, however... she'd be sending Lutz to his death. Probably all their deaths. But what choice did she have? Eventually they would have to stand and fight somewhere and the voices of the two men above them sounded calm and relaxed. They didn't know death was close.

Lutz continued to stare down at her. Waiting. He was an experienced soldier. He'd been to war, fought on the battlefield, seen and done things beyond her imagination. He'd killed men. He'd killed men tonight, in front of her, with a speed and savagery belying his age and gruff, grudging good humour. He could be a curmudgeonly grandfather, coarse of tongue and soft of heart. But he wasn't. He was a soldier. Her soldier. And he was looking at her to make a decision that might very well cost him his life.

All she wanted was to run back to her books and her embroidery and daydreams of handsome young princes. She couldn't. It was a luxury she didn't have any more.

Kill them.

She mouthed the two little words. When Lutz continued to stare, she mouthed them again. He nodded. No expression ruffled the deep lines embedded into his face. Then he handed her the pistol he carried in his left hand.

For a moment she thought he was just going to turn and run up the stairs, instead he bent down, close enough for the coarse bristles of his beard to scratch her ear.

"Fire one of the pistols and then scream as loud as you can. When they come, I will drop low and take the first one, fire your other pistol at the second man. You will not miss at this range..."

"Wait."

Turning around she handed one of the pistols to her brother. Torben looked at it with interest.

"When I nod, fire this down the stairs, 'tis important. Do you understand me, Torben?"

Her brother raised his head and nodded, pointing the gun behind him.

The look on Lutz's face spoke volumes when she turned back.

She smiled, reassuringly, then tugged one of Lutz's spare pistols free from his belt.

Somewhere beneath his bristles the Sergeant pulled a disapproving face. He didn't trust Torben with a gun. He probably wouldn't trust him with a spoon either. But her brother wasn't the simpleton everyone thought him; she felt a lot better about having two chances to hit whatever came hurtling out of the gloom towards them on the narrow staircase.

Solace met the old soldier's eye, raised her chin, and held it.

A half twist of a smile flickered beneath his beard, and he drew a long-bladed dagger from the rough leather sheath hanging from his weapon belt. Then he turned his back on her, placed one foot on the next step, bent his knees and lowered his shoulders, pistol in his right hand, dagger in the left. And waited.

Setting herself as best she could, she waited. Holding one heavy pistol was awkward, firing two together suddenly seemed a mite ambitious. Both were longer than her forearm and the triggers were stiff.

Lutz's broad shoulders blocked most of the narrow staircase in front of her and she tried to control her nerves, afraid she might end up shooting the old man in the back.

Lutz should have been more worried about giving her a gun than Torben.

Taking a deep breath, she steadied herself. The voices came again, this time accompanied by a laugh. A low dirty chuckle that held more malice than mirth. What was there to laugh about amongst the horror and bloodshed engulfing her home? Anger welled inside her and it steadied her more effectively than the cold damp air she had just sucked into her lungs.

Looking over her shoulder she found Torben hadn't moved a muscle, he was still pointing the pistol behind him, still looking at her, his face as expressionless as always, save for his eyes which were wider and brighter, glimmering in what little light snuck around the curve of the stairs.

The light was so poor it would be hard to identify whoever came down those stairs. If they were her men...

No. She was certain. She felt it. The dread stone felt it. They were the enemy. The invaders. The Devil's rogues. Men who served monsters. Men they must kill.

She held her brother's eye and nodded.

The crack of the pistol shot breaking the stillness made her jump and she screamed without thought.

"Help!!!"

Lutz hadn't told her to say anything, but she guessed the sound of a woman in distress would bring the men above down the stairs more eagerly. She'd spent most of her life cocooned within The Wolf's Tower, but she understood enough about the world to know what men like these did to women in distress.

Sure enough, the thump of nailed boots hurtling down the stone steps instantly replaced the echo of her scream.

"Who's there?" a gruff voice she didn't recognise rolled out of the darkness.

"Please! Help, they hurt me!" She hoped she wasn't overdoing it, but the distress and fear in her voice were genuine. And that should bring men such as these to her like wasps to fruit rotting in the summer sun.

Her grip on the pistols tightened.

She didn't see the first man till Lutz shot him. A snarling face momentarily illuminated in the flash of the Sergeant's pistol as he careened around the curve of the staircase. Lutz then put his head down and cannoned into the soldier, shoulder hitting his midriff, propelling him backwards, into a second man. Like the first he wore the uniform of a von Tassau man at arms, but not the face.

Pulling both triggers on the cumbersome wheellock pistols took all her strength, but they fizzed and fired true. The man screamed, stumbling backwards and landing on his rump as acrid white smoke billowed from the guns. She didn't know if she'd hit him once or twice, or where she'd hit him, but she'd done enough. Or so she thought.

The first man was still alive and grappling with Lutz. The Sergeant was on top of him, he'd lost his dagger and was throttling the rogue. He was trying to push Lutz off, but the tight confines of the staircase didn't give him enough room to swing a punch.

"Die you fucker! Die you fucker!" Lutz screamed into the soldier's face. She couldn't see much of the man bar his thrashing legs, but he didn't seem inclined to die quickly enough for her liking.

Metal clanged as their helmets clashed, the soldier trying to head butt Lutz.

Solace dropped the empty pistols and twisted around to her brother, who was craning his neck to see. He didn't always appear to pay much notice to what happened around him, but he was taking an interest now.

"Give me your sword!" she cried.

The weapon was too large and unwieldy to be of much use in such a tight space, but she could at least slash at the man's legs. Every little would help.

Torben, however, had other ideas.

Sword in hand he pushed past her to get into the fight.

She could have stopped him, but there was no time to squabble. Instead, she flattened herself against the curving stonework and allowed her brother by.

Torben didn't often smile, expressing emotions was something else he struggled with, but he was grinning from ear to ear as he scrambled past her, raising the heavy weapon to hack at the enemy.

That was when Solace noticed the second rogue was still alive after all. He had flopped on the steps above Lutz and the man he was trying to strangle, slumped against the outer wall and head lolling, but still very much taking an interest.

And even as the blood bubbled through his lips, he raised a pistol towards them.

*

Ulrich stood, unsure what to do.

Running away was a promising idea. But that scream had been the Lady Solace, he was sure of it. He'd barely exchanged a word with her and wouldn't know her scream from the next wench's, but she'd been heading up those stairs, so it seemed likely it was her.

So? It solved his dilemma, didn't it? He didn't have to betray her if she'd already stumbled into the hands of the masters.

If you are not an asset, you are food...

They didn't really need him anymore, did they? Despite their setbacks the castle was theirs. Maybe they'd hang him up by his ankle along with everybody else. But if he proved his worth? And how else might he prove his worth?

What if it wasn't the masters on the other side of the door, but Red Cloaks? Men who might decide they'd rather enjoy the beautiful young woman themselves before taking her to their masters.

Pistol shots, shouts and cries echoed through the castle.

He should run. He should help. He should do whatever he needed to survive.

His father's words, always spoken with a quiet awful bitterness, came to him. He'd always been too young to understand what he'd meant. He probably was still too young. But the wretched sadness of them had always haunted him.

Honour is the only thing that cannot be taken from a man. He can only give it away...

The choices you make in a moment can break the rest

of your life. You think you are going to live a good and virtuous life and end up tormented by the fact you never did, rotting away in a stinking little room, surrounded by flies, with nothing but regrets to hold your hand as you slip screaming out of a world you left no worthy mark upon.

"Damn you..." he spat, taking the few strides to the door at a run and ripping it open.

The landing inside was empty, the sounds of fighting were clear enough however and he took the steps leading down the spiral stairs two at a time, tugging the pistol he'd taken from the dead man in the Darkway free from his belt.

It must have taken only a handful of seconds to charge down the stairs, but it stretched like an age as the shadows blurred past him. The candles in their worn little niches conjured faces in their wavering light; Old Man Ulrich, Kadelberg, Vinzenz, Holger, the dark pits of their dead eyes full of mocking scorn alongside the distorted, too thin faces of demons hungry for his blood and his soul.

As usual, he had no idea what he was doing, or why he was doing it, but he ran all the same, his shoulder bouncing off the stonework as he giddily sped down the stairs.

Finally, a real figure emerged out of the shadows.

A mortally wounded man slumped on one of the steps was levelling a pistol at someone out of Ulrich's sight around the corner.

He wore the garb and wolf rampant insignia of Tassau, but he was one of Saul's men right enough. Ulrich recognised him from *The Bear Pit*, standing in the background, watching the masters sucking blood from the two plump whores hanging from the rafters with casual disinterest.

Ulrich shot him in the head.

The bastard's head jerked into the wall and the pistol tumbled from his grasp before he slid back on the steps.

The sound of fighting continued.

If one of the masters stood around the bend of the stairs, he was a dead man. But if one of the demons was there Ulrich thought the fighting would have been over in seconds. No mere man could stand against them, he'd seen that well enough during the massacre in the village.

He continued down the steps, rounded the bend and hoped no one shot him.

Clank, clank, clank.

The noise reverberated through the stairwell as Ulrich edged around the corner to find Lutz trying to kill one of the Red Cloaks. Tangled together on the steps beneath the man he'd just shot, the Sergeant was smashing the Red Cloak's helmeted head against the step. The Red Cloak had got one hand on the old man's throat and was pushing him away. His other hand grasping for a dagger laying behind them.

The Lady Solace and her half-witted brother stood below the struggling men; the girl, wide-eyed and ridiculously beautiful, clutched her brother, trying to pull him back while the simpleton stood and tried to figure out how to work the sword hanging from his limp wrist.

Scooping up the dagger the Red Cloak's fingers groped for, Ulrich put one hand on the cold metal of his helmet and pushed his head back before slashing the blade across his throat.

If the man recognised him before he died, he didn't have time to say anything about it.

Lutz continued bashing the man's head against the step as if not noticing Ulrich, the dagger or the blood that had sprayed his face.

"You should stop that," Ulrich pulled the blade clear, "the demons have excellent hearing..."

Lutz grunted and looked up, eyes full of fury. For an instant, he thought the old soldier was going to throw himself at him, assuming he could get his fat arse off the ground of course. Then the light of both sanity and recognition returned to his eyes.

Satisfied Lutz wasn't going to try and start smashing his head against the stonework, Ulrich turned his attention to the *Freiherr's* children. Solace had composed herself, Torben still looked like a slack-jawed simpleton. Strange how so many men had died tonight and yet this fool still breathed. Aristocratic breeding for you.

"My lady," he nodded, before adding, "my lord."

"A timely intervention, Renard," she replied.

The fact she knew his name took him aback. Lady Solace had never displayed the aloof disdain most of the nobility reserved for commoners like him, but he'd never had cause to think she'd ever even noticed him.

Lutz managed to pull himself free of the Red Cloak's corpse, his bulk filling most of the stairwell and blocking the *Freiherr's* children from view. He inspected both the dead men, before returning his attention to Ulrich.

"Good work," he growled. It was, by Ulrich's reckoning, the first time Lutz had complimented him on anything since he'd joined The Wolf's Tower garrison. Everything he'd done previously had been a source of ire and scorn to the old fart.

It was, indeed, a night of surprises.

Part Two

Blood

Chapter One

"'tis nothing, my lady," Lutz reassured her, spitting out blood along with one of his remaining teeth, "I've hurt myself worse farting."

She raised an eyebrow and suppressed a smile. She doubted Father would approve of such language. However, thoughts of her father made the urge to smile evaporate.

The door to the South Wing was locked and barred. It didn't budge a fraction when Lutz rattled the handle in frustration.

"Where do we go now?" Renard asked. He stood at the top of the stairs, reloading his pistol with powder and shot taken from one of the dead rogues.

"Through this damn door!" Lutz barked before she could answer.

"If you have a magic key, now would be the time to use it. We will not be alone for long," Renard didn't look up as he rammed the shot down the muzzle of the wheellock pistol.

The expression on Lutz's face suggested he was

sucking up some more blood to spit at the young man. Torben followed the exchange, moving his head back and forth between the two men the way he did when something interested him enough to pay attention to the world around him.

"Your attitude hasn't improved any..." the old man said, before demanding "You rode with Kadelberg? What happened?"

"Later!" she snapped at them, "We need to get to the Chapel first."

"Those two..." Renard indicated the corpses on the stairs with a nod, "...were guarding the door, waiting for one of the demons to break it down. They know people are on the other side of it. One, or more, will be here soon."

"Knock on the door," she ordered, "he's right, that door didn't lock itself, some of our people must be in there. Maybe my father..."

Renard looked up from his pistol and stared at her. Then he shoved the gun into his belt and started checking the weapons he'd taken from the two dead rogues.

The dread stone moved in her guts. Renard's look chilled her, but now wasn't the time to question him. Once in the Chapel, they would be safe. For a little while at least.

"Knock on the door!" she repeated, loud and harsh enough to make Torben jump.

"Open up!" Lutz hammered on the door, "Open this fucking door in the name of *Freiherr* von Tassau!"

"I'm not sure that would encourage anyone to let us in," Renard noted, his tone as dry as the powder he'd poured into the gun, "you sound like one of them."

Lutz shot another baleful look over his shoulder, but Renard was right, again. In the circumstances, she doubted she'd be inclined to open the door to the bellicose sergeant either.

She slapped her own palms against the unyielding wood, "Open the door! 'tis the Lady Solace! Open the door!"

The door remained closed.

Did anyone remain alive on the other side of it to hear their pleas? If people cowered in the Chapel, they might not even hear. Or think it another trick if they did. Or had lost their minds with fear. Or the demons had smashed through the door at the other end and only corpses awaited them.

She glanced back at Renard. The young man was bright. He wasn't still alive due to luck alone, but he offered no advice. Instead, he stared down the shadowy well of the stairs, distant eyes peering out of his bruised face

"Renard...?"

He looked up with a start before shaking his head, "No... No one's coming yet, but soon. Perhaps we should go somewhere else? Is the Chapel any safer than the rest of the castle? We could go down and hide in the cellars...?"

She shook her head, hard enough for her long white-blonde hair, which had worked itself loose, to dance about her head, "Nowhere in The Wolf's Tower is safer than the Chapel."

She returned her attention to the door.

"This is not a deceit! I am the Lady Solace, daughter of Rainer von Tassau, granddaughter of Jorg von Tassau. I am with my brother, the Lord Torben... and... and... men at arms! I command you to open this door!"

A faint scraping sound came from the other side of the door and her heart quickened. Then a voice, hesitant and uncertain.

"My lady?"

"Yes, let us in!"

"Is it... really you?"

"Dolman?" Lutz glared at the door, jaw jutting forward.

A pause.

"Yes..."

"Then open this fucking door or I'll rip your worthless intestines from your worthless guts, wrap them around your worthless neck and choke the worthless life out of your worthless fucking hide!"

"Yes, Sergeant!"

She'd never heard a man sound so relieved to be threatened and insulted in her life.

*

The household's survivors huddled around the Chapel's small altar.

Two men at arms, two maids and the *Freiherr's* steward, Strecker, a pinch-faced man whose responsibilities included paying the castle's garrison; a task undertaken as begrudgingly as any miser forking out clipped coins from his own dusty purse.

Ulrich stood in the doorway, listening in case more survivors hammered on the locked doors at either end of the corridor, or, more likely, the Masters started smashing them down.

The fact everything remained quiet suggested no one

else was alive and the demons were too preoccupied with getting the Outer Gate open to bother with them just yet. It wasn't as if they were going anywhere.

The Chapel door was as thick as the ones sealing the corridor. It might keep the demons out for a couple of minutes. It didn't seem much of a plan.

He could slip away. Unbolt the doors and find the Masters, tell them where Solace was hiding, or take her to them himself and claim the glory.

Neither were honourable choices.

His father, who he worshipped as a boy and pitied as a man, had been obsessed by the concept; the way a man should conduct himself in the world, the way he should be seen and remembered. Honesty, integrity, sincerity. How he loved to weave those words into the spellbinding tales he entertained Ulrich with when he'd been little.

Old Man Ulrich tried to live by those principles and ended up a broken, friendless, ale-sodden wreck, selling his sword to whoever was in the most desperate need for men at arms.

Perhaps if he'd betrayed a few more people along the way, he would have died a happier man...

Ulrich leaned out of the door and checked the corridor again. Still empty. Still quiet. Nothing moved bar the candle flames. When he looked back into the Chapel, Lutz was glaring at him.

From his first day at The Wolf's Tower, Lutz had taken against him. The Sergeant had known Old Man Ulrich, a long time ago, and not been much impressed. Sergeant Lutz seemed to feel Ulrich was an apple that had fallen remarkably close to the tree.

Of all the people who might have survived the attack, he would have placed everything of worth he owned (which didn't amount to much more than his father's sword, a fair pair of boots and the few coins Strecker gave him that hadn't gone straight to *The Bear Pit*) that the old bastard would be one of them.

Ulrich smiled at the old man. Lutz's tongue and temper had always scared him, but that fear seemed absurd now. What was to fear about one fat old soldier when creatures like the Masters roamed the world? They were far more worthy of his fear than Sergeant Eugen Lutz.

Lutz spat on the floor, then remembered where he was and looked slightly abashed beneath his blood-caked beard. Then decided nothing really mattered as they were all going to be dead soon anyway.

Well, maybe not all of them...

He dropped his gaze, in case betrayal was something you might glean from a man's eyes. When he looked back, the Lady Solace was walking toward him. She'd been talking to the other survivors, listening to their tales, offering comfort, even to the two lowly maids. Her brother remained on his knees in front of the altar. A fat lot of good that would do.

As she came to the door, Lutz pushed himself to his feet with a grunt and followed her.

"We have little time," she said in a hushed voice, "so my expression of gratitude has to be brief, but I thank you, Ulrich Renard, you saved at least one of our lives tonight."

"Everything was in hand," Lutz growled at her

shoulder.

"I was only doing my duty, my lady."

As an honourable man should...

"Talking of duty," Lutz jumped in, "what happened in the village?"

"It was a trap. The church had been set afire with most of the peasants inside. The doors barred by nailing Pastor Jonathan across them..."

Solace pressed a hand to her mouth, Lutz sucked at one of his teeth.

"They came at us from all sides, musketeers from the cottages, demons amongst us. It was a slaughter..."

"And yet, you are here?" Lutz asked.

"I fought my way clear."

"You ran away."

"I killed the men who got in my way; I'm no coward."

"No one is suggesting that you are," Solace said with a soft smile, despite the fact the hairy old bastard next to her had just implied precisely that.

"So, you came back here to warn us?" Lutz asked, still working at the tooth. Maybe he was going to spit that one out too.

"I lost my horse, I ran into the woods..." Ulrich didn't want to lie, but he didn't want to admit the terrible truth he had helped the Masters into the castle to save his skin either, "...I got lost in the darkness..."

That, at least, was true.

"And the men we let into the castle?" Lutz continued to stare at him, hand resting lightly on the pommel of his sword.

"I guess they stripped the dead of their armour and clothes and pretended to be us."

"But Captain Kadelberg was with them?"

"The Captain is dead."

"I spoke to him before we opened the gates!" Lutz insisted.

"I saw one of the monsters rip the Captain's throat out with his teeth. These are demons. They have many tricks."

"May the Lord deliver us from evil," Solace interrupted, before the Sergeant could get any more belligerent. He muttered a begrudging, "Amen," instead.

"And when you finally made it back to the castle?" Solace asked.

"The Outer Gate was open, bodies filled the Darkway, more corpses in the Courtyard. I wanted to run, but the portcullis came down..."

"How many bodies in the Darkway?"

"Six or seven. The bodies in the Courtyard were all our people."

Lutz scratched his chin through his blood-caked beard, "Twenty-eight riders came through the Outer Gate, at least nine are dead, plus, with God's grace, a few more in the Wheelhouse."

That would be three, but he decided not to venture that nugget, enough holes gaped in his story as it was.

"That leaves nineteen, at most," Solace did the sums for Lutz who had fallen silent. The fiendish calculation clearly too much for the old bastard.

Sixteen...

Assuming Callinicus really was dead. Fifteen if you

counted the wounded Red Cloak Callinicus had carried from the Darkway. Ulrich cast his eye around the Chapel, the odds remained poor. Especially as half that number were demons.

"Until the ones outside get in," with the arithmetic out of the way, life returned to Lutz's eyes.

Solace took a deep breath, "Then we must leave before then."

Ulrich stared at her. On the face of it she didn't seem as simple as her brother...

"There is a horde of them outside the gate, which is now sealed. The only other way would be to climb down from the roof, cross the frozen moat and hope none of them notices us running through the snow..."

Lutz bridled at his tone, but Solace raised her hand before the Sergeant could remind him of his lowly station.

"No, there is another way."

Lutz's big head swivelled towards the young woman.

"There is, my lady?"

"My forbearers built The Wolf's Tower to be secure, they didn't build it to be a prison. There is a postern gate, known only to the family. We can escape."

"What of the men locked outside?"

"'tis a tunnel, built to take defenders beyond the siege lines of any attackers, either to escape or assault their rear. It comes up in the woods to the east. They will not see us."

Ulrich sagged against the door.

Ever since Saul made his bargain in *The Bear Pit,* his choice was a stark and simple one. Serve the Masters or die. Horribly. The possibility of another option flooded him with unexpected hope.

"We should leave at once, my lady..." Lutz said, his voice low.

Solace nodded, looked around the Chapel and then back, "There are so few of us, there must still be other people alive...."

"My lady, I'm afraid we cannot tarry here," Lutz shook his head, "there are not enough of us left to fight. Not against these demons. If there is a means of escape, we should take it. That is what your father would want."

Solace turned her soft, bright eyes on Ulrich, "Did you see anyone else?"

"No one alive, my lady."

"My father?"

"He is in the Great Hall," the words escaped him without thought, or perhaps some dark part of him blurted them out, either way, Solace's eyes both widened and brightened. Lutz's on the other hand, narrowed considerably.

"How do you know that?"

"I overheard it, they said he'd been taken to the Great Hall..."

"Then we shall rescue him!" Solace whirled towards the others gathered around the altar.

"No," Lutz's word stopped her.

"I am sorry, Sergeant?"

"I cannot allow it."

Her delicately plucked eyebrow inched up a fraction, "You... *cannot?*"

"I have my orders."

"My orders are that we will rescue my father!"

"My orders are from the *Freiherr*."

"From my father?"

Lutz nodded, "'tis your safety that is paramount, above all others, including my own. And including his. Those are the orders he gave me if the castle were ever to fall. They apply as well to demons as the Imperial Army."

"My father is in danger."

"We are all in danger, my lady. He would not want you risking yourself to save him. Besides, 'tis impossible. Even if we faced men, it would be difficult, as we are not..."

Solace drew her mouth into a thin tight line. She probably didn't have much experience of someone refusing her wish.

"I-"

"I'm sorry, we must leave."

Her nostrils flared. She really didn't like being told what to do.

"What do you think?" she asked, turning to stare at Ulrich.

I could deliver you to the demons and hope they are creatures of their word...

"It would be very difficult to rescue the *Freiherr*..."

"But not impossible?"

He ignored Lutz's glower, "Very difficult."

"What he thinks is irrelevant, I have my orders. We must leave, so please, my lady, show us how to access this tunnel."

"No."

"I'm sorry?"

"Not without my father."

"My lady..."

"I suggest you start preparing for the rescue... alternatively, we can just wait for the demons to come..."

With that she spun away and went to pray alongside her brother.

Chapter Two

She needed to talk to God before she spoke to the others. She also needed to calm herself.

Kneeling beside Torben, she closed her eyes and prayed. She prayed for salvation and guidance. She prayed for the strength to do what was right. Mostly, however, she prayed for her father.

Beyond her closed eyes she heard little above the soft rhythm of Torben's breathing; the occasional whisper of scuffing feet, a cleared throat, a sniffling nose. No one spoke. She hoped they were all praying too. If anyone in the whole wide world needed God's help tonight, then, surely, it was this small band of survivors.

Soon the demons would come, and the doors would not hold. They all knew that. What they didn't know yet was that her father was alive.

And they must save him!

In the quietness of prayer her blood cooled and instead of God's voice came the demon's.

We are death, Lady Solace... but not for you...

She shivered. Not for herself, but for everyone else. Is that what the demon meant?

Behind her one of the maids, she couldn't tell whether Karina or Erna, started to sob.

She peeled open her eyes. It was Erna, who was young and pretty. Kapsner, a dour-looking man at arms with a bloodhound's face, tried to comfort her, one hand resting awkwardly on her shoulder. He looked like he wanted to cry himself.

Was it possible she could save her father?

Lutz didn't think so. And it wasn't cowardice making him say that. She commanded four men at arms, plus her brother, who could barely carry a sword, Strecker who was skilled only in quill and ink and two red-eyed maids. A poor army to throw against the demonic creatures invading her home.

Erna shuffled on the pew and swallowed back her sobs. She'd noticed Solace watching her and took her stare for annoyance. Solace smiled and nodded. Then she closed her eyes again.

Whatever she decided, she must decide it fast.

She could save these people, or she could try and save her father. She couldn't do both. And if she tried to save her father at least some of the people huddled in the Chapel - who turned to her for protection as much as God - were likely to die in the attempt.

Her brother knelt before his new sword, both hands wrapped around the blade, forehead resting against the hilt. He'd always wanted his own sword. He'd always wanted to be like other men. Now he could pretend he was.

She reached across to tug the sleeve of Torben's tunic. It was about the most physical contact he could suffer.

Torben opened his eyes and turned his head to stare at her, his eyes their usual unfathomable selves in the light of the few candles flickering in the Chapel.

"We need to talk..." she rose from her knees and patted down her skirts while she waited for him to rise too. When he didn't, she added curtly, *"...now!"*

Her brother put his weight on the sword and pushed himself to his feet. She led him to the far corner of the Chapel, feeling the eyes of the other survivors on her along with the weight of their desperate hope. Torben followed her. Until he realised his too-large helmet was still on the floor by the altar and scurried back to get it.

By the time he joined her, dented steel framed his face and the burgonet's rim hovered over his eyes. She reached up and took it off. A flicker of something childish crossed Torben's face. She ignored it.

"Father is still alive. The demons hold him."

She waited for a reaction. None came. At least the expression of childish pique faded back into the slack expressionless pond Torben's features usually amounted to.

"We can try to rescue him or..." her voice dropped even lower as she leaned in close enough for him to shuffle his feet in discomfort "...we can try to leave the castle... through the back ways?"

Torben continued to look at her with his big, liquid eyes. He displayed no more emotion than if she had asked him whether chicken tasted better than fish.

"If we leave, we might get away from the demons, if we

try to save father everyone might die, but if we leave him in their hands... he will die. Torben, I don't know what to do?"

She glanced across to the doorway, where Lutz had come into the Chapel. For a moment she feared he brought news of the demons arrival, but though he moved directly towards them there was nothing in his demeanour to suggest their situation had become even worse.

When she returned her attention to Torben he was holding out his hand. Resting in his palm was a small wooden carving.

The Horse.

The Horse meant *be quick*. It also meant *run*.

It meant abandon their father to his death.

*

"And you don't know where this tunnel is?"

"If I did, I'd just throw the girl over my shoulder and fucking carry her out of here..." Lutz snarled.

They had moved out of the Chapel and into the corridor. Lutz didn't want the others to hear there was a way out of the castle, or that Solace wasn't prepared to reveal where it was unless they all went and got themselves killed trying to rescue the *Freiherr* first.

The Sergeant probably suspected it might not go down too well.

The door at the far end of the corridor tugged Ulrich's eyes.

The heavy oak bar still rested snuggly in place. No one, even a demon, was getting through that door without making a lot of noise. Still, he didn't like turning his back on it.

Instead, he rested a hand against the outer wall. As this wing housed the private rooms of the von Tassau family, panels of dark walnut covered the walls.

Lutz was looking at him again.

"How'd you get by the wagons and the rest of the demons?"

"Pardon?"

"You said you entered the castle just before the portcullis dropped. We did that. To stop the rest of those bastards getting in. Wagons and a column of horsemen were approaching the castle from the village. How'd you get by them?"

The good Sergeant was a suspicious sort of fellow...

"I came from the south. I lost my way in the woods..." he touched his bruised face and swollen nose "...I ran into a tree as I fled in the darkness. Knocked the senses out of me for a few minutes... more maybe... when I eventually found the castle I was to the south, I came around the side, didn't see the riders till the last minute..."

His words petered out with a shrug. He wasn't sure he'd believe himself and Sergeant Lutz was a man who carried a lot of scepticism along with his pot belly, broad shoulders and thick neck.

"And how-"

"Perhaps we should concentrate on getting out of The Wolf's Tower. Afterwards you can interrogate me at your leisure..." his eyes drifted back to the East Door, "...because we're going to be enjoying the company of demons soon..."

"I don't like you, Renard. Your father was a

troublemaker. A drunkard. A liar. I fear you're your father's son. I told the *Freiherr* as much..." Lutz chewed at his bottom lip and looked like he wanted to say more.

Caught between wanting to thump the old man and pretty much agreeing with him, Ulrich offered a shrug, "A thank you for saving your life is sufficient, really..."

The bits of Lutz's face visible between beard and helm grew red.

"You've been here but a few months, you ride out with forty men and are the only soul to return, even though I spoke to Kadelberg, who you insist is dead. And then The Wolf's Tower is assaulted by a plague of demons..."

"Are you implying something, Sergeant?"

"I'm implying nothing. I'm saying something stinks like my feet after a long march on a hot day."

Lutz's eyes were dark, intense pools beneath his heavy brows. Ulrich struggled not to squirm under their scrutiny. The fact the Sergeant didn't like him was no revelation, but Lutz didn't know what he'd done or that he still teetered on the precipice of betrayal. Lutz's dislike didn't give him insight, it just tainted his view of everything Ulrich did. Even killing two of the Red Cloaks hadn't been enough to win the old man's trust.

Although Ulrich still didn't know whether he'd killed the men to save Solace or so he could give her to Saul himself.

"When the demons finally come through one of those doors, they will kill us all. Convincing the Lady Solace to reveal the way out of the castle will serve you better than telling me you don't like me very much. We both knew that already."

Lutz didn't look happy. In truth, Lutz never looked happy, but Ulrich's logic was undeniable. In the end, the old man's only response was a wet noise in the back of his throat that sounded like someone was throttling a small animal. He spun away. The dirty hem of Lutz's cloak slapped against Ulrich's knees as the Sergeant stomped into the Chapel to find Lady Solace and their way out of The Wolf's Tower.

As soon as the shadowy archway swallowed Lutz, Ulrich's eyes snapped back to the East Door. They would come that way. He knew it. Perhaps they were at the door now. Listening. Maybe they could look through solid wood. What were the limits of their strange and terrible powers? Perhaps it was a test to determine what he would do. Whether he was worthy.

More likely they didn't care one way or the other and would kick their way in when they were good and ready.

He was surprised to find he was halfway to the door.

Ulrich stopped, blinked and looked around him. He didn't remember walking towards the door. Given all he'd endured it was hardly surprising his mind wasn't working as it should.

He put a hand against the wall, the walnut panelling smooth upon his fingers. He felt exhausted and ached from head to toe. His eyes felt raw in their sockets and his broken nose throbbed. He wanted to sleep.

He wanted to lift the bar and let them in...

He imagined the feel of the wood, not smooth like the walnut panelling, but coarse and worn. And heavy. He felt the weight of it, his biceps tensing as he lifted it away, and the relief of dropping it. The burden, released, not just from his arms, but from his shoulders, from his neck, from his legs. From his soul. That weight always pushed down on him, making every single step slow and laboured and painful.

The weight of his father's expectations.

The weight of a broken man's hopes and prayers that his son would be a better man than he. That he would be a good man, a brave man, a pious man and, above all other things, an honourable man.

If he cast aside that bar on the door then the expectations of a dead man would no longer weigh upon his shoulder, because there would be no more pretence that he was the man his father failed to be. He would no longer need to strive to be a better man because he would have become a man so very much worse than his father.

What would Old Man Ulrich's misdemeanours be in comparison? Why, nothing at all! Was there a greater failing than betraying your lord, your oath, your God and your very own soul to demons? Possibly, as it was, after all, a terrible world. But he couldn't think of one.

Fingers brushing the walnut roses scrolled along the wooden panels of the wall, Ulrich's feet begun moving towards the East Door again...

Chapter Three

Lutz headed straight for her.

"My lady," he said, breathing hard, "we must leave. Now."

"My father-"

"Your father would not want you to risk yourself. He would want you safe."

"I believe we have already enjoyed this conversation."

Lutz sucked in air. He looked a lot older than he did a few hours earlier. They probably all did.

"I gave my oath to serve your family a long time ago. To your grandfather. I have honoured that oath as best I can. I fought alongside your grandfather, I have fought alongside your father and, now, I fight alongside you and Lord Torben. I will give my life, gladly, to protect yours. That is as it should be. My life for yours, my lady..."

Lutz's eyes didn't waver; she clamped down on the temptation to pull her cloak tighter to stifle a shiver. The Chapel had always been the coldest room in The Wolf's Tower.

"...but I will not discard my life without purpose, on a fool's venture that will see me, you, the Lord Torben and everyone else here die. The *Freiherr*, who it is my greatest honour to consider my friend, as well as my lord, would not want it. You are his line, you are the future, without you, this place is just a pile of cold stones. So, you will show me the way to the postern gate and we will leave."

She raised her chin and set her jaw. Everyone seemed determined to abandon her father. She would not. Her cheek tingled and the hard slap of glove on face rung in her ears again. Their last moment together unless she convinced Lutz and her brother of a way to save him.

She held her tongue as she fought to find the right words, but Lutz saw her response well enough in the set of her face and fire in her eyes. When he continued a cold, suppressed anger sharpened his tone.

"My lady, what do you expect to happen if we try to rescue your father? The plucky and headstrong young woman leads the reluctant old warrior, the troubled prince, the handsome stranger..." he jerked his head towards the door to indicate Ulrich Renard before jabbing a finger at the others huddled around the altar and watching them with haunted eyes, "...and a ragtag bag of survivors, against a terrible foe and somehow, through cunning and trickery, overcome overwhelming odds and unnatural powers to win the day?"

"Why not?"

"Because, my lady..." Lutz growled, stepping forward to loom over her, "...this isn't that kind of a tale..."

Something crumbled inside her. Only her

stubbornness prevented her yielding. The same stubbornness that had made her set men afire without knowing for certain whether they were friend or foe.

That time, at least, the dread stone turned in her guts to tell her she was right. Now... now there was nothing. If she possessed any kind of *sight,* it was not helping her to see a way forward. Other than the one Lutz suggested.

"I do not expect to live out this night," Lutz's gravel-scoured voice softened, "I've seen my last sunrise. But I don't want my death to be leading you to yours. I want it to mean something. I want to die with honour. I want to die well..." the old man raised his head and straightened his back.

She closed her eyes. In the darkness she imagined her father facing a terrible death at the hands of demons and knew, in her heart, Lutz was right. She could do nothing to save him. When she opened them again, she saw the drawn, terrified faces of the survivors, the last of her people, the souls now in her care, expecting the same fate. There was nothing she could do for her father, but there was something she could do for them.

Reaching out she rested her hand on Lutz's arm, found a smile and a nod before crossing to the altar. It took a moment to find the catch, cunningly hidden beneath the rim. The click echoed in the cold silence of the Chapel. When she pushed, the altar moved a fraction. Then Torben joined her, and they pushed together. The altar moved jerkily aside.

The others scrambled to their feet and gathered around the hole in the stone floor.

"God be praised!" Strecker cried above the hush.

"'tis not God's work," she said, stepping back, "thank my ancestors. They have saved our lives."

*

Let us in, Pretty Thing...

Ulrich's hands rested on the heavy wooden bar. His head jerked up and stared at the door. Had the voice come from the other side or from somewhere in his head?

The demons didn't need him to open the door, it represented no more than an inconvenience, so maybe it was only imagination. Unless, of course, it wasn't the door that mattered. It was his soul. His honour. By opening the door, he wouldn't only be letting them in, he would be giving himself to them.

A man's honour is the only thing that can't be taken from him...

That voice, Old Man Ulrich's, had been in his head, right enough. But, as with many things in his life, his father was wrong about that too. Honour wasn't the only thing. A man had his soul and, that too, could only be given away.

Why would he even want to? He knew what they were. Satan's creatures. Abominations on God's Earth, things that had crawled out of the Pit to wreak havoc and horror upon the world of men,

He closed his eyes and listened to the slow, rhythmic creak of a rope swinging in the draughts of *The Bear Pit*, one end tied to the rafters the other to a plump whore's ankle.

Would that be his lot? To string up the wretched for demons to feast upon. Would he travel so far from the man his father wanted him to be just to free himself of the old man's expectations? The inevitable, crushing disappointment of his own petty failings leading him, in the end, to the same bitter, broken fate as Old Man Ulrich.

Or was it just the promise of life? A demon who drank human blood, a demon with a handsome face and a liar's eyes. He did not want to die, he didn't want to be a servant of the Devil, he didn't want to be the weak, dishonourable man he feared he was destined to be.

But which was the lesser evil?

That, really, was the question.

"Renard!"

He jumped back from the door, his head snapping around. He hoped he didn't look guilty.

Kapsner leaned into the corridor, one hand wrapped around the Chapel's doorway as if afraid the darkness might sweep him away if he let go. He was a hung-jawed, thick-headed, dour-hearted oaf. They had both tried to woo Erna and judging by the way she gravitated to him in the Chapel, Ulrich suspected Kapsner had enjoyed a lot more success than he had.

"Yes?"

"There's a way out. We're leaving. You can stay if you wish..."

"I'm coming..." Ulrich snapped back, but found his legs still rooted to the spot.

"What's wrong?" Even the greyness drained from Kapsner's face, "Is someone there?"

Ulrich's gaze flicked to the door and then back to the gloomy man at arms again, "No... I thought I heard something... but no..."

Let us in... Give them to us... Let us have them...

He forced himself to turn and run back towards the Chapel.

"No... there's nothing..."

The faces of the survivors in the Chapel had changed; hope now illuminated them like the dawn's first light. They clustered around a hole in the floor where the altar formerly rested. He joined them and stared into it. A few handholds jutted from the roughly hewn stone before darkness consumed the shaft.

"It leads down to a tunnel running out of the castle and into the woods to the east," Lady Solace was saying.

Erna, pretty and fey, clutched Kapsner's hands and smiled as bright as a maid on her wedding day, "We are saved from Satan!" she gushed. Kapsner grinned back, his eyes darting towards Ulrich. It seemed the slaughter of most of their comrades and demons hunting them wasn't enough to stop him looking smug when the opportunity arose.

Dolman stared at the hole in the floor as if it were a unicorn playing the pipes, Strecker muttered a prayer of thanks, Karina sobbed into her hands, the Lord Torben had returned to looking like a statue, while his sister was ashen-faced. In her mind she was abandoning her father to a terrible death. Everybody else was too concerned about saving their own hides to worry about the *Freiherr*. Lutz just glared at him.

"We should leave at once," Strecker said, patting down what remained of his hair while trying to look dignified in his night robes.

"Yes..." Solace nodded.

Ulrich cast his eye around the little party and, not for the first time in his life, wondered if he was the only person in the world who wasn't a fool.

"There are a few problems," he said, when no one else ventured any sense.

"Apart from bloodthirsty demons?" Lutz asked.

Ulrich ignored the barb. If he wasn't going to betray them, he should at least do his best to keep them alive.

"First, 'tis winter. It would be a shame to escape the bloodthirsty demons only to freeze to death," he pointed at Strecker's night-robes, which undoubtedly kept him warm in his bed, but would be little good in the snow-crusted woods, and the two maids who, unlike the Lady Solace, Torben and the men at arms, had no heavy cloaks to protect them from the cold. The steward looked down at himself as if realising for the first time he'd been snoring in his chamber when the attack had come.

"Erm... well..." was the best he could come up with.

"Second, torches or lanterns might help. It looks dark down there."

A round of nods at his wisdom.

"But the third problem is the worst."

"Spit it out..." Lutz sighed, from the set of his face Ulrich guessed he'd probably worked it out for himself.

"Can the altar be pulled back in place once we go down?"

They all stared at the hole. Then at Solace.

"No..." A coin dropped, loudly, somewhere behind her eyes.

"So, when the demons break down the doors, they will find the hole and follow us. Instead of dying in the Chapel, we'll die down there..."

He met Lutz's scowl and smiled darkly.

Chapter Four

"One of us will stay behind and push the altar back in place," Lutz offered the solution with an air of grim resignation.

"There must be another way!" She gave the altar a hefty shove. It didn't move.

"There isn't," Lutz said.

"Couldn't we use ropes to pull it back over?" Dolman asked.

"Even if we had any rope to hand, someone has to stay behind to remove them..." Renard cocked an eyebrow at the young, gangly soldier.

"Oh..."

"Then who should stay?" Strecker raised his chin and both eyebrows.

"I will," Lutz's eyes swept the room, challenging someone else to offer. No one did.

"No. You're too important!" Solace shook her head vigorously.

"Well, if the good man is willing..." Strecker said with a

thin smile of encouragement.

"It can't be you or the Lord Torben," Lutz's said, his voice softer than usual, "nor Karina or Erna. Even if I were less gallant, they aren't strong enough."

"Then one of the other men," her eyes flicked around her. Only Renard met her gaze.

"We need all the men at arms..." Erna piped up. Strecker glowered at the girl's impudence.

"No," Lutz said, "It must be me."

The thought of losing the old man, who'd she'd known her entire life, made her shiver, "We should draw lots. 'tis the fairest way."

"No..." Lutz, said again, this time his voice was a growl, "I don't trust anyone else."

"Trust?" Strecker bridled.

"Yes, Herr Steward. *Trust*. When the demons come, I will take this secret to the grave. The rest of you..." he shrugged "...I can see blubbing and begging for your worthless lives," his eyes fixed on the Steward, "You in particular."

"Well, really!"

Her brother moved to the altar, rested his hands upon it, looked at her and then pointed to himself.

"No!" she said in unison with Lutz.

"I'm certain *he* won't talk," Strecker sniggered before covering it with a cough.

Given their situation the Steward was by far the most useless man in the room. If she could trust him, she would order him to stay, but Lutz was right. He was a coward. Faced with the demons, would he fight to the death or sell them out along with his soul? She didn't need the dread stone to provide the answer.

"The Lord Torben is the *Freiherr's* heir," Lutz pulled his burning eyes away from Strecker, "for all we know he may already be the *Freiherr*. He cannot stay behind."

Torben stared at the old man. It was often difficult to discern her brother's feelings, but the sadness etched upon his face was clear. He lowered his head towards the dark pit on the floor.

A roar reverberated around the Chapel, curtailing further objections.

"What was that?" Erna cried, moving closer to Kapsner.

"The demons," Renard's hand moved to the pommel of his sword, "they're using gunpowder to blow down the Outer Gate."

"Then they will be here soon..." Lutz said, "...we cannot tarry any longer. You must leave. Now."

If Strecker could jump headfirst down the hole, she suspected he would. The others shuffled their feet. And looked at her.

She groped for another way. Perhaps one existed. Maybe it would come to her in a few minutes or hours, or many days hence when she tortured herself with this moment again and again. But she didn't have one now and there was no time to wait for inspiration.

"Very well..." she said, unable to look at him.

She should say something, *anything*, to recognise his bravery and acknowledge his sacrifice, but her throat was suddenly too dry and too tight for any more words to come.

First, she'd abandoned her father, now she was abandoning Lutz. How many more sacrifices did God expect of her tonight?

When she did drag her eyes back up, Lutz was smiling.

"My life for yours, my lady. As it should be..."

*

Ulrich watched Lutz as he prayed.

He didn't like the old man. Never had. From the moment he arrived at The Wolf's Tower the Sergeant treated him with nothing but contempt, a contempt many of the other men noticed and replicated. His attitude rankled. Indifference and dislike he could suffer, the constant criticism and distrust he could withstand, but the barbed asides about his father, whose wretched death in a piss-stained, flea-infested bed was still a raw wound, cut deep into his soul.

But now, as he watched, he had to confess a grudging admiration for the man's dignity and calmness. Lutz was making his peace with God before he died, without fear or remorse. There was no rage, no complaint, no wavering in the face of his end. The Lady Solace had given him a way out, her feelings for the old bastard all too evident in her ashen face and shaking hands, but he'd refused.

Looking at the men around him it was obvious none owned the mettle required to make such a sacrifice. Not prissy Strecker, dour Kapsner or wet Dolman. And certainly not him. He'd already betrayed his oath to save his skin once and didn't doubt when Alms or Wendel or, worst of all,

Saul the Bloodless, came crashing through the door he would point meekly to the altar in the hope they might spare him again.

No, only Lutz could be trusted, because he was a man of honour. A man who had made his oath, had lived his life by it and was prepared to die for it even though the man who had knelt to make that oath had been a young man, with a young man's hopes and dreams and ambitions. That young man was long gone, as were those hopes, dreams and ambitions.

And soon the old man would be gone too.

Old Man Ulrich would have admired him, wishing he could have lived his life as Lutz lived his and died with his sword in his hand, rather than rotting away in a stinking tavern attic room, weeping with pain and tormented by the inadequacies and weaknesses that had broken him. Leaving nothing behind but his sword, an almost illegible letter begging the *Freiherr* of Tassau to take in his son and a bucketful of regrets for a life that had not been lived well.

The others waited in silence, praying for the old soldier, or praying for themselves. The demons were not here yet, but they would not be long. He could feel their approach like a storm boiling out of the sea.

Karina and Erna fetched heavy cloaks for themselves from Solace's chambers and clothes from the *Freiherr's* for Strecker. The *Freiherr* was a bigger man than his steward and they hung loosely from Strecker's gaunt frame, but he liked their finery well enough. His hands continually brushed down the sides of the hunting jacket and fur-lined cloak as if to show the world how much they suited him.

The maids found three heavy lanterns, once lit they pushed the shadows back into the corners of the Chapel. Solace disappeared for a few minutes also, returning empty-handed, but from the bulges in her cloak it was clear she'd decided that even if she had to abandon the castle and her father to the demons, she was not leaving them the family's wealth as well.

All the eyes in the room, save Dolman's who watched the corridor, followed Lutz as he climbed to his feet and then turned to them.

He pulled pistols from his belt and handed them to Kapsner, "My sword will do me good enough, you may need these."

"No," Ulrich snapped, and the eyes, save Torben's who continued to stare at Lutz like he was some mythic being rising from the deep, moved to him.

"There are two corpses on the stairs with lead balls in them. If they find no pistols here, they will know you were not alone."

Lutz continued to hold the guns out for a moment, then nodded and returned them to his belt.

"I'll put them to good use. With God's favour I'll send a few of the bastards back to Hell with them."

"I'm sure the Good Lord would approve," Solace found a watery smile, "though not of the language."

"'tis a little too late to change my rough ways, my lady, God will have to take me as he finds me."

Solace looked away and blinked.

Lutz clapped his hands. The sound startling in the heavy silence of the Chapel, "Now be off with you and God's speed. I have work to do..."

"Sergeant..." Solace swallowed, "...Eugen... we all thank you for what you are doing... I... my father..." and suddenly she was just a girl; not a noblewoman, not a leader, not a warrior who had slain demons. Just a girl, beautiful and fragile, overcome with tears.

"There is nothing to be said, my lady..."

Solace threw her arms around the big old man in a manner unbecoming for a woman of her rank and hugged Lutz fiercely. Strecker looked aghast, everyone else bar Ulrich looked away. Torben took a hesitant step forward, lightly placing a hand on Lutz's shoulder as if afraid his fingers might burn.

"My lady... my lord..." Lutz appeared embarrassed, which didn't seem befitting for a man about to sacrifice his life.

Torben dropped his hand and shuffled backwards; Solace pulled away a moment later.

"It has been my honour to serve your family," Lutz lowered his head towards each of them in turn, "you are your father's children. I can think of no greater compliment I can pay."

Lutz glanced at the shadow choked hole in the floor before bellowing, "Now all of you, fuck off!"

"Well..." Strecker shuffled forward, evidently relieved the goodbyes were over so he could get as far away from the demons as possible, "...who goes first?"

From the way Lutz glowered at Strecker he looked like he wanted to give the Steward an opportunity to stay behind and fight some demons.

"Do you know the way, my lady?" Ulrich asked.

"My father showed me how to open the entrance, but I never went down. I was never a girl much inclined to spend her time in the company of rats and spiders."

Ulrich looked at Torben, who, eventually, shook his head.

"I believe we need to keep going till we reach the bottom, the shaft joins the tunnel out of the castle below the dungeons. My father said it was straightforward, but never took us down. I don't believe he thought we'd ever need it..."

Lutz scooped up one of the lanterns and handed it to Kapsner, "You go first, lad."

"Me?" Kapsner took the lantern with evident reluctance.

"Are you afraid of rats and spiders too?"

"No, sir," Kapsner shook his head, sat on the floor, legs dangling down the shaft. He lowered the lantern and peered down, "I can't see the bottom."

Lutz tapped the soldier's side with his boot, "I'd better not have to kick your arse down there then, had I?"

Kapsner nodded, started to push himself into the shaft before pausing and looking up, "Goodbye, Sergeant, it has-"

"Been a fucking torment putting up with your slothful ways. Move!"

"Yes, Sergeant!"

Kapsner carefully tied the lantern to his belt, he would need both hands for climbing. The lantern clanked against the stonework as he disappeared.

One by one they followed Kapsner; Dolman next, then

Torben, Solace, Strecker, Karina and Erna until only the two of them remained in the Chapel. Lutz gave his last order, "You can bring up the rear."

Ulrich nodded and tied the final lantern to his belt. He had no goodbyes to say to the old man. He sat on the edge of the shaft, but before he clambered into it, Lutz bent down and gripped his shoulder.

"You make sure she gets away. The demons want her and if you let them get her, I'll fight my way out of Hell to come and drag you down into damnation with me."

"Why do you hate me so much?" Ulrich snarled, shrugging off the old man's hand.

"I don't hate you boy, I just don't trust you."

"I've done nothing to make you think that," he lied.

"Your father was a good man once. He fought at my side, and I was proud to call him my friend. But he was weak, and those weaknesses destroyed him, drove him to feckless ways. He lost his honour. You remind me of him before he lost himself, I see it in your eyes."

"Pity the *Freiherr* didn't listen to you when I came then."

"The *Freiherr* did listen to me," his voice softened, "I vouched for you and persuaded him to take your oath."

"Why?"

"Because I owed your father one last favour, and good soldiers are hard to find these days... and you are a good soldier, Ulrich. So was your father, but he wasn't a good man. You deserved a chance to show you could be both..." Lutz straightened up and stepped back, "*This* is your chance, boy. Save her and you save yourself."

Ulrich held the man's eyes and didn't know what to make of his words.

From the corridor came the sound of cracking wood.

"They're here..." Lutz said, eyes darting to the doorway for an instant. It was the first time Ulrich had ever seen a flicker of fear in the man's face, but it vanished in a heartbeat "...go."

He slid into the shaft, arms braced on the edge until he found the first foothold and eased himself down. Before he disappeared, he glanced at Lutz for the last time.

"Don't let them take you alive..."

Lutz nodded, "I'll save one of the pistols..."

The frenetic banging from the corridor grew louder. It wouldn't hold long.

Ulrich eased himself into the shaft, looking up all the time as Lutz heaved the altar back into place until the light vanished.

Chapter Five

The descent was painfully slow.

Groping for each foothold whilst clinging to the one above, her arms soon ached, while the cold seeping from the damp stone numbed her fingers. The shaft was narrow enough to brace her back against the other side when she needed respite. The skirts and tight restrictions of her dress did not make things any easier. Solace tried not to think how long a drop it must be to the bottom and ignored the little trickles of powdery dust and flecks of stone dislodged by those above.

She prayed nothing more substantial came down on her head.

Lanterns glowed above and below, casting enough light to reveal the rough stonework of the shaft and the shadows of her companions. There was nothing else bar stains birthed by centuries of damp.

How long had it been since anyone had come down here? Only the family knew of the shaft, but she and Torben had never done more than peer into the hole. Her father, in his more adventurous youth, had apparently climbed down, but no one since. How long would that be? Thirty years? A long time for a place to be devoid of use.

A couple of the stone ledges shifted under her weight, but none felt like they might come away.

Nobody talked, more from concentration and exertion than the fear they might give their presence away to the demons. The castle boasted thick walls. As they inched down The Wolf's Tower, she doubted the scrape of metal on stone, the grunts of effort, the sniffles or dislodged pebbles would betray them.

The shaft was well disguised, if the Good Lord scattered some luck, it would be many hours before the demons discovered she was no longer in the castle. Perhaps they never would. Most castles had secret places for concealing people or valuables, the demons might think she was hiding in one. They could rip the castle apart looking for her without finding this shaft.

Her ancestors had been cunning. The Chapel wall was thinner than the rest of the castle, the shaft concealed by the altar dropped through the thicker walls below to connect with a tunnel beneath the dungeons. With God's grace they would be long gone before the demon's found the shaft. If they ever did.

Unless someone told them of course.

Her father had been explicit only the family should ever know of its existence. She'd never told anyone and Torben definitely hadn't. Lutz hadn't known about it, and he'd been in The Wolf's Tower for decades, neither had Strecker, and the Steward considered it his business to know everything. The tunnel's builders died centuries ago. No one else could tell the demons about it.

Other than Lutz or her father.

The old Sergeant would die before falling into the demons' hands, the certainty of his death was a hollow reassurance that left her heart as numb as her cold fingers, but the demons now held her father. Would he tell them? If they hurt him enough? He would know she and Torben would be using the shaft to escape. It would be his one hope.

Her father, to her, was as resolute and unyielding as The Wolf's Tower itself. She couldn't imagine him breaking, even to whatever horrors a demon might inflict, but then The Wolf's Tower itself had yielded to the monsters. All things, and all men, broke. But her father? No, that was unimaginable.

Wasn't it?

She tried to push her doubts and fears away, burying them deep within herself along with the horror and heartbreak of the night. Instead, she thought only of the climb. Of the next step, of stretching into the void and finding the worn, old stone with her toe, securing a foothold and lowering herself on to it. Again and again.

She was aware of her brother below her, as silent as ever, and Strecker above, breathing hard, but each step she made was as true as her own. Of the others all she knew was none had fallen yet.

They were going to make it to the bottom. All of them. After that, she only had hope to cling to.

And hope, she knew, was a fickle master.

*

The others were some way ahead of him thanks to his final strange conversation with Lutz.

The sounds of their descent floated up alongside ghostly, distorted shadows set a dancing on the ancient, stained stonework of the walls by his companions' lanterns. Nothing suggested they had run into trouble. If Karina and Erna could make the climb, he was damn sure he could.

The shaft was so narrow he could descend it without the little jutting ledges, simply by bracing his back against one wall, feet against the other and shuffling down.

For the first few minutes he strained to hear anything from above. But no screams came, no pistol shots rang out. The heavy altar sealed them from the sounds of the castle as effectively as it did in every other way. Lutz was either dying up there or running to lure the monsters away from the Chapel.

He hoped the old man enjoyed a quick death either way.

If he'd been the one to stay behind...

He shook the thought aside. If he were going to betray Lady Solace, the black deed would be done by now, wouldn't it? He retained his honour. He retained his soul. He would keep his word, keep his oath, he would not succumb to the lies of demons. He would keep Solace from whatever foul purpose Saul planned for her and that would be vengeance for what he'd suffered, for what all the dead had suffered this night.

He would make his father proud.

Not by making a noble sacrifice like Lutz, but by living, and keeping the Lady Solace from the demons.

Wouldn't he?

He hoped so. Lutz saw the weakness in him, the same weakness that had run through his father, a weakness that meant his death had been so different and so much less than the one Lutz had chosen. They may have stood together as young men, but the paths they had elected to walk had been vastly different ones.

But he was not his father, even if he was not Lutz either.

He would charge the enemy line, he would defend the breach. To the last. He would keep his honour. He would keep his soul.

In time, the sounds from below changed and the shadows ceased dancing beneath his feet. There was only a soft glow of light.

They had reached the bottom.

Above him the darkness remained intact. The altar still concealed their escape. No demons pursued them.

Finally, he emerged from the shaft. The stone steps continued down to a floor of hard earth, and he gratefully planted his boots on it. His legs and arms ached and sweat bound his shirt to his back beneath his cuirass, but he'd made it.

They found themselves in a tunnel, too narrow for a man to stretch his arms fully to either side. Slabs of stone lined the walls and ceiling, which was too low for him to stand straight.

Most of the others slumped upon the floor, staring at

him, red-faced in the light of his lantern. Only Solace remained on her feet, strands of damp hair plastering her face.

"Did you hear anything?" her voice sounded hollow, whether from the stones entombing them or from within herself.

He shook his head, "No. The altar remains in place. They are not following."

"God be praised," Strecker panted from the ground, leaning against the stonework.

"And Sergeant Lutz," he replied.

"Amen..." Solace agreed.

"We should push on," he said, when no one rose to their feet.

"A minute or two if you please, let us take rest," Strecker asked, "the climb was hard on the women."

Karina and Erna sat huddled together. They looked a lot fresher than the Steward. They were far more used to physical labour after all. He suspected Strecker's chivalry might not be genuine.

"No," Solace said, "we go on, let us find the exit and then we will rest a little. The going should be easy from here."

Ulrich eyed the tunnel. It was ancient. Several slabs had cracked, allowing dark earth to leech inside. He was more concerned about the ceiling, however. Even in the small section illuminated by their lanterns it sagged in several places. No doubt lintels ran along the length of the tunnel to reinforce it. Two of the three in view sported a black web of cracks.

He thought of the weight of The Wolf's Tower above them - they were below even the dungeons here - and shuddered. Being buried alive might be an even slower death than the ones on offer from the demons.

Solace followed his eyes towards the ceiling, "It has not collapsed in centuries, I doubt it would be so inconsiderate as to do so now."

Ulrich nodded. And wondered how long it had been since the tunnel suffered the footsteps of eight people walking through it...

Chapter Six

"I shall go first," Renard squeezed by them to reach the front of their little column.

"Shouldn't we keep a man at the back, in case...?" Strecker's words trailed off as he raised his eyes towards the dark hole of the shaft.

"Then you can go last," Renard replied, "we're more likely to encounter trouble ahead than behind."

"But surely-"

"The demons don't know about the altar, but other entrances are hidden in the castle that give access to these tunnels," she pressed herself against the wall to allow the young soldier to pass, "'tis unlikely they have found one, but..."

"Wonderful..." Strecker rolled his eyes to the ceiling.

"I'm more concerned about our footsteps bringing the roof down..." Renard said, as Dolman and Kapsner shuffled aside. They were both senior to Renard but appeared content to defer to him now Lutz was gone, "...best we have the important people at the front, it will give them a chance of getting past if it starts to go. Better than being trapped down here and waiting to see if you starve before the demons find this place."

Strecker jumped to his feet.

Renard smiled back at her in a manner reminiscent of Lutz, despite the fact the Sergeant was fat, old and ugly, while Renard was slim, young and quite dashing.

Dashing?

She shook *that* pointless thought away. The young soldier's good looks were of no concern to her. Getting everybody out of The Wolf's Tower alive was.

She almost clapped her hands to get everyone to their feet, but, eying the ceiling brushing the top of her head, made motions with her hands instead.

With varying degrees of reluctance, they prepared to continue. Once ready, she pushed her way forward to stand at Renard's shoulder. When he raised a quizzical eyebrow she announced, "The important people need to be at the front..." when that didn't raise a smile, she added, "...besides, I am the closest we have to someone who knows the way."

"It would be safer if you stayed with your brother."

She gave him a glacial stare, "I was never inclined to do what Sergeant Lutz told me, you... even less so."

Renard nodded, "My lady..."

No one spoke, only their footsteps echoed in the confines of the tunnel. Occasionally, metal scraped against stone when one of the soldier's helmets brushed the low ceiling. Here and there dripping water broke the silence. They stepped over dark puddles collected in depressions in the uneven floor. The walls slimed green where moisture seeped down from the world above.

She kept looking up, despite herself. How deep were they? Below the lowest dungeons, certainly, beyond that she didn't know. Close enough for rain and snow to seep down into the tunnel. And it had for centuries, the evidence of its slow corrosion was everywhere.

The weight of the earth above must be colossal. And all held by slabs and lintels put in place centuries before. How many centuries? She didn't know if the tunnel was as old as The Wolf's Tower itself or a later addition. However long ago, it was *very* old.

Renard was right, it could come down at any time...

She concentrated on the young soldier's broad shoulders, at least she didn't have to walk with a stoop. A small mercy.

After five minutes another tunnel joined theirs from the right.

"Where does that go?" Renard paused to thrust his lantern into the entrance and peer into the shadows. It was identical to the one they followed.

"It must lead back to the lower entrance to the tunnels."

"Are there any other ways in?" Renard glanced at her, before adding, "My lady."

Deference didn't appear to sit comfortably with him.

"No. There are hiding holes throughout the castle, but no other ways down here but these. That I know of, at least. The lower exit is for men to sally out against besiegers and the Chapel for the family to escape."

He nodded and begun walking again.

The tunnel was narrowing, and she started wondering how much further they needed to walk to reach the exit. She imagined the view from atop The Wolf's Tower and tried to calculate the distance to the eastern woods reserved for hunting game. They weren't far away, but she had no idea how deeply the tunnel penetrated the woods before emerging back into the world of light and life.

"An impressive feat," Renard muttered after they had walked further.

"My family was much wealthier in the past, before the silver from our mines was exhausted and most of the barony sold or lost... we could afford such things then."

"'tis lucky for us..."

Five minutes later they found her ancestor's engineering was not as impressive after all.

The tunnel had collapsed.

*

Dolman was swearing, someone else was praying, one of the maids, Karina he thought, sobbed. None of which helped getting them beyond the blockage ahead.

Rubble filled the tunnel from floor to ceiling, allowing dark black soil to flood in. Water trickled down the shattered chunks of stone and clods of earth to pool before the obstruction. To Ulrich's, untrained, eye, the collapse looked fresh. The broken lintels gleamed white in the lantern light, no lichen grew over the exposed surfaces and the seeping water had yet to smooth or wear the edges.

Perhaps the demons brought it down before they

attacked. If not them, then their master. It smacked of the Devil's work one way or another.

"Can we not clear it?" Strecker called from the back of their ragbag column of the damned.

Ulrich lowered the lantern and turned around. Ashen faces peered back at him.

"'tis more likely we'd bring more of it down on our heads," he waved a finger at the jagged crack running through the sagging ceiling-slab. As if to emphasise the point, a small pebble plopped into the water, "Perhaps it would be wise to retreat a little..." he added, in a lower voice.

The group shuffled back up the tunnel in silence, save for Karina's sobbing. Solace's hair shimmered in front of him as he stooped over her. It shone as if threaded with strands of silver in the restless light of his lantern.

Once they moved back far enough for the darkness to consume the wall of rubble blocking their escape, they drew to a halt.

"We must clear it. What other choice is there?" Strecker's voice, which was thin, reedy and increasingly irritating, broke the silence.

"Renard is right," Kapsner sunk to the floor so he could straighten his neck, "we'd just bring the roof down on us."

"How can you know that?" Strecker asked.

"My father was a miner, as was I for a while. We have no picks or shovels and, worse, no wood to shore up the ceiling. The lintels and ceiling-slabs are gone. Take the rubble away and there is nothing to hold up all the dirt above the tunnel. It would be suicide."

When Strecker didn't reply, Dolman spoke, "Then we must stay here, wait for the demons to leave. They won't stay forever. Will they?"

"We have no food..." Ulrich replied, "...we can live on puddle water for a while, I suppose..."

"Well, I'm not hungry," Strecker said, with a thin little laugh.

People eased themselves to the ground as if that settled the matter, until only he, Solace and her brother remained standing. The simpleton picked a way through the hunched forms to stand next to his sister. Surprisingly, he managed the feat without stepping on anyone.

Solace tried to take her brother's hand, but he snatched it away before settling himself at her feet to stare into the darkness towards the collapse. She smiled weakly and then turned her eyes on him.

"So, Lutz sacrificed himself for nothing."

"We're still breathing," he felt exhausted and wanted to flop to the damp floor along with everybody else. Instead, he remained on his feet. He could see Solace's face better from here.

She was beautiful, even after the horrors and travails of this night she was more vibrant and alive than most women he'd ever seen. More importantly, the demons wanted her. But why? Surely it was not her beauty that interested them? It didn't matter why. They were here for her, maybe for silver as well, maybe for the women and children too, but mostly they were here for her.

And when they couldn't find her, would they shrug

their shoulders, pack up their weapons and leave?

No. They would tear the castle down stone by stone until they found her hiding place. No one was coming to relieve The Wolf's Tower, there were no friendly forces nearby and it was the middle of winter. The demons wouldn't be here forever, but they would be in no hurry to leave either, not without Solace anyway.

"And what say you? What do you think we should do?"

It took a moment for Ulrich to realise she was talking to him.

"Dig? Hide? Something else?" she prompted when he didn't answer.

Give you to them?

"If we stay here, they will find us. We'll be like rats in a trap."

"They won't find us down here!" Strecker tried to mask his lack of conviction with a sneer, "They will think everyone dead and leave after looting the castle. We're probably safer here than tramping through the snow for days anyway."

"They might not miss your corpse, Steward, but they will miss the *Freiherr's* children. And they *will* keep looking for them."

Strecker fell silent. The children had worth. They were the heirs to the estate and enjoyed a hefty ransom value. But he didn't think that was what the demons were after. They hadn't shown any interest in Torben. Only Solace.

"We are well hidden here..." Solace's eyes returned to his. He was unfamiliar with a woman looking at him so boldly, but then his experience of noblewomen was no more than remembering not to stare at them for fear of a flogging. He was only expected to die for them, after all.

"All castles have hiding places, if not a means of escape. The demons will be looking. And they will be asking..."

"My father?"

He nodded.

"He will not talk."

"There is a reason they took him alive. All men will break in the end, because all men have a weakness running through them, just like those lintels that gave way. If you apply enough pressure for long enough, they will break. 'tis only a matter of time..." he struck out a hand towards the rubble choking the tunnel just beyond the light of their lanterns "...time we no longer have."

"So, what do you suggest?"

"We can dig and die buried alive, we can stay and hope to die of starvation before the demons find us or... we can find another way out?"

Dolman and Kapsner raised their eyes and even Karina stifled her muffled sobs to hear better.

"There is no other way out of The Wolf's Tower... unless you know more about my home than I do?" Solace's gaze was unwavering, by turns he wanted to avert his eyes or tumble into hers.

Save her and you save yourself...

"My lady, there is always more than one way out..."

Chapter Seven

"You're moon-touched!" Strecker cried.

She looked at the other faces staring up at them, they kept their opinions to themselves, but they appeared no more enamoured with Renard's suggestion than the Steward.

No expression flitted over Torben's face one way or the other, but as he stared at the young soldier, he turned one of his carved animals over in his hand. The Fox.

Her eyes slid back to Renard, "'tis a plan reeking of desperation..."

The man at arms appeared exhausted, the bruises on his face swelling and tugging his countenance. The ceiling was too low for him to stand straight, and one shoulder rested against a wall as if to keep him on his feet. But, unlike everyone else, he remained standing. Did that say something about the man? His idea suggested he was a fool, but nobody had offered anything better than hiding down here in these dank, dark tunnels with the rats and hoping the demons would go away.

Maybe that *was* a better plan, but the dread stone in her stomach whispered otherwise. It swelled and hardened deep in the pit of her gut whenever she concentrated on the idea of just sitting here and waiting.

Renard was right. Whether by breaking her father or the Devil's luck, the demons would find their way down here.

And then?

And then they were all dead. She suspected whatever the demons wanted with her didn't involve her death, not immediately anyway. But whatever it was, it could only be something worse. Like Lutz, she would not let them take her alive. Of that alone, she was certain.

"My lady," Strecker craned his scrawny neck, "we must remain here. We will be safe-"

"I am not so certain."

Karina decided it was time to start sobbing again.

"My lady!" Strecker protested.

"You may be happy to die in a drain. I find the prospect... unappealing."

"But what this young fool suggests is impossible. We will all die!"

"Possibly," the young fool said before she could speak, "but we will all die if we stay here. I'd rather at least try to live."

"'tis impossible to-"

"Silence!" she barked, the coldness in her voice alien to her own ears and, judging by the way her brother's head jerked around, to Torben's too.

The steward flinched like she'd slapped him, but he

nodded and sank back until his back rested against the stonework. His eyes remained fixed on her. Not for the first time since entering the tunnel, rats came to mind.

Strecker, however, was the first she'd actually seen.

"We will do nothing rash. We have a little time, let us contemplate and pray before we make any decisions."

It wasn't exactly befitting for a *Freiherr's* daughter, but dignity being the least of her concerns she hitched up her skirts, folded her legs and eased her backside down on the cold damp floor next to Torben.

After a moment's hesitation Renard sat next to her.

Once he settled himself, Renard turned his lantern down as low as it would go.

"Our oil will not last forever..." was his only comment.

Kapsner snuffed his lantern's flame out and the shadows rushed in. Strecker held the last lantern, but he made no move to turn it down. The darkness loomed above them; giant shadow wolves waiting to pounce once the alien light retreated from their realm. Perhaps Strecker was right to leave it burning.

"Are you certain we cannot dig our way out?" she asked Kapsner, grasping for any alternative.

The soldier nodded, his glum, melancholy face, enlivened only by soft liquid blue eyes, "Aye, my lady. My father died underground. So did my brother and two of my uncles. I know mines. I took up arms to escape the same fate. I reckoned soldiering was likely safer than mining..." when he noticed the enquiring eyes around him, he added with a shrug "...a soldier has only to survive a few battlefields in his life. A miner can die any day..."

"And yet here you are, trapped underground..." Renard smiled softly.

Kapsner snorted, "Aye, seems 'tis impossible for some men to avoid the fate God and their fathers intended for them, no matter what."

The smile vanished from Renard's lips and his eyes dropped to stare at his soiled boots. For a moment he looked as far away as the stars in heaven.

In time, he returned his gaze to her. Carefully, he undid the clasp on his helm, before tugging it off to reveal a shock of blonde hair, darkened by sweat and plastered to his forehead despite the bone-numbing chill.

"I don't suppose a secret passage leads back up to the library, does it, my lady?"

She shook her head.

"And we can't go back up to the Chapel with the altar in place."

She shook her head a second time.

"But we can enter the castle through the dungeon?"

"There is a door that can be opened from either side."

"So, we have to get to the library from the dungeon..."

"Or we go to the battlements."

"The library is three floors lower; it would be a much easier climb," Renard said.

"Assuming we can find rope..."

"There is rope in the stores, that will not be a problem."

"Getting past the demons and their rogues, I think, will be the problem..." her voice dropped to a whisper, and she found herself leaning in so close to the young soldier their heads touched. Which was not at all seemly.

She coughed and straightened up. Torben watched her with uncharacteristic interest. She smiled at him. He didn't smile back. Her brother continued to turn The Fox over and over in his hand.

The fox was clever. Clever and sly. She felt neither clever nor sly. She felt afraid, not just for herself and Torben, but for all of them. The last of her people.

Renard's suggestion was to go up to the library and climb down the outside of the castle. The library was one of the few rooms in the castle to face outwards and the only one with windows large enough to clamber through. Both due to the whims of a forbearer who had wanted better light to read by and a grand view to enjoy when he wasn't.

The library was on the third floor of the South Wing. Even if they got there, they would have to negotiate a climb down the wall, cross the frozen moat without drowning and get into the woods. All without attracting the demons' attention. The chances of achieving such a feat seemed slim.

She leaned into her brother and whispered, "Will they find us if we stay here, can you see?"

Torben's lips trembled, his eyes glistening with tears. He lowered his face to avoid her gaze. Then he nodded, once, before returning to stare into the darkness towards the collapse.

However desperate Renard's plan, if they stayed down here, they would die. She was sure of it. And so was her brother.

That was enough to make up her mind.

*

Steward Strecker was becoming more and more agitated.

Whether it was the idea of climbing down the side of The Wolf's Tower to escape a pack of blood-thirsty demons or the fact nobody considered he was in charge that upset him the most, Ulrich couldn't decide.

"My lady, I am not sure you are the best-placed person to make this decision," Strecker said carefully.

"And who, pray, is, *Herr* Strecker?"

"You are of the fairer sex and barely more than a child. Given the Lord Torben's... *deficiencies*, the burden of leadership should fall to me in the *Freiherr's* absence. I have the experience-"

"You have experience of counting beans," Solace said, "not fighting demons!"

"My lady-"

"One more word and I'll strip you of both your rank and my father's clothes."

On the basis he'd never much cared for the prissy steward, while he was liking the Lady Solace more with every passing second, Ulrich stood up, grinned thinly and made a show of resting a hand on the pommel of his sword.

Strecker, who had squeezed along the tunnel to stand over Solace as she explained what they intended to do, went pale and sank back down onto his skinny haunches.

"I may suffer from being the fairer sex..." Solace cast an eye at Strecker before sweeping her gaze over the little group huddled around the single lantern burning in the narrow tunnel "...I may also be barely more than a child. My brother may also suffer from *deficiencies*, but we were the only ones who tried to stop the demons entering the castle. If... if people had listened to us then, the demons would still be shivering out in the snow or dying on our walls. But people didn't and here we are. Just as I knew we should not let those riders into the castle, I know we cannot stay here. Call it a hunch, call it the *sight*. Call it witchcraft if you must. You have all heard the rumours about my brother and I. But I know. And so does Torben. I will not stay here... but I will not force any of you to leave this place against your will. All I will say is that if you stay here, eventually, the demons will find this tunnel and you will die..."

Torben sat, hugging his knees and playing with one of his wooden toys. He gave no sign of agreeing to anything, but he didn't dispute his sister's claim either.

"My lady..." Erna asked, "...how can we climb down the castle wall? We will fall!"

"We will tie a rope around you and lower you down," Kapsner jumped in, "you will be safe, I swear!"

Erna smiled at him. Although she didn't look convinced, she clearly wanted to be convinced.

Such a hero...

The thought twisted, bitter and hard, inside him. He'd never loved Erna, he'd just wanted her to warm his bed and she hadn't seemed hostile to that idea, but now it was Kapsner she turned her doe eyes upon. Kapsner who she looked to for protection, Kapsner whose hand she reached for in the darkness. Dour, dull, dismal Kapsner with his hangdog face and flat eyes. Why would she choose Kapsner over him? He was younger, better looking, smarter. So why?

Because she sees the weakness in you? The cracks that run wider and deeper than the ceiling slabs and lintels keeping the earth from crushing us flat... she knows you're not a man to be trusted...

"And what of the moat?" Strecker, considering his silence served, demanded.

"We hope the ice is thick enough to cross," he pulled his eyes away from Erna.

"And if it isn't?"

"Don't scream too loudly as you drown. It might attract the demons."

Solace shot him a dark look.

He sighed, "We will send the lightest across first with a rope. The heaviest last. Crawl across to distribute weight evenly and those of us with armour will discard it. With God's grace we will all get across."

Solace nodded. Her look more approving.

Strecker didn't look convinced. Neither did Karina and Erna. Dolman looked like he was still trying to figure it all out and Kapsner was always miserable regardless. Torben stared too intently towards the collapsed tunnel to be paying much attention to anything else.

"If we are going to do this, we should not tarry. The more time that passes, the more time the demons will have to get their men into the castle and start searching for us properly."

And more time to torture your father...

Solace stooped and picked up the only burning lantern, before handing it to Dolman, "Light the other two. As we will not be staying there is no purpose in saving the oil."

Karina gave out another strangled little sob. She possessed an impressive repertoire when it came to blubbing.

One by one, and with increasing degrees of reluctance, everybody hauled themselves to their feet until only Strecker remained on the ground, glowering in silence.

"Leave me a lantern... please..."

Solace's face hardened and for a moment he thought she was going to kick the dog where he sat. Instead, she turned to Dolman, "Leave whichever has the least oil..."

She didn't wait to hear the Steward's thanks.

He took one of the remaining lanterns and pushed his way through to lead the way back, Solace at his shoulder. Karina and Erna stared at the Steward, hands clamped around the black metal of the lantern Dolman had given him. Then Erna pulled Karina's sleeve and they too left the Steward sitting alone in his pool of light.

They walked for less than five minutes before the tunnel shook and a deep throaty roar rumbled and rolled out of the darkness behind them. Karina screamed, Erna seized Kapsner's hands and even Solace's fingers momentarily dug into his own arm.

Dust motes rained down around them in a grey drizzle.

As the sound subsided to first an echo and then a memory, Solace let her hand fall away.

Ulrich stared over his shoulder, past Solace and beyond the others to the darkness trailing in their wake. No lantern glowed in the distance.

It appeared Strecker hadn't been prepared to sit and wait in the dark after all.

Chapter Eight

Another death.

And this one was solely her fault.

She wanted to save everyone left alive. This small band who had survived the demons' assault upon The Wolf's Tower and then placed their trust in her. And she'd left one scared man alone in the dark, because he annoyed her, because he wouldn't obey her, because he thought he knew better.

He'd convinced himself he could dig his way out and brought the tunnel down on top of him instead. Now there was one less life to save.

No one had said a word by the time they retraced their steps to where their tunnel met the one going to the dungeons.

They paused at the branch, Renard walked back towards the shaft that climbed to the Chapel, not to see if they could go that way, they couldn't, but to listen for pursuers.

Torben moved next to her, his hand softly brushing up

and down her arm. His fingers grazed her sleeve. His head bobbed a couple of times. It was his way of offering comfort. She stared into his wide, unblinking eyes and, not for the first time in her life, wondered what it was he saw through them. In the faltering lamplight, they looked both impossibly sad and impossibly knowing.

"We're still alone," Renard confirmed, returning to her side.

Her brother dropped his hand and shuffled back a few steps, eyes narrowing against the glare of Renard's lantern.

"Perhaps we should wait, let them... preoccupy themselves looting the castle..."

Renard shook his head. The soft skin beneath his eyes was the colour of bruised lavender in the swinging lantern light.

"This isn't a normal army, my lady, I doubt they will be distracted by looting and pillaging until they have what they came for."

"And what did they come for?"

After a heavy pause, "You... my lady."

She knew that anyway, but the young soldier's words knotted her stomach around the dread stone all the same.

"And you know this how?"

"I heard them. The demons. Ordering their men to find you."

"You heard a lot while you sneaked about..."

"I'm good at hiding."

He was lying. She was sure of it. As sure as she'd been that her father was letting dead men and devils into The Wolf's Tower. But if he was lying, how did he know they wanted her?

Lutz hadn't trusted this man. There was history of some kind, she suspected. She'd thought the Sergeant was just being overly protective, but perhaps not...

"We should push on, a lot of their men might still be trying to get in. Even if they blew the Outer Gates open, they would still need to cross the moat. And they had their wagons too..."

Should she trust him? She didn't believe staying here would save them. The dread stone told her that and Torben agreed. But her *sight* was warning her not to trust Renard either. Not completely anyway.

Two of her enemies had died at his hands. She'd seen it with her own eyes. So why should she not trust him? One of her own soldiers. A man who had given his oath to her family.

"My lady...?"

She nodded. Hiding down here was not an option. The demons *were* coming.

Renard turned down the side tunnel, lantern in one hand, pistol in the other. She let Dolman go with him. She glanced at her brother; his right hand rested on the pommel of his dead man's sword in the manner of someone who had an inkling how to use the thing. In his left hand another figure had joined The Fox. It was The Goat. He rubbed the two wooden animals against each other between his fingers and thumb.

He'd used those figures before. *Clever Devil*, she thought he'd meant earlier.

The Goat and The Fox...

The Devil and The Fox.

Torben's soft eyes held hers before sliding away as he shuffled past, boots hissing as he dragged them over the floor, stooped slightly forward, clutching the figures to his chest.

"My lady?" Kapsner asked when she didn't follow her brother. Karina and Erna stared over the soldier's shoulder, the younger maid holding their other lantern.

"The Devil and The Fox..." she whispered, eyes widening. Her breath steaming before her eyes in the glare of the lantern.

"My lady?" Kapsner repeated, frowning beneath his helm as he leaned in towards her.

She shook her head and hurried after the others. Her brother and Dolman. And Renard.

Renard. Which her tutor Magnus long ago taught her was French for fox...

*

As they approached the end of the tunnel Ulrich turned down the lantern.

He neither knew how well concealed the door was nor how sensitive the demons' eyes were. Turning the wick down probably wasn't going to make any difference, but it was best not to make too many assumptions.

The door was unremarkable. Thick oak reinforced with strips of black iron, sitting atop half a dozen high stone steps. It looked no different from most of the other doors in the castle. Just older.

They waited at the foot of the stairs. Dolman stared

fixedly at the door, both pistol and sword drawn, expecting a demon or two to come bursting through at any moment.

Ulrich swivelled around and rested his back against the wall. If something did come bursting through the door, best Dolman had a clear shot. Behind Dolman, Lady Solace's idiot brother stood square across the narrow tunnel. Slack jaw agape, he was staring pointedly at him from beneath his ill-fitting helm.

Ulrich waited for the bobbing lantern that signified the rest of their party was catching up with them.

"Are we going to die?" Dolman asked suddenly, his voice wavered, but his eyes and hands remained steady enough, at least.

"Of course we're going to die. Everything dies..."

Except demons, maybe...

"Are we going to die today?"

"I don't know. But the more you chatter the more chance someone will hear us and the more chance we'll all die today."

Dolman swallowed and kept quiet.

The rest of the group arrived with scuffling feet and steaming breath. No one thought to turn their lantern down. Solace led the way, Kapsner behind with the two maids at the rear.

He placed his lantern by Dolman's feet and squeezed past Torben, whose head swivelled to follow him. It was far from the most unsettling thing he'd seen recently, but the way the boy's eyes never moved in their sockets, only ever staring directly ahead, still unnerved him.

"My lady... does the door open into the dungeon?"

Solace's eyes, on the other hand, were restless. Darting over him as if looking for something. She shook her head and flicked some stray licks of blonde hair from her face. He'd never seen her look dishevelled before. He wondered what her hair looked like when she woke up in the morning, which didn't seem the most pressing of questions, all things considered.

"It opens into a tomb in the family crypt, which is the lowest part of the castle."

"A tomb?"

"Bernard the Black, one of my ancestors. He built most of The Wolf's Tower."

"And the door is unlocked?"

"The tomb is hidden from the castle, anyone coming this way wouldn't get any further into The Wolf's Tower without knowing how."

"Why did he hide his tomb?"

"The story goes he detested the rest of the family, he hated spending time with them in life so much he didn't see why he needed to be bothered by them in death."

"Very well, we need to be silent from here on in," he raised his eyes from Solace to address the others, "there are storerooms above the crypt, we will get rope before taking one of the southern staircases to the third floor and the library. If we see anyone we hide, if they don't spot us, leave them be. A fight will more likely just bring more of them. So, we avoid it unless we must. Does everybody understand?"

Once everyone nodded, he turned to lead them up the stone steps, but Solace gripped his wrist, "Let Kapsner and

Dolman go first and check the tomb."

"My lady-"

"tis what your lady wishes."

There was a coldness in her tone he hadn't heard before, "Of course."

"Or do you think as Strecker did? That I am of the weaker sex and no more than a child to boot? That I should not be trusted with anything of importance?"

"No, my lady."

"Good," she continued to stare at him, then, as if realising she still gripped his wrist, her fingers sprung open and she took half a step backwards, before blurting, "Why didn't Lutz trust you?"

His first instinct was to lie and claim he wasn't aware Lutz didn't trust him, but suspicion clouded her eyes where none had been a few minutes before. What had changed? She'd seemed happy enough to put her faith in him earlier.

"He knew my father. They were friends once but... things soured. I believe he feared I might be the same manner of man as my father."

"And what manner of man was your father?"

"He was... in the end... a dishonourable man..." the words tightened his throat, but they were undeniable. He'd told her enough lies.

Tell enough lies and they'll start to stink like bad fish on a hot day.

"Are you a dishonourable man too?" Her eyes bore into him, challenging him, cutting him open in search of who he really was.

"I... don't yet know, my lady..."

It'll swing on whether I betray you or not.

Ulrich swallowed and tried not to flinch.

"As there is a good chance none of us will live to see the dawn..." she brushed past him, "...now might be an opportune time to decide."

Chapter Nine

Kapsner and Dolman returned through the door after just a few seconds. Dolman remained in the archway atop the steps, lantern in hand, while Kapsner hurried down to where she waited with the others.

"'tis as you said, my lady, just a tomb with no exit. Nobody's been inside for years by the look of it."

"Good," she hadn't expected anything else, but every step they now took was upon a bridge that could collapse at any moment. And below lay a chasm ending in the fires of Hell.

"Do we continue?" Renard asked. Which was preferable to the assumption they were here to do what he said.

"Yes."

Kapsner held his ground before them, "My lady, we can defend the tomb as well as anywhere in the castle, *if* the demons found us..."

She looked at Renard, "How many men do they have?"

"Maybe a hundred in total, a few less perhaps, but not

many."

She returned her attention to Kapsner, "Even if we only faced men, we couldn't hold the tomb indefinitely. They could starve us out if they wanted, no one is coming to our aid. However, I suspect the demons are not that patient."

Kapsner didn't look happy. It seemed safe down here. The idea the demons wouldn't find them and return from whence they had come was achingly plausible. And if it wasn't for the dread stone in her stomach and the look in her brother's eye, she would never have agreed to Renard's suggestion.

A suggestion from a man she didn't trust.

Out of the corner of her eye she could see her brother was turning The Goat and The Fox over and over in his hands.

I... don't yet know, my lady...

The strangest look crossed Renard's face when he'd said that, some hidden torment fleetingly bubbling up from within him before sinking back down into his soul. She didn't know whether those words made her trust him more or less.

If only Lutz were still here...

But, of course, he wasn't and now everything fell to her.

"Trust me. If we stay here, we die."

"And if we try to escape?"

"We will probably die."

"'tis not a great bargain."

"Better to die trying to escape than being slaughtered

cowering in the dark," Renard growled the words so deeply in his throat it seemed Lutz was still with her, but when she turned Solace found only the fair-haired soldier with the busted nose and bruised eyes behind her.

Kapsner nodded and turned back towards the steps, his hangdog face even longer than usual. Solace followed with the others.

It had been five years since her first and only visit to the tomb of Bernard the Black. On her twelfth birthday her father decided she was old enough to know The Wolf's Tower's greatest secret.

Nobody appeared to have visited since. The dust her feet ploughed as a child was now as undisturbed as fresh snow. Her visit had been fleeting. The tomb scared her, something she'd never experienced anywhere else in the castle. She suffered nightmares about the sightless, cobweb-cloaked statue of her ancestor for weeks. She hadn't understood why it frightened her so much. It wasn't the only tomb in the crypt, and while the others held an eerie fascination, the tomb of Bernard the Black terrified her.

As she stood on the threshold she wondered if that terror had been a premonition of this terrible night rather than a child's fear of death and dark places.

Her ancestor's tomb dominated the small, vaulted room. A stone sarcophagus upon which a life-sized statue of Bernard in full armour, cut from black granite, lay, sword clutched to his chest, stern sharp features staring sightlessly towards heaven.

Her childhood nightmares came flooding back, of

standing barefooted on the cold stone as Bernard's head turned to stare at her, mouth opening and closing as he tried to warn her about something, something important and dreadful, but no words ever came out of his mouth. Only spiders, a stream of black spiders, filling the room like water from a pump to slosh and heave around her ankles.

She swallowed. Renard was moving around the walls, running a hand over the stonework, everybody else stared at her. Torben, standing next to her, had neither concern nor interest on his slack features.

"My lady?" Dolman asked from the other side of the tomb. Two statues of gowned women, faces raised to the ceiling and hands pressed together in prayer, stood against the wall opposite Bernard's mailed feet. Otherwise, the room was empty save for dust and cobwebs.

"A moment..." Bernard's stony face dragged her gaze back. Whatever he'd been trying to tell her in those dreams, he was silent now. She reached out and run fingers down his face, cutting two trails through the dust from his eyes to his chin.

"He looks... sad," Erna pushed herself gently against Kapsner and rested her head against his arm.

"I'd look sad," Karina sniffed, "spending eternity down here alone in the dark."

"Not totally alone," Dolman conjured a toothy grin as he rapped a knuckle against the stone breast of one the female statues.

Karina shot him a withering look. Both Dolman's grin and hand fell away.

"Even at times like this, men can still think of nought

but tits!" Karina spat, before glancing at Solace and blushing, "Sorry, my lady."

She turned away from Bernard's stern, unhelpful features and crossed the tomb to stand before the statue Dolman had been fondling.

"'tis not her tits, however fulsome, we are interested in, but her hands," she reached up and pushed the clasped hands of the statue to the right, they moved only a fraction, but the click echoed in the silence of Bernard's tomb.

"The way is now open..." she indicated the slice of wall between the two statues. It looked no different from the rest of the tomb, just rough, featureless stone blocks.

Renard moved to her shoulder and pressed his hand against the wall. At first nothing happened, but with more effort the wall began to pivot.

"Clever..." he said, before meeting her eye, "...you should stand aside, we don't know what is on the other side."

"Just more dead relatives, hopefully," she replied, but her voice was a whisper and she moved back beside Bernard the Black and her brother once more. She wasn't sure which figure was more lifelike.

She placed her hand on Torben's elbow, his lips quivered several times, but he didn't flinch.

"We must go and face the demons again," she breathed.

Torben turned his head to look at her. He nodded. Put The Goat and The Fox back in his satchel and pulled his sword free with a couple of clumsy tugs.

Renard had to use both hands and all his weight to get

the door to open enough for them to squeeze through one at a time. The three soldiers went first. A long silent minute passed before Dolman's head popped back through the door. He summoned them with a flick of his hand, "The crypt is empty..."

Solace nodded, then she and Torben left Bernard the Black to meet more of the dead.

*

They closed the hidden door behind them.

In the main crypt two statues of armoured knights marked the secret entrance to the tomb of Bernard the Black, one folded his hands over the hilt of an upturned sword, the other held a shield bearing the rampant wolf of Tassau.

After they heaved the stone door back into place, Solace pulled the hilt protruding through the knight's hands and something clicked like an old dry bone snapping in two.

Ulrich looked around, but the only figures in view were stone ones. If any demons lurked down here, then the light of their lanterns would have alerted them before the noise of the ancient locking mechanism returned Bernard the Black to his dark slumber.

"'tis a shame..." Solace stared up at the knight's sightless stone eyes visible through his helm "...that my ancestors did not allow *both* entrances to the tunnels to be opened and closed from either side."

She was talking about Lutz, of course.

"It could not be helped, my lady," he said, fingering his

sword as he continued to cast an eye around the shadow-laden crypt.

"But if we had come here, rather than up to the Chapel, he would not have had to die for me."

"Had you come down here, you wouldn't have found the rest of us. We would probably all be dead by now. The tunnel would still be blocked and you'd still be facing finding another way out."

Dead or damned...

She didn't look convinced. Perhaps Lutz's life carried more weight than the other survivors put together. Either way, this wasn't the time to discuss past choices.

"We need to move, my lady."

She nodded, reluctantly.

"I've never been down here, which way do we go?"

"There is one set of steps on the far side of the crypt leading up to the next level."

"The cellars?"

"I know them well enough," Erna said, "the stairs go up to the kitchens from there."

He nodded and handed the maid his lantern, "I need both hands free."

Erna accepted the lantern and Karina took the other. He was afraid the light would give their presence away, but no torches burned in the crypt and blundering around in the dark would not hasten their escape.

Most of Solace's ancestors boasted less elaborate tombs than Bernard the Black's, the majority no more than an inscribed slab on the floor, but there was no shortage of stone knights, angels and cherubs heralding their path across the crypt. A few sneering gargoyles too. The ceiling was higher than in the tunnels, but he didn't need to hold his hand far above his head to touch it.

The crypt was less dust smothered than Bernard the Black's tomb, but their footsteps echoed just as hollowly on the flagstones. Each time the lantern light danced across one of the stone statues he expected it to reveal itself as a snarling demon, but they made their way across the crypt without incident. Whatever Saul and his bloody company were doing in The Wolf's Tower, they hadn't yet reached these silent catacombs.

He hoped getting men and wagons through the Outer Gates still preoccupied them. It was their one chance. If Saul had kept the bulk of his men working to open the gates, in the expectation they could hunt down whatever survivors remained once the castle was secure, then they still might escape. If not, then they had embarked on a desperate gambit. If finding Solace was Saul's priority, then whatever men had made it through the Outer Gate would be scouring the castle and it would be impossible to fight their way through them all.

The three men at arms fanned out across the crypt, Solace and Torben, who were both armed, behind them, Erna and Karina carried the lanterns at the rear.

They gathered together at the foot of the rough stone steps that, on any other night, led up to the world of the living. A closed door barred their way at the top.

"Where can we get rope?" he asked, not taking his eyes from the door.

"I know," Erna offered, "I spend half my days fetching

and carrying from the cellars."

"Will there be torches alight?"

"Not normally..."

Pity.

"If the demons are about, our lanterns will give us away."

"Can you find your way to the rope in the dark?" Solace asked.

Erna shook her head, "I don't think so."

"Then we need to move with all haste, get the rope, go up through the kitchens to the south-west stairs and then to the library," he said.

"Without anyone seeing us?" Kapsner's doubt was plain on both his face and in his tone.

"We don't have another choice," Ulrich snapped, although both Kapsner and he knew other choices existed. Kapsner's preference was to hide and wait for the demons to leave.

His choice was something else entirely.

Chapter Ten

Solace tightened her grip on the bulky wheellock pistol. It was a heavy and cumbersome contraption. She wasn't sure whether she carried it to help her escape the demons or to kill herself if they couldn't.

They hurried up the stairs from the crypt, Renard taking the lead, and entered the series of low-ceilinged rooms making up the cellars. Most of the castle's supplies were down here, along with any other sundry items the family had collected over the centuries but no longer used.

They decided to keep the lanterns lit and move fast. Sometimes relying on luck was the only option available.

To her eyes everywhere appeared much the same, but Erna insisted she knew where the rope was.

The cellars were a maze of vaulted alcoves, each recess a black maw capable of hiding an army of demons. The lanterns jigged and danced as they scurried through the darkness, casting their own deformed shadows onto the walls, columns and arched ceilings.

Several times she missed a heartbeat as something

monstrous jumped out at them, only to find it was just her own shadow dancing in the lantern light.

Their panted breath misted in ghostly halos around them as they ran, the nailed boots of the soldiers echoing on the straw dusted flagstones. The air hung damp and thick; pungent aromas rose as they passed each vaulted room. Bunches of dried lavender and rosemary warded off evil spirits from the castle's food supplies, their scent mixing with stale water and the stink of the castle's cesspools that didn't manage to empty everything into the moat. The tang of woodsmoke mixed with the acrid reek of tallow and rushlights, even down here where no fires or candles burned. Other smells she couldn't identify rose out of the shadows; sweet, musty, bitter, waxy, all combining together into one nauseous whole.

Above all those smells, however, one sliced through the others.

The stench of fear.

Somewhere in this old, cold, damp castle she'd always loved, things waited to kill them.

She expected grasping hands and screaming mouths to explode from every foreboding pool of shadow they passed. The darkness seemed somehow heavier and more intense here, as if its enormous weight was too much for the feeble light of their lanterns to overcome. It was probably because the lanterns were at the rear of their group rather than the front, but no matter how many times she told herself, she couldn't shake the feeling there was a more malign reason. That the darkness had taken on form and consciousness, that it was aware of their presence, of their trespass into its realm.

And the darkness was hungry.

"Here!" Erna said, indicating the next alcove on their right. Her quietly spoken words made Solace jump.

The maid shoved her lantern inside, weakly illuminating the building materials haphazardly stored within. Lumber, bricks, slabs of broken stone, a pile of cracked flagstones and various tools littered the vault. Supplies for repairing the castle presumably.

Kapsner ducked inside and after a mercifully brief rummage found several coils of rope.

He tugged dubiously at one length, "This will be strong enough?"

"It will have to be," Renard took the rope and wrapped the coil over his shoulder and across his chest.

"And long enough?" she asked. She thought of the drop from the library window. It suddenly seemed an awfully long way down, even more so when all you had to save yourself was a length of rope that had lived with the damp and the rats for years. Maybe decades.

"Take all we can carry, if it isn't, we'll tie them together."

Renard made it sound so simple. Whether confidence or bravado propped his words, she couldn't decide. But as she didn't know if he'd been lying through his teeth since he'd found them, it probably didn't matter anyway.

Kapsner and Dolman coiled lengths of rope around themselves. She picked up the remainder and handed it to her brother. Torben stared at it with mild disinterest.

"We cannot have too much," she said. Torben neither

smiled nor nodded, but at least allowed her to wrap the rope around him in the same manner as the other men.

"The kitchen is the best route?" she asked Erna when they finished.

The maid looked awkward. The novelty of the lady of the house asking her opinion evidently enough to momentarily dispel the terror they faced.

"Yes, my lady, the other stairs lead to the Courtyard."

She nodded. Of course they did. She'd spent her life in The Wolf's Tower, but she knew little of this underground world, other than part of the cellars had once been dungeons for holding wrongdoers, but they had only housed stores and victuals in her lifetime.

"The Lord has preserved us thus far..." apart from poor Steward Strecker and Sergeant Lutz of course, but their deaths were more her doing than God's "...let us pray he continues to cast his hands over us to shield us from the evil we face."

Everyone muttered, "Amen," aside from Torben and Renard.

"The fact the demons are not down here is a good sign," Renard said, "this is an obvious place for people to hide, they must still be too occupied with the Outer Gate to begin searching the castle thoroughly."

His words should have provided some reassurance, but every time he opened his mouth the dread stone rumbled faintly within her.

Don't trust this man.

Don't trust him, but don't cast him out or cut him down. That was what her senses whispered. It confounded her. Either he was with them, or he wasn't, but however long she had until her final breath she was never going to doubt her instincts again.

"Then we are ready..."

Her companions nodded and they headed towards the stairs at the end of the cellars. She gripped the wheellock tightly in both hands.

Her eyes never left Renard's back.

*

However much you tell yourself what you are going to do when the moment arrives, once all is said and done, fear boils off the meat and the gristle of your certainties until just one thing or the other remains.

You either run or you stand.

His father had said that to him more than once. Always with a mug of ale in his hand, but never the first of the day. Each time he uttered those words it was if he uttered a great and secret truth. A great and secret truth he couldn't recall he'd revealed to his son many times before.

Old Man Ulrich never told him what happened when his moment came. He didn't need to. It was as clear as the stubble on his face, the vivid scar above his right eyebrow that curved like a crescent moon and the shake in his hand as he raised the mug to his lips.

His father could not change the things he'd done. Whatever they'd been, whatever he'd seen, whatever had made him cast aside his honour and run, but he'd spent the years afterwards travelling the low roads to sell his sword to one master or another, scratching for redemption in the life his son would lead. The honour he was unable to recover himself could be redeemed by the son who padded dutifully at his side, sharpening his sword, polishing his dented armour, and trying to keep him sober enough to do their current master's bidding, at least until his next pay was due.

The fact most of the lessons he tried to teach young Ulrich had been given while too drunk to stay upright and piss at the same time, never lessened his father's sense of righteous, fervent, desperate hope that when his son's moment came, he would make the honourable choice.

He would charge the enemy line, he would defend the breach against all odds...

As they crept up the stairs towards the kitchen door, Ulrich knew his moment loomed. The moment that would boil away everything he thought he was and leave only the truth of him behind; cold, naked, shivering and undeniable.

Stand and fight for his mistress or run and deliver her to his master.

He went up the stairs first, there was a small stone landing at the top before the door that opened onto the kitchen. It was just big enough for them all to squeeze together. Karina and Erna put the lanterns down on the last step. If they came across an unlit part of the castle, they would do without them, the risk of drawing attention to themselves was too great now. Solace insisted she and Torben knew The Wolf's Tower well enough to move through the rest of its levels even without light.

Holding up his hand he showed three fingers and placed his other hand on the latch. He heard nothing on the other side, but that didn't mean much. Dolman and Kapsner each nodded grimly and readied their weapons, Torben played with his sword and at least managed not to send it clattering back down the steps. The Lady Solace held a pistol with both hands, the muzzle pointed at the ceiling, her eyes, however, remained fixed on him.

She was an incongruous figure with her fine clothes and delicate features, clutching that ugly, ungainly weapon. She should look ridiculous, but every cut of her, from her stance to the set of her mouth, to her unblinking gaze, spoke of someone you did not want to cross. She might only be a young woman, a feted and privileged one to boot, but she was both capable and prepared to kill.

As Callinicus and the Red Cloaks in the Darkway had found.

Ulrich still didn't know what he would do when his moment came, but he'd no doubt about the Lady Solace. She wasn't going to flinch, or budge, or cower, or plead. She wasn't going to sell her soul and give away her honour.

She was always going to stand.

Three fingers... two fingers... one finger...

He pushed open the door and they rushed through together.

Chapter Eleven

The kitchen was one of the few rooms in The Wolf's Tower that was never empty and never dark. Pots forever boiled over the great fire, there were always meals to prepare, things to dry and cure, salt and pickle. Things to cut and scrub and wash and clean. Even in the smallest hours a servant or two would be toiling at something or other in the greasy tallow light of cheap candles.

As they burst through the door Solace found, as she always had, the kitchen was neither dark nor empty.

The great fire still cracked and fizzed, though no pots hung above it tonight. Instead, hesitant flames licked around a body sprawled headfirst in the hearth. It was difficult to tell for sure, but it looked like Herman the cook, whose head was now roasting in the fire he'd prepared so many meals on.

It wasn't the cook's charred body that held the eye, however, but the figure sitting cross-legged upon the huge table dominating the kitchen, it's thick oak top scoured and dented by decades of chopping, cutting and pounding.

The man's head shot up as they rushed into the kitchen. He did nothing bar smile amiably at them, though the blood smearing the lower half of his face undermined the amiability of the smile somewhat.

He had a shock of spiky red hair and skin as pale as dirty chalk. A string of sausages lay across his lap, which he studied with a pinched look of intense concentration as they burst into the kitchen.

They had agreed to keep moving or hiding before fighting. No one had considered the option of coming to a halt and gawping.

The man wore her father's colours, but even without the blood-smeared face it was obvious he was not one of their men at arms. He was a demon.

Dolman raised his pistol and Kapsner hefted his sword, knees bent in the fighter's stance, but when the demon only smiled and stared back at them, they shuffled uncertainly.

"You can tell a lot about a man by what he eats..." the demon told them in accented German.

It took her a moment to place it. Her father had entertained a foreign gentleman a few years earlier, a boorish brute who drunk almost as copiously as he passed wind. As the man enjoyed some wealth and status, her father had ignored his uncivilised ways. His German had been poor but understandable, the demon's was better, but had the same inflexion.

She'd always assumed demons came from Hell, not England.

"...this man ate too much meat and too many sugar

fancies, I'd wager he was quick to temper and slow to labour..."

Her stomach rolled as she realised it was not a string of sausages in the demon's hands, but intestines, the contents of which he squeezed out with gore-blackened fingers to examine.

"My lady?" Dolman asked, pistol still raised.

It was a fair question.

The demon wasn't threatening them, but it was a monster all the same. Even if they somehow dispatched it cleanly, gunfire would soon bring others down upon them. But if they left him, he would raise the alarm.

"Do you plan to try and kill me?" the demon asked, sensing her dilemma, his voice low and pleasant. Bloody face and fingers aside, his manner was much better than the last Englishman she'd met.

"'tis a quandary..." she admitted.

"I can see that," his eyes fell back to his lap to examine something, "hmmm... he didn't chew his food sufficiently. A hasty soul too I'd say!"

"What would you suggest?" She inched forward and placed a hand on Dolman's forearm despite the young man at arms alarmed look.

"'tis hard to kill a vampire, I would probably slaughter you all before you could accomplice the task," his eyes, which were uncommonly dark against his pale skin, fixed upon her, "but as you have managed such a feat once already this evening, you present me with a dilemma too."

"You are a creature of darkness; it would be expected by all that is holy that we should try."

The demon - or vampire as he called himself - laughed.

"You are the Lady Solace, are you not?"

"I am."

"My lady!" Erna cried. Everyone knew you shouldn't give your name to the Devil.

"That one such as mighty Callinicus should be dispatched by so sweet a countenanced child. 'tis a delight! Though one he was far too boorish and boring to appreciate."

"If you value your life, perhaps you should not have come here."

The demon shrugged, "Oh, I just tag along for the fun. No one asks my opinion. They think I'm mad," he twisted a loop of intestine around his hand, "And they are right. What they don't appreciate..." he leaned forward to add in a conspiratorial whisper "...is that we are all mad, 'tis the nature of the beast..."

"Do you have a name, demon?"

"Of course! How rude of me not to introduce myself! My name is Henry Cleever," he dropped the intestines and waved at them.

She nodded. She could feel the tension in Dolman and Kapsner, who stood either side of her. Renard was out of her eyeline so she couldn't tell, but it was the nature of fighting men to fight, and she feared they would strike at any moment. And if they did, she was almost certain they would die at Henry Cleever's bloody hand.

"So, Mr Cleever, what would you do if we tried to leave the kitchen? Would you want to see what fills our stomachs too?"

Cleever thought about things for a moment, straightened his back and placed a hand on each knee.

"I *should* try to stop you, or call my fellows given you are why we are here."

"I asked what you would do. Not what you should do."

"If you escaped Saul's clutches, he would be terribly angry. His reputation has become rather important to him since he formed our Company..." Cleever's words dissolved into a boyish giggle "...his fury is very funny to behold. So long as you remember only to laugh behind his back, of course."

"Who is Saul?"

"Saul the Bloodless. The leader of our Company."

"Pray tell, what is his interest in me?"

"Oh... I wasn't really paying attention; I'm cursed with a traveling mind. Not that he tells me much. I told you they think I'm mad, didn't I? You must forgive me. I forget a lot. So many memories you see, too much for this old noggin," he rapped a knuckle hard enough against his head for the sound to echo around the kitchen.

"Perhaps you might forget you saw us?"

Cleever grinned, "'tis possible, these innards are *fascinating...*"

"And if Saul finds us, we won't tell him you saw us."

"That would be obliging, though if Saul finds you... well, you'll tell him whatever he asks. He has a way like that. The clever fellow ensures Saul never has cause to ask them a question in the first place. That's the trick!"

A scream rang out before she could ask anything else.

"The festivities seem to be starting."

"Shouldn't you be there?"

Cleever pulled a face, "I don't really like the screaming to be honest. I kill quickly, suffering does not interest me."

"What does interest you?"

"One day one thing, the next another. I'd love to talk to you more. You interest me."

"I do?"

"Oh, not like that! I grew bored of fucking centuries ago. You have a mind, my lady, and you have guts," he glanced at the intestines spread before him and giggled again, "to tarry here and talk when those about you would try to kill me without thinking, *that* is most interesting."

"I don't really have the time to stand and chatter."

"No," Cleever said, "you don't. Best be off with you. There are still yards of guts for me to go through here and they're remarkably interesting too."

With that, the demon picked up the intestines and started squeezing their contents out again.

"Move..." she hissed when she looked around and found everyone staring at her.

"My lady," Henry Cleever said, without looking up, "one last thing. You can tell a lot about a man from what he likes to eat. Saul the Bloodless likes eating children. I think that tells you all you need to know about him..."

*

Ulrich expected Cleever to mention his treachery, but the demon didn't seem to recognise him.

Cleever was one of the demons he hadn't spoken to and hadn't even known his name till he'd told Solace. He'd been in *The Bear Pit,* swinging the two plump whores back and forth like human pendulums; Ulrich Renard had been of a lot less interest to him.

Although they had agreed they would only fight if they had to, he almost shot the demon on sight, better they die than know of his disloyalty, but Solace's reaction had stayed his hand. She'd not flinched or cowered before the monster, despite the horror of their encounter. She faced the demon and understood him in a moment. He suspected she had saved their lives, even if only for a few minutes. If they encountered one of the other demons, however, he doubted they would be as obliging as Cleever.

Solace hadn't seen the way the demons fought, the unnatural speed, strength and reactions he'd witnessed as they had slaughtered the rest of Kadelberg's men in the snow before the burning church. And yet she *had* known. Cleever would have been picking through their entrails by now if they had tried to kill him. Partly it was the fear of bringing more of Saul's Company down upon them, but not entirely. She'd known, somehow, it was a fight they couldn't win.

How could a slip of a girl know such things?

And what else did she know?

They moved warily past Cleever, the fact their pistols remained levelled at him didn't seem to bother the demon in the slightest. He continued to examine Herman the Cook's intestines with immense fascination, whistling through his teeth. Whatever powers these "vampires" enjoyed, the ability to carry a tune wasn't one of them.

Once behind the demon, Kapsner looked imploringly

at Solace, lifting his sword to suggest he could kill the creature without a sound. Before she answered, Torben reached out and gently pushed the blade down. His face was as blank as it usually was, whatever emotions the *Freiherr's* peculiar son enjoyed they only ever fleetingly crossed his features, which were as soft and somehow unfinished as his fuzzy beard. However, there was a sense of rare certainty in that movement; it brooked no argument.

Kapsner made no move to raise his blade again, but his eyes remained on Lady Solace. She shook her head and indicated the door with a jab of her pistol. The deal she'd made with this devil was one she intended to keep.

Kapsner nodded his reluctant acquiescence and alongside Dolman they moved through the doorway out of the kitchen, Torben and Solace followed. Ulrich ushered the ashen-faced Karina, who clamped a hand to her mouth in a vain attempt to silence her sobs, and Erna who refused to meet his eye as if her toying with his affections before this night mattered a jot, after them.

He backed out of the room. Solace was keeping her end of the bargain, but he kept watching Cleever to the last minute. Demons might be more fickle when it came to their deals. Particularly insane ones.

Before he ducked out of the kitchen, Henry Cleever twisted around and looked over his shoulder at him. The demon's whistle faded away as a slow smile spread across his bloody face.

Then he winked at him.

Chapter Twelve

The scream stopped them in their tracks.

A short passage led from the kitchens towards the Great Hall. Where it turned sharply to the left, the door to the south-east stairwell sat. The corridor continued to a preparing room the servants used as they attended the Great Hall during banquets. Beyond was the Great Hall itself. Where the demons had taken her father. Where the scream had come from.

The scream had been a man's and it had been long and terrible.

She didn't know if it had been her father or not, she had never heard him scream after all. But then she'd never heard anyone scream like that either.

The door to the stairwell hung invitingly open, they couldn't see what was around the corner. And nobody wanted to find out.

There was no other route they could take. The kitchens and associated pantry, larder, buttery and storerooms occupied the entire ground floor of the East

Wing, the only exits were to the Great Hall and out onto the Courtyard. There had once been an exit to the North Wing, but one of her ancestors bricked it up decades ago for some long forgotten reason.

"My lady..." Renard mouthed, coming alongside her.

He was right, they couldn't hesitate. Move or die. They were their only choices.

Instead, she looked at Torben.

"Father?"

"We can't save him!" Renard cried, while her brother stared blankly at her, "Or the children."

The children. Of course. The children from the village loaded on the wagons. The demons were going to feast upon them. In the Great Hall. She wondered if they would wait until they found her before starting. Perhaps she was the main course...

"We can't leave them..."

"Yes, we can!" Renard returned, leaning in close enough for her to smell his breath.

"But-"

"If we go around that corner, we're dead. All of us. Just like your father."

His words stung, but he was right. She didn't command an army. She had three soldiers, two maids, one mute brother and no plan whatsoever for saving anybody.

"God, forgive us..."

"If God gave a damn about us, he wouldn't have let this happen in the first place!" Renard spat.

She'd seen too much to be concerned by either blasphemy or disrespect, Erna, however, muttered under her breath and gave the soldier a scabrous look.

Ignoring her, Renard leaned in even closer, the cold metal of his helm grazing her forehead, his eyes filling her vision, "'tis not what your father would want, 'tis not what Lutz sacrificed himself for. They wanted you to escape. If we try some cack-handed rescue, not only do we die in vain, they will have died in vain too."

"The children..."

"...will die anyway! We *cannot* go in there! I've seen what the demons can do! We cannot stand against them; we cannot stop them. We can only save ourselves. You *must* trust me..."

There was certainty in his voice, but there was pleading too. He didn't want to face the demons again, she understood that, but it wasn't cowardice in Renard's eyes. Some other kind of fear twisted inside him.

She nodded and allowed him to push her towards the stairwell door.

No more screams emanated from the Great Hall, but now laughter fractured the silence. Satan's feast was beginning and all they could do was run away.

They moved. As quickly and silently as possible. Dolman and Kapsner reached the door first, Kapsner ducking inside to check the stairs were clear. They were. Renard pushed her and the maids after them.

"Lock the door behind us," she said as she passed Renard. Who nodded, though his eyes remained on the south corridor leading to the Great Hall. No candles burned here and there was nothing to see beyond what light leaked from the stairwell and the east corridor.

"Go," Renard said, hand briefly on her back as she started scrambling up the stairs. She could hear Karina's never-ending sniffling behind her and the faint clank and scrape of metal from Kapsner and Dolman ahead of her. Between the first and second floors, blood splattered and smeared the wall, running down the stonework in dark rivulets., but otherwise there was only the worn twisting steps and the occasional candle.

With each slap of foot on stone she expected to hear a shout or a scream, the clash of steel or the retort of a pistol. The dread stone rocked and rolled within her, or perhaps it was just fear now, swamping the *sight* along with any coherent thought. Just run. That's all they could do. Climb the stairs, run from the demons. It was the only victory left.

Her father was dead, the women and children from the village would soon be as dead as the rest of the castle too. There would be no daring rescue, no saving souls, no snatching triumph from defeat. Lutz had been right; this wasn't that kind of a tale.

And if they lived... if she lived... it would be because of the blood of others. Her father and Lutz. And the blood of innocents. If the demons were too preoccupied with Satan's feast, then they might have a chance. And her conscience would have to cope with that knowledge till the day she died.

By the time she reached the third floor landing her chest heaved and she cursed the heavy skirts she wore. Kapsner and Dolman waited at the door, the younger man turned towards her as she appeared.

"The corridor is empty, my lady, the way to the Library

is clear!"

"God be praised," she gasped as first Karina and then Erna joined them. Karina panting so hard she'd even stopped crying. She turned and grabbed the younger maid's arms to save herself from falling as her knees buckled.

"We are nearly there," Erna managed a smile of encouragement and hugged Karina.

Solace, however, could find no smile.

Her brother and Renard weren't behind them...

*

For one awful moment he thought Solace was seriously going to suggest trying to rescue her father and save the village children. He imagined her fearlessly striding into the Great Hall, pistols raised, telling the demons to get out or they would be in serious trouble.

Thankfully, sense prevailed, saving him from having to throw the girl over his shoulder.

Once Karina and Erna disappeared up the stairwell, he looked behind him, expecting Torben to be there. He wasn't. His stomach gave a sick lurch. Had one of the demons dragged him away? He would have heard something, surely? Although, of course, the Lord Torben, unlike his father, couldn't scream.

Ulrich stared towards the Great Hall. The candles leading to the Preparing Room and the Great Hall had either burnt out or been put out. The windowless corridor was as dark as Saul's heart. He squinted, was that a figure almost consumed by the shadows or just his mind's conjuring?

The sound of feet pounding upon stone faded as the others disappeared up the stairs, thankfully no screams or sounds of fighting replaced them.

He should hurry after them, whatever the demons were up to, one of their company would pass this way sooner or later and he shouldn't tarry for the sake of a half-wit.

Instead, he took a hesitant step into the darkness.

"My Lord...?" he hissed at the shadow.

He took another step. It *was* a figure; he was sure of it.

But who? Solace's simple brother or a demon? A demon waiting to drink his blood or do a deal for his honour? Which would he prefer? Would he run or stand, fight and die or deal and live? He should leave before he found out. What did it matter if Torben was gone? What use was he anyway?

Except, Solace might not come back for her father, but for her brother? His oath was to the family, not just Solace. Honour dictated he find the boy and honour was what mattered most if he wanted to avoid his father's fate. Fear had led him to break his oath and aid his Lord's enemies once tonight. If he abandoned Torben then what hope was there for him? He might as well just give his soul to the demons. Go and find Solace and bring her back to the Great Hall as well, so she might see what the monsters had done to her father and what they intended to do to her.

The figure remained motionless and silent. A demon would have made himself known by now, one way or the other. It must be Torben. He took another reluctant step forward. He didn't know if he hated himself or the simple fool more. At least Lord Torben had the excuse of being a half-wit. He was just a coward who had sold his soul to the Devil. He knew which was worse.

He walked further into the darkness. He couldn't go without Torben. Solace would never forgive him for abandoning her brother. It was a lesser sin than the one he had already committed, but the thought of it seared, nevertheless. Hauling the fool up the stairs would not bring him redemption, but it was, perhaps, a step backwards from the precipice of damnation his cowardice had brought him to.

Old Man Ulrich would approve. Even if it was from behind the miasma of beer fumes and weakness that ruined his own life and broken the honour he cherished so much.

"Damn you..." He didn't know if he cursed Torben or his father, either way, he gripped his sabre all the tighter and plunged into the darkness.

The figure coalesced from shadow and terror into the form of Torben, standing with his back to him. He knew the boy - he thought him a boy even though he was older than him - could not tolerate a hand upon him. It was just one of the devilments plaguing the poor wretch, but this was no time for niceties.

He grabbed the half-wit's shoulder with his free hand and hauled him around, "We must go, there is no time for foolery!"

The boy's eyes were just wet glinting suggestions in the dark. Torben whimpered briefly, but neither resisted nor made a move to comply with Ulrich.

"Come! Your sister needs you!"

His body turned to face him, but Torben's head, Ulrich sensed as much as saw in the dark, looked back over his shoulder towards the Great Hall. Towards his father. Towards the demons and damnation.

"We cannot, my lord, we cannot..."

Torben shuddered. A wretched silent sob racked his frame, but he made no move one way or the other.

"If we go in the Great Hall, we die. If we stay here, we die. Please..." Ulrich was torn between punching the idiot and dragging him upstairs or punching the idiot and leaving him on the floor for the demons' amusement. Not that they wanted this half-wit, they wanted his beautiful little sister and the longer Ulrich stayed this close to their malign presence, the more the faults and fractures in his soul shifted, the more he wanted to give them what they desired in the hope he might live to see another day.

Another terrible scream rolled out of the Great Hall.

Save her and you save yourself...

"They want her..." he pleaded, "...they're here for her, I don't know why, but they are. That's why we can't hide. We can't hide because they won't stop looking till they find her. Do you want that? Do you understand that? Do you understand *anything?*"

He blew out his cheeks as Torben started walking in his strange shuffling gait back towards the stairs and the soft light that snuck around the corner from the corridor leading to the kitchens.

Ulrich moved at his side, one hand hovering behind

the boy's shoulder blades in case he changed whatever passed for his mind, constantly looking back for signs of his would-be new masters erupting from the shadows.

Instead of climbing the stairs, the boy stopped in the doorway and fixed his strange motionless eyes on Ulrich. His face was wet with tears. He held up his hands, palms outstretched. In each sat one of his wooden toys. They were how he communicated, but only Solace really understood them. Ulrich certainly didn't.

In his left hand was what looked like a goat, in the right a fox. A skilful hand had carved them, but this was no time for such foolishness. Before he could knock the things from the boy's hands and kick his stupid arse up the stairs, Torben held the goat towards the Great Hall and thrust the fox towards Ulrich.

Fox. That was what his name meant in French, the tongue of his forefathers. Was the boy referring to him? And the horned goat... the devil? He shook his head, "Not now, my lord, come show Lady Solace and she can tell me what you mean."

It was Torben's turn to shake his head, hard enough for it to rattle around inside the oversized burgonet he wore. He seized Ulrich's hand, his boyish features twisting into a grimace of distaste beneath his fuzzy beard as they touched. He pushed the carving into his palm, before poking his finger into Ulrich's chest and then jabbed it up the stairs.

"You must come with me, my lord..." Ulrich's eyes darted in the direction of the Great Hall; voices drifted out of the darkness, muffled and indistinct.

Torben held up the goat, cradled it to his chest, pointed to himself and then down the corridor.

"You want to go to... the Devil?"

Lord Torben nodded again.

"You can't save your father."

A smile, timid and sad, haunted the boy's shadow softened face.

"You cannot... they are monsters... they will kill you..."

"He sees the future, you know?"

Ulrich whirled around to find Henry Cleever standing behind him. The demon still bore his blood-drenched grin. At least he'd left the cook's intestines behind.

He half raised his sword, but Cleever shook his head.

"They say his mother foretold her own death. Torben saw his too, didn't you, lad?"

Torben nodded.

"I heard the stories..."

"Such things are usually just the whispers of fools in the shadows. But sometimes they turn out to be true," Cleever leaned against the wall and Ulrich hesitantly lowered his blade.

"Is that why you came here?"

"No. We came for his sister. For silver and gold. And for the blood, of course, though we can get that anywhere. Saul likes to play the soldier, likes to play games for his blood."

"Because she has the sight?"

"Oh, she's wanted for far more mundane reasons, I'm afraid."

"You said you didn't know why. That you hadn't been

listening."

Cleever offered an apologetic shrug, "Vampires lie. A lot. It makes all these damn years a little bit less boring."

The demon didn't seem as insane as when he'd been picking through Herman's intestines.

"Then why?"

Cleever rolled his eyes, "Oh, it's too, too dull to explain. Ask young Solace about *Graf* Bulcher though. She'll work it out. She's a clever girl."

"You knew all this was going to happen?" he demanded of Torben.

The young man stared at him with tear-filled eyes.

"And he wants to walk down that corridor to his death?"

Cleever shrugged again, "The future is not a book. 'tis but a series of possibilities and that is what he has seen. Possibilities. He could walk down that corridor and Saul might roast him over the fire, like his father, or he might become what he has wanted above all other things. To be a man. Not a man like other men, admittedly, but not the broken, pathetic thing he is now."

"I don't understand."

"A vampire's blood is a gift as well as a curse. It has the power to heal as well as to destroy. Remember the three men you put down in the village? Our blood restores and two of them will be walking again by morning, though it will take a few days for Gustav's fingers to grow back. That, I believe, is what Torben has seen. The possibility of being whole."

"But..." Ulrich shook his head "...he poured oil on you,

he helped kill some of your Company. Why?"

Cleever fixed his eyes on him. Even in the thick shadow it was clear the demon possessed the most extraordinarily beautiful eyes, "All men have a destiny and sometimes we try our hardest to fight against it even when we know what it is. I think you understand that, don't you, Ulrich?"

The winter had seeped into the bones of The Wolf's Tower, but it wasn't the cold that made Ulrich shiver.

"Do you have the sight too?"

Cleever pursed his bloody lips, "I have inklings and I have curiosity. I'm a great student of nature. Particularly the nature of men. Sometimes I know more than I should, but never as much as I desire."

Ulrich pulled his gaze towards Torben for fear of what he might find in the dancing light of the demon's eyes.

"And this is what you want? To be with them? The creatures that are killing your father? That slaughtered everyone in these walls? That are going to feast on the village children?"

Torben's only response was the tears rolling down his cheeks.

"He wants to be whole. 'tis all he has ever wanted. A voice that can be heard, a mind that isn't choked and hazed by clouds, a body that obeys its masters will. He has lived his life as a figure of ridicule, contempt and pity. Even in the eyes of his father. But he is not a fool, he is not a child, he is just broken. In that respect, he is no different from other men. We are all broken, after all. 'tis only the nature of our fractures that vary."

"But-"

Cleever silenced him with a shake of the head. He reached out and put a hand on Torben's arm. The boy didn't flinch.

"Come. 'tis time."

Cleever begun moving towards the darkened corridor leading to the Great Hall, Torben turned with him.

"Wait. The tunnel! Did you know it was blocked? Did you let Lutz die for nothing?"

Torben stopped. He shook his head.

"He wanted to escape his destiny. To stay with the sister he loves, I believe, truly. Do not judge him too harshly."

"Harshly?" Ulrich spat, "You're going to slaughter women and children and he is going to be part of it!"

"That, I'm afraid, is going to happen anyway. 'tis not to my taste either... but," Cleever shrugged, "cruelty is in our nature. Most of us at least. And not just vampires. I've seen such terrible things in my long life, most of them done by your kind rather than mine. Cities put to the sword, innocents slaughtered, women raped, people tortured and burned because they worshipped God the wrong way or were seen to be different or just for the damn fun of it."

Cleever wiped the back of his hand across his gore-splattered face, "We just possess a talent for it. Vampires and humans both."

Ulrich clenched his sword and strangled the urge to strike them down with it.

Cleever's eyes flicked to Ulrich's hand and back again, "Torben has betrayed no one. He fought against us, and he fought against himself. You helped us into the castle in return for your life. Who among us is without sin, Ulrich?"

He lowered his father's sabre till the tip clanked against the flagstones.

"Do we get out of the castle? Do you know? Have you seen it?"

Torben hesitated, then nodded. But his eyes drifted away.

"Whatever else Torben is doing, he is buying you time," Cleever said, "most of the Company are still trying to get across the moat and into the castle. Torben and I will keep Saul occupied. There are still men searching the castle, but if you know a way out, take it now. 'tis your only chance. That or coming with us. You put three of our men down. Saul likes you. He always requires more swords."

"I... I will not betray her... again..."

"Good for you. Find your own path, Ulrich. 'tis all any of us can do."

The demon put his arm gently around Torben's shoulder. The young man made no attempt to squirm away from the demon's touch, but before walking with Cleever he shrugged off the satchel carrying his carvings and let it clatter to the floor.

"Goodbye, my lord..." Ulrich whispered, as more screams rolled out of the Great Hall.

Torben nodded. The vampire at his side, they turned the corner and walked together into the darkness.

Chapter Thirteen

"Where are they!?" she asked, not for the first time.

Kapsner hovered on the stairwell landing, peering down the steps. He looked up, the candlelight playing over his grim face, "I can hear nothing, my lady."

"We would hear fighting, wouldn't we?" Dolman offered from her shoulder.

"Only if they had a chance to fight..."

Dolman bit his lip, he was shaking slightly, she noticed. They probably all were.

"We must go back and find them," Solace announced.

Karina let out a pitiful little whimper. She'd once owned a hound that made a similar noise from under her chair during thunderstorms. Dolman and Kapsner exchanged a look. Nobody moved to go back down the steps.

"We cannot abandon them!"

Kapsner straightened and turned towards her, "My lady, if men found them there would be sounds of fighting, but if a demon found them..."

"And there's nothing we can do to save them if that's happened!" Dolman squeaked, "'tis already too late!"

She slapped his face, the sound echoed between the old stones of her home.

"Coward!"

Dolman recoiled, eyes wide, cheek instantly reddening.

Kapsner moved to stand between them. He was a tall man, but then everybody towered over her.

"No one here is a coward," the calmness in his voice drained her anger. Leaving room for despair to pour in and take its place.

"Torben..."

She wanted to slump to the floor and curl into a ball. He couldn't be dead. She would know. The *sight* would tell her. It had shown her other things, so why wouldn't it tell her if the person she loved the most in the world was dead? What use was it, if it didn't tell her that? It wasn't telling her he was dead, it wasn't telling her he was alive. All she had was the huge weight of the dread stone in her guts swelling inside her like a malevolent child, as it had for weeks.

"We must go on, my lady," Kapsner continued, in his calm reasonable voice, "'tis what he would want."

Kapsner might not have the *sight*, but he'd decided her brother and Renard were dead all the same.

"You have no idea what my brother would want," she snapped. She never had, so she was certain one of their men at arms, whose only thought for her brother was to laugh behind his back with the other soldiers while they supped ale in the village tavern, didn't.

"No, I don't, but I know what I want. I want to live. So, I'm not going back down there..." Kapsner's voice hardened, then he looked at her in a way few men ever dared, "...my lady..."

Dolman and Erna stared at her, only Karina refused to meet her eye, instead looking at her feet while she drew her sleeve back and forth over her reddened nose.

Silence descended; a silence undisturbed by the sound of feet coming up the stairs. Erna shuffled to Kapsner's side and slipped her hand into the soldier's.

"We're leaving," Erna said, chin raised and nostrils flaring, "you're welcome to come or to stay, but we'll go looking for your brother no more than we did for the *Freiherr*. And no more than you would for us. We should have stayed in the tunnels, where it was safe, but we listened to you instead. This is our last chance, we're not going back for them," the maid smiled coldly, before adding, "And if you try to slap me, my lady, I *will* slap you back."

She wanted to push past them, to tell them to go to Hell, that they were nought but traitors and cowards, to run down the stairs, find her brother and drag him from the clutches of the demons with nothing to help her bar one pistol and a lifetime of getting whatever she wanted.

But she didn't.

Instead, she nodded, "We go on... if they still live, they will find us."

A little of the tension eased from her companions, save Dolman who still glared sulkily at her.

"Lock the door," Kapsner ordered, immediately turning towards the library halfway along the corridor.

"No!"

Her shrill voice stopped him. He looked over his shoulder, already pulling off the rope coiled around him, "We have to seal it... and the one at the other end too. It will take time for us to climb down..."

"Torben won't be able to get in!"

"Your brother isn't coming, my lady. The demons are..." He nodded at Dolman, who shut the door, lowered the bar and pulled the bolts across.

Erna hurried after Kapsner, while Karina whimpered, "Sorry, my lady..." before scurrying after the younger maid.

"I'll wait here, if they come, I can open the door."

Dolman sucked in his cheeks, "As you wish."

"Tell me when you're ready, I owe it to my brother to wait that long."

Dolman nodded.

"I shouldn't have hit you. I'm sorry. Truly."

The young soldier shrugged but didn't reply. As he turned away, he spat on the floor.

She watched them retreat down the corridor, crossing the little pools of light cast by the candles in their sconces and traversing the shadows in between. Kapsner and the two maids disappeared into the library while Dolman sprinted down to the other end of the corridor and bolted that door too.

All the time she listened for the sound of her brother's footsteps on the stairs, for Renard to call out for her to open the door for them. But she heard nothing until Dolman ran back along the corridor and ducked into the library. A moment later the door slammed shut behind the young soldier.

Then the screaming started.

*

Ulrich took the stairs two at a time, concentrating on not falling over and not thinking about how he was going to explain what had happened to Lady Solace.

He should be taking more care; he was making too much noise charging up the stairs. He wouldn't hear someone coming the other way, but he'd lost so much time and the others should be at the library by now. They certainly hadn't come back to see what delayed Torben and him.

All men have a destiny and sometimes we try our hardest to fight against it...

Cleever's words reverberated around his head with the force of his nailed boots hammering on the stone steps.

But what destiny did he fight against? The honourable man his father yearned for him to be in recompense for his own failings or a servant of demons? Which one was he running away from? Which did he run towards?

Surely, he'd made his choice. He could have gone with Torben. Gone to the Great Hall, gone to the slaughter, bent his knee to Saul the Bloodless and told him where Solace was.

He hadn't, but part of him - the weak, fractured part - begged, squirmed, and screamed to go with Solace's brother. To walk into the darkness, for in the darkness there would be life. At the end of these stairs there might be honour, but there would also be death.

When he'd asked Torben if they escaped, the boy had nodded, but there had been a hesitation. The young lord might be mute, but that hesitation spoke volumes.

Would Torben betray them? If Saul wanted Solace badly enough, perhaps he would deal for her. Give Torben what he wanted, for their demonic blood to cure his afflictions - or whatever Cleever had meant - in return for his sister.

Saul the Bloodless told him he could make any man talk and it seemed he had a way to make even the mute Torben speak.

Running up three floors of spiral stairs wearing a cuirass, helmet, with a sheathed sword swinging at his side and loaded pistols in his belt soon made breathing his only concern.

By the time he reached the third floor he was panting heavily and sweat slickened his brow. His gratitude at finally reaching the door tarnished by finding it shut in his face. And they would only close it if they intended to lock it.

They thought we were dead...

It was a fair assumption, he supposed. When they got up here and realised Torben and he were not behind them, they must have thought a demon had got them. They'd been right too. Though the demon was the one who'd tormented Torben all his life as much as the ones with fangs and a taste for blood now stalking The Wolf's Tower.

He slowed, stopped and leant forward, resting his hands upon his knees, as he sucked in air through his nostrils, eyes fixed on the closed door.

Why did he hesitate? Because he'd have to tell Solace

about Torben? That her beloved brother had given himself to the demons who slaughtered their father so they might fix the broken parts inside him. Or was it that he was following the wrong sibling? That the only thing behind the door was death.

He straightened up and walked the last few steps to the door.

Save her and you save yourself...

"I will not betray her..." he whispered, before hammering on the door.

When no response came, he rapped his fist harder and rattled the latch. They couldn't have gotten out of the library window yet, could they? And Solace would wait for her brother.

He was about to kick the door in frustration when the sound of scurrying feet came from the other side.

"Thank God..." he muttered, looking over his shoulder as the heavy bolts and bar on the other side were pulled clear. He gripped the handle and wrenched the door open to reveal a blood-soaked figure waiting for him in the shadows on the other side.

"Ah, at last, the Pretty Thing..." Alms hissed...

Chapter Fourteen

The screams were terrible, but they didn't ring out for long. The following silence was worse.

You run or you stand, you run or you stand, you run or you stand...

The words echoed around her, filling the silence as the final scream was cut short. The voice in her head belonged to Renard, for no obvious reason.

She found herself walking down the corridor towards the library, the pistol she had carried for so long gripped in both hands, the muzzle raised upwards.

Dolman and Kapsner both carried pistols too, but not a shot had rung out from the library.

There was no one left now. She was the last. Her father, Torben, Lutz, her little band of survivors she'd so foolishly thought she could save. The Wolf's Tower was no longer her home. It was her tomb.

She stopped halfway to the library and stared at the pistol in her hand. She had one shot. What was the best thing to be done with it? Maybe she'd get lucky and kill one of them, but she'd killed already tonight; the men roasted in the Darkway, the soldiers in the Wheelhouse, the demon blown up with the gunpowder that destroyed the mechanisms for opening the Outer Gates, the two men in the stairwell Renard had dispatched. And yet here she was. Alone. Alone with something that had just slaughtered the last of her people in the library.

What was the best thing she could do with her one shot?

We are death, Lady Solace... but not for you...

That was what the monster behind the door had said. Whatever foul purpose they had for her; it didn't involve killing her. If you could believe the things monsters whispered in the darkness of course.

You run or you stand.

"But what do you do when you can do neither, Ulrich the Fox...?"

No answer came, bar a distant moan of wind.

Her feet stopped. She didn't need to go any further. She didn't need to see the corpses. She didn't need to see the blood-splashed books her father professed to love but rarely read. She knew. It was strange she didn't know for sure if Torben was dead, her *sight* would not whisper that into her ear, but she had no doubt the four people who had gone into the library had died there.

What do you do if you can't stand and you can't run?

What choice remained?

We are death, Lady Solace... but not for you...

You took the only course left to thwart your enemies, to stop the monsters, to claim a victory, however hollow.

The Wolf's Tower had been her home and it would be her tomb.

She placed the pistol under her chin, closed her eyes and pulled the trigger.

*

Although the creature wore its human face, in the shimmering candlelight the demon was hard to mistake for a man. Alms' eyes burned with feverish delight as his crimson-stained lips twisted into the smile of a lunatic. Everything about the way he held himself was wrong, as if he'd found a way to contort every aspect of the human body ever so slightly into the wrong angle.

When Ulrich could only stand, mouth agape, his last forlorn hope of escape crumbling to dust around him, the demon laughed. It was the kind of high-pitched giggle he might associate with flirtatious ladies-in-waiting if the humble young soldier had ever met any.

They were dead. All of them. He was too late.

Alms raised a hand and beckoned Ulrich through the door with fingers as stained as his lips. In the ill-formed light, they appeared as hooked and jagged as old broken claws.

Unable to resist the command, Ulrich walked through the door. Alms moved only fractionally to one side forcing him to brush against the demon to get by. His skin crawled and his stomach roiled at the smell of him. A scent of rich dry exotic spices mixed with the stink of an abattoir. Alms' breath played over his face.

It was as cold as a January breeze.

"The Sweet Little Thing is close..." Alms slithered after him. When Ulrich stopped, the demon leant over and placed his chin upon Ulrich's shoulder before whispering in his ear, "...I can smell her..."

She's still alive!!

Ulrich tried to step forward, but Alms' fingers snaked around his arm and tightened like bands of iron, "...I can smell the Sweet Little Thing on you. She stinks like a bitch in heat..."

"I-"

"If the next thing to come out of your mouth is a lie, I'll crush the bones of your elbow to dust..." the pressure on his arm intensified enough for Ulrich to know the demon wasn't exaggerating.

"I... couldn't betray her. She has my oath."

"I do wonder... would your nobility stretch so far if it was as fat as a pregnant sow with a face to match?" Alms snickered, "I must confess, the world would be less complicated with fewer pretty things in it..."

The demon released his arm, then reached up and pulled Ulrich's helmet free. The burgonet clattered to the floor and the demon stroked the back of Ulrich's head. Cold, fat worms pushed through his sweat-tousled hair and pressed into his skull.

"I can crush your head as easily as I can crush your arm."

"Why don't you?"

"I like pretty things... 'tis a weakness of mine."

"I am not pretty."

Alms tittered and his hand fell away.

"Master!"

The demon twisted around at the sound of the voice. Ulrich let out a slow, shaky breath. He stared down the corridor. A discarded pistol lay on the floor halfway towards the library, otherwise nothing was out of place. He suspected that wouldn't be the case inside the library.

"Master Saul wishes you in the Great Hall," the voice said as the rap of nailed boots, the clank of steel and the creak of leather filled the corridor. Red Cloaks. He didn't feel the need to turn around.

"I'm busy," Alms snapped, "the girl thing, Solace, is nearby."

"Saul insists," the man said evenly. No fear or wariness registered in his voice, just the familiarity of doing something many times.

"What is so important I must stop looking for the thing we came here to find?"

"'tis her brother..." Ulrich said before the Red Cloak replied.

Alms leaned in towards him again. Ulrich tried not to flinch at the demon's breath, it stank like warm, fresh blood poured into a cold, old grave, "And why would her worthless brother be so important? It's a half-wit and a simpleton! You said so yourself?"

"He's given himself to you. He wants your blood to make him whole."

"It really is a fool then."

"A fool who can see the future..."

Alms was silent, then, "Truly?"

"That was why they poured the oil on us, Torben

foretold your coming, but only his sister believed him."

Again, silence broken only by the shuffling soldiers behind him. He thought there were three, but he still stared in the opposite direction. He didn't want to see any of them or what might be reflected in their eyes.

"Then why did it burn us? 'tis an unusual way to ask for help, no?"

"Men fight against their destinies sometimes, so Cleever believes."

"Cleever?" Alms voice dropped a notch, "What is this to him?"

"Torben went with him."

"Cleever has him?"

"I assume he is with Saul now."

"He is, Master," the same Red Cloak said, presumably in response to a questioning glance from Alms.

"But the half-witted thing gave itself to Cleever?"

Ulrich nodded. He wondered what politicking played out between demons.

"Then I must go. Find the girl thing," he addressed the Red Cloaks, "this one will help you. If it doesn't, kill it."

"Yes, Master."

"Is he valuable to you?" Ulrich asked, finally turning as Alms made to leave.

"A man that can see the future has value. If it can be turned... well, a vampire that can see the future..." he smiled grimly.

"Would Saul deal for him?"

"Deal?"

"Our freedom for Torben's fealty?"

Alms laughed, "We already have its fealty. There is nothing to negotiate."

"He loves his sister. Kill her and he won't serve you."

"We have no intention of killing it. And this is none of your business."

"And the children? Torben won't-"

Alms hit him. He suspected it was intended as a light slap, but it sent him first careening against the wall and then on to his knees. Searing daggers of pain tore through the side of his face. He wondered if he'd managed to pick up a broken jaw to compliment the broken nose Alms gifted him earlier.

The demon loomed over him, "You are in no position to demand terms. And even if you did, Saul would never give up the children. He has a taste for them you see. Picked it up after he kissed the vein and became vampire. Not to my liking, but each to their own..." the demon bent down, a slow grin spreading over his strange, boyish features, "...personally, I much prefer just fucking them."

He laughed and swivelled away, before he left, he barked at one of the men, who Ulrich recognised as Bekker, the Red Cloaks captain.

"Find the girl thing. It's close. If the Pretty Thing here doesn't help you, I've changed my mind. Don't kill it. Bring it to me and I'll kill it. If it doesn't co-operate, just cut something off. I don't mind what..." Alms brushed past the Red Cloaks, but then stopped after half a dozen paces to twist around "...as long as it's not its cock. That's mine..."

"Yes, Master," Bekker nodded, before turning back to Ulrich. He looked down and smiled fulsomely, "Welcome back."

Then he kicked Ulrich in the face.

"Now get to work, we have a bitch to hunt."

Chapter Fifteen

The trigger clicked, the wheel turned, the powder fizzed.

Nothing else of note happened.

Solace peeled open an eye and lowered the pistol. Unless very much mistaken, she appeared to still be alive. She dropped the gun and was mildly surprised it didn't go off and shoot her foot.

Was it a message from God that she should not give up so easily, or merely the mindless happenchance of a dumb mechanism choosing a completely random moment to fail?

It was probably not the most opportune moment to ponder such a question. She felt tired beyond words. Perhaps she should just curl up on the floor until the demons found her. That would be easier than this. Of fighting and running and striving and seeing everybody else die.

As if to underline the thought, the sound of breaking glass came from the library, followed by a woman's scream, a scream that faded to nothing. It sounded like Karina. It sounded like Karina being thrown out of the window.

If she'd gone to the library to try and save her instead of attempting to kill herself, would the pistol have fired?

She listened to her thudding heart and then to the library door creaking. Someone was coming. Something was coming.

The door to the nearest room hung open and she ducked inside. It was a study. The library of The Wolf's Tower had once been renowned and scholars regularly visited to read the old tomes. This was one of the rooms set aside for them. It was dark and unused. Nobody came to the library anymore and many of the books were now rotten with damp and mildew.

But she knew the room well enough, she knew every room in The Wolf's Tower. The study was empty, whatever furniture it had once held had long since disappeared; sold, thrown away or burnt. The hearth was large and had never housed a fire in her lifetime.

She moved across the room, there was no light, but she found the fireplace without pause as it dominated the room. Those old scholars had liked their warmth. She ducked under the lintel and stood in the hearth. Reaching up she located the ledge hidden inside the chimney. It was smaller than she remembered, it had been years since she decided she was too old for games of hiding with her brother.

She boosted herself up, the constraints of her dress made that harder too, but she managed to swing her legs up at the second attempt. She didn't think she'd made too much noise...

Drawing up her knees she hugged them tightly. The scent of ancient fires haunted the chimney, their soot still gritting the brickwork. The Wolf's Tower had many such secret places for hiding people and things from the minions of emperors, kings and bishops. She was sure there were more than even she knew of.

None, other than the tunnels, were big enough for hiding seven people, but now it was just her she had an abundance of hiding places to choose from. Even her father probably didn't know all the places she did...

She blinked in the darkness and tried not to think of the dead.

Instead, she strained her ears to listen for them.

*

He spat blood. Several teeth followed onto the floor.

Not even his mother or Alms would think him pretty now. He'd never known his mother and wished he could say the same about the demon.

As Ulrich climbed back to his feet, Bekker cast an eye over him in the manner of a man checking to see if what he'd just shat out of his backside met with his approval.

"Stupid bastard..." the soldier sneered.

Bekker boasted a hard-chiselled face and cold eyes the same colour as the tarnished steel of his stolen burgonet. The two men with him wore the red cloaks of Saul's Company rather than the clothes pulled from the corpses of the Tassau men slaughtered in the village. So at least some of the demons' minions had made it through the Outer

Gates.

Ulrich opted to say nothing. He didn't want to lose any more teeth before he died.

"Where is she?"

"I don't know... I was downstairs with her brother."

Bekker chewed the answer over. He didn't seem to like it, but at least didn't feel the need to kick him again.

"They were making for the library. I think they run into Alms."

"Master Alms..."

"Yes... Master Alms..." the words hissed strangely through the unfamiliar new gaps in his teeth.

"But Master Alms didn't find her..." Bekker looked up and down the corridor. The door at the far end remained closed, the one he'd come through was still open, but nobody had come in or out since him, other than Bekker and his two Red Cloaks.

Bekker pulled the pistols out of Ulrich's belt and handed them to the two soldiers. Then he unbuckled the weapon belt and took his father's sheathed sabre, which he held onto.

"Hagan guard the door we came through, Lohmus the other one. If the bitch tries to get out, make sure you stop her," he glared at the two men, "but if you kill her, Master Saul will be roasting *you* over a fire. Understand?"

The soldiers nodded and hurried to either end of the corridor.

"Was that an idle threat?"

Bekker just smiled and shoved him towards the library.

Unlike most of the corridors in The Wolf's Tower, there were rooms on both sides. In the rest of the castle the rooms were all on the inner side, looking down on the Courtyard, but someone had wanted a view from the library. It wasn't the original design; that someone had gone to a lot of trouble to get their view.

The library ran the entire outside length of the corridor. After the Great Hall, kitchen and the stables, it was the biggest room in the castle. Half a dozen smaller rooms occupied the inside length. Ulrich didn't know what they were as he'd never been in them. He'd only seen the library once, during a brief tour of the castle after the *Freiherr* took his oath. Men at arms had little need for books.

Bekker pushed him in. A couple of candles burned on the big mahogany reading table dominating the room, their light didn't reach far along the shelves lining the walls, but they danced merrily in the wind gusting through the shattered window. At first, he thought his companions had smashed the window to escape.

Then he saw the bodies.

"Take a candle," Bekker said, "My eyes aren't as keen as the Masters..."

Reluctantly he picked up the candle, which was beeswax rather than tallow. Old Rafael must have been working in here, though working involved no more than reading old books from what Ulrich knew of him. One laid open on the table, a bone aestel rested between the pages of faded text and illustrations of saints.

Bekker flicked through the heavy vellum pages of the

book, more interested in the drawings of angels and cherubs than the corpses decorating the library.

Kapsner's head was a bloody mess, his dour features pulped beyond recognition against one of the few pieces of wall not lined with books. What looked like blobs of grey matter crawled down the wall. Dolman laid at the foot of the table, an expression of mild surprise on his usually slack disinterested features. His right eye was gone, blood and goo seeped down the young man's cheek. A dagger through the eye and into the brain.

He found Erna further along the library, perhaps she'd tried to run as the two soldiers died. She was on her back, her throat a savage ruin. A blade hadn't crossed it.

He stared down into her sightless eyes. He'd never loved her. He wasn't sure he even liked her. But he'd wanted her, and she'd played him along without ever telling him she wasn't interested. Still, her lifeless face turned something inside him.

"That's a shame..." Bekker came over to stand at his shoulder, "...they usually save a couple of the pretty ones for us," he sucked at a tooth before dropping the book on Erna's corpse. It disintegrated into a flurry of pages that settled around her like giant yellowing leaves.

There was no sign of Karina. He thought the maid might have somehow escaped the slaughter alongside her mistress, but when he walked to the main window, he found her white cap on the floor and jewels of blood on the broken glass. Leaning out he narrowed his eyes against the winter's bite to peer down into the moat. Something had shattered the ice.

"The bitch we want isn't down there," Bekker told him.

"No..."

"The plan was to climb down?" he nodded at the rope still coiled across Ulrich's torso.

"Yes," he looked out of the window again. The frigid breeze ruffled his hair. It was a long way down, but they could have made it. He raised his eyes to the trees beyond the pasture. It would have had been hard, but they might have done it. So damn close.

"Did Master Alms know we were coming here?"

"No," Bekker snorted, prodding the leather spine of the book he'd dropped on Erna with his boot, "he's a book collector, would you believe..."

Ulrich found a grim, humourless smile worm itself on to his face. If the bastard had just stuck to killing, he might not have been here and they would have escaped, but no. He'd decided to take in the *Freiherr's* collection of old, mouldy books instead.

The candle in his hand blew out in the cold restless breeze. He stepped back and returned to the table to relight it from the one still burning there. Bekker's eyes followed him.

"You should have brought her to us, like they told you to."

"I gave my oath."

"The *Freiherr* is dead, or as good as. Your oath is discharged."

"Lady Solace isn't."

"Just a bitch. Not worth dying for. 'tis a good life serving the Masters."

He stared over the flickering candle flame at the soldier, "Serving demons? Your soul will burn in Hell for all eternity."

Bekker laughed, "Only if I die."

"Everybody dies."

"The Masters don't. They pay well in gold, silver and women, decent food, good ale and their blood heals our wounds. Unless you're stupid enough to get your head cut off, blown to smithereens or some other wound that will kill you before they can heal you. And if they like you enough, they can make you one of them."

"A demon."

"A vampire," Bekker shrugged, "I suppose there's not much difference."

"They slaughter the innocent, they're going to kill children, they roasted the *Freiherr* alive. How can you serve them?"

"You've not been a soldier long, have you?"

"Long enough to know I couldn't do such things."

Could I?

"If you're a soldier long enough, you'll end up doing most anything. There's no honour in it. No glory. Maybe those knights of old were different, but I doubt it. Reckons the likes of us got slaughtered much the same. And our women and children."

"I have honour..."

Bekker laughed, "You know, I can see why Master Saul likes you... shame you can't see your way to serving him..."

Ulrich looked around the corpse-strewn room but didn't reply.

Bekker sighed, "I guess we can debate this like we're in some fancy university for the damned, but we ain't got hours enough for clever words..." he pulled a pistol from his belt and swept the room with it, "Where is she?"

"I don't know, I wasn't with them. Maybe she got out the window..."

"No, don't think so. Would you tell me if you did know?"

"Probably not."

"Your attitude isn't exactly helpful, friend."

"I've already betrayed her once in helping you get in. I'll not do it again."

"Fine words right enough, not sure I believe them though. Give her to us and Saul will hand you a red cloak. As I said, 'tis a good life. Better than any soldiering I ever done before. Gold, women, good ale... maybe get to live forever..."

But no honour.

"I don't know where she is," he said, not meeting Bekker's eye.

The sagging lintels in the tunnel, struggling to bear the colossal weight pushing down from above, came to mind as he thought of the cracks and weaknesses inside himself straining under the pressure of temptation.

Save her and you save yourself...

Bekker shook his head, "We'll check this room first, a candle in both hand if you please. I'll be behind you..."

Ulrich picked up the second candle and together they checked the rest of the library. There were a lot of books. A hearth that still faintly smouldered. A broken window and a couple of portraits of men as glassy-eyed and expressionless as corpses.

There weren't any obvious hiding places, unless the shelves concealed a secret compartment. Which was possible. All castles had their hiding places.

When they finished in the library, Bekker tossed Ulrich's sabre onto the table before they left.

Six other rooms made up the remainder of the floor, all empty, some of them even of furniture. They didn't seem to have been used much. Two were completely bare, one appeared to be a storeroom for books too decrepit to go into the library. One seemed to be a workroom for binding and restoring and two were studies with small desks and uncomfortable chairs.

The hearths all sat cold and no lights burnt in any of them. In the room closest to the pistol in the corridor, his candles picked out a few black lumps soiling the floor. Soot from countless fires clogged the chimneys and the detritus often fell to scatter over the floor. He skimmed the candlelight over the dirt, pushing it back into the hearth with his boot while Bekker tapped the muzzle of his pistol against the room's wood panelling.

The Red Cloaks' captain was looking for a hollow space behind one of the panels. If he found one, Solace wasn't going to be in it.

She was hiding up the chimney.

Chapter Sixteen

The tears came in the darkness.

They rose and swelled without warning. A vast dark bubble of grief expanding to the point it consumed her, overwhelming even the dread stone in her stomach. She felt nothing but a pain ripping deeper into her soul than anything she'd ever physically experienced in her life.

She could do nothing to prevent the heaving spasms racking her chest and jolting her shoulders up and down. She hugged her knees fiercely and pushed her face hard against them to stifle the sound of her sobs.

Tears soaked her face and the heat in her cheeks made it feel like someone had lit a fire beneath her. Her nostrils clogged with snot and every breath became a wet, rattling wheeze.

They were gone. Everybody she knew and loved was gone. Her home was gone. Her life was gone. And God had not even granted her the mercy of letting her die before she fell into the hands of the demons.

Why was He punishing her so? What had she done to

deserve this? Why had she been unable to save anyone? Not her beautiful, troubled brother? Not her father with his stern countenance and soft eyes whose last memory of her would be slapping her face? Not craggy loyal old Lutz? Not dour Kapsner or Karina whose constant tears she'd silently cursed and now aped? Not simple Dolman or pretty Erna? Not prissy, whinging Steward Strecker. Nobody. Not even Renard who the dread stone warned not to trust but whose strength of purpose gave her a glimmer of hope they might escape. All dead, all gone.

Now she was alone. In the darkness. Waiting for the demons to find her.

She sucked in air and forced herself to calm. When they found her, she didn't want to be blubbering like a child. If that was the only victory left open to her, then she would claim that at least. She would keep her head high; she would damn their names and she would spit in their faces.

The tears slowed and faded. She wiped her sodden face with her skirts. When she looked up there was nothing to see but darkness.

She straightened and rested her back against the soot encrusted brickwork. The ledge was no wider than her hips. She shuffled a fraction, dislodging detritus to rattle into the hearth below. She stilled herself till the only movement was the slow rise and fall of her chest and the drumming of her heart.

There was nothing to do but think.

How long could she stay here? How long would they look for her?

She suspected the answer to the first question would be the opposite of the answer to the second. The dread stone turned inside her as if to confirm the suspicion.

Why don't you do something useful and tell me what I can do?

The dread stone, of course, didn't answer. It, whatever in God's grace it was, did not work like that. It talked to her only in feelings and dreams. It did not come in the precise, clipped purposeful words of her old tutor Magnus, but in the vague whisperings of a lunatic muttering the same words over and over again, but so softly you couldn't be sure you really heard anything at all.

Think! Think! Think!

If the *sight* wasn't going to help her, then all she had was her brain. She'd never considered that to be one of her most winning attributes. Even though her father hired Magnus to teach writing, arithmetic and her Bible, thinking was not a skill expected of the daughters of *Freiherrs*.

Magnus' teachings seemed no more useful right now than the womanly pursuits of embroidery, singing, playing the harpsichord and looking pretty; all considered far more valuable things for a girl to learn, particularly when their father was actively trying to arrange an advantageous marriage for them.

Perhaps she might lull the savage demons' hearts by playing a fugue?

Her music had always calmed Torben. Music had been one of the few things that had made her brother smile.

Had...

She bit her lip and stared into the darkness

surrounding her. She was not going to cry again. Was not. Was not. Was not...

Dismissing the idea salvation might lie in fetching her harpsichord, she turned every other possibility over in her head. Each and every one involved moving. There were better hiding places scattered around the castle, but none the demons wouldn't find if they wanted her badly enough and had time to rip the castle apart. The most secure and best hidden were the tunnels, but she'd left those because the dread stone whispered the demons would find their way in. Her insistence they leave had cost the lives of everyone who had trusted her.

Would she have been better off staying? How could it have worked out worse?

With nowhere to hide, the only other course was getting out of the castle. But how? The tunnels remained blocked and the Outer Gates would be full of the demons' rogues. The library window was no longer an option. Her ancestors had neglected to furnish her with another exit. Other than jumping off the battlements.

She turned the idea around in her head. Could she survive such a fall? The moat was deep and the ice not thick. She remembered leaning over the battlements and dropping stones down into the moat when she'd been younger. Watching them tumble and turn before splashing into the dark green water so far below, fascinated by how the tiny ripples disturbed the stillness.

If she survived without being seen and didn't drown... then she would need to cross the pasture to the woods unseen. Soaking wet in the middle of winter. If they didn't find her, she was likely to freeze to death. Would such an end be worse than whatever the demons had in mind for her?

She closed her eyes and thought of Karina's scream fading to nothing. They'd thrown her out of the window. Could she do that from twice the height?

We are death, Lady Solace... but not for you...

The demon's voice came again, unbidden from her memories. Her death was the only victory within her grasp. They wanted her. For what reason and purpose, she didn't know, but the dread stone told her that was true. Its jabbering, lunatic whisper was clear on that point, at least. Did the manner of her death matter?

In a moment of black despair, she'd pressed the cold metal of a pistol's muzzle against her chin and pulled the trigger without hesitation. If she could do that, she could jump from the battlements and put her fate in God's hands once more. He'd seen fit to make the gun fail, so maybe He would deliver her from darkness again. And if He didn't? Well, she would still have won. She would deny the beasts what they sought.

But, of course, she had to get to the roof first.

She looked up. Pulled from her thoughts by the sound of voices and footsteps. The voices of men. The voices of demons.

She stilled her breathing and wished her drumming heart would calm. It seemed to echo in the dark, sooty confines of the chimney.

The voices faded after a while, and she let out a breath. Whatever she planned, for now they were too close.

She had to hope they would think no one else was here and search another part of the castle. Would they believe it had just been Kapsner, Erna, Dolman and Karina trying to escape? Or would they suspect others were with them? She thought of her pistol discarded in the corridor and cursed herself.

She strained her ears. There was only silence beyond the thump of her heart. Should she go now? No. Too soon. They would still be close. Wait until they move on. Wait until they grew bored. Be patient. The moment will come. That would be Lutz's advice, wouldn't it? Wait until your enemy is looking elsewhere and then act. Surprise was the only weapon she had left.

She moved, unable to resist the need and a few more grains of soot trickled over the edge of the ledge.

Be still! In the name of the good Lord be still girl!

A smile dusted her lips despite everything. That had been Lutz alright. The old man might be dead, but surely his shade would stay with her. Loyal, dutiful, crusty old Lutz, watching over her till the very end.

The voices came again. Then just footsteps, but closer. They were in the room now.

Oh heart! Be silent, please!

Cobweb grey light played across the hearth below her. Men with candles or lanterns. Searching the room. She could hear tapping, metal on wood. Checking the walls.

Ha! I'm not there. Tap all you like; you won't find me.

The light grew stronger, the footsteps louder and she silenced even her mind for fear her thoughts might somehow betray her in the absolute silence of the dead castle. The footsteps stopped, though the tapping continued. Two men at least. One checking the walls, one now standing in front of the fireplace, removed from her by only the brickwork of the chimney.

Even if he ducks inside and holds up his candle, he won't see me... will he?

Then another sound. Soft as sighs. A boot rubbing over gravel, the faintest patter of tiny stones. The heart she'd been willing to silence missed a beat.

The dislodged soot!

Grains and granules stuck together over centuries, sent tumbling to the floor as she clambered up into the chimney.

The man or demon by the fire had noticed and ran his boot curiously over them. She rested her head against the chimney wall. It was over. They would find her and pull her out. She was done. Her final battle was as lost as all the others endured this terrible night.

Then the light receded and the footsteps with them.

She would have let out a shaking sigh of relief if it would not have given her away. She forced herself to be still. No fidgeting now! He might be too stupid or unobservant to work out someone climbing into the chimney had dislodged the grit under his boots, but such luck would not hold if she sent out another signal to her presence.

And when they left, she would need to move. Not all the demons would be so careless.

"She's hiding here somewhere," a voice said, deep and gruff. Not the demon who had whispered through the door, but whether it was a man or a monster she couldn't tell.

"Probably run when Master Alms killed the others," came the reply. Her eyes widened in the darkness. *Renard?* That sounded like Renard, but...

"Nowhere to run. Locked doors at each end of the corridor. She's close... when more men get here, we'll pull this floor apart stone by stone till we find the little bitch."

"And then what happens to her?"

That is Renard!

"We give her to the man who paid us to come and get her."

"What does he want with her?"

"You ask too many fucking questions. My advice is that unless you really want Master Saul to cut you into strips you should realise you don't need to know everything."

Silence. Then footsteps moving away. Then stopping.

"What about the chimney?"

"What about it?"

"Did you check it?"

A pause, "She isn't there."

"How'd you fucking know?"

Another, more prolonged, pause, "I'd see her feet..."

More silence, "Don't be so stupid, these old shit piles are stuffed with hidey holes. Best for you we find her quick if you want to live."

The footsteps grew louder.

"Give me one of those candles, I'll look..."

*

This was the moment.

The thought struck home as Bekker snatched one of the candles from him. He either let Bekker find Solace and throw in his lot with the demons, or he tried to stop him. He sold his oath, or he honoured it.

It was time to run or stand.

Old Man Ulrich would have told him to stand by his honour, but he would have said it with beer froth around his whiskers and bleary eyes incapable of meeting his son's, because standing by his honour was something he'd been unable to do. Everything was easy when you cradled an ale pot, but the distance in his father's gaze said some things were much harder to do when you weren't sloshed full of tavern bluster.

And it was always the things you couldn't do that haunted you for the rest of your life.

Torben had given himself to the demons in the hope of becoming something he was not. But the price he would have to pay would be to become something so far removed from what he had been that there would be nothing left of him at all.

What had remained of his father in the end? Bitterness and regret. Nothing else. A long, long road had taken the young man he'd once been to that wretched place.

Whatever failings his father suffered, whatever mistakes he'd made, whatever poor decisions he'd taken on that road, none could possibly be as grievous as giving yourself to demons who slaughtered the innocent. Even if it was the only way left to stay alive.

Bekker ducked down under the fireplace's stone mantel, raised his candle and looked up the chimney. He should have called for Hagan and Lohmus before going up the chimney, but, of course, the world was full of fools.

As Ulrich placed his candle on the mantle and stood by the fireplace, the voice whispering in his ear wasn't his father's, it was Eugen Lutz.

Save her and you save yourself...

"Ah-ha, there you are... there's someone who wants to meet you..."

The soldier straightened up until only his legs remained visible. There was a muffled cry and the sound of a struggle, a clang as something connected with Bekker's helmet, Solace's boot probably. A series of curses and laughs floated out with the soot as Bekker managed to haul Solace from her hiding place.

Landing with a yelp and a flurry of soot in the hearth, Solace tried to stand, but Bekker got his hands on her collar first and threw her out into the room.

"Keep hold of the bitch!" Bekker laughed.

Solace looked about the room. Wide, frightened eyes behind her blackened face finally focused on him.

"You bastard!"

He ignored her as Bekker ducked out of the chimney place. When the Red Cloak's captain straightened up Ulrich came at him from behind, hooking a hand over his mouth as he yanked Bekker's dagger from his belt.

Bekker tried to stamp down on Ulrich's foot but missed. The dagger flashed across the Red Cloak's throat as Bekker's teeth sank into the meat of Ulrich's hand. Searing pain lanced up his arm. Ulrich ignored it, sawing the dagger deep into the older man's flesh. Blood sprayed the room in a crimson arc, splattering floor, wall and Solace alike.

The man's muffled cries and struggling subsided, the pain in Ulrich's left hand lessened as Bekker's jaw flapped open,

"Let us see demon blood cure you of this..." he spat in the dying man's ear. The pungent stink of shit filled the room as Bekker's bowels opened.

He held the body tight against him until Bekker's final spasms subsided and the bastard's soul was on its way to Hell. His eyes never left the door in the expectation of Hagan and Lohmus having heard the struggle. No one came. The door had swung shut and Bekker hadn't had the chance to cry for help. They would be dead if he had.

Panting, he lowered Bekker's body to the floor. Blood dripped from his fingers as he straightened up. His eyes moved from the door to Solace. She was still on the floor, resting on her side, back arched, two sooty hands pressed hard against the floor like a cat tensing to spring.

"If you're going to hate me, save it until we're safe."

"I thought you had betrayed me?"

"No time..." he bent and retrieved the two pistols in Bekker's belt and placed them on the floor.

"Did you betray Torben?"

"No."

"How did he die?"

Ulrich paused as he pulled Bekker's sword free, "He didn't."

Solace sprang to her feet, "Where is he? We must find him!"

"We don't have time."

"We are not leaving him!"

He placed the sword next to the pistols and started undoing Bekker's weapon belt, he didn't answer until he yanked it free. When he looked up Solace had taken a step towards him, hands balled at her sides and shaking visibly. He straightened up and flexed his left hand. Blood bubbled out of the wound to mix with Bekker's.

"He went to them freely. He gave himself to them."

Solace's mouth popped open, "Why would he do such a thing?"

Ulrich bent over and wiped his bloody hands on Bekker's cloak.

"Partly to buy us time, but mainly because he wants them to cure him."

"Cure him!! Cure him of what?"

"His... afflictions," Ulrich stood up and buckled on Bekker's belt, "there's something about their blood. It has the power to heal... I presume he thinks it will give him his voice, give him his mind, give him the things other men have. Cure him of his torments. Make him whole."

"I don't understand..."

"He saw the future..." when Solace just continued to stare, he sheathed Bekker's sword and slid the pistols into the belt, "...you know he can do that?"

She nodded. Her bottom lip quivering as a tear fell from her left eye. It washed a stream through the soot upon her cheek. The memory of Bernard the Black came unbidden, Solace's fingers cutting through the dust beneath the eyes of the statue.

"I don't know what the demons will do. Someone who can see the future would be useful to them. That's what Cleever said. Alms - the demon that killed Kapsner and the others - was summoned downstairs. I assume they want to decide what to do with Torben..." he bent down and pulled off Bekker's helmet, he wiped off the worst of the blood splattering it on the dead man's cloak "....and while they're preoccupied, we can escape."

"But... what will become of him?"

Ulrich stood up and slipped the helmet on. Bekker still wore the uniform of the Tassau soldiers. He tried not to think about the fact two men had already died wearing the burgonet that night. He grunted. It was a good fit.

"I don't know. Unlike your brother, I cannot see the future. But if we tarry any longer, they will find us. They know you are here, and they'll send more men to look for you. There are two in the corridor, one by each door. I can deal with them. Once more come..."

Tears flowed down her cheeks, "But he is the gentlest creature in the world..."

She didn't appear to be listening to him.

Ulrich crossed the room and seized her arms, squeezing hard enough to make her gasp and him grimace from the wound in his left hand. It wasn't the way a common soldier treated a noblewoman. But they were beyond such things now.

"Listen to me. We go now or you submit to whatever it is they plan for you. Someone has paid them to take you. I don't know why. Do you want to stay and take your chances? I could have betrayed you. They offered me a place in their ranks, like him..." he jerked his head towards Bekker's corpse "...I decided my oath to you means something. I decided to keep my honour rather than save my skin. Don't make me regret my choice."

"How can I leave him to them?"

"You left your father to them."

Solace's beautiful eyes widened as if slapped. He took a breath and tried a different approach.

"Torben knows the future, or some of it at least. Presumably he knows what they intend for you. Do you think he would have fought so hard against what he sees as his own destiny otherwise? That he would have poured oil over them? That he would have attempted to escape if he didn't know their intentions for you were worse than what we will have to endure to survive? He didn't go to them just for his own reasons. He's giving us time. He's sacrificing himself. Like your father did. Like Lutz did."

She looked up at him, eyes wet and uncertain.

"My lady, please, tell me what you want to do?"

Chapter Seventeen

She'd never known the workings of Torben's mind. Not really.

Sometimes she fooled herself she understood him, but he had always been a mystery a bag of wooden carvings and a small repertoire of expressions and gestures never allowed her to fully unravel.

But this?

Where had this come from? Was he so unhappy that he wanted to sell his soul to the Devil? For what? A voice? To look like other men? To walk like other men? Why would he desire such a thing, especially if the price was to become something that was no longer a man at all?

Part of her wanted to shrug Renard away, stomp down the corridor and demand to know what her brother thought he was doing. Not so long ago she'd cowered in a chimney, stifling her tears. Before that she'd put a pistol to her chin and pulled the trigger. Now the fear for her brother's soul scoured such indulgences away.

Fear and anger too. Anger that he would give himself

to the creatures who had killed their father, killed Lutz, killed everyone they knew.

Renard squeezed her arms again. Sharply. It was entirely inappropriate, but he sensed her mind slipping away. He needed a decision. Not that she owed him anything, given he had given himself to the demons too.

Her eyes moved past Renard to the corpse on the floor.

Well. Perhaps she did owe him something.

"Why could he not find contentment being who he was?"

Renard's grip loosened, "Who among us truly can?"

"My brother chose to stay, for reasons I'll never understand. I choose to leave."

"Good..." Renard stepped back and pulled off the rope still coiled across his chest, when he was free of it, he threw it behind the door, "...but we must be swift."

"Can we still get out of the library window?"

He nodded as he grabbed one of the dead man's feet, "Yes, but we need to deal with the two men guarding the corridor first. Grab his other foot."

Together they dragged the body behind the door, so it was out of sight too.

She wrinkled her nose as she straightened up. Blood stained her hands.

"How do we deal with the others?"

"You make a fuss..." the smile he shot her revealed the bloody stumps of his newly broken teeth, "...I'm sure you know how to do that."

*

He grabbed her arm and dragged her out into the corridor.

Solace screamed and tried to claw his face.

It appeared the art of making a fuss was one Lady Solace was well acquainted with.

One of the guards, he couldn't remember which was Hagan and which was Lohmus, laughed and started down the corridor towards him.

Ulrich shared a similar build to Bekker, the light was poor, and they both wore the Tassau colours. With the dead man's helmet on, he hoped Hagan and Lohmus would mistake him for their captain struggling with their quarry, at least from a distance.

Solace enthusiastically kicked his shin and twisted out of his grasp. He made a grab, her hair, which still shone in the candlelight despite the soot, teased his fingers, then she was gone. Running for the library.

Renard didn't trust they would mistake his voice for Bekker's - he was no Wendel after all - so he signalled for them as he ran after Solace. Another roll of laughter suggested their suspicions had not been raised. Hopefully they wouldn't see Bekker's body when they passed the study, nor wonder where the traitor Ulrich Renard had gotten to.

The world was, of course, full of stupid people.

He chased Solace into the library a few paces behind her. She was staring at the corpses of their companions.

"My lady!" he said, pulling out a pistol and thrusting it at her.

She took it and stepped around the table. His father's

sword lay where Bekker had discarded it on the long reading table.

Ulrich pulled the blade from its sheath and waited behind the door until Hagan - or Lohmus - bundled into the room. The soldier, who was tall and spare, slowed and grinned as he saw Solace apparently cowering behind the table (which shielded her pistol from his view).

"Bekker?" he glanced left for his captain, when he looked right Ulrich slashed at the man's neck. Hagan - or Lohmus - wore a lobster-tail helmet, but the venom in Ulrich's two-handed blow smashed through the plates protecting the soldier's neck and he went down stunned. Ulrich crashed his blade into the man's neck and blood spurted across the floor to mix with Kapsner's.

He dragged the sword clear and span around in expectation of the second Red Cloak. Solace had raised her pistol in case Ulrich hadn't finished with the first by the time he arrived.

The seconds ticked by. They exchanged a glance.

No footsteps pounded down the corridor. Ulrich winced as he pulled a pistol free with his wounded left hand before cautiously peering around the door.

"Shit..." Ulrich slammed his hand against the door.

"What is it?"

"The other one's gone. He either guessed the ruse or was just eager to take the good news to Saul. Every Company has rats like that..."

"So, we must hurry."

He stood by the door and stared at her.

"You know any other good hiding places?"

"We can't. They will be here soon!"

Ulrich pulled out Bekker's sword, dropped it and slipped his father's sabre into the scabbard, "They will know where we've gone and hunt us down. If we leave the rope hanging out of the window, they will search for us outside, and when they don't find us, they will leave."

"There's nowhere else on this floor bar the chimney in the study."

"We can't go there; the floor is awash with Bekker's blood... soot from the chimney too. Somewhere else?"

She turned her attention to the window, "No."

"My lady!"

"We cannot," slowly she turned back to him, her voice steady, but her eyes glistened again, "Torben knows every hiding place in the castle. All the ones I do. They won't fall for such a ruse. Snow covers the ground, when they find no tracks, they will soon deduct we haven't left the castle..."

"And when they see tracks in the snow, they will follow them."

"If we can make the woods..."

No good options remained. He'd burnt the last one when he killed Bekker. If awarded the luxury of time to sit down and think everything through, he'd probably conclude either choice was terrible.

"I'd rather die on my feet in the snow than cowering in a hole," Solace raised her chin, defying him to argue the point. When he didn't, she hurried over to the door, skipping around the bodies of Kapsner and Hagan- or Lohmus - slammed it shut and locked it.

Either choice might be terrible but standing and

arguing with Solace was worse.

"Yes, my lady..." he sighed. Ignoring Dolman's single remaining eye, staring at him with blank accusation, he started pulling the coil of rope free of the dead soldier's corpse.

Chapter Eighteen

It quickly became clear one length of rope wasn't enough.

Renard tied Dolman's rope around the heavy table and then added Kapsner's to it. While he worked, she used the butt of one of Renard's pistols to knock out more of the window - particularly the bits darkened by Karina's blood - she tried not to wonder how skilled Renard was in the art of knot tying.

As the good Lord hadn't let her shoot herself, it seemed unlikely He would allow a weak knot to do the job, although given the night's events trying to understand God's intentions seemed an even more fruitless pursuit than usual.

"You go first," he tugged at the rope until satisfied the knot was strong enough, "don't wait for me at the bottom. Just run for the woods. I'll be behind you."

"Will you?" The words were out before she had time to think about them.

Renard carried the rope to the window, "Why wouldn't

I be?"

"I do not trust you."

He stared pointedly at the corpse of the Devil's rogue, blood pooling dark and slick around his half-severed head.

"If I was going to betray you..."

"I heard you, with the other one. You have not been honest with me."

"I did what I needed to do to stay alive. I haven't sold them my soul..."

Renard's eyes remained on the corpse.

Before she could say anything, or even decide if she wanted to say anything. The sound of running feet echoed down the corridor.

"They're here..." she mouthed.

Renard took the rope and flung it out of the window.

"Go," he drew his sword and turned to face the door as fists started hammering on it.

It was too late. She saw that in his eyes and felt it in her heart.

Perhaps his idea had been better. Solace always thought she would die in The Wolf's Tower, that it would be her home for life. The prospect of living anywhere else always seemed absurd, even after father started looking for an advantageous husband for her. Now she wanted to die with the air on her skin, away from these old stones the demons had transformed from her home to a charnel house in a matter of a few terrible hours.

"Open up!!" a harsh, accented voice demanded.

She grabbed the rope, its rough, hairy sinews scratched her palms.

"Loop it around yourself," Renard did not look up. He was busy collecting pistols off the fallen.

She stared at the broken window, the night's freezing breath caressed her face, tugging at her dishevelled hair.

The door thudded and shook. It was heavy, but nowhere near as thick as the doors that could seal the corridors from the stairs. It wouldn't hold long. Even against men.

Renard lined the pistols up on the table. She dropped the rope and picked one up.

"What are you doing?" Renard demanded.

She might prefer to die with the winter's breath on her face, but what you desired and what life gave you rarely married.

"tis time for us to stand, Ulrich Renard," she whispered above the sound of pounding fists, "'tis time to defend the breach..."

The little colour left in Renard's battered face, beneath the blood and bruises, drained away. She smiled without quite knowing why. The pounding ceased for a moment. Then the door shook hard enough to dislodge dust from its ancient planks. They'd moved from the futility of their fists to shoulder charging it. The door groaned in protest but held. No demons had arrived yet.

Renard swallowed, "You can still get away, my lady..."

She looked behind her at the beckoning window, feeling its breath on her face. When the Reaper came for you, leaning over and reaching for your hand, would his breath be hot or cold...

"They will hunt me down like a dog. If I am going to

die..." she fingered the heavy pistol in her hands "...I desire to take a few more of them with me."

"They do not intend to kill you."

"I know. I heard. They're going to give me to the man who paid them to come here. Do you know who?"

Renard shook his head, "No, my lady, I am not one of them."

"Yet you called them *master.*"

"They spared my life in the village in return for my help..." his eyes flittered away from hers "...I'm sorry, my lady."

"And yet here we are."

"My lady?"

"Standing together at the end."

"We make our choices."

"And I choose to stand."

Renard nodded as the door shook one more time before falling still. They both glanced at the door. The silence was more ominous than the pounding.

"And so do I."

They readied the pistols and waited for the demons to come.

*

"The demons can die..." he said, "...but I think they must die instantly, or they will heal. Aim for the head."

Solace nodded but didn't reply. He glanced at her, half expecting her to be trembling with fear or staring over her shoulder wondering if there was still time to get out of the room. Women, he knew, were prone to change their minds.

Solace, however, was dry-eyed and straight-backed. She looked like someone who had made peace with the prospect of their own death.

He sucked in a breath and willed his hand to stop trembling.

His father would be proud. At least. In the end, when the moment came, he had chosen to stand. He could have forgone honour and lived, in some blighted fashion or another, but perhaps all Old Man's Ulrich's drunken ramblings, recited on a bitter breath of stale ale and regret, had worked after all.

"Who is *Graf* Bulcher?" he asked, as much to fill the silence and still his own thoughts as anything else.

"A vile pig," Solace grimaced, "why?"

"When I asked Cleever who was behind this, he said to ask you about *Graf* Bulcher."

Her frown deepened, "He wanted to marry me... at first he claimed the arrangement was for his son and Father was open to the suggestion, given Bulcher is rich, our circumstances are reduced and the *Graf* seemed prepared to accept a minimal dowry, but I knew it was he that wanted me from the start. When Father found out the truth of it, he refused. Bulcher is old, fat, charmless and cruel, and he sent the *Graf* away with a flea in his ear, Bulcher was not... best... pleased..." Solace's eyes widened "...this is all because-"

The door bulged inwards, the wood screaming and cracking beneath a ferocious blow.

"Aim for the head..." he repeated, raising his pistols towards the door. He would fire both then grab his father's sabre from the table and rush whatever came through the door.

Charge the enemy line, defend the breach against all odds...

The door bulged inwards from another blow, its wooden planks shattering and showering the library with splinters.

Is this what Lutz saw at the end? What went through his head when the demons came for him? Terror? Regret? Defiance? A lifetime of memories surging through the narrow channels of his mind like a spring flood?

Ulrich felt... nothing.

His hands stopped trembling, his back straightened, his eyes narrowed. He would stand. He would die with honour. He would fulfil his oath. That was better, wasn't it? Better than a life racked with guilt and remorse. He would never sit in a tavern and drown his regrets, wishing he'd stayed true to what he believed.

At the end, the very end, that was all that mattered.

They flinched in unison as a final blow sent the door flying inwards, skidding across the room, and smashing into the other side of the table before pirouetting to crash upon the floor.

The corridor outside was empty.

"Whoever comes through that door is going to die. Man or demon!" he bellowed.

The only response was laughter; rich and good-humoured.

Saul the Bloodless.

"Come on in Saul, roll the dice, let's see how fast you

really are... or do you fear death too much to try?"

The laughter faded.

"Ah... the mouse that learned to roar like a lion! You are a fool, Ulrich, a brave fool, but a fool nevertheless..." Saul's voice floated out of the shadows, "...of course, the Devil has always suffered a weakness for brave fools..."

"I guess he'll be able to tell me himself soon."

"Put down your guns."

It was Ulrich's turn to laugh, "Why would I do that? You're going to kill us anyway."

"We were never going to kill Lady Solace. That has not changed."

"So you can give me to Bulcher?" Solace asked.

"You worked that out? Clever girl! Though you weren't supposed to. Bulcher wants to buy you. A ransom. Your gratitude would be so great you would gladly leap into his bed. That was what he hired us for."

"In all the sweep of time, no one has ever been *that* grateful!"

Saul laughed, "What a delight you two are!"

"All these people died just because Bulcher wants... wants to fuck me!"

Ulrich glanced at Solace; the coarse words grated upon her lips. Her eyes bulged and the chords of her neck stood out vividly. She was beyond fury. If Saul came through that door, he doubted he'd even need to fire his guns.

"Oh please. Give the *Graf* some credit. He is an honourable man. He doesn't *just* want to fuck you. He wants you for his wife."

"That is insane."

"Oh, completely. He is quite the lunatic, and, believe me, I know what I'm talking about in that regard. I've met a lot of those in my time. Men's cocks can make them do the most absurd things. Still, it has a certain romance. Helen may have launched a thousand ships; you launched a company of vampires. You should be flattered!"

"Trust me, I am not."

"Of course, it wasn't *only* you. Your father insulted the mad *Graf* most grievously in refusing his offer, not just in substance, but in the manner of his dismissal, in Bulcher's deranged eyes anyway. He will be disappointed not to get his demanding little cock into you, but your father has been dealt with to his satisfaction."

"My father is...?"

"He made the mistake of calling the *Graf* a pig, among other things... quite tactless in my opinion, albeit fairly accurate... so Bulcher wanted him slow roasted like one, with a salted hide, basted in rosemary oil and an apple in his mouth. Apparently 'tis an old family recipe. Cooking isn't my greatest talent, I must confess, but he does smell rather delicious now..."

Solace let out a hiss of air through her clenched teeth. Ulrich thought her legs were going to buckle and for a heartbeat she sagged against him.

"What of Torben?" she managed to ask; her voice carried a calmness not apparent in her blazing eyes.

"Yes, your brother. Now that was all a bit... unexpected."

"Have you murdered him too, you bastard!?"

"No. He has presented us with a dilemma."

"What dilemma?" Ulrich asked before Solace could find the spit to respond.

"He has offered his considerable talents to my Company. In return for you being allowed to leave unharmed."

"No!" Solace screamed, "Let him go!"

"'tis not in my gift. He came willingly, eagerly. The chance to be whole. The chance to be a man. Something your father always wanted. Something your father could never forgive him for not being. 'tis funny how life can turn out. Don't you think?"

"He is a gentle soul, he is harmless, he is not a monster!"

"My lady..." Saul's sigh carried from the shadows, "...we all have a monster within us. The only difference is whether we choose to unchain it or not. Your brother has chosen. And perhaps he is not quite the gentle soul you believe. He offered no bargain for your father's life after all, he seemed content enough to let him burn..."

"Let him go! Let him go and I will do whatever you ask!"

Solace fixed her eyes on someplace between the shadowy doorway and damnation. Ulrich doubted she was even still aware he was at her side.

"To be Bulcher's wife? Go to his bed with a skip and a smile? To sire his brats? To submit to whatever despicable practices his black heart desires? The man who has paid for all this to befall you and yours? All for your brother?"

"Yes!"

"Love, when all is said and done, makes people do

even stranger things than men's cocks."

"I can't live knowing he has become something like you!"

"'tis a tempting offer. Bulcher will pay us a lot of silver for you and silver is always useful. But a man who can see the future... that is worth more than every bean Bulcher owns. And Bulcher owns a lot of beans..."

"Please..."

"Go, Lady Solace, trust me, this is the best offer you are going to get. This or any other night."

Solace lowered her head, the pistols falling to her sides.

"Why should we trust you?" Ulrich demanded.

"Sometimes you just have to show a little faith. Besides... Torben's deal was for his sister. Not you."

Solace lifted her head, "'tis both of us or neither of us."

"Such loyalty! You know he has betrayed both of us tonight. Between you and me, I fear he isn't a man upon whom you can place a great deal of trust. You'd be better leaving him to me. The main course is coming on nicely, but we do need a starter..."

"He comes with me. And I want to see Torben before I leave."

The only response was a faint repetitive tapping noise; fingers drumming against a wall.

"Oh, very well, you can have him. I hope it works out splendidly for the two of you. Your brother, however, isn't available. He's sleeping."

"Then I'll stay here until he wakes up."

"Oh, Lady Solace when he wakes up, Torben won't be

the same man at all. If he had a broken arm, a few drops of our blood would mend it and he would be the same merry soul he was before. But Torben's malady runs far, far deeper, he can only become whole by becoming one of us. A vampire. When you kiss the vein it changes you, you think it won't, that your soul, your essence, your core, call it what you will, is immutable. But it isn't. Once you let the chains run free and the monster is loose... how could you be? Go now. When Torben wakes up he might decide the deal isn't to his liking at all anymore. If I were you, I'd be as far away from this place as you can get before the sun comes up."

"Torben would never hurt me!"

"You remember Wendel, don't you, Ulrich? That talented fellow of many faces. The first thing he did when awoke after kissing my vein was to rape his little sister. Of course, Torben might be different; different monsters like different meat. But take my advice. Go. Your brother, the one you know, is as dead as your father. Just not as well cooked..."

Solace turned her eyes upon him, they were unreadable in the candlelight.

"My lady?" he asked.

Chapter Nineteen

"My lady?" he asked.

Renard's eyes were hooded, the right bruised and half closed. He still held his guns levelled towards the door.

"Do you trust them?"

A crooked half-smile twisted his swollen lips, "No. But they can kill us easily enough without tricking us. Perhaps Saul doesn't want to lose any more men... if we refuse, we *will* die. If we agree... perhaps we live. I suppose it depends on how much we want to live."

How much did she want to live?

Everything was gone. Her life was a ruin, the question was whether it was a ruin she was prepared to live in. What purpose would it serve? Simply to exist? Or let the bitter hope she might one day bring an equal ruin down upon Saul and his demonic Company preserve her? That appeared a distant and forlorn hope, but it was the only thing of worth she could grasp to make taking the hand Saul offered worthwhile.

Lutz had died for her. Torben had sold his soul, in

part, for her. Renard it seemed, in the end, was prepared to die for her. Stand or run? Standing meant death or *Graf* Bulcher's bed, running meant life. If she trusted a demon's word. A demon who had roasted her father like a pig and turned her poor, sweet, broken brother into a monster.

"I..."

The words dried in her throat. The dread stone was gone. The black swelling that had filled her so completely for weeks had dissipated. Not with some calamitous explosion that had ripped her limb from limb, but like a stealthy, tip-toeing thief that had snuck into her chamber, stolen her jewels and stood at the foot of her bed watching her while he decided if there was anything else she owned that he had a fancy for, before slipping away back into the night.

It was over.

Carefully she placed her pistol on the table.

"I accept your terms."

Renard bit his bottom lip, but if he had any further reservations about her decision, he kept them to himself. He lowered his guns, slipping them carefully into his belt rather than laying them down.

He picked up the sword from the table before them and was sliding it into his scabbard when a figure she assumed was Saul appeared in the doorway. He did not look like the embodiment of evil. Tall, good-looking, easy on his feet and with a smile that would be charming if she didn't know better.

Renard shuffled forward and put his shoulder between her and the demon. A pointless gesture, but strangely touching all the same. Saul looked amused.

A sword hung at the demon's waist, but he made no attempt to draw it, instead he entered the library and stood across the table from them, slipping his thumbs into his belt. Other figures followed him, none made any threatening move, but it was Saul who held her eye.

"My, my, you are indeed a pretty one..." Saul's smile grew wider as his eyes slid up and down, "...to think such a delightful looking creature could cause so much trouble. You've led us a merry dance. And if that tunnel hadn't been blocked you might even have slipped away..."

"You knew about the tunnel?"

"Your father was quite talkative before we stuffed the apple in his mouth..."

"Tell me," she asked, straightening her back and folding her arms across her chest as she sucked in air to drown any quiver from her voice, "what would it cost me for you to roast *Graf* Bulcher over a fire?"

"Ah, but if only I could. He is, I am sorry to say, a remarkably unpleasant man, but killing your employer, well, that would be bad for our reputation."

"Perhaps you should take greater care in whose coin you take."

"I do not need to like a man to take his coin. Such is the mercenary's burden."

The others formed a semi-circle behind Saul. One of them was Cleever, a few of the others were red-cloaked soldiers, most were not. Demons like Saul and Cleever she assumed. One improbably tall, bare-chested and encased in tattoos, another curly-haired with a boyish femininity, another a sour, brooding face and cruel eyes. She stopped looking. Saul was the only one that mattered.

"Are you going to honour our deal?"

Saul placed a long-fingered hand over his chest, "You wound me, my lady, like a stake through my heart..."

"Your heart is on the other side."

His grin was full of boyish good humour as he let his hand fall back to his belt, "It has been said I own a wandering heart..."

"You haven't answered my question."

"If I didn't intend to honour our deal, he would be dead," Saul jerked his head in Renard's direction, "and you would be starting your journey towards *Graf* Bulcher's bedchamber. A fate, I can say with some assurance, much worse than death. Your brother is important to me. An hour ago, he wasn't, but now, everything has changed... I will do as he has requested in return for his fealty."

"So... we are free to go?"

Saul offered a shallow bow and a deep smile.

"I do not see you standing aside."

"Given the trouble you have caused us, including the death of a friend I have known for nearly two hundred years, as well as my loyal captain, there is a degree of... ill-feeling amongst the Company. My men usually do what I tell them, but, when the blood is up..."

The tall demon with the bare chest hissed... and then his face changed into something monstrous, devoid of colour, thin as a blade, marbled with throbbing veins. He opened his pallid slash of a mouth to reveal the fangs hiding behind them.

She throttled her fear and held the demon's gaze.

Renard's sword hissed half out of his sheath before Saul raised a hand, "Enough!"

The demon's black eyes shimmered in the shadows before his shoulders relaxed and his face melted back into something human.

Renard eased his sword back into its scabbard.

"As you can see. There is some dissent. So, 'tis better you leave by the most direct route. For your own safety, of course."

"The most direct route?" Renard growled in a fair imitation of Lutz, hand still curled around the hilt of his sword.

Saul smiled fulsomely enough to reveal his bright, but otherwise human, teeth. Then he nodded towards the window...

*

He stood in front of Solace as she undid her tight bodice. The purpose of a noblewoman's clothes was flattery, not climbing out of windows.

"Such a gentleman..." Saul chuckled.

Cleever started flicking through a book, Alms grinned thinly at him while Jarl concentrated on cracking his knuckles. The rest seemed to be hoping Solace would be taking more clothes off.

"You're playing games," he hissed at Saul, who smiled his amiable smile while his liar's eyes lingered on Solace.

"Of course! When you've lived as long as I, you find your amusement where you can."

"That is all this slaughter is to you? Amusement?"

"Rich men hunt and kill dumb animals for their amusement. So do I."

Ulrich's grip tightened on both his sword and his tongue. Anger, it seemed, could usurp even fear.

Saul's infernal smile widened, but Solace forestalled further comment by dropping her bodice to the floor. The petticoats and skirts of her gown would not make the climb any easier, but she'd given the demons as much of a show as she intended.

Ignoring the circled demons, she stepped to his side, "How do we do this?"

He didn't want to do this at all. It had a ripe stink. He didn't trust Saul any further than he could spit into a gale, but they had little choice but hope the demon wasn't playing a game, toying with them like a cat torturing a mouse before it bit the head off.

"As before," he said in a low voice, "you go first. Do not wait for me at the bottom. Just run."

She nodded and the strangest urge to hold her surged through him. He ignored it. It wouldn't be the worst thing that had happened to her this night by a long and bitter league. But she'd suffered enough indignities all the same.

"No need for grand goodbyes, my lady," Saul beamed, "you'll be seeing loyal, faithful Ulrich at the bottom soon enough. One way or another..."

Wendel, who no longer wore Kadelberg's face, laughed. Cleever's eyes shot from the book he held open in his hands. Something akin to distaste flickered along his dark lips.

Solace brushed past him towards the demons. The table still separated them from Saul and his Company. She pressed herself hard against it, hands splayed across the lacquered top.

"Two matters before I take my leave. A request and a promise."

"We are gifting you your life and your liberty, Sweet Little Thing. We are generous enough..." Alms placed his own hands on the other side of the table, mirroring Solace's stance.

Solace ignored him; eyes fixed on Saul. Alms' smile evaporated.

"Firstly, the request. Tell Torben I love him and I always will."

"Love is not what it was after you kiss the vein, my lady..." for once Saul was not smiling and if Ulrich didn't know better, he'd have thought melancholy tinged the demon's words.

"Tell him! You have butchered my father, taken my brother and slaughtered everyone in the world I care about. 'tis not much I ask."

Alms let out a strangled little giggle and looked sideways at Saul, but when the demon nodded the grin faded into a sneer.

"And the promise, my lady?"

"One day I will destroy you and your wretched Company of monsters."

"I've garnered a number of regrets over the centuries," Saul's smile returned, "letting you live will not be one of them. We will leave this place, you will never see us again and I will forget you."

"We shall see..." Solace walked to the window. Her lips quivered only after she turned her back on the demons.

He had looped the rope around two of the table legs and tied a knot where the rope met itself again. The table was a massive beast, he was confident it weighed more than Solace. Whether it would bear his own weight was not his first concern.

"Ever climbed down a wall before?" he asked.

It took a moment for Solace's eyes to focus on him. She shook her head. It was a stupid question. But she'd never killed a demon before tonight either and she'd managed that feat.

He pulled his gloves from his belt and handed them to her. They were too big and stained with blood, but she took them without comment, "Keep a loop of rope around one hand and brace your legs against the wall. Go slowly, ease yourself down only a little at a time. The gloves will protect your hands from a rope burn."

She looked up at him as she pulled on the blood-stained gloves, "Have *you* ever climbed down a wall?"

"'tis easier than it looks."

She stared doubtfully at the window and then her long skirts brushing the floor, "Simply getting out of the window may be the hardest part of the journey..."

She was right. It was an awkward and undignified business, even freed from the constriction of her discarded bodice. It amused the demons no end as she hitched up the folds of her skirts and clambered out of the window, avoiding the remaining glass.

"It still wears far too many clothes," Alms said. They both ignored him. Ulrich felt horribly exposed with his back to a room full of lunatics and murderers, but he concentrated on Solace's eyes as she gripped his forearm, the rope looped around her other hand.

A bitter gust of wind teased her hair as she wriggled backwards out of the window. The clouds parted, the moonlight turning her hair to silver as she stared up at him, lips pressed hard together, beneath the soot and dried blood her cheeks flushed to rose petals at the winter's kiss.

He leaned further out of the window as her feet found the wall and her skirts and long cloak billowed about her. Below, the frozen moat beckoned, the black hole Karina's body had punched through it still visible.

"One step at a time. Do not look down!"

She nodded and her right hand started to slip from his forearm. He loosened his grip in return, he felt the sleeve of her gown slipping away, then the rough leather of the glove he'd given her. For a moment their fingers brushed and then she was gone. The only remaining touch was from the eyes locked with his.

Ignoring the glass biting into his hands he leaned further out and watched her, she moved slowly. She looked scared, but not terrified, beneath the determination etched onto her young, flawless face.

"My lady..." he whispered.

Then he turned back to face the demons.

None had ventured to his side of the table, though Cleever now sat cross-legged upon it, reading his book. The rope vibrated and twanged as Solace made her way down, but the table - heavy even without Cleever's added weight - hadn't budged.

Saul, however, had drawn a dagger.

"It wouldn't take much for you to cut that rope..." the demon's eyes remained on the blade, which he span on its tip.

"And why would I do that?"

Saul raised his eyes, "To prove yourself to me."

"I proved all I needed to when I slit Bekker's throat."

"That proved you have initiative. And loyalty to your oath..." Saul rested his palm against the bottom of the dagger's hilt, "...but if you cut through the ties binding you to your mistress..."

"Why are you so interested in me?"

"You have... *promise*. I lose few men, most wounds we can heal, and I don't select men who aren't skilled warriors for our Company," his eyes shifted to the corpse of the Red Cloak on the floor, "but you have killed a number of my men. You survived the ambush in the village, you were smart enough to stay alive and you escaped to help your mistress when you could. I am impressed. Not an easy feat. You are a warrior, Ulrich. And I have men to replace."

"The Devil knows how to flatter..."

"As I have said before. I am not the Devil. I used to be a man. Like you. Now I am something more. As can you be."

The rope jerked and shuddered. Grew still and then resumed twitching.

"One swift cut is all it requires..."

"You have a deal with Torben."

"I promised to let his sister leave the castle and not pursue her. I will keep that promise. If that rope accidently snaps however..."

Ulrich shook his head, "No..."

"You don't sound so sure? I can offer you such a life, young Ulrich! All you've ever dreamed of. Riches, power, women, respect. And, maybe, one day I might let you kiss my vein too and you will not grow old, you will not weaken, you will not die. Really, 'tis quite the deal."

"And all you'd want in return is my soul?"

"I have no interest in your soul. 'tis your sword I want. Our Company needs men like you. We are in great demand. All the pious lords of Christendom have black deeds in mind and dark desires to sate. The war is a perfect cloak for their ambitions. It is how powerful men are. The Red Company takes their darkness and turns it into bright silver. In times like these, when all else has fallen, the strong will rise...."

Saul's voice was a soft, seductive lullaby. For a moment he imagined doing what Saul asked and sending Solace to her doom. In truth, he hardly knew her.

Riches, power, women, respect...

All the temptations of the world, in return for one small, black deed.

Saul let the dagger fall to the table and then slid it towards Ulrich.

What would Old Man Ulrich have done? Had the weakness in him been so great he would have taken Saul's blade and used it to slice through both the rope and his soul in the same moment? Did the same weakness that fractured his father run through him too? He suspected it did. Lutz had too.

But he'd seen what letting those weaknesses win did to a man.

"If Torben can see the future, you know I never cut that rope..."

"He's not really in a position to elaborate on the details yet. That will change."

"You have nothing I want... even if I was a man bereft of honour."

"A pity..."

Saul's lying eyes remained on Ulrich. He wasn't smiling anymore.

Ulrich inched back towards the window, the rope twitching against his leg. The demons started edging around the table towards him like a pack of starved hounds awaiting their master's command. Apart from Cleever, who still sat on the table, his eyes only following his finger back and forth across the book. He tutted and shook his head at something on the page.

When his back pressed against the window he felt for the rope with his left hand, which was throbbing from Bekker's bite, and curled his fingers around it. He kept his right on his sword's hilt.

A thought struck him.

"How did Torben tell you he could see the future? The boy is mute," when Saul said nothing, he continued, "And he persuaded you very quickly to let his sister go. 'tis unusual to see such eloquence from someone who cannot speak or write?"

"I told you he was clever...." Cleever muttered, not looking up from his book. Alms stopped and stared at Saul.

"His talents weren't *entirely* unknown to me," Saul admitted.

A frown now furrowed Alms' brow. The other demons were looking at their leader with interest too.

"Can you see the future too?" The rope in Ulrich's hand stopped twitching.

"That is a talent I don't possess."

"Then how did you know?"

"Rumours of witchery travel far and fast in these accursed times. Usually, they are the baseless fantasies of fools, but now and then... given his mother's reputation for the sight... it was another reason to take Bulcher's commission."

"You knew their mother?"

Saul's smile returned.

"In truth I have done them a service. If such tales found my ears, they will reach the Churchmen's too. It wouldn't have been long before the witchfinders came with their questions and pyres for Torben and Solace."

"But-"

"That rope has stopped moving. Lady Solace must have reached the bottom. Time for you to take your leave too. I wouldn't linger, all that broken glass around the window, it could easily have frayed the rope."

Ulrich didn't know what games Saul played, he suspected from the looks on some of the other demons' faces they didn't know either.

"You can take my life, you can take everything I have

and everything I might become," he dressed his fear in a smile and hoped it shone as brightly as the demon's own, "but the one thing that can't be taken from a man is his honour, he can only give that away..." Ulrich grabbed the rope and swung out of the window, "...and I choose not to give you mine..."

The rope burned his fingers and pain lanced up his arm from his wounded left hand. He ignored it as he ignored the winter ripping into his flesh. The old stones of The Wolf's Tower flashed by him as he discounted every word of advice he'd given Solace. He wrapped the rope around his forearms and slid downwards, his feet found the rope too and he pressed his heels into it.

From somewhere above he fancied he heard a hissing scream of rage, but that might just have been the sound of the rope catching against the coarse linen of his jerkin and the wind ripping into his billowing cloak.

He tried to look down to see how much further there was to go, but the motion twisted his body one way and then the next and all he saw was the faintest flush of light to the east.

Then the rope went slack and he was falling.

Chapter Twenty

Renard's voice stayed with her all the way to the bottom.

She didn't look down. She went slowly. She kept her feet planted against the wall. She kept calm. She listened to his voice and imagined him at her side.

The wind was light, but it clawed at her skin all the same. Her hands became slick with sweat inside the blood-stained gloves her fingers could not find the ends of. She eased the rope through them a little at a time and ignored her protesting arms.

She kept glancing up hoping to see Renard emerge from the window, but there was nought but scudding dark clouds interspersed with a scattering of stars soaring above The Wolf's Tower.

Was he waiting for her to reach the bottom? Defending the rope from the demons? As if his one sword was enough to fight them off if they decided not to honour Torben's deal after all.

The thought of her brother cut her deeper than the

bitter air whistling around her ears.

She paused, squeezed her eyes shut and tried to feel nothing but the wind tugging at her clothes. Perhaps she should just let go. What was the best she could hope for if she made it to the bottom? Her father slaughtered, her brother had given himself to monsters, her home in ruins, everyone she knew dead. What kind of life would she have left? Death would be kinder.

One day I will destroy you and your wretched Company of monsters...

Her defiant words swirled around her, a whistle on the wind. And then another voice, growling out of the darkness.

...this isn't that kind of a tale...

Lutz had been right. She was never going to defeat Saul's bloody company here, not this night. But she'd hurt them all the same. She'd killed a demon and a score of Saul's rogues too. Not a mortal wound, but more than a scratch. A lot more.

She couldn't guess Torben's motivations and didn't know how much of the future he saw behind his strange, motionless eyes, but she prayed it had been more than a simple desire to be like other men. That he had done it to keep her alive because it was the only way they might avenge their father. To live, by whatever means, to fight another day. That's what Renard had done, after all. Lived to fight.

God had spared her when she'd tried to take her own life in a moment of bleak despair. There had to be a reason for that. A purpose, a purpose she could not thwart by releasing the rope and plunging to her death.

This was not that kind of a tale, but if she lived to see the dawn already tentatively flushing the eastern sky with the first kiss of a new day, then she would have other tales to tell.

Solace opened her eyes and resumed her descent, moving the rope quicker through her hands, feet pushing off the cold, lichen flecked stones of The Wolf's Tower.

She kept her eyes fixed on the window above, but there was still no sign of Renard.

"Come, Ulrich, now..." She needed him, she realised. A man who had helped the demons, but in the end had saved her. Her tale would be all the harder without him.

She hit the ground with a surprised thud, her backside dumped into the snow. She let out a shuddering breath, gathered up her skirts and scrambled to her feet.

Turning around she expected to find some grinning demon bearing his fangs, but there was no one bar Karina, face down and half-submerged beneath the shattered ice. The only thing biting her was the wind teasing ripples of dusty snow back and forth across the frozen moat.

A narrow strip of ground, little more than two paces wide separated the castle wall from the frozen moat. Beyond was the snow-covered pasture and then the dark line of the woods.

The lowering moon starkly lit the towering bulk of the old castle, she placed a hand against the stonework and leant against it, exhausted.

"Please Lord, by your grace, do not take him from me too. I cannot do what you ask of me alone... I cannot..."

Still no one came.

He'd told her not to wait, to cross the moat and run for the woods as soon as she was down, but her legs wouldn't move. What if he didn't come? Or they tossed his corpse out of the window like poor snivelling Karina? Then what?

Before she could answer that question a figure emerged above her, cloak flowing around him as he began sliding down the rope.

He was going too fast!

She put her hands to her mouth, convinced he must fall. Rather than her own careful descent with feet braced against the wall, Renard wound the rope through the arms he clutched to his chest and around his ankles and was letting it run through his grasp.

She was on the verge of shouting at him to slow down when a second figure appeared at the window, leaning out to watch. She edged to the left for a better view and cried out as she saw the figure, who had to be Saul, bright in the moonlight, start cutting the rope with a dagger.

Renard began twisting from side to side, losing control. He was nearly halfway down, she wanted to shout, to tell him to hurry, that the demon was cutting the rope, but her voice deserted her. Instead, she scurried back a few more paces.

There was snow on the ground, but it was old and icy, crunching beneath her feet, if he fell it wasn't going to soften his landing much.

Renard got his descent back under control but almost as soon as he did the rope parted and he was falling. Her hands pressed against her mouth, tainting the sharp, frigid air in her nostrils with scents of leather and blood.

His arms flayed as he fell but there was no scream, he twisted in mid-air and hit the ground shoulder first with a crunch. Now he screamed. He half bounced, half rolled down the shallow slope and slid into the moat, plunging into the hole Karina had made.

Solace threw herself forward, reaching for him, for a moment she locked with pale blue eyes staring wildly from a face ashen beneath its blooming bruises. Then his head slipped below the water.

"No!!!" she cried, lunging for his flailing hand, their fingers snagged, and she managed to grip his wrist with one hand and then the other. She tugged as hard as she could. Even without his cuirass, sword and nailed boots he weighed twice as much as her.

She screamed again, trying to wrench him back, fighting against the weight trying to drag her into the moat too. Karina's corpse, disturbed by Renard's thrashing, floated further under the edge of the ice.

Renard's head reappeared - at least he'd lost his helm - gasping for breath.

"Use your other hand!" she shouted, feeling herself sliding towards the rim of broken ice, Renard's only response was an incoherent cry of terror. Of course, he couldn't, he'd landed on his left shoulder, it must be broken.

She ground her teeth together and tried to both pull him out and lever herself onto her knees. That was when the gloves Renard had given her slid from her hands and the young soldier splashed back under the water.

She only just managed to stop herself sliding in after

him. Renard's hand still reached for hers out of the water but less and less of his arm remained visible. His armour was dragging him down.

"Don't you dare drown!" she screamed.

She grabbed the severed rope that had fallen with Renard and threw it towards his submerging hand. It missed.

"Grab the rope, Ulrich, please!"

She threw it again; it snagged his fingers but slipped from his grasp. She leant out as far as she dared and threw it once more. This time Renard's hand closed around it. She scrambled to her feet, coiled the rope around her, leant back and hauled with all her strength. Renard looped the rope around his wrist and pulled back.

Her feet slid and she dug her heels into the snow. She thought she was screaming but couldn't be sure. The weight of the soldier dragged her towards the black water while the rope dug into her waist. She leaned and pulled hard enough to stagger backwards. Renard's head erupted out of the water.

Even in the silver moonlight he looked blue.

She tried to take another step but ended up on her backside. Her feet found the ground and she pushed herself back, shuffling across the snow until her spine pressed against the castle wall. Renard threw his good arm out over the bank and lay panting, face down in the snow.

"You have to get out of the water," she sobbed.

At first, he didn't respond, then he levered himself upwards, found some purchase with his feet and managed to haul himself out of the moat.

After discarding the rope, she crawled across the snow on all fours to him. He'd rolled onto his back and was staring at the sky, great shuddering breaths racking him as steam twisted from his body.

"Move," she commanded.

"Can't..." he shivered.

"Stay there and you die. And I will *not* allow that."

He swallowed, then coughed a cloud of breath into her face, "Yes... my lady..."

With his face disfigured by pain he pulled himself to his feet, one arm clinging to her, the other hanging limp and useless by his side. He was shivering and every movement contorted his features.

They shuffled along the edge of the moat, away from the hole Karina's body had made. Carefully she unbuckled his heavy cuirass and let it fall to the snow, but he wouldn't allow her to take his sword.

"We must reduce your weight, else the ice might break," she told him.

"Not the sword," he said through chattering teeth, allowing her only to pull the pistols from his belt and drop them.

"You... first..."

She didn't care to leave him, but they could not cross together, and he would not hear of going first.

She tied the rope around her waist and the other end around him. If the ice broke, she doubted he had the strength to save her, but, again, he insisted.

"The ice will not break," she said.

He nodded but she wasn't sure he heard her.

She hauled up her skirts and petticoats, put her knees on the ice and then her hands and crawled across as fast as she dared. The ice groaned under her weight; beneath the snow it was perilously thin. If she brushed away the covering, she fancied she might see Karina's dead eyes staring up at her.

Silver and jewellery weighed her heavy winter cloak, all she'd been able to grab from their chambers before descending the shaft. She should throw it aside, but it was all she had left. And she would need it. Destroying Saul and his foul Company would not be a pauper's task.

The ice creaked and complained as she crawled. Several times she heard it crack but she made it across and scrambled up the far bank. She rolled over and climbed to her feet on the far side.

Renard was still on his feet but swaying from side to side like a sapling in a stiff breeze.

Above him The Wolf's Tower rose out of the snow, the stars around its battlements fading as the eastern sky became a smear of dark blue. A few tendrils of black smoke curled up from the Barbican on the far side of the castle She scanned the windows. No one was in sight, but she felt eyes upon them all the same.

"Walk further!" she cried, "I've weakened the ice here!"

Renard made no response, but managed to shuffle along the bank, dragging the rope binding them over the snow.

They'd almost reached the corner of the castle when he stumbled to a stop. She looked over her shoulder towards the treeline, the birch trees bone-white against the shadows. Even if he managed to walk that far he still needed shelter and warmth. An old hunting lodge lay in those woods, her father had taken her to it a few times when he'd been more interested in riding with his daughter than killing things. Could she find it?

She shook the thought away. One obstacle at a time. If the ice broke it wouldn't matter, rope or not, she didn't think either of them were strong enough to haul him out of the icy water a second time.

"Here!" she shouted.

Renard stood on the edge of the moat swaying gently, staring at the ice like she was asking him to swim across an ocean. He dropped the rope and stepped out of it. She wanted to tell him to keep it, but if the ice broke the water beneath was deep and he would just drag her back into the moat. Then he stepped forward on to the ice.

"Crawl!" she shouted, "you must crawl!"

Renard shook his head and took another step. His left shoulder drooped and he cradled the limp arm with his right hand. He couldn't crawl, not with his ruined arm, he'd be dragging it along the ground.

She swallowed and prayed. As the wounded man shuffled forward, his boots cut drag marks through the snow. Should he walk fast or slow? What would be safer? She didn't know.

Renard hung his head, but his eyes remained upon her as he took one precarious step after another, following the discarded rope as he approached the middle of the frozen moat. Would the ice be thicker at the centre or the edges? Something else she didn't know. How many winters had she lived here? That was a more straightforward question, but she'd never once noticed where the ice was thickest.

She thought of Torben again. It was just one of the many things she hadn't noticed...

Renard was slowing. Head still lowered, eyes still on her. The only sound to reach her ears was the mournful wail of the ice protesting its burden. The only disturbance visible was Renard's footsteps in the thin, crusty covering of snow, whatever was happening below remained hidden from her eyes.

But not her ears.

A crack rang out and her heart skipped a beat, expecting the ice to part and the dark water to swallow Renard. The young soldier stopped, steam curling off his body, wet hair plastered about his battered face.

He shuffled forward again. His expression suggesting each step hurt him a lot more than it hurt the ice. Another crack. Followed by a pained groan. He was over halfway across now. She moved forward to the very edge of the ice as if closing the distance between them might aid his crossing.

"Pick up the rope! I can pull you out if you fall through!"

The slightest shake of the head. His eyes remained on her, his face contorted with pain and effort. He dragged his feet further across the snow, then winced and stopped.

"I can feel... the ice... moving..." he was close enough now that he didn't need to shout.

"Please... take the rope!"

His head dropped to the rope as if seeing it for the first time, "If the ice breaks... I am dead... too weak..."

"Then move your wretched feet and get off it before it breaks!"

He conjured a smile through his pain and found the strength to take another step, "Anger suits you well... my lady..."

Then the ice shattered, and he fell into the black waters below.

Epilogue

Nine Months Later

"I knew you would come. I dreamed of you again last night..."

The woman regarded her; the dancing firelight reflected in the black mirrors of her eyes.

"Do you know who I am?"

"You are the rider on the black horse... you are the night's breath... you are vengeance..."

"Vengeance..." the dark-haired woman muttered, the thinnest and bitterest of smiles dusted her lips. Slowly she shook her head.

Solace huddled by the fire on the best chair she had left, the autumn was fading into winter and its cold fingers seeped deep into the ruins of The Wolf's Tower this late into the night. She reached down and tossed a log on the fire, orange sparks shot upwards as it ignited instantly. She threw in another.

Wood she had plenty of; everything else was in short

supply.

The woman sat further back from the flames, eyes narrowing as the fire brightened greedily around the fresh wood. She sat cross-legged on the floor, hands resting on her knees. She dressed like a man. Britches, riding boots and a simple cotton shirt beneath her hooded cloak. Her hair was dark and wild. She was beautiful.

She was a demon.

She'd ridden out of the shadowy woods a couple of hours after sunset upon a huge black stallion. Solace waited for her beneath the cracked, fire-blackened arch of the ruined Outer Gate, as she had every night for the last month, ever since her dreams started foretelling the stranger's coming.

"You've come for Saul the Bloodless, haven't you?" Solace asked after the hooded rider dismounted and carefully crossed the remnants of the drawbridge.

The stranger nodded.

Solace held out her arms to either side, palms turned upwards and looked over her shoulder at the ruin of her home.

"You are too late..."

*

Solace run a grubby hand through what remained of her hair. She'd hacked off her long silver-blonde locks months ago. Like the stranger, she dressed like a man now. She just didn't do it half so well.

The woman said little while listening to her tale, but Solace knew why she'd come here. She was following the bastard. Her dreams hadn't told her everything, they never did, but they whispered that much.

It was a pity they hadn't told her more about Saul beforehand, maybe her life wouldn't be as ruined as the crumbling castle around her if they had, perhaps it would have made no difference. But in the months following the fall of The Wolf's Tower, her dreams had grown stronger and louder, perhaps that was what the *sight* demanded in order to reveal the future more clearly. Fire and blood.

"Why are you looking for Saul?" Solace asked.

"I intend to kill him."

She smiled, "I hoped you were going to say that. My dreams whispered of vengeance. I want vengeance too."

The woman shifted on the floor and tilted her head slightly, "I do not seek vengeance."

"Then why do you want to kill him? What other reason could you have?"

"Atonement..." the woman said. The firelight danced across her face. No expression followed.

Her dreams hadn't mentioned that.

"Vengeance is more straightforward."

"Vengeance will never bring you peace. Do not pursue him. Take what remains of your life and live it the best that you can. Even if you do manage to kill Saul you will find no peace. That is the nature of vengeance, my lady. One death is never enough.

"You think it will heal you, but it won't, it will leave you empty and the only way to fill that emptiness will be more killing. Kill the rest of the Red Company's vampires and then you will want to kill all the soldiers, kill all the soldiers and you'll want to kill other vampires, other soldiers, their sons and brothers, wives and daughters. Vengeance is a dark god that can never be sated."

"tis better than sitting here surrounded by nought but rubble and ghosts."

"Trust me, Solace, if you stare into the darkness long enough you allow that darkness to creep into your soul..." the demon leaned forward a little, her eyes, which sparkled like black diamonds, bore into her, "Your desire to destroy this monster will consume you and burn away who you are. You will cross any bridge, break any taboo, do whatever you deem necessary to find your vengeance, to feed your rapacious god, until, one bitter day, you find *you* have become the monster..."

"I am not sure there is anything left of me to burn away..."

The demon didn't reply.

Solace listened to the fire instead. Sometimes, in the darkest, quietest hours, she fancied the echo of her father's screams rolled beneath the hiss and crack of the flames. It was probably better to be cold, but she always piled on the logs so she might hear better. The flames didn't just heat her body and cooked what little food she had; they stoked her hatred of Saul the Bloodless too.

"Why are you not like them?" Solace asked when the crackle of the fire became too much to bear.

"How do you know I am not?"

"My dreams tell me I can trust you. I listen to my dreams more closely these days, besides, if you were, I would be dead on the floor by now. Or worse."

The stranger regarded her. Solace thought she was going to ignore her question until she spoke a single word. It was not a word she'd had much cause to think about lately.

"Love..."

"How?"

The demon straightened her back, "I came here to find answers, not give them."

Solace leant back and stared at the shadowy ceiling. The room was one of the few in the castle still to have one, "My family have lived here for five hundred years, give or take. You will be the last guest we will ever entertain in The Wolf's Tower. After we leave it shall crumble away in the company of rats and shadows. So, humour me with a tale this dark night in return for the final hospitality of the von Tassaus..."

"It is too long a tale for one night and each night I linger is another night I am further from atoning for my sins."

Solace leant forward, eyes unwavering, "Tell me..."

The demon's eyes slid away to stare into the shadows, "Once, a long time ago, I wasn't so very different from how Saul is today... vengeance took me from the person I was when I walked in the sunlight and it made me a monster... I was lost... I was an abomination that existed only to bring death and suffering. Love was the light in that darkness for me, a beacon that brought me home from furious seas..."

"What happened?"

"A good man saved me from myself. He died a long time ago. I loved another good man, many years later. My love for him created the monster that did this..." she cast a hand around the room that stank of smoke and damp decay "...love can redeem, love can destroy, that is what I have learned. We things of the night fool ourselves... what we feel... what I felt... was not love, just its echo. It saved me. It destroyed me... There is no more of it in me now. The echo has faded to silence. I will have no more of the love of monsters than I will of vengeance."

Her dark eyes returned to Solace, "That is all I have to say."

"I would know more of you?"

The demon jumped to her feet, cloak flapping back to briefly reveal the sheathed short sword tied to her left leg, "You said Saul headed north when he finished here. I will head north. That is all you need to know of me."

"What is your name?" she asked as the woman drew her cloak about her.

The demon's face was expressionless as she looked down at her, "Morlaine," she said after a long pause.

"I will come with you."

Morlaine's expression didn't alter, she just shook her head, "No. My road is walked alone."

"I-"

"Solace..." the demon crouched in front of her, easy on her haunches, she appeared to be only a few years older than her, if you didn't look too deeply into the demon's eyes, "...I cannot see the future. But I travel the Night's Road and I know it will lead anyone else who follows it to their deaths."

"I cannot stay here, I have lost everything, everyone..."

Her eyes flicked to the room's shattered door as it creaked open; a hunched figure shuffled in from the shadows.

Almost everyone...

*

Both the women in the room terrified him.

He'd made an excuse about finding some wine for their guest. The stranger said she didn't want any, Solace said they didn't have any. He'd gone to look regardless.

The dark-haired woman scared him because she was a demon. She drunk blood and slunk in the shadows, like Saul, Alms, Cleever and the rest of that dark Company. She didn't appear insane, but an intensity haunted everything she did. Every action considered, every word weighed. She listened to their story without expression and yet he sensed a taut, restless energy building within her. He doubted she'd allow anything or anyone to stand in the way of her finding Saul the Bloodless.

He'd thought Solace beautiful once, but the demon would have taken his breath away if he hadn't already been breathless with terror at the sight of her.

Solace scared him because she wanted to pursue Saul's Company. She wanted to kill the demon and save her brother. That was all that occupied her mind now and it had only been his slow convalescence that had kept them here. Soon it would be winter again and that would bind them to the broken shell of The Wolf's Tower until the spring.

She'd saved his life; nursed him, cared for him, kept

him alive when all he wanted to do was slide into the comforting oblivion of death. He was both honour-bound and oath-bound to her. Now he was in her debt too. Wherever she went, he was bound to follow, even to the last place on earth he wanted to go. Which happened to be wherever Saul the Bloodless was.

He didn't want to pursue demons. He didn't want to live in the crumbling ruins of The Wolf's Tower either, but he would take the life he shared with Solace here over trying to find those wretched creatures. If they ever did, they would not survive a second time. Not in mind, body or soul.

"I found a bottle!" he declared. Neither Solace nor the demon pulled their eyes away from each other.

He'd come across the wine months ago, sitting alone in a cobwebbed corner of the cellars. Saul's Company had stripped the castle of anything of worth they could carry; they'd tried to destroy everything else, but a few things had escaped them.

"Our guest, Morlaine, is leaving..." Solace said of the demon standing over her, "...we are going with her."

The demon's eyes followed him as he shuffled across the room. Her gaze felt like cold spiders scurrying across his skin. He eased himself into the lesser of the two chairs Solace still owned and placed the wine on the floor between his feet. He didn't trust himself to open the bottle. His good hand trembled too much.

The creature's eyes crawled back to Solace, "No, you are not."

Solace rose slowly to her own feet, she was shorter

than the demon, fair where the demon was dark. They both looked like monsters, framed by the glow of the firelight and the single candle burning on the scorched table.

Beautiful monsters, but monsters all the same.

"'tis not just vengeance. I want to save Torben."

"Your brother is beyond salvation now. If he still lives, he is not the man you once loved. Grieve. There is nothing else of worth you can do for him."

"Could they do what he hoped? Fix him?" Solace asked.

"Our blood can cure physical ailments, disease, injury, even ageing, to a degree, but conditions of the mind..." she shrugged, "...the only way to be sure of curing him of such afflictions would be to make him a vampire too. But that is fraught with danger, most do not survive the rebirth. You should hope your brother did not."

"And if he lives, Saul will have a man who can see the future."

"No," Morlaine shook her head "he will have a monster who can see the future. That is much worse."

"My brother is a kind and gentle soul; he could never become... like them..."

Morlaine pursed her lips, "Saul was a kind and gentle man once..."

Solace snorted and looked away. Her eyes fell on him, and he tried to shrink back into the shadows.

"Could your blood heal him?"

The demon's eyes followed Solace's, "Yes."

"I don't need to be fixed!" he cried, aghast at the suggestion.

"A one-armed swordsman is not much use to me."

"My sword arm is good," he insisted, cradling his withered left arm and flexing the numb fingers that no longer gripped properly. A jolt of pain lanced down his arm. He tried hard not to wince.

"Make him whole again," Solace said to the demon, the matter settled.

"Only if he wishes it."

"I do not want your cursed blood inside me!" he sprang to his feet, knees nearly buckling. He grabbed the chair with his good hand to stop himself falling.

"I will take that as a no," Morlaine turned for the door.

"We *are* coming with you," Solace's lips curled into a snarl, her eyes narrowing. There was something feral about his mistress now, like a cat that had gone back to the wild.

The demon shook her head again.

"You can't stop us following you..."

Morlaine looked more than capable of stopping them. He slumped back into the chair and stared into the fire. It would have been better if he'd died. He hated feeling weak, hated it so much part of him wanted to take the demon's blood if it meant being whole again.

Then he reminded himself of the horrors the demons had wrought here. The things that lay beneath the rubble of the Great Hall. Those small, shattered bones. He shuddered, no, some things were worse than being weak. Worse than being broken. If only Torben had known that...

He closed his eyes and listened to the fire rather than the monsters' voices. A log cracked and spat. The sound an echo of the one the ice had made when it collapsed under his feet.

He'd expected to die.

Plunging into the frozen moat for a second time. The black water rushing up to consume him. The water reached his chest before his boots plunged into the sticky goo on the bottom.

The moat, centuries old, had silted up, in that spot at least. It had been much deeper beneath the walls where he'd gone in the first time, but there, whether by age or design, he could keep his head above water. His left shoulder and arm were shattered and he was numb with cold, but he'd managed to draw his father's sabre and hack through the ice towards Solace. He'd expected each step to be his last, through exhaustion or the bottom disappearing beneath his feet.

He retained only a hazy recollection of reaching the bank. Another agony crawling out of the water, Solace hauling him up by the collar, his broken arm screaming in protest. He'd blacked out, but Solace slapped his face and made him stand.

"We shall not die today! God has saved us both! He has plans for us!!" she'd said. Over and over again as they stumbled through the snow, the brooding presence of The Wolf's Tower, wrapped in a thin shroud of smoke, receding behind them with every faltering step.

He'd only the vaguest memory of that walk. Solace could not have carried him, but how he stayed upright he'd no idea. Good arm slung around his mistress' shoulders, her arm around his waist. He remembered nothing else save Solace's mantra, repeated over and over in his ear in hoarse, harsh pants as they ploughed through the snow.

We shall not die today! God has saved us both! He has plans for us!!

When he lay awake, alone in the night, he still heard those words when he closed his eyes and held his breath. Either her words or the screams of the ghosts echoing around the broken castle. He'd never been able to decide which frightened him the most.

He couldn't remember making it across the pasture or entering the woods or stumbling through them. He had no memory of reaching the *Freiherr's* hunting lodge at all.

He just remembered the cold. Burning with it, numb with it, weighed down by it. His flesh cut to ribbons by it.

The first thing he recalled with certainty was waking up in a narrow bed piled with coarse blankets, Solace curled next to him asleep. Both of them naked. It was the sort of thing a man would remember, he supposed.

Sometimes when he couldn't sleep, which was often, he would think about her naked body and imagine it was close to him again. He had been weak and racked with pain, but the caress of her skin, the softness of her hair splayed over him, her gentle breathing next to him.

It was the last beautiful moment of his life.

The lodge was small, a wooden cabin where the *Freiherr* took guests to kill things, drink, sit around a fire and talk of manly concerns. It had been emptied for the winter; no provisions, no wood, no clothes, no weapons. Just a few musty old blankets.

Solace had stripped him of his wet, freezing clothes and piled the blankets on him. She hadn't been able to light a fire and when he'd continued to shiver uncontrollably, she'd done the only thing she could think of to keep them both warm. Strip off her own clothes and curl around him so they might find warmth from each other's bodies.

That was probably the second time she'd saved his life. The third was when the fever struck. He didn't know if it was a result of the cold, the filthy water of the moat, his broken arm or Bekker's bite. Wherever it had come from it had all but killed him.

He remembered hot feverish dreams, he remembered ranting incoherently. He remembered sweating and freezing by degrees. Solace had kept him warm and made him drink water from snow melted after she'd collected wood and eventually started a fire.

They had no means to hunt for food even if Solace had known how to track and kill deer or boar in the woods. After three days his fever broke, but with no food and winter still gripping the land he faced starving to death instead.

On the morning of the fifth day Solace declared she was returning to The Wolf's Tower in search of food.

He'd tried to stop her, but barely had the strength to speak. His arm sent spasms of pain through his body and violet lights flashing behind his eyes.

She was gone for most of the day, returning at dusk with a sack of things scavenged from the castle and village. When he'd asked what had happened, she had said only that the demons were gone, their tracks heading north through the snow. Her face had been ashen as she emptied the meagre supplies on to the floor.

It had been a month before he'd been able to venture out of the lodge. The first spring flowers were emerging by the time he was strong enough to return to The Wolf's Tower. All the time Solace talked of killing Saul and rescuing Torben. And little else.

We shall not die today! God has saved us both! He has plans for us!!

The Wolf's Tower had been a blackened shell. Not only torched, but, in places, filled with gunpowder and blown apart. The Great Hall had collapsed and was nought but rubble. He thought of the women and children Saul had brought from the village and wondered what horrors laid buried within.

Solace had wanted to find her father's body so it could join their ancestors in the crypt. When he tried to look, he found things in the rubble. Things that had once been children. Parts of them at least. He hadn't told Solace; he'd just said it was too dangerous. The gunpowder had loosened the walls and digging through the rubble would likely bury them too. She'd believed him.

Occasionally, screams or sobbing echoed around the broken castle at night, sometimes it was Solace in the next room, tortured by her nightmares. Sometimes it wasn't and he pushed his hands against his ears, especially when the crying sounded like children.

The children they'd done nothing to try and save.

Outside the castle walls pyres had burned; greasy ash still darkened the soil. The demons had been as thorough in covering their tracks as they had in laying waste to the castle. The village had fared no better, every building torched, every corpse burned.

A few of the rooms in the servant's quarters still had glass in their narrow windows and they had taken shelter there, scavenging what they could. Solace found a couple of chickens in the ruined village and they planted seeds. When he recovered enough, he'd shown her how to snare rabbits in the woods and take fish from nearby ponds well stocked with trout for the castle.

The plan had been to stay until he was strong enough for them to begin their pursuit of Saul and Torben. His arm was never going to mend, it had set badly and the muscle wasted from the bone. His fingers were numb and clumsy. He was still weak and doubted he'd ever be as strong as he once was. He'd developed a shuffle and a slight stoop. He was no longer sure whether they were real or affectations to convince Solace he wasn't strong enough to pursue Saul. And he never would be.

Then Solace started dreaming of a demon who would help them and talk of leaving abated. Each night she awaited the demon's arrival in the lee of the Outer Gate and each night she'd returned alone.

He'd begun to hope she was wrong and no demon would ever come to drag them away from the relative safety of The Wolf's Tower. Perhaps she couldn't see the future at all. Perhaps only Torben had that gift.

Then this beautiful monster rode out of the night, and he knew the madness would start anew.

*

"You can't stop us following you..."

Renard slumped back into his chair as if to suggest he couldn't follow anyone, anywhere.

"You wouldn't be able to follow me for long; I have a horse, you don't, I am strong, you two aren't. I doubt you'd last a day travelling across this blighted land. You are safer staying here."

"I'll be able to find you wherever you go," she raised her chin and took a step towards the demon, "I possess the *sight*, remember. I knew you were coming here; I know where you're going next."

Nothing so obvious flickered over Morlaine's expressionless face, but for the first time Solace sensed uncertainty.

"I can help you find Saul. It will be much easier if we work together."

"I travel the Night's Road alone..."

Solace smiled, "My brother is with Saul. He will see you coming. You'll be dead before you get anywhere near Saul."

"And your brother won't see *you* coming?"

"He will, but he won't tell Saul. He'll know I'm coming to save him."

Morlaine's dark eyes fixed on her, unblinking, unwavering, "Tell me where I am going next?"

"To find a man who loves songbirds too much."

"Where is Saul now?"

"I don't know," Solace admitted, "but my dreams will tell me when we pick up his trail."

The demon looked at her for a long time. Behind her dark eyes, wheels turned, eventually she said, "You can accompany me as far as the next city, you will be safer than in open country, as you will see when we travel."

They'd seen so few people since the attack she'd started to wonder whether Saul and his Company had emptied the world of souls. She supposed another season of war would have taken one more step toward that goal without the demon's aid.

She had no intention of staying in any city, but it would get them out of the ruined castle and give her a chance to prove her worth to the demon.

"Be ready to travel in thirty minutes," Morlaine nodded at them both and left the room without another word.

Renard sat slumped by the fire, hollow-cheeked and weary-eyed. He was unrecognisable from the handsome young man of the previous winter. He had shrivelled and aged like soft fruit left in the sun, his withered left arm was next to useless, any physical exertion exhausted him quickly and he trembled and quivered like a mouse hiding from a cat.

In dark moments, she wondered if it would have been better if he'd disappeared under the ice.

But no. God had saved them both for a purpose; that purpose was destroying Saul and saving Torben.

"We're leaving, get your things together."

"I have no things. Neither do you..."

"Ulrich, this is what we've been waiting for!"

Sad, tired eyes peered up at her from between puffy lids, "Yes, my lady..."

He wanted to say more, she knew. It didn't matter. Nothing mattered bar finding Saul and saving Torben.

Nothing.

She turned and hurried out of the room.

*

For a while Ulrich sat and stared at the fire.

Somewhere in the ruined castle a child wailed, begging him to help. He listened until the child stopped. They always stopped in the end. Usually abruptly.

He asked Solace about the ghosts once; she'd shaken her head and claimed to have heard nothing. Just the wind playing tricks, she said. Perhaps she was right. Or perhaps her curse was to see the future while his was to hear the past. Hear the cries and the pleas of the dead, hear their anguish and deaths over and over again. Hearing them asking why he'd run away and left them to the monsters.

Was that what honourable men did?

Save her and you save yourself.

Lutz had told him that and, in the end, he'd believed him. He raised his withered left arm, he had to prop it with his right to keep it there. He stared at the skeletal fingers. Now and then they twitched like bare twigs in a midwinter gale.

Would he have been more broken if he'd taken Saul's dagger and cut the rope? He would be free of her now, free of this place, free of the broken body he now endured, free of the ghosts of children.

He doubted anything haunted Saul's monsters.

They never found Lutz's body. The old man's corpse had no doubt burned with most of the others in the pyres the demons built in the pasture. He was at peace. Ulrich often tried to imagine what being at peace felt like. He never managed it.

There was no peace for him. In this world at least. He had tied himself to Solace and they would both slide into madness together. He didn't know if he loved her or hated her. He just knew he would never be free of her.

He sniffed, rubbed his good hand over his eyes, then hauled himself to his feet. He made sure he wiped all the tears from his sunken cheeks, before stepping out of the light and hobbling into the darkness after Solace.

Author's Note

I've never been one of those writers who meticulously plans everything out in advance, the kind who always know exactly what's lurking around the dimly lit corner or behind the next locked door. The characters usually come out of the darkness and let me know. I just tag along and tell their story.

Unusually, when I sat down to write *Red Company,* I quickly developed a very clear idea of how it was going to end, I even wrote the final paragraph with only a couple of chapters in the bag. This seemed quite liberating. No groping around in the dark, no waiting for the characters to tell me what was going to happen, I was going to be the boss for once!

I worked for months towards that ending and it was a good one, I thought, poignant and gut-wrenching. And there would be no possibility of continuing the story, *In the Company of Shadows* was supposed to be a collection of standalone stories and short ones at that. Job done.

The short story *Red Company* started out as eventually grew into a full novel, then, a couple of chapters out from the finish line, Solace, Ulrich and Torben had other ideas, they didn't seem so keen on my ending after all. They wanted to do something different. So that final paragraph, which had been waiting so patiently at the end for the rest of the story to catch up to it, got deleted and something else was born.

I'm not going to say what the original ending was, I don't want people telling me "Hey, that was much better, doh!" but I will say it involved a lot fewer people making it alive to the end. It was dark and it was final, but somehow I think the ending I went with is bleaker. Two broken people locked together by the need for vengeance and all-consuming guilt over the choices they made. When people find themselves in such dark places there are consequences for the soul... and if you've read any of my other books, you'll know that's right up my street.

I've taken a light touch to the historical background in *Red Company*, in the preceding series, *In the Absence of Light,* I weaved a lot of background into the tale, but here I didn't think it was so necessary, given the story never leaves one remote castle. The war alluded to in *Red Company* is the Thirty-Year War, which tore apart The Holy Roman Empire (modern day Germany, Austria, the Czech Republic and bits of other surrounding countries) between 1618 and 1648.

Initially a conflict between Catholics and Protestants in the Empire, it quickly dragged in most of Europe's major powers, who took the opportunity to use the war to further their own interests.

The result was one of the most brutal, blood-thirsty and destructive conflicts in human history (which is a depressingly high bar) that killed around eight million people - between a third and a half of the inhabitants of what is now Germany are estimated to have died, as largely mercenary armies rampaged far and wide, stealing food, livestock and valuables, killing, raping and committing terrible atrocities against the local populations regardless of whose side they were supposed to be fighting for. Plague, pestilence and famine followed hot on the hoofbeats of the war. When religious zealotry and a craze for burning witches were mixed into the brew, the results were three decades of appalling cruelty and suffering

It will be into this maelstrom of violence and terror that Solace and Ulrich follow Morlaine in their search for Torben, Saul and the Red Company in future books.

If you're not familiar with my earlier novels, Morlaine is a character who features in the latter books of *In the Absence of Light*, which are set some 70 years after the events of *Red Company*. There's no need to have read *In the Absence of Light* to enjoy this book, it was written to stand perfectly well on its own two feet, but, of course, I hope you liked *Red Company* enough to want to explore the same dark world further. There are also two novellas available that feature Morlaine, *The Burning* and *A House of the Dead* which are available free from my website andymonkbooks.com.

I'll be returning to *In the Company of Shadows* shortly, both to continue Solace and Ulrich's story and in other tales, both short stories and novels. You can receive updates on forthcoming work by signing up for my mailing list, again either via this book, from my website or Facebook page.

I hope you enjoyed *Red Company* and that our paths cross again soon somewhere along the Night's Road...

Andy Monk
October 2019

In the Company of Shadows

If you'd like to read more dark tales from the world of *In the Company of Shadows*, there are currently two free novellas (available as eBooks only) – *The Burning* & *A House of the Dead* – available. Both are set shortly before the events of *Red Company*. To get your free copies just visit andymonkbooks.com. or scan the QR code below and join Andy's mailing list for updates, news of forthcoming releases and bonus material.

The Burning

The madness of the 17th Century witch burning frenzy has come to the sleepy village of Reperndorf.

Adolphus Holtz, Inquisitor to the Prince-Bishop of Würzburg, is keen to root out evil wherever he deems it to be. His eye has fallen on young Frieda and he fancies she'll scream so prettily for him when the time comes.

Frieda has already witnessed one burning and knows from the way her friends and neighbours are looking at her that she will be next. She seems doomed to burn on the pyre until a mysterious cloaked stranger appears out of the depths of the forest...

The first novella of *In the Company of Shadows* expands the dark historical world of *In the Absence of Light* and the shadowy relationships between humans and vampires

A House of the Dead

All vampires are mad...

The weight of memories, loss, the hunger for blood, the voices of your prey whispering in your mind, loneliness, the obsessions you filled the emptiness inside yourself with, the sheer unrelenting bloody boredom of immortality could all chip away at your sanity.

And love, of course, one should never forget what that could do to you...

Mecurio has hidden from the world for twenty years in the secret catacombs beneath the city of Würzburg known as the House of the Dead, a place of refuge for vampires away from the eyes of men.

He tells himself it is so he can complete his Great Work without the distractions of the mortal world. But it isn't true. Time is slowly stealing the woman he adores from him and he has hidden their love away in the shadows of the House of the Dead to await the inevitable.

When a vampire whose bed he fled from a hundred and twenty-seven years before, arrives in search of information, he sees the opportunity to do a deal to save the woman he now loves for a few more bittersweet years. But all vampires are mad, one way or another, and when you strike a deal with one you may not end up with what you bargained for...

Books by Andy Monk

In the Absence of Light
Book One: The King of the Winter
Book Two: A Bad Man's Song
Book Three: Ghosts in the Blood
Book Four: The Love of Monsters

In the Company of Shadows
The Burning (Novella)
A House of the Dead (Novella)
Red Company (The Night's Road Book One)
The Kindly Man (Rumville Part One)
Execution Dock (Rumville Part Two)
The Convenient (Rumville Part Three)
Mister Grim (Rumville Part Four)
The Future is Promises (Rumville Part Five)
The World's Pain (The Night's Road Book Two)
Empire of Dirt (The Night's Road Book Three)
When the Walls Fall (The Night's Road Book Four)
Darkness Beckons (The Night's Road Book Five)

Hawker's Drift
Book One: The Burden of Souls
Book Two: Dark Carnival
Book Three: The Paths of the World
Book Four: A God of Many Tears
Book Five: Hollow Places

Other Fiction
The House of Shells
The Sorrowsmith

For further information about Andy Monk's writing and future releases, please visit the following sites.

www.andymonkbooks.com

www.facebook.com/andymonkbooks

Printed in Great Britain
by Amazon